ACKNOWLEDGMENTS

"Introduction" copyright © 2013 by Elisabeth Waters
"The Damsel in the Garden" copyright © 2013 by Pauline J. Alama
"Ru's Bad Day" copyright © 2013 by Lorie Calkins
"The Vine Princess" copyright © 2013 by Steve Chapman
"Tear-Stained Sword" copyright © 2013 by Jessie D. Eaker
"A Variation in Silence" copyright © 2013 by Rebecca G. Eaker
"Trading Gifts" copyright © 2013 by Rabia Gale
"Justice" copyright © 2013 by Suzan Harden
"Promises and Pastry" copyright © 2013 by Melissa Mead
"Ghost Spike" copyright © 2013 by Jonathan Moeller
"Where There's Smoke" copyright © 2013 by Michael H. Payne
"Pearl of Tears" copyright © 2013 by Deborah J. Ross
"What's in a Name?" copyright © 2013 by Katharina Schuschke
"Dead Salt" copyright © 2013 by Jonathan Shipley
"The Tavern at the Ford" copyright © 2013 by Dave Smeds
"The Rolang of Taiyung" copyright © 2013 by Catherine Soto
"A Drink of Deadly Wine" copyright © 2013 by Michael Spence & Elisabeth Waters

CONTENTS

INTRODUCTION

by Elisabeth Waters

I have been known to define an editor as a collection of prejudices. Marion Zimmer Bradley certainly was, and I learned most of what I know about editing from her. What this means in practice is that we, and our readers, like a certain kind of story and dislike other kinds. Zombies are popular at the moment, but I personally don't like them. I wouldn't buy a book about them to read myself, and it's unlikely I'd buy a story with them for SWORD AND SORCERESS. It's just not the kind of thing I buy—usually expressed as "this doesn't have the feel I'm looking for." I still have a copy of MZB's rejection paragraphs, but it's rare for me to use any of them, because I think many of them were unnecessarily harsh. "'Willing suspension of disbelief' does not mean hang by the neck until dead" may be amusing, but not when it's applied to your story. I may not always be able to put into words exactly why I like or dislike a story, but it takes me only one reading to decide if there's any possibility that I'm going to buy it. If I know I won't, I send it back right away, so that the author can find a better home for it.

I firmly believe that any good story can find an editor who will buy it. I grew up on A WRINKLE IN TIME, and later Madeleine L'Engle became a personal friend as well as one of my favorite authors. More than two dozen editors rejected her novel before it was published, won a Newbery Medal, and became a classic that is still in print and selling well more than 50 years later. She said to me once that she had asked an editor who originally rejected it if he regretted his decision. He said no; he knew it would either bomb or be a terrific success and at that time his publishing house couldn't afford the risk of its failing. (This may be why movie theatres this year are showing

Despicable Me 2, *Iron Man 3*, *Fast & Furious 6*, another *Star Trek* movie, another *Superman* movie, another *Hobbit* movie, another *Oz* movie, another *Die Hard* movie, and a number of recycled fairy tales.)

Not that I'm in any position to criticise the movie industry (but how many times do they have to destroy New York?—I think Superman did more damage than *Al Qaeda*). This volume contains at least one recycled fairy tale, a new "Temple Cats" story, a new "Ghost" story, a new "Treasures of Albion" story, and the further adventures of Cluny the sorceress squirrel. Of course, it also contains new stories by authors who haven't sold to us before. One of MZB's aims when she started this series was to encourage new writers, and that's certainly a tradition we want to continue.

I'm sure there are many editors who would run screaming from this collection, but these are all stories I like. I hope that you will enjoy them as much as I do.

DEAD SALT

by Jonathan Shipley

For Jonathan Shipley's fourth appearance in SWORD AND SORCERESS, he has written a new story about Jenna, the young exorcist with a difficult calling, continuing her adventures from "Grave Gold" in SWORD AND SORCERESS 27. Since last year, he has published three more speculative fiction short stories, with another three pending, pushing his list of short fiction towards the three-dozen mark. His World War II occult fantasy REICHSBLOOD has also been short-listed by a major New York publisher for what may be his first novel publication. I'm keeping my fingers crossed for it.

Jonathan lives in Fort Worth, Texas, and has a web presence at www.shipleyscifi.com.

The towers of the old Commandery came slowly into view above the surrounding forest as the wagon trundled along the pocked road.

Pacing the wagon on horseback, their Knight-Guardian Trayn gave a little whoop. "Almost there—oh, for a hot bath and a close shave." He took off his helmet to let loose a shaggy mass of sandy-brown hair. "And a little less mane would be welcome."

"I told you I can clip it," Herrin retorted from the seat of the wagon.

"And end up with a priest's tonsure—no thank you," Trayn snorted. "I have my pride."

"Entirely too much sometimes—"

Jenna ignored their bickering. Her young brother and her Knight-Guardian were always arguing about something and she was too tired to care. It was the end of the road and, like Trayn, she wanted a good wash and an end to travel grit. Ah, to be back in her room in the Cold Wing with a fire roaring on the hearth.

Then she shook her head.

What did it say about her life if she looked forward to a drafty room in a haunted wing of a barracks? A few weeks of "home" and she would be ready for the road again, harsh as that could be at times. The vagabond life of riding around in an open wagon wasn't exactly pleasant either. A month of that and she would be ready to come back to the Commandery. It was an idiotic cycle. But if she wanted pleasant, she should never have accepted the life of a Church exorcist.

Beside her, Herrin had stopped complaining and was whistling a glum, tuneless melody. The Commandery barracks wasn't a pleasant place for him either. A priest-acolyte didn't fit in well with the soldiers. The only one of their trio that looked genuinely pleased was Trayn, who was a Knight through and through and fit in quite well with barracks society.

The gray walls of the Commandery drew closer, and by late afternoon, their little caravan was rolling through the front gate. Trayn was immediately in his element, swinging down from his horse to embrace his fellow knights like lost brothers. With a sigh, Jenna and Herrin gathered their bundles from under the tarp of the wagon and headed for the abandoned north wing of the fortress. The Cold Wing.

Passing through the main block was the expected mix of draftiness and woodsmoke and food cooking. But the moment they pushed through the heavy door connecting to the north wing, the temperature plummeted. Jenna set her jaw and kept on going, refusing to give in to the urge to shiver. In her profession, cold spots were common enough. Beside her, however, Herrin shivered violently.

They didn't speak until they reached the room they had claimed amidst the many empty rooms. They could have taken the biggest and grandest but had chosen small instead because heating would always be a problem in the middle of a cold spot. At least the room wasn't directly above the old torture chambers, so the unnatural chill wasn't as bad as other rooms.

Herrin went directly to the hearth to build a fire. "Definitely," she nodded encouragingly. At least the Knighthood didn't begrudge them plenty of wood.

"You'd think Sir Knightly Horsely would help once in a while with the bags and the fire," Herrin grumbled through chattering teeth.

The unflattering nickname came out whenever Herrin was irritated with Trayn. The countercharge was usually "damnable acolyte." They probably had names for her as well, but she wasn't privy to them. It was all part of the joy of constant companionship, which could grow very thin indeed on a rough road in bad weather. "Trayn does his part," Jenna shrugged. "He manages all the campfires when we travel, so I can forgive him not managing this one."

Like most of the Knights, Trayn was terrified of the Cold Wing. Considering it was haunted by souls tortured to death by the Knighthood in earlier generations, they were smart to be wary of the place. The dead did, she could professionally attest, hold grudges.

When the fire was blazing, they unpacked their bundles from the wagon. Neither had much, just a change of clothes or two and some personal odds and ends. Jenna also had a sack of "professional equipment," as she called the salt and knife and books that she used in her exorcisms. She also used bread with the salt, but that she acquired fresh for every exorcism. The dead might not actually care, but if she were a spirit, she would be insulted to be offered stale bread as a prelude to negotiation.

"I suppose if we want to eat, we should go mix with the rowdies," she said after they had sat silently by the fire for a while. "If we're lucky, there might even be...potato soup."

Herrin gave a short laugh as he got up and led the way to the door. Potatoes were the staple of the Commandery diet. There might also be meat of the day or fish, but always potatoes. "See you back in the land of the living." He flung open the door and charged into the frigid corridor.

She closed the door and followed at a less frantic pace. Then it happened—a cloud of mist rose from the floor and hovered before her. Wisps, she called them when they had so little form. This one was less vague than many others with even the semblance of a face atop a runny body.

"Ill met," it wheezed at her. There was hardly enough of it left to qualify as a he or a she. "The dungeons have been opened. Stop it before it starts again..." The words faded into silence as the form faded into nothingness.

Jenna frowned. Spirits did not make idle chitchat, and she felt obligated to take these words seriously. But later. She was tired and hungry and could not be an exorcist every moment of the day. So she hurried. Now that one had found her, others would come if she tarried. Passing through the doorway connecting the wing and main block of the castle felt like crossing the threshold of life and death. Here it was merely drafty with none of the unnatural bone-deep chill, but with sounds and the smell of potato something wafting up from the kitchens. And always people. The Commandery was tightly quartered when everyone was in residence, and not much better at any other time. Occasionally a new recruit would attempt quarters in the Cold Wing but always moved back to the cramped barracks soon enough.

"Exorcist!" a sharp voice called from down the corridor.

She turned and waited for his approach. Obviously an officer from the bearing and uniform, but not one she knew...and she thought she knew the upper echelon at the Commandery.

"It's good I caught you early so we won't have to discuss business at dinner," he said, coming abreast of her. He had the lean, iron-gray look she associated with long-time professional soldiers, without a speck of friendliness to his demeanor.

"And you are?" she prompted.

"Frant, the new Commandant," he said briskly. Then added more deliberately, "*Your* new Commandant."

That spoke volumes in itself. As an exorcist, her chain of command went to the Exorcist-General in King's City, not the military arm of the Church. This might not be the moment, however, to point that out.

"Your mission here seems to have bogged down under my predecessor," he continued. "I want it back on track with a timetable of results. Is that clear, Exorcist?"

"No," Jenna said with a frown. "Not at all. What mission are you referring to?"

Frant looked irritated. "Exorcising the Amantias Wing, of course. To my knowledge that's been pending the eighteen months since you took up lodging at the Commandery with few visible results."

Now Jenna was irritated. Exorcising the Cold Wing had always been a very informal task, to be worked on between her official duties. It had never been a condition of her lodging. "I manage a few more exorcisms every time I'm in residence," she said stiffly. "I assume you're aware of that."

"And at this rate, how long before the Amantias Wing is purged?"

"About three hundred years," she said with a certain satisfaction. "The Knighthood's torturers created a huge population of unquiet souls over the centuries. Advise your predecessors to kill fewer prisoners, and we could all be more comfortable."

"Three hundred years is not acceptable," he returned coldly. "And though you may regard this as a joke, I assure you that I do not. This is now to be your top priority."

"And you have that in writing from the Exorcist-General?" Jenna pushed back. "That is the only office with the authority to set priorities for me."

"You're very sure of yourself, young woman, for one dependent on my good will."

"My job is negotiating with the dead, and often the vengeful dead. That is my only..."

He walked off while she was still speaking. "If you have reports for King's City," he called back over his shoulder, "have them in my office *now*."

Jenna bristled, but held her tongue as she turned and retraced her steps to the Cold Wing. She'd already made a mess of this meeting. She knew the type, knew that she should have limited herself to yes sir, no sir. But no, she had to throw in three hundred years and get the new Commandant's back up. Now she would have negotiate herself to calmer waters with the man. It might not be the vengeful dead, but the stiff-necked living had their own challenges.

When she returned from her quarters a second time with a sheaf of reports to be forwarded to the Exorcist-General in King's City, the amanuensis was not even at his desk in the Commandant's office. No one was there. The Commandant himself was already at dinner as she should have been if not for this fool's errand. But this attitude led nowhere good. She had to remember that there was constant frustration within the Commandery over all those empty rooms in the Cold Wing when the barracks was overflowing.

But it was equally frustrating that the Knighthood in general—this Commandant in particular—didn't seem to grasp the magnitude of exorcising a killing field. *The dungeons have been opened.* The ghostly words came back to her as she walked, making her wonder. Would this new, stiff-necked commander be so foolish as to re-open the old torture chambers? The thought sickened her. She both wanted and did not want to ask, but knew she would have to sound out Trayn on the topic fairly soon. If the dead were more restless than usual, she had to know why.

At the refectory door, she spared a glance at the high table of ranking officers where the Commandant was comfortably ensconced, then searched the benches for Herrin. She spotted Trayn mid-table, kept looking, then her eyes returned for a second look. This was no longer the familiar, scruffy Trayn of the road. He'd evidently found his bath and shave and was looking sleek and civilized as he traded stories with his brother Knights. She tended to forget how well he cleaned up and that he was really much younger than his road-weary, battle-ready self usually looked. He looked odd out of boots and armor. Not like the real Trayn at all. But even in soft clothing, he was friend enough to field an awkward question...but later.

She kept searching for Herrin, knowing his dark priest's cassock ought to stand out among the brighter clothing of the Knights. Ah, there by himself on a bench in the corner, looking completely unsociable as he pushed food around on his plate.

"Why aren't you sitting with the others?" she demanded as

she joined him.

He shrugged. "I was told I wasn't welcome." He nodded at the head table. "Seems the new Commandant doesn't care much for exorcism assistants."

"Or exorcists," she added in an undertone. Witch...exorcist—some people saw no difference. *Stop it before it starts again.* The wisp's words echoed ominously. It seemed to be a new regime of intolerance at the Commandery.

"Have you eaten anything at all?" she asked, nodding at his untouched food.

Herrin shrugged. "Not much appetite at the moment."

"No, we traveled all day with barely a bite and you must eat for your strength. We both must. Then you're going directly to my chamber and locking the door. This feels wrong...unsafe."

He looked at her with wary eyes, sensing her urgency. "And you? If I'm not safe, neither are you."

"I'll join you as soon as I can. But I have to talk to Trayn first. He needs to know what's going on."

The meal dragged on. Finished with her dinner and sitting alone in the corner, Jenna felt every second tick by. She had planned to simply interrupt Trayn at his table talk to tell him her concerns, but every time she stood to do that, she felt the cold eye of the Commandant on her and sat down again. There was something unnerving about that man. Finally she simply left by the nearest door. She wasn't giving up, but she couldn't sit there any longer. So she made the trek back to the opposite side of the building and passed through the barracks to the row of monks' cells where she knew Trayn had his own cubicle. While the barracks was not an appropriate place for a young woman, it still seemed the best place to force a meeting. Left to himself, Trayn would never come to the Cold Wing.

The cell itself was not hard to find. Each Knight hung his shield on the outside of his door when he was in residence, and she was very familiar with the quartered chevrons of Trayn's family arms. Slipping inside, she waited by the single, narrow window, taking in the view of the Commandery courtyard from an unfamiliar angle.

Eventually she heard multiple footsteps coming down the corridor and tensed as the door opened. "Aye, and the same to you," she heard Trayn call out as someone kept on going down the corridor.

He entered, gave a long sigh, and sank down on the narrow bedstead.

"Trayn, it's Jenna," she said softly.

"Hmm?" he mumbled, then sat bolt upright. "You can't be here," he exploded in a savage whisper. "A lady does not come to a man's room uninvited and unchaperoned. It spawns unflattering rumors."

"I realize that," she shot back. "But this is too important to wait on proper protocol. Things have happened. I had an unpleasant introduction to Commandant Frant. He believes I am here solely to follow his orders and cleanse the Cold Wing. But more distressingly, a spirit waylaid me on my way to dinner and warned that the dungeons have been opened again. I don't think these are unconnected events."

Trayn mumbled something under his breath.

"I did *not* bring this on myself," she snapped. She actually hadn't heard his words, but she knew the type of thing he tended to mumble to himself.

"I said, 'please just one night of quiet before I die'," he retorted. "I know full well you did not bring this on yourself because I've been hearing all evening about this jackass of a new Commandant. It's not good, Jenna. He was fine the first week, then suddenly got a wasp up his trews about something. Unfortunately, you're just the type of person to draw his fire."

"Because I'm a woman or because I'm an exorcist?"

"Either...both," Trayn shrugged. "But mainly because you have opinions and don't keep them to yourself."

"And have the dungeons been reopened?"

He nodded slowly. "Talk is that the Commandant has a witch down there. Holding her with cold iron until a specialist can come hear her confession."

A cold chill ran up Jenna's spine. "A specialist—a torturer, you mean?"

"That would be my guess, though that word wasn't used."

"Then it *is* starting again," she murmured. "That's the problem with the Cold Wing, you know. It was used to torture and kill witches, people with Talent. And believe me, if there's anything more difficult than an unquiet spirit, it's a dead witch with a grievance." Then she paused and cocked her head, considering. "Is it possible that this is being done without authority?"

Trayn frowned. "The Commandant has complete authority over the Commandery."

"But only over the Commandery. My point is that there are policies that come down from King's City. I know the official instruction of the Exorcist-General to all exorcists is to cleanse hauntings, lay the vengeful dead to rest, and not stir up trouble with the Other Side. How can Commandant Frant be going in a completely different direction from official Church policy?"

"A very good question," Trayn nodded. "Perhaps you and I should investigate the dungeons in our own respective ways tonight."

"A summoning, you mean." Jenna didn't look forward to that. With so many unquiet dead wandering around, it was like opening a floodgate.

"A summoning for you; a casual chat for me. Where there's a prisoner, there's a guard. And where there's a guard, there's always room for a mug of ale. And the sooner done, the better. If you've already crossed Frant, he'll be looking for charges to bring against you."

Charges to bring against you. The phrase kept rattling in Jenna's head as she trekked back to the Cold Wing. If she'd had any idea, she would have bypassed this homecoming and kept going on the road. But now that she was here, it would be awkward to leave again so soon...maybe not even possible. The Commandant was correct that she was dependent on his good will for horses and supplies.

Upon reaching her quarters, she rapped on the door and

waited for the bolt to be pulled back. “That took a long time,” Herrin said nervously as she entered and bolted the door again. His face looked pale and pinched.

“Yes, mostly waiting for dinner to end. I am going to do a general summoning,” she said to get that unpleasant fact out there. “And I need your help, so don’t even think about leaving. Besides, you’re safer with me and the dead than with the living at the moment.”

“Trayn knew something?”

“He’s hearing unpleasant things. We suspect that the new Commandant has opened up the dungeons for torture again. Yes, exactly,” she added at her brother’s shocked expression. “This is grim, and it may not be official. If the worst proves to be true, you need to be prepared to run for Mechon Abbey down by the river, carrying a complaint to the Exorcist-General.”

“This shouldn’t be happening,” he murmured, sounding very young.

“No, it shouldn’t,” she agreed. “Now, help with the salt circle. And when the spirits come, I’ll need you to scribe everything I say. There will much too much for me to remember.”

They laid the protective circle quickly with themselves safely inside—or as safe as one could be amidst a crowd of restless souls. Jenna took a moment to focus herself, then intoned, “Spirits trapped between one world and the next in this building of stone and pain, heed my voice. Come to me, speak to me, and I shall listen.” Three times she spoke the invocation, each time feeling the temperature in the room drop, despite the roaring fire on the hearth.

By the third time, it was as if Lord Winter had come to visit in all his icy majesty. And they were no longer alone. To Jenna’s eyes, it was a throng of pale, transparent bodies pressing forward in all directions, held off only by the salt circle surrounding the two of them. “What do you see?” she whispered at Herrin, who sat cross-legged beside her.

“Mist rising from the floor,” he murmured back. “Very dense. How many are here?”

“Scores, maybe hundreds. They run together. Here we go.

Spirits," she said, raising her voice. "I have been warned that the dungeons have been reopened and a prisoner now sits in a cell of cold iron. Tell me how and why this has happened. And how it can be stopped."

A wave of thin voices washed over her in a jumble. She concentrated on a word here, a phrase there, until she found a coherent voice. "You," she said, pointing a finger at a wispy figure in a bonnet. "Speak."

"I was accused when I was innocent," the figure whined. "I was tortured when all I wanted was to live in peace with my children."

"You have been heard and I grieve with you at the injustice," Jenna intoned after repeating the words for Herrin's record. "Lay down the burden of your grievance and move to the Other Side." The figure gave a wispy sigh and faded away. Some spirits merely wanted to be heard. Those were the easy cases. Another voice pushed into the void. Another story of injustice and torture. One after another, she repeated them for the record. Later she would comb through them for common elements. Then a stronger voice.

"I was taken and my body broken for following the Old Ways," this new spirit—definitely a woman—began. "I was held in the cell of cold iron for they feared my powers, even though I was dying. But one thing I was able to do—drag my torturer into the limbo of undeath with me, so that he also can find no rest."

Jenna felt her whole body tense as she realized what the spirit was saying. This was what the living feared most from the dead—not death, but eternal undeath. "Does the cycle begin again?" she asked after again repeating the spirit's words. "Is the living woman now being held in the cell of cold iron also a witch?"

"I told her what I did to my torturer...and how," the witch spirit wheezed. "Now she lies in wait."

Jenna shuddered. This was the worst of everything repeating itself. She had to warn Trayn to warn the other knights to stay clear of the witch on pain of damnation. "How can I stop this cycle?" she cried to the circle of spirits. She felt her concentration, her ability to hold their attention, faltering. "How can I persuade the Commandant?"

"The Commandant is as good as dead," a voice whispered as the ghosts began drifting away, many sucked into the floor like unwary travelers into quicksand.

"Did you get an answer to that last question?" Herrin asked, quill poised over the parchment.

"Not a good one," she muttered. "Decidedly not a good one."

As the last spirits faded, she felt warmth creep back into her body and was able to brew them cups of tea from the kettle steaming away on a hearth trivet. The hot liquid was like life itself after the unnatural cold.

She felt herself sag into a comfortable drowsiness, then abruptly came awake at a soft tapping on the door. But she never had visitors of the living sort. Exchanging a puzzled glance with Herrin, she unbolted the door. A shivering figure darted into the room. "Trayn? What's happened?"

"Tea first," he said through chattering teeth. "How can you abide this place?" He sipped from the cup Jenna offered and added, "There is indeed a witch incarcerated in the dungeons. And there's worse—the interrogatory specialist arrives in the morning. I knew you needed to hear that immediately."

So they were out of time, and still no answers. No, she did know a few things, like a dead witch who had cursed her torturer. She straightened as another odd bit came into focus. "Who calls the Cold Wing the Amantias Wing?"

"That's the original name for it—inscribed on the cornerstone, even. But no one's called it that in years. Not since—"

"The persecutions?" As Trayn slowly nodded, she grimaced. "That's what Frant called it earlier today. Twice in fact. I would lay money that he's a blood descendant of one of the Knighthood's torturers from back then. And his coming here woke up some old evil. We need to break that connection."

Trayn raised an eyebrow. "How?"

Jenna sagged onto a stool near the door. "I don't know—yet. If this is just a form of possession, dead salt and Holy Water could break it, but it might be more curse than simple possession.

To break that, we might need a—"

"—a witch?" Trayn supplied.

She grimaced and nodded. Suddenly she stood and lit a chamber lamp from the fireplace. "And we shouldn't delay." She turned to her brother. "Organize the notes from the summoning and attach a letter of complaint against the Commandant. Then ready yourself for a quick departure. If all this goes wrong, you have to make it through the woods to Mechon Abbey. Oh, and Holy Water. A small vial from the chapel should be enough. I'll meet you in the Great Hall when I'm back from the dungeons."

"This is crazy," Trayn protested. "Trying to get into the dungeons is crazy and enlisting the help of an angry witch is even crazier."

"Doing nothing is crazier still," Jenna retorted. "We only have until morning."

Unexpectedly, Trayn dropped the argument. "Let's go, then."

She had envisioned doing this part alone, but one look at Trayn's face dissuaded her from mentioning that. He had his "it's my duty" look on his face and in truth, it made sense. He was, after all, her sworn protector. But this might be awkward.

"I'll try to persuade the guard that our exorcist needs to inspect the dungeons for official purposes," he offered as they moved into the corridor. "But at this hour, it's a thin argument."

Very thin, she thought. "No need, Trayn. There's a concealed spiral staircase in the corner of the Cold Wing that leads directly to the dungeons below."

"Truly?" In the lamplight, he looked amazed. "How is that not known?"

"Because no one comes to the Cold Wing and until recently, no one used the dungeons. But spirits told me about it when I first moved in, not that I've had had any desire to use it." She found the hidden door and planting her feet carefully on the steep stone steps, she made her way downward by the dim light of the lamp.

Cold. Cold. Cold. Even as used as she was to the chill of death, this coldness was heart-numbing. She must be close to the torture chambers themselves where so much violence had occurred. She pulled her cloak closer and walked the length of the twisting corridor. Beside her, Trayn was shivering violently. Then she heard moaning from within one of the cells. "Stay here," she whispered to him.

She backtracked, unbolted the door, and pushed it open. A plump, matronly woman was strung up by her wrists in an iron box. Where the shackles touched, her arms showed burn marks. The bite of cold iron on those with magic. "Don't do it," Jenna muttered in a low voice. "I'm trying to help, but damning a soul will just make it worse."

The woman's eyes popped open. "Who are you?"

"An exorcist. I talk to the dead and they told me. I don't know why you are imprisoned, but none of this is right. The persecutions ended generations ago. This is like an old curse someone has stupidly released. I'm trying to make it right. Will you help me?"

"Are you blind?" the woman snapped bitterly. "I can do nothing but hang here, bound by cold iron."

"Well, there's cold iron," Jenna said, opening her cloak to reveal an earthenware jar where she had scooped up salt from the circle. "And there's salt recently used in the summoning of the dead. My Gran used to say that as salt corrodes iron, so dead salt corrodes the numbing power of cold iron."

"Your Gran was a witch?"

"Gran talked to the dead, just like me. To my knowledge, that was her only talent. Do we have agreement about setting things right without vengeance?"

"If you knew half the—"

"I *do* know," Jenna insisted. "I live above these dungeons with every dead witch who was ever tortured to death whispering the bitter details in my ears. Vengeance leads nowhere good, either in life or in death. So I ask again, do we have agreement? And I ask all who have suffered in this cell to bear unseen witness to our words."

The witch's eyes narrowed. "You're very savvy for one so young."

"I negotiate with the vengeful dead as an occupation. One

learns to be very careful with words and agreements."

"Hah. Well said. You just might be the one to set this mess aright after all. No vengeance—you have my word."

Jenna stepped closer, set the lamp on the ground, and began flinging handfuls of salt at the iron box. "Let the salt of the earth ease the bite of cold iron," she intoned ritually. It wasn't a ritual she knew, but she had gotten very good at improvising. When the jar was empty, she asked, "Better?"

The witch gave a long sigh. "Much. I don't suppose you have the key to these manacles?"

Jenna shook her head. "The guard must have the key. What can you tell me about your capture? Why you? I can think of half a dozen witches within easy range of this Commandery. But only you were captured."

"True." The woman thought a moment. "My family is well known locally. The power has passed mother to daughter for many generations. My grandmother was a victim of the old persecutions. Died right in this very cell."

Jenna gave a start. "Is she the one who whispered to you about dragging the soul of your persecutor into damnation with you? Yes, it must be. Blood speaks to blood, even without any special talent to speak to the dead."

"Is that important?"

"I think so. I'm guessing your ancestor cursed the Commandant's ancestor, and now both those ghosts are fighting on through their descendants. But this is more than simple possession, and that's where I need your help—"

"Someone's outside the door," the witch hissed suddenly. "If you've betrayed me—"

"No, no," Jenna assured her. "It's just my Knight-Protector who is my ally in trying to set this right. Trayn," she called in a soft voice. "Come inside."

He entered warily, eyeing the witch as suspiciously as she was eyeing him. Jenna was exceedingly glad she'd obtained a binding oath of non-vengeance. "Breaking the curse," she prompted. "Dead salt and Holy Water are my usual tools."

"Blood," the witch said. "A curse like this would have been

written in blood and only blood can break it."

"Whose blood?" Trayn demanded. "Not Jenna's."

"No...mine. A little blood, freely given, should offset the generational curse when combined with words of release and the name. And quickly now." The clang of a metal door far down the corridor underscored her last words.

Trayn unsheathed a dagger from his belt and pricked the witch's forearm. Jenna caught the trickle of blood in her empty salt jar before it slowed and thickened. Then she scooped up the lamp. "Be brave," she urged at the door.

"You—young Knight—tarry a moment," the witch urged and whispered something at Trayn when he stepped closer.

"We need to hurry," Jenna reminded them.

"Yes, we're done—let's go," Trayn said, setting a quick pace. They hurried up the twisted corridor to the steep, spiral steps and climbed as fast as prudence allowed.

"Damn, you play a dangerous game, Jenna," Trayn muttered as they reached the floor above.

"The danger is this blood curse driving the re-opening of the dungeons. Here, you take the blood and meet me at the door of the Commandant's sleeping chamber. I need to stop at my chamber for more salt and a quick summoning."

"A summoning?" Trayn looked uncertain. "Why? We have everything."

"Except a name." He seemed to accept that, and as their paths diverged, she asked quickly, " What was your little heart-to-heart with the witch? Did she hex all your toes to fall off?"

"No, she said you were a rare gem and my body should be your bulwark in the darkness."

Jenna stopped, startled. "What? No, later. I'll see you upstairs in a few moments."

"Where we'll be breaking into the bedchamber of my commander. It's indefensible if I'm caught, you know."

"So don't get caught," she advised. "And I don't know why you're raising a stink when you've already decided that helping me is the only way to fix the Commandery."

"Oh, absolutely," he agreed with a shrug. "You just need

reminding from time to time how insane your plans are."

Jenna rolled her eyes.

The brass Vogelclock over the front door struck midnight. *How appropriate*, Jenna thought as she crossed the Commandery's Great Hall. *The witching hour for undoing some old, wicked witching.* Herrin was waiting in the shadows near the door, dressed for traveling in cloak and boots.

"Remember—don't wait," she told her brother as she accepted the vial of Holy Water and mounted the broad staircase. "If Trayn and I don't come back down these stairs, go to the abbot at Mechon and—"

"—don't stop for anything. I know, I know. Good luck, Jenna," he added as he melted into the shadows of the hall.

At the end of the third-floor corridor, Trayn was pacing nervously. "Is the door bolted?" she whispered as she approached.

"If it is, I shall simply batter it down at your command."

She gave him a sharp look. "Is the door bolted?"

"No."

"Then"—she produced a small bowl and held out her hand for the jar he was holding, adding blood, then Holy Water to the dead salt. It fizzled encouragingly, showing that something was happening with mystical potency. "Open the door."

She knew something was wrong the moment she stepped into the dim bedchamber. The bed was empty. And there was a figure coming at her in the dark with dagger drawn. Then Trayn shoved her aside and tackled her attacker.

All that happened in a blink. On second blink, time was back to normal with Trayn calling up to her, "A little help, if you please." The scuffle was not going well.

Jenna dumped the salty concoction over them both and recited loudly, "Earth-bound spirit, by the water of the Church, be absolved. By the salt of the earth, be absorbed. By the blood of your condemner be released. Arteus of Kithorn, be gone!"

The sounds of fighting subsided into a snuffling and coughing. She lit a lamp on the bedside table and turned to survey the damage. The Commandant lay twitching on the rug, his eyes wide and baffled. Beside him, Trayn was sneezing frantically from salt water up the nose.

"Are you all right, sir?" she asked, stooping down beside Frant.

He blinked a few times, seemed to realize he was lying on the floor, and managed to sit up. "I remember investigating the Cold Wing, finding the staircase down to the dungeons, and then...nothing. What happened?"

"Possession," she said. "Not common, but possible when there's a direct blood-link involved. You were possessed by an ancestor of yours whose spirit was trapped in the dungeon by a witch he tortured to death. But he's gone now, and you are yourself again."

He gave a snort. "I take it you're our resident exorcist of the Cold Wing."

"I am. Jenna by name. And this is my Knight-Guardian Trayn."

Trayn stopped snuffling just long enough to say, "Sir."

"And there is a woman currently in the dungeons who needs to be released immediately with restitution for indignities visited upon her by the Knighthood." She decided to leave it at that. The less said about witchcraft, the better. "And with that, sir, we shall take our leave."

She gave Trayn a hand up and got him out into the corridor between sneezes. "Thank you. I would have been dead by dagger if you hadn't been there."

He gave a shrug. "Thank the witch. She was the one who told me to use my body to protect you in the darkness."

Oh. That was what he meant.

"But she wasn't all that good a seer," he continued after another sneeze. "Absolutely no warning about salt water up the nose."

THE ROLANG OF TAIYUNG

by Catherine Soto

Lin Mei's brother is away, serving in the Emperor's army, so she's working solo. That's not likely to stop her from doing what needs to be done, however. She was always the brain to his brawn. Besides, she has both the cats.

Catherine has been pretty busy this last year. Lots of overtime at work (i.e.: more money, less energy), but got some comp-time from it, which allowed her a rare day of self-indulgence at the Asian Art Museum in San Francisco, where she saw the Terracotta Warriors from China. She also has a blog, catherinesoto3.blogspot.com, and is on Goodreads as well. Has not done much on either for a few months (overtime again) but plans to get back to them soon.

I know the feeling.

The crickets had fallen silent. Lin Mei set down her brush and looked up, puzzled. It was a warm summer night and the sound of their chirping had been almost a din, for crickets. The sudden cessation of the sounds had fallen like the drop in conversation at an awkward moment at the dinner table.

In the corner Shadow and Twilight stirred out of their semi-sleep, looking about. Lin Mei sat up straight; her hand reached out for her dagger and thrust it in her sash. Shadow's tail twitched. His eyes were wary slits. Next to him Twilight sat up, looking about. That decided her. Grasping her sword she rose and went to the sliding door, slowly pushing it open and stepping out onto the veranda.

Outside the night was warm and still. Across the small courtyard a stand of bamboo stirred slowly in a vagrant breeze that did not reach beyond its confines. A rock garden filled the space between it and the veranda. Overhead a full moon lit the area.

Ordinarily such a peaceful night scene would have been pleasing. The caravan had stopped for a few weeks in the shadow of the Loksangha Monastery on the side of the mountains south of the city. The annual Taiyung silk fair had drawn merchants from as far as Kashmir to the west and Dunhuang to the east, and a city of tents had arisen in the open land around the city. The days were filled with raucous bargaining and trade, with good-natured insults and curses enlivening the din, followed by rowdy carousing into the evening. But by late night everyone was in an exhausted torpor.

The Taiyung Guard was more than adequate to secure the lands about the city, and only a nominal guard was needed for the caravan pickets. At night the more valuable goods were stored in safety inside the city walls. Lin Mei was second in command of the guards, reporting to Shin Hu, the guard commander. Aside from a round on horseback she had no duties after sunset. Her quarters were more than adequate, especially compared to what a caravan guard usually enjoyed, and she had spent the prior two nights in rare ease and comfort.

Beside her the two cats slipped out into the shadows cast by the railing, their attention on the bamboo. Shadow's tail twitched. At that Lin Mei drew in a deep breath and pressed the guard of her sword forward with her thumb, loosening it in the scabbard.

It was a few short steps from the veranda outside her rooms to the one next door. Beside her Shadow twitched his tail and crouched low. She went up the three steps slowly, eyes casting about. So far she had not melded her senses with the cats. With possible danger so imminent she did not want to lose focus or concentration by taking the few moments needed to join their senses to hers. They followed along behind, one to either side.

On the veranda she stopped, eyeing the sliding door. The hair on the back of her neck prickled. Scowling, she looked about. The cats had eyed the bamboo suspiciously just a few moments earlier but now their attention was on the door before her. But nothing had moved between the two. So whatever was making them uneasy was inside. She studied the door.

That moment saved her life. Suddenly, someone, or something, slammed the door completely open and leapt out, arms forward, as if to reach for her. With reflexes honed by years on the frontier she dropped to one knee, her sword coming out and slashing to her right side, and into the torso of her attacker.

Ordinarily such a strike should have been fatal, but her arm throbbed with pain as her blade slammed into her attacker. It felt as if she had hit a tree trunk. Only the high quality of the steel kept it from shattering. But the impact threw her to the floor of the veranda. She kept on rolling, her blade tucked in close to her.

When she felt far enough away to feel she could safely stop she leapt to her feet, her sword arm swinging in a wide arc to clear the space about her.

It was unnecessary. She was alone on the hardwood flooring. But inside the building she heard screaming and yelling as men rushed about, lighting lamps and gathering weapons. In moments one was out, eyes casting about. His gaze rested on Lin Mei.

"He went past me," she shouted, before he might get the idea she was responsible for whatever had happened inside, "in that direction!" She pointed out toward the sand garden. He looked past and his face contorted in what might have been anger, or horror. Puzzled, Lin Mei looked past him. On the sand were footprints. It took a moment for Lin Mei to notice what might be the cause of his reaction.

The prints were in a pair, as she might have expected. But instead of being those of a walking or running man, they were side by side, as if the intruder had hopped away. Still, she could not think why that should be so alarming.

Other men rushed out, all armed and one carrying a lamp. "Where did he go?" one asked, brandishing a lance. Lin Mei pointed off into the darkness. The lancer rushed off, the rest following. She was alone on the veranda, save for Shadow and Twilight. She sheathed her sword and stepped inside. Women were moving about, hurriedly but with more composure than that exhibited by the men.

"What was that?" she asked a maid carrying some coarse

cloth. The girl merely bowed her head and gestured toward the inner hall. Lin Mei strode through the entry. Inside there was a knot of women in silk robes at the far wall. A man lay on the matting. It did not take one with Lin Mei's experience as a guard to see that he would not last long, even with the expert ministrations of the women about him. A corner of her mind noted the expertise they showed. So they were not new to this. That was interesting.

"What has happened?" she asked. The women all looked up at her. Finally one of them, of some importance judging by the costly robe she wore, spoke. "The Rolang came in and attacked us," she said calmly, as if discussing a spilled cup of tea. "This man," she gestured down at the supine form, "was wounded defending us." It was perhaps doubly tragic that the valiant man chose that moment to let out his last breath in a death rattle that sent a shiver down Lin Mei's back no matter how often she had heard it before. She took a moment for a quick prayer.

Behind her she heard the door bang against the frame as it was thrown completely open. She turned. It was Dorpak Champa, her host, flanked by two heavy-set guardsmen armed with swords. She saw three more behind him. She bowed quickly as he strode past her to stand over the dead man and the women around him.

"It has come," he said. "It managed to escape over the west wall." Lin Mei's mind raced. He did not seem surprised. Now that she considered it, no one so far had shown any shock or surprise at the night's grisly events. Her hand tightened on the scabbard of her sword. Behind her she could sense Shadow and Twilight prowling about nervously. Dorpak turned to face her.

"How is it that you are here?" he asked.

"I noticed that the chirping of the crickets had stopped," she said, carefully considering her words as she spoke. "I stepped outside to investigate." Dorpak looked at her for a long moment before nodding.

"Please return to your quarters," he said. "I will speak with you later." Lin Mei bowed and left, the two cats padding along behind. Back in her rooms, alone but for her feline companions, she pondered the situation. Despite the tragic nature of the night's events everyone else seemed strangely composed, as if they had been expecting the attack. And now that she thought about it, the presence of so many well-armed and capable men in the compound of a merchant, even one as wealthy as Dorpak Champa, was unusual. She took up her brush and with a few strokes finished the report she had been writing, setting her seal upon it in red before rolling it up.

A soft knock on the veranda floor outside made her look up. "Enter," she called. It was a maid, with tea. She saw the tray held two cups. Well. She waited until the maid had left before setting her sword behind her, hilt to her right. She did not have long to wait. In moments Dorpak Champa arrived, sliding the door open and entering without ceremony. As he slid it closed behind him she saw two of his guards standing outside. She bowed low in greeting. "Please," he said, his hand moving in a gesture of dismissal, "you are my honored guest."

"It is you who honor me, sir," she replied politely, gesturing to the mat opposite her. "May I offer tea?" He nodded politely and sank to the mat. There was silence as she set out cups with tea leaves and poured hot water from the pot into them. She saw the way he watched her as she did so.

"You know how to serve tea," he said, lifting his cup for a polite three sips. She kept her face impassive, nodding in acknowledgment. "It is unfortunate that your stay here has been marred by such a tragic event," he said, setting his cup down.

"The generosity of your hospitality makes any unpleasantness trivial," she replied, weighing her words carefully. "But it is unfortunate that such a brave man met his end," she added. He nodded, eyeing her.

"I have heard much about you," he said, "and your brother, Biao. Wang Liu speaks highly of you." His eyes shifted sideways to the cats, who sat impassively watching from the far corner.

"My brother is at present serving in the army of the August Throne," she said. He nodded.

"Yes, the armies of Tifun once more stretch the borders, and the August Throne must send forces to chastise them. I have heard of your brother's sword, and his speed and skill with it. He will be helpful in the campaign." He stopped to take another sip. "But I suspect that his knowledge of the land, and its people, will be more useful to the commanding general," he added. "Both of you have traveled long in those regions, and are familiar with them. And Wang Liu writes that you have often dealt with problems of various sorts, both in this world, and the other one." She nodded in polite acknowledgement, her face placid while her mind rapidly went over all the implications of his comments. None of them looked good.

"You are most gracious," she ventured. He smiled and took another sip.

"I must confess I had ulterior motives for inviting you to be my houseguest," he said. Lin Mei raised a quizzical eyebrow. Dorpak Champa was a wealthy merchant and an associate and trading partner of Wang Liu, her sometime employer in far-off Kendar, on the western fringe of the Empire. Wang Liu had sent a shipment of silk for Dorpak Champa to sell on consignment, a shipment so large and of such quality that Dorpak had been pleased enough to have offered Lin Mei quarters in his compound. Apparently there was more than gratitude behind the offer of hospitality. He looked at her face and smiled, although with a touch of grimness.

"There is disquiet in my household," he said. "The woman you have met, Pakchen Dgorge, is my first wife's cousin, and a member of the knightly class. She was recently married to four brothers, Jampha, Palden, Sousom, and Tsering. They are men of the Kalden Clan. They are also of the knightly class." Lin Mei nodded. She knew of the mountain people's customs. Such arrangements were not rare.

"Tsering is also a monk, a Geshe of the Loksangha Monastery. He is at present in a cave above the monastery, meditating, and is not to be disturbed."

"A Geshe?" Lin Mei asked. "I have heard the word, but am not too familiar with the meaning."

"He is a sorcerer, and Geshe means that he has taken advanced training, and is most adept," her host replied. She nodded.

"He is allowed to marry?' she asked. "Even as a monk?" Dorpak nodded.

"The Akung sect allows monks to marry, with the permission of their abbot. For that matter, Jampha and Palden were also monks at the Loksangha Monastery, but were released from their monastic vows when their family arranged the marriage, so that they would be fully able to participate in the affairs of the household without distraction. And that brings us to the hub of the problem," he said. Lin Mei sat up straight, a small part of her mind noting that the cats were also paying rapt attention, and wondering why. "It appears that Tsering does not seem interested in fulfilling his matrimonial duties," Dorpak continued in a lower voice. "In fact, he plans to marry a young woman of another knightly family here in Taiyung. His family does not approve, but his reputation as a sorcerer is such that he feels he will be able to support his own household in proper comfort and in a manner appropriate to her station."

"He is allowed to marry another woman, even if he is already married to Pakchen Dgorge?" Lin Mei asked.

"The customs of the mountains allow that," Dorpak replied.

"Is there anything the customs of the mountains do not allow?" Lin Mei asked.

"Apparently not," Dorpak replied, wryly. Lin Mei chuckled.

"Pakchen Dgorge is the woman in the red robes?" she asked. He nodded. "She does not seem unattractive." Lin Mei noted, "I cannot see why Tsering would not wish to carry out his matrimonial duties, all the more so if he is also allowed to marry another woman. And Pakchen has three other husbands. I imagine she can spare one."

"The Kalden are prominent in this region," Dorpak told her. "While this would not qualify as a mortal insult, it will cause upset. Also, Sousom is not yet of age to fulfill the more intimate duties of a husband."

"But he was still married to Pakchen Dgorge?" she asked.

"The marriage contract represents an alliance between two noble and wealthy families," Dorpak replied, "and as such his name was on the contract despite his young age." Lin Mei nodded; that was not unusual.

"And the Rolang?" she asked, bringing the conversation back to the night's events. Dorpak took a deep breath.

"Do you know what one is?" he asked. She shook her head slowly.

"Powerful magicians are reputed to be able to bring the dead back to life," he said slowly, "or at least to some semblance of life. Such creatures are under their control, and will do their bidding." Understanding dawned in her.

"Is Tsering suspected of involvement?" she asked carefully. Dorpak nodded his eyes grim.

"So I hear. It appears he is determined to marry the young woman with whom he is taken," he said.

"But if the local customs allow him to be married to her, even if he is already married to Pakchen Dgorge, how would that cause problems?" she asked. Dorpak let out a sigh.

"Trade partnerships often follow family ties," he replied slowly, as if carefully choosing his words. "If Tsering were to split his affections between two women of different trading families, there might be some concern if trade was to be seen as being unfairly apportioned." Lin Mei settled more easily on her mat. So it was out. This was about trade. Somehow that did not surprise her. Dorpak looked at her, his eyes measuring her.

"You have sometimes dealt with complex matters," he said. "I would be most grateful for your assistance in dealing with this one." Lin Mei bowed low, partly to hide her face. Danger lurked in the offer, no matter how desperate Dorpak might seem. But as a guest she could not easily refuse his request. "I will tell everyone to cooperate with you," he went on, "and you will have any assistance my household can offer."

"I am most honored by your request," she said.

"And I am honored by your assistance," he replied. And so it was done.

After he had gone she sat back to consider the matter. Suddenly she was consumed by feelings of loneliness. For most of her life she had traveled the western lands, always in danger and surrounded by the unknown and the mysterious. Now she was once more in the midst of mystery and menace. Alone in her quarters, with only Shadow and Twilight to see, she surrendered to her emotions, letting silent tears fall to her lap.

After a while she used a scrap of cloth to dry her tears. She was investigating a matter of life and death. And apparently she had a reputation in such matters. It would not do if people suspected any weakness on her part. She drank the last of the tea and tossed the cats some scraps of dried meat. After checking her appearance in a mirror she stood, thrust her blades in her sash, and stepped outside, leaving the cats to settle back into a semi-somnolence. She had no worries of another attack anytime soon. In her experience the supernatural needed time to rest, just as mortals did, and their actions did not come too frequently.

First was a visit to Pakchen Dgorge. The two Kalden brothers, and husbands, met her at the door and let her in without delay, as if they had been expecting her, which was probably the case. She noted that one was the lancer she had seen earlier. They escorted her inside. The noblewoman was waiting on a black cushion which contrasted with her red robes. A tea set waited before her. Her men sat down on mats on either side of her. Lin Mei noted the strong family resemblance.

"May I offer tea?" Pakchen said, by way of greeting. Lin Mei bowed low.

"If I may be allowed to enjoy it with you," she replied. Pakchen smiled and poured for all of them. Lin Mei noted her movements were graceful and economical. So she was most likely born to the title and rank, and not of some merchant family who had purchased them by whatever means. She filed that datum away in the back of her mind. Lin Mei took the moment to evaluate the woman. Pakchen was, like the two men with her, tall and graceful. She accentuated her height with an elaborate hairdo around a split bamboo frame. She introduced her husbands. Palden, with the topknot, was the lancer. Jampha wore his hair short.

"May I be allowed to offer condolences on the death of your

servant?" Pakchen nodded in acknowledgement.

"Darten was a brave and loyal soldier, who had served our family loyally and well for years, as did his father before him," she replied. "His death is a great loss."

"All the more so as it came at the hands of the supernatural. Will such an unnatural death cause complications in his after-life?"

Pakchen set down her tea cup.

"It should not," Jampha interjected. "He was a good man, and his actions in life had earned him much merit. He will have a good rebirth."

"I am not familiar with the type of creature that visited earlier," Lin Mei went on. "May I be enlightened?"

"You mean the Rolang?" Pakchen asked. "It is a supernatural creature, a dead man brought back to life by sorcery or magic."

Lin Mei considered her next words carefully. "I noted a lack of surprise earlier. Was the attack expected?"

"There has been much talk in the town that it would come," Jampha said again. "Our brother's name, Tsering, was mentioned many times. He has been seen visiting the compound of the Gharlen Clan, for the purpose of seeing Tiniki, the youngest daughter of the clan elder. All know he has feelings for her. Despite our precautions, the Rolang penetrated this compound."

"Jampha is adept at gathering gossip in the markets and teasing truth out of it," Pakchen said.

Could that have been a smile on her lips? Lin Mei could not tell.

"I heard he was in a retreat in the mountain, above the Loksangha Monastery," Lin Mei said.

"That would not be a problem for such an adept," Palden said, speaking for the first time.

"Could such magic be done from such a distance?" Lin Mei asked.

Pakchen looked at her across the tea set, her eyes level. "If you are asking if my husband, Tsering, could be the one responsible," she replied, "I must say yes. A powerful and adept sorcerer can wield such power, even from a great distance. Even from a faraway mountaintop."

Afterwards, back in her rooms, Lin Mei pondered the meeting. There had been little of interest in the rest of her meeting with Pakchen, aside from learning that the wedding had been recent, and had not been attended by Tsering or Sousom. She blew out the lamp and went to sleep, her blades within easy reach.

The next day dawned bright and clear, and the haggling outside the city walls began early. Lin Mei made her rounds of the silk fair, checking with the guards under her command. The night had been uneventful; the guard was mainly for form. Taiyung was a wealthy and powerful city, and its reach extended far into the surrounding countryside. Brigands were rare. The ruling clans of the city were known for their passion for justice, and their ferocity in enforcing it.

That thought took her to the graveyard north of the city. A quick search led her to what she was looking for. In the section set aside for condemned criminals she found a grave that had been recently dug up, with shovel marks still fresh in the ground. She looked at it thoughtfully for a short while before entering the town though the East gate. There she stopped at a street vendor's stall and bought some roasted meat and barley bread. The stall was in a busy part of town and the man was busy. But not so busy he could not spare time for gossip.

"There is news of strange events in the compound of Dorpak Champa," the vendor ventured. Lin Mei looked up at him.

"Gossip outruns a fast horse," she replied, quoting a mountain proverb. "What is being said?"

"Much talk of unnatural things, a dead man brought back to life. Bad thing, that. The dead should stay dead. But now we know why Dorpak and the Dgorge woman brought in extra guards two days ago. People wondered why. Now we know."

"It was the Rolang," a nearby street urchin piped up, "a dead man walking!"

"And what do you know of Rolangs?" she asked.

"That they cannot be killed easily, because their flesh has

hardened as they lay dead, so that magic must be used. And that they don't walk like normal men, because their legs are not as bendable as they used to be. So they hop like this!" The boy held his feet together and took three hops, to the amusement of all nearby. Lin Mei laughed and bought him a scrap of bread. She stopped at other stalls, making more purchases, but learned nothing more.

On the way back into town she tried to see Tiniki Gharlen but was not allowed into the compound. Some maids shopping at a vegetable vendor nearby were more forthcoming, describing a shy and pretty young girl, the sheltered daughter of a wealthy and proud family. They also confirmed that a man had been seen visiting of late, with the family's blessing.

A temple sat on the street near the compound of Dorpak Champa. She stopped there, and after making a modest but significant donation to the place, spoke at length with the priest, leaving with a small sealed jar, which had also cost a modest but significant donation.

Back in the compound Lin Mei stopped at the Dgorge household and spoke with Palden, leaving the jar with him before returning to her own rooms. There she gave the two cats some scraps of meat she had brought for them, then bathed and changed into clean clothing. Out on the veranda, with a cup of tea, she considered the matter. Across the sand garden she could see the bamboo stand. The sand had been raked smooth. The tracks left by the Rolang were gone. She brought up her memories of the night before, her eyes thoughtful. Finally she went back inside and took a nap. She would need the rest later.

Evening came late. It was midsummer and the air was warm and thick. She changed into thick rough clothing, what she normally wore on the trail. It had been cleaned by the maids, and the cloth felt pleasant against her skin.

The compound was settling down for the night, but she could see lamps burning within the Dgorge household. Occasionally armed men opened the doors and looked outside. She saw to her blades, checking the long dagger with special care before thrusting it in her sash. She was as ready as she could be. Nearby

Shadow and Twilight prowled about the room nervously. She sat on a mat on the veranda.

She did not have long to wait. A sudden roar split the night air to her right, and a long shadow cast by the torches near the gate speared across the sand before her. Lin Mei grasped her sword and leapt from the veranda to run out onto to the sand, the cats following. There she confronted the Rolang, which landed before her with a single leap that spanned the length of a man.

"Yah! Yah!" she yelled, waving her arms about. "Yah! Yah!" The dead man turned blank staring eyes at her, his mouth emitting a horrid stench as he growled. Around his ankles Twilight bounded about, slashing at his feet and legs. Lin Mei jumped to the side and ran to the bamboo. If she was right, the creature would have to follow. Sparing a look back she saw that it had. Reaching the bamboo she struggled for a moment to pass between the stalks. Behind her she could hear the monster coming closer. Suddenly there was a squalling sound and she spared a look back. Shadow had jumped onto the Rolang's head, grasping it while he chewed on its ear and clawed at the eyes. Twilight was still shredding the trousers. She slipped between the thick stalks and silently sent a command to her feline companions. They cut off their attack and retreated to the safety to the veranda. They had accomplished their mission.

Behind her she heard the Rolang crash into the bamboo. The tough plant stalks bent, but did not give way. Unable to move in any way but hopping he continued to crash into the stalks. Behind she could hear shouting and yells, as the armed men of the compound rushed out, Palden in the lead with his lance. But she had no thoughts for that. She had her own quarry to hunt.

She ran into him just a short way further. Drawing her dagger she held it before her.

"I don't think you should," she said as he attempted to draw his sword, difficult to do in the close confines of the bamboo. "Drop your blade. It's all over." With an outlet of breath that might have been a sob Jampha did as she bade.

They were gathered in the Dgorge hall. Pakchen sat against

the wall, her long black hair loose and held back by a silver headband. Palden sat to her right, his lance on the mats beside him. He had taken time to clean the head of the potion Lin Mei had given him. She sat to Pakchen's left. Jampha was between them, facing Pakchen. His face was a pale mask showing what might have been numb shock.

"I would know more," Pakchen said, speaking to Lin Mei.

Lin Mei settled back on her heels, carefully arranging her thoughts.

"Last night when the attack came," she began, "I noticed the bamboo stirring, despite the lack of a breeze." She did not add that the cats had noted something odd in the bamboo first, before turning their attention to the house. The less said about them the better. "But the Rolang emerged from the house itself. So who was in the bamboo? And it was Palden who emerged from the door, with the other men. I did not see Jampha until later."

"Also, all the talk about Tsering did not seem true to me. And most came from Jampha. While monks may sometimes be distracted by the pleasures and temptations of this world, to become an adept such as a Geshe would require such a level of commitment that it seemed improbable." She stopped to spare glances at the two brothers.

"I noticed a strong family resemblance. Does Tsering also share that resemblance? Enough so that Jampha could pass for Tsering as he visited the Gharlen compound?" Pakchen nodded slightly. "Then might they also share a talent for magic? Both Palden and Jampha were monks with Tsering at the Loksangha Monastery. Did Jampha progress further than he may have admitted to?"

"I would have been a great Geshe!" Jampha spoke at last. "Tsering was always my inferior! But he was allowed to stay, and I was brought here to marry that..." He stopped, pale at what he might almost have said. Before him Pakchen sat very still, her face cold and still.

"What did you mean?" she asked slowly. "When you said 'that...'?"

"Tiniki is a sweet young girl," Jampha said, "and her family would have allowed me to pursue my studies." Lin Mei noted that Pakchen was a formidable presence, bordering on intimidating. She wondered if that might have been a factor in the drama that was unfolding.

"You have betrayed me and both our families," Pakchen spoke in a voice as cold as the winds of her mountain home. "You also caused the death of a loyal and valued servant, who died bravely in my defense. You will leave this house, and go to the Loksangha Monastery. There you will take Tsering's place in the cave. You will stay there for the rest of your life, praying for forgiveness, and for the soul of Darten." She waved her hand. Two large guards took him away.

The next day dawned clear and bright. With it came an offer to join Dorpak Champa for breakfast. Lin Mei changed to suitable attire and followed the maid to the main hall, the cats following along behind. Something told her not to make them stay.

Dorpak was in an amiable mood. Trading had been good, profits were more than satisfactory, and his household was once more at peace. Lin Mei was amused to see two small bowls with meat stew on the floor in the corner. The cats settled down to eat. Dorpak gestured to the mat opposite him. After soup and pickles the rice was brought in, hot and steaming. Both dug in with relish, chopsticks clicking. After the bowls had been taken away and tea served he dismissed the maids.

"This matter is well-settled," he said. "Tsering has been sent for. He will take Jampha's place in the household. Also, another Kalden, a cousin of the brothers, is coming down to join the household. All appears to be well."

"Pakchen wishes another husband? Three are not enough?" Lin Mei asked, eyes wide. Dorpak laughed at her surprise.

"The mountains are a hard and dangerous place," he said. "One cannot have too many good men about."

—or good women, Lin Mei thought.

TEAR-STAINED SWORD

by Jessie D. Eaker

For every spell there is a counter-spell. The trick is knowing when to use it. This is Jessie's first submission to SWORD AND SORCERESS in several years. His previous stories were in SWORD AND SORCERESS 6, 7, 9, 11, 14, and 15, as well as the anthology MARION ZIMMER BRADLEY'S FANTASY WORLDS. Despite the feminine spelling of the first name, Jessie is male. The last name is pronounced "acre" with the *E* being silent. Jessie lives in Richmond, Virginia, with his wife Becki. This past year they have become empty nesters as the youngest of their children moved away to college. This has been quite a challenge since they've been surrounded by kids most of their lives, but they're adapting and discovering the joys of cats and of being grandparents. His youngest daughter Rebecca also has a story in the book. Jessie says, "It is a unique privilege to share the pages with a talented writer who just happens to be your child."

My prey was close.

Drawn by the magic that bound me, I gradually made my way toward the back of the hall. The white lace scarf affixed to my right wrist tingled in delight as I spied my target. I instantly recognized her. *Faydra! It couldn't be her!*

She stood alone and beautiful, waiting for my arrival. Her gown was bright green, embroidered at the sleeves and hem in white ancient patterns. She wore her hair long, with her wavy red locks held back with two emerald combs. Her youthful face had gentle freckles sprinkled across the pale complexion of her nose. Her eyes held an expression of deep sorrow.

I sprinted toward her—the spell of compulsion on me was irresistible. The world around me grew suddenly quiet, as if the goddess herself held her breath. I heard no sound other than my own pounding heart.

Twisting my blade flat, I leveled my sword to strike. At the moment before...our eyes met. Faydra's brilliant green eyes loomed before me. And they swam with tears.

I plunged my sword deep into her chest, with just a hand's breath of sword remaining. The task completed, the compulsion broke, and the scarf affixed to my wrist loosened and drifted free.

"Oh Goddess, what have I done!" I whispered.

Faydra's lower lip trembled. The tears filling her eyes became dislodged and rolled down her cheek. In the horrid silence, I heard a tear, then another, splat loudly against the exposed flat of my sword. Her trembling hand slowly rose and gently touched the side of my face. "These tears are for you, Kerrin, my foolish sister...."

I bolted awake, gasping for breath. My heart hammered in my chest and my hands shook. I threw back the covers and sat on the edge, cradling my head in my hands, as I waited for the dream to fade. It had been months since I had been sent to find a rebel leader. Months since Faydra's body had been laid to rest. Yet the dreams still came the same one over and over: the taking of my sister's life.

The room was dark except for the few coals in the fireplace and a lantern turned down low next to the door. I looked toward the room's narrow slit of a window, and sadly found it still dark outside—dawn would be a while coming. I rubbed my eyes. There would be no further sleep for me. I got up and padded in my bare feet to the window, where I opened the shutter and gazed out across the dark courtyard. A faint breeze tugged at my loose shirt, smelling of cool mist and damp earth. I breathed deep the chill spring air, trying to shake off the dream. If my servants caught me such, they would scold me, saying the night vapors brought evil spirits. But I knew ghosts didn't come through a window. They haunted my dreams.

No official reason had been given for Faydra's death. But rumor had it she had been plotting to overthrow the king. Even though we hadn't seen each other in over five years, I knew that wasn't Faydra. It just wasn't in her character.

I had tried to confront King Liam as to why he had ordered her death but found myself barred from his presence. The one time I crossed paths with him, he refused to even look at me. I suspected my presence reminded him I went there by his command.

I shook my head. She could have stopped me—countermanded the order and halted the Huntress spell. But she didn't. "All it would have taken was a single word," I whispered. "But you didn't. Why?"

Only silence answered me.

I drew the shutter and went to the hearth, where I found a few embers ready to be awakened. I stirred them to life and fed them a few pieces of oak. The reborn flames danced prettily. As always, Faydra sprang to mind when I did this, reminded of how we first met.

In my early years, I lived quietly with just my mother in a small cottage. But one day during my tenth year, she took to her bed and shortly died. While my cheeks were still wet with grief, the men arrived. And I learned the truth. My mother had been a mistress of the king, and I, his illegitimate child.

I was straight away taken to my father, King Liam. He gave me one look, said I looked like my mother, and dismissed me with a wave of his hand. I was assigned a room, fed and bathed with nary a kind word. I later learned the servants were terrified to show me any favor lest they bring down the Queen's fury. She had not been a kind lady.

And so I found myself in a strange room, in a strange bed all alone. I still remembered how terrified I was that first night. The bed had seemed huge. The shutter creaked in the wind and the room was cold, so cold I could not get warm. Yet I was determined not to cry and denied the wet streaks sliding down my face. Maybe I dozed, I'm not completely sure, but a loud pop from the fireplace startled me. I bolted upright to find someone stoking the fire. A girl just a few years younger than me squatted in front of it in nothing but her nightdress. The orange light from the fire illuminated the fabric and seemed to make her glow with warmth. She must have heard me sit up and turned to look at me. “I thought you might be lonely,” she said and grinned. She ran to my bed, and giggling, jumped under the covers beside me. Suddenly the bed had seemed snug and warm. “I’m Faydra. We’re sisters. I’ve always wanted a sister.”

I smiled to myself. She had gotten a severe scolding for that trick. Her mother forbad her to have anything to do with me. (Not that it stopped her.) I was, after all, her competition for the king’s favor.

I sighed. Little chance there had been for that. I learned early on that in my father’s eyes, daughters were nothing but brood stock for alliances. And that was one fate I was determined to resist.

I went to the foot of my bed where I kept my gear. I took up my sword and carried it back to the fire along with some oil, rag and whetstone. I pulled my sword from its scabbard and began to rub it down. The servants would do this for me, but I insisted on doing it myself. Your weapons are your life in a fight and I didn’t relish trusting mine to servants who were more interested in their next cup of ale than keeping me safe.

I swore I wasn’t going to look, but I did anyway, finding them exactly as before: two irregularly shaped spots on the blade just shy of the guard. They looked like where drops of water had wetted it, yet for some reason refused to roll off. Two of them. One for each of the tears my sister had shed.

Afterwards, on the night of her death, as I cleaned my sword (and shed my own tears), I noticed them for the first time. *How had they gotten there?* I tried to clean them off with oil, but they stubbornly remained no matter how hard I rubbed. The next day, I went to the blacksmith and he tried various methods including heat and scouring, but neither worked. He suggested I see an alchemist to perhaps try acid, but warned it could permanently weaken the blade.

I next went to a priestess, reasoning it must be some kind of magic. My sister did practice—some said she was very good. The priestess confirmed it was indeed some kind of sealed spell with some sort of trigger. But as to what the trigger was, she had no idea.

"You say she died when these were made," the priestess had asked.

I could only nod.

"That would explain their feel. A casting quite powerful is locked inside one of them. Whoever did this must have been desperate, because she poured the remains of her life into it." She looked up into my eyes and found something painful. She immediately glanced away. "But other than that, I cannot tell you more."

So what exactly had my sister done? I didn't think it was to harm me. To me, she had always been sweet and gentle. Only once had she been short with me. Not too long after my sister reached marriageable age, she was bargained off to one of my father's stronger lords to consolidate an alliance. With the queen having died the year before and no one to intervene on her behalf, she had resigned herself to her new fate. She had come to see me the day before she was supposed to leave.

As soon as I saw her, I could tell she was angry. At first I thought it was at me, I had by that time made myself quite undesirable as a bride.

"No, my sister," she shook her head. "I'm not angry with you. It's father I'm angry at. This alliance is only for war and his foolishness will ruin the land."

"But you are going in my place," I protested. "I'm the one that should be leaving. I can understand why you might be angry with me."

Her expression softened and a sad smile touched her lips. "Your destiny is much different from mine. You have a great duty ahead of you. A very important one." And with that she pulled me forward and gave me a kiss on the forehead. I felt it tingle. "Our time together has been short. Never forget that I love you. I have from the first time I saw you enter father's court. Just remember that I will always protect you." I could see tears in her eyes.

I remember watching her turn and walk briskly from the

room. I think I heard her give a single sob as the door closed behind her. Why? Why five years later did she have to die?

Why did father order me to kill her?

I went back to cleaning my sword. These were the questions I pondered until the horizon began to lighten. And I was no closer to an answer than I was several months ago.

When it was light enough to see, I pulled on a loose shirt and trousers and went out to the practice yard. I faced the rising sun and stretched as my old tutors had instructed to prepare for the more complex moves to come.

Father had thought it amusing that I took up the sword. A girl. It provided him great entertainment to watch me fall on my backside while I learned. *That will teach that girl her place,* I could hear him say. To discourage me, he sought out the cruelest tutors he could find. And for the first few years, my backside stayed quite bruised. I cut off my hair and would dress like a boy, almost always covered in bruises and dirt from the practice yard. The servants constantly talked about me. *The Wild Girl*, they called me. Those in my father's court laughed. But I ignored their chattering. I persisted and grew stronger.

One day a minor lord boasted to the king he would show me my place. He was good...but I was better. Another came forward days later and I beat him too. Perhaps a little more soundly than I should have.

Suddenly no one laughed anymore—including my father. Shortly after, he ordered me to start wearing dresses and sent servants to bathe and dress me. I kept the bath, but sent the dresses back.

Next, he found me a husband. When I refused, my father decreed that the first man to best me, could bed me. I did not think that was amusing. And the first few challengers did not think their method of losing was amusing either.

Angry now, father sent me into battle. I returned victorious. But instead of the recognition I craved, he decided that I was too dangerous to leave unchained.

Oh, how I cursed that day.

"Mistress!" I jerked at the sudden interruption of my thoughts. I slowly turned to find a servant at the edge of the practice field. I glared at him coldly and he swallowed nervously. "Mistress. His majesty requests your presence in his quarters."

"What does he want with me?" I wiped the sweat from my forehead, watching the servant dance nervously from foot to foot.

"Mistress, I do not know. But he did receive a visitor late last night."

I frowned. This could only be trouble. Yet it would give me a chance to finally talk with my father. "I will be there after I get my coat."

The servant took a step back. "He said to tell you to come now." He swallowed nervously. "He said he didn't care if you were stark naked in bed with your lover or straining over a chamber pot, to get there *now*."

Typical father. I sheathed my sword. "Lead on."

I expected to go to his court, but instead I was led to his private chambers. Two soldiers stood either side of the door: my father's personal guards. They barred my entrance. "Your sword, Mistress Kerrin," said the one on the left.

I knew no one was allowed to bring a weapon into the king's presence. Not even his daughter. Or more likely, *especially* this daughter. My first impulse was to say something rude and refuse, but I decided that today perhaps I should play along. I unbuckled it and handed it to the guard. He seemed relieved and stepped aside.

Knocking once and entering, I found father sitting in his favorite chair, and strangely, still in his bed clothes with his gray hair still unkempt. He also seemed thinner and his eyes had dark shadows under them. I blinked in surprise. Normally, he was up and fully dressed before the sun. *Was father ill?*

My half-brother Prince Cavan lounged across from him in all his richly dressed, royal splendor. Their conversation stopped immediately.

Goddess, could this day not get any better? Cavan was very much the spoilt child: extremely impatient and expecting to be pampered and flattered. In appearance, he took more after father with light brown hair and a handsome face (or so the ladies said). He also had father's temperament. Only Cavan was crueler. Much crueler. I dreaded the day he became king.

"Good day to you, sister." Cavan smiled, but his eyes glinted with malice. "Are you feeling any better? I heard you've been having nightmares."

I stiffened. *How did he know?* He always did have a knack for finding out secrets. Cavan was using that knowledge to try and goad me into losing my temper in front of father. But I held my tongue and kept my expression blank. I didn't want to spoil my chance to question father.

King Liam leaned forward. "Kerrin, we've found a task for you. We've gained a clue as to the whereabouts of the rebel leader. You're to leave immediately to find him. Now hold out your arm."

I didn't move. "The last time you did this, it cost me my sister's life."

He paused in mid-motion. "*That* was a mistake!" He spat out. The venom in his voice surprised me.

"A mistake! You used that damn spell to make me kill my sister, and it was a mistake!"

He looked up at me with fire in his eye. "Yes, a mistake. Somehow the traitor managed to switch the anchor with another. Unfortunately, it was one of Faydra's old scarves she left behind."

He pulled out a small silver box with a hinged lid. "But with this, we'll have our revenge." He opened the lid.

The inside was lined with black velvet and laying across it, I could see a single long hair, light in color. He carefully lifted the hair and looked up. He seemed surprised I hadn't already extended my arm.

"I don't want to do this...."

"*Huntress*," he commanded and I instantly stiffened as the spell seized me.

He didn't even seem to notice. "It is not your place to question me. I have this on the best intelligence. *Now, extend your arm!* I want you on your way within the hour. I want my revenge!"

The spell would not allow me to disobey. I extended my right arm and he carefully draped the long hair over my wrist. He smiled wickedly up at me. "By my command, seek and kill. *Huntress.* Get the bastard that caused Faydra's death."

Spurred by father's anger, the binding spell hit me hard. By itself, the hair wrapped itself tightly around my wrist where it would stay until my task was completed. I spun on my heel and stepped toward the door.

Cavan called after me, his voice dripping in sarcasm. "I do hope this hunt doesn't make your nightmares any worse!"

I ignored him. My concern at the moment was to control the spell long enough to get my gear together.

The horse trotted down the road at a good clip. After a week of travel the prey had grown very close. The spell wanted my mount to run, to gallop until his heart exploded. But I resisted, knowing, as the spell did not, that pushing the animal to death would not help.

I shifted in my saddle. I also rode alone, with my father's guards several hours behind me. They had long since learned to stay out of my way.

Damn this spell—this collar of magic my father had put on me. I cursed myself for being a coward.

Several years ago, on the day after I returned from my last battle, I was called to my father's court. I had expected to be rewarded for my bravery, but instead I was surrounded by twelve of his personal guard. My weapons were taken and my hands bound. Father then announced to his court that I had become a threat to him, and especially, his heirs. I had grown too powerful, and, with my bastard status, he feared I would challenge his legitimate children for the throne. But he was merciful and saw usefulness in my service. So he gave me the choice: die...or receive the Huntress Collar.

And in my cowardice I chose to live.

I shook my head. The Huntress Collar was a powerful spell, more curse actually, which would force me to obey not only my father's orders, but those of his children, Faydra and Cavan. I also was prohibited from harming them without a direct command.

And use me, my father did. I became his assassin: a deadly weapon with no mercy and no choice. All he needed was an object that belonged to the person, and I would track them down. I was no stranger to killing, having survived a few battles. But there is something very different about facing an armed soldier on the battle field and some terrified minor lord in his bedroom.

Faydra was horror struck by what father had done. Until she left to be wed, she would seek me out after I returned from a hunt, and we would weep together.

On this day, the sun was high overhead and pleasantly warm for early spring. Some of the trees beside the road had already started to bloom. This had been Faydra's favorite time. As a child, she had so loved to watch spring unfold. We often snuck away to help with the horses and maybe get a brief ride if we were lucky. It was on just such a day as we walked back from the stables that she stopped and squatted beside a tiny purple flower poking up from the ground. She looked at it for quite a while, carefully studying it, until I prompted her that we had to be back. Her mother would discipline us both.

But Faydra did not move. She had always been a little strange for a child. I supposed it was her magical abilities, which had awoken so very early. She would just sometimes go elsewhere in her mind.

Suddenly, the moment broke. She looked up at me with a very serious expression, and then she said something which I only recently understood the meaning of. "You know I can do magic, don't you."

I nodded. Suddenly afraid to speak.

"I can even see into the future. Take this flower. It will be crushed under some cow's foot before the week is out. But that is all right, because that trampled flower will have managed a single seed. Then, next year, from that seed, another flower even prettier and stronger will grow. And from that daughter flower, seeds will spread which will turn this entire meadow a beautiful shade of deep purple."

I held out my hand to her. "We must be getting back before they find us missing."

She ignored me, continuing in her speaking. "I also know you're going to kill me one day. I've known since the first day I saw you. But don't worry, it's not for many years yet and it's not your fault."

"That's nonsense." I said, thinking her playing some prank on me. "I'd never hurt you." I reached for her hand. "We have to go."

She snatched my hand tightly and rose, pulling me close. "But remember sister, I will protect you...."

I shook my head to clear the painful memories. She had known I was her death. And yet she befriended me. Sought me out even. Why had she done it?

The Huntress Collar jerked me out of my thoughts. A side road appeared to my left, and it was insisting I take that direction. I could feel we were very close and I urged the horse into a gallop.

Rounding a clump of trees, I spied a cottage just up the hill and knew my target lay just inside. I urged my horse even faster and felt the familiar spell fall in around me. I couldn't suppress the evil grin which spread over my face.

I reined in just before the door, trampling several rows of flowers just starting to bloom, and dismounted before the horse had even stopped moving. I ran to the door, shoving it open with my shoulder where it banged loudly into the wall. I scanned the cottage's interior noting the single hearth on the far wall, a single bed with two pillows to the right, meal preparations scattered on the table before me. Two bowls sitting out.

I heard a frightened sob and glanced to the corner where an older woman huddled in terror. I drew my sword and prepared for the death blow....

When a small red haired child, with vibrant green eyes, rose over the woman's shoulder to stare at me. And I was so taken off guard I froze for just a moment. The old woman wasn't my target. *It was the child!*

And there was no mistaking those eyes, that hair, that face. She had to be my sister's child.

The spell reoriented itself and I drew back to strike the girl. *Oh goddess, not again!*

Out of the corner of my right eye, up towards my sword, I saw a brief white flash and heard a sound like water sizzling on a hot iron. Then I heard a deafening voice....The voice of my dead sister, "Stop *Huntress*, my dearest Kerrin," it said calmly. "By my command, I say stop."

And the spell suddenly released. The hair which anchored my hunt drifted free from my wrist.

I lowered my sword and cradled it in disbelief. What had just happened? Then I saw. On the blade just shy of the guard, one of the two tear stains was gone.

My world suddenly wheeled. *Faydra had saved them!* I stumbled to a bench and sat down on it heavily. I laid my sword across my lap and put my head in my hands. Exhaustion was heavy on me, as was usual for when the spell completed. My mouth felt as dry as high summer, and my stomach felt unsettled and hungry at the same time.

I considered the pair before me. Some of the terror had left the old woman's eyes, and the little girl watched me warily. She was the spitting image of her mother. I guessed her to be three or four years old. Her hair was lighter than Faydra's, but definitely her mother's red hue. She was dressed in a plain blue dress with feet bare and her hair loose. There looked to be flour on her nose.

I never knew that Faydra had a child. She had stayed with her husband for almost a year, before he mysteriously died. Her husband's brother took the throne of that kingdom, and about the same time, Faydra vanished. Father refused to talk about her and would not allow me to hunt for her. I feared her imprisoned or dead. But a year after her disappearance, I received a lone letter saying very little except she was alive, well, and unable to return. There had been no mention of a baby.

Which meant she fled the new lord, afraid for her child. That also explained why she hadn't returned home, since our Father would have either quietly killed the child, or used her as an excuse to challenge the new lord's power.

I slowly stood and sheathed my sword. "I'm sorry for breaking into your home," I said to the woman as I stood. I reached down and began to gather the things I had knocked to the floor in my rush to enter. "The girl is Faydra's daughter, isn't she?"

The older woman's eyes went wide and her mouth drew into an *ohh* before she nodded.

The little girl scooted out from behind the woman and wagged a finger at me. "Don't be mean to Nanny. That's not nice!"

I couldn't help but smile. The girl had her mother's temperament too. I went to one knee in front of her to bring her more to eye level. "And pray tell, what is your name?"

The girl stood up straight and pushed her hair out of her eyes. "Veretie. And what pray tell is yours?"

I nodded at the direct question. "I am Kerrin. I was your..."

"You're my aunt! My mother's sister!" she blurted out. She stepped forward a huge smile on her face. "She told me stories about you. I especially liked the one where you were hiding in the stables and got stung by bees." She emphasized the point by pinching the air.

My heart twisted in my chest. She was so much like her mother. And I nearly killed her. If it hadn't been for Faydra's magic, she would be dead. Why would father consider the girl a traitor?

One thing was sure, I couldn't leave her here. Father's guards were not too far behind and they would report my failure. I looked to her guardian and knew there was no way they could run fast enough to get away even with my help. And if I tried to run with them, the Huntress Collar would drag me back.

No, there was only one path forward. I had to take Veretie to my father and pray I could convince him something had gone wrong.

I leaned forward and ruffled the girl's hair. "Have you ever ridden a horse before?"

A week later, I strode into my father's court holding Veretie in my left arm. I had been walking much too fast for her so I just scooped her up and carried her. She did not complain and instead, rode on my arm in silent dignity, as if she were the queen and I her mount. I had stopped outside the castle and changed her into her finest dress (a long light green one) and matching slippers. I had pulled her hair back in tight braids just like Faydra had worn in her youth. To me, she looked like a vision of the past.

Unfortunately, I found the throne room was completely empty. Strange. Father would normally be in court at this time of day. "Where is my father?" I asked the guard by the door.

The guard glanced to the child, clearly curious. "He is likely in his chambers. He's been ill since you left."

"What's wrong with him?"

The guard shrugged. "No one knows. Rumor says poison."

I thanked the guard, and with a growing sense of unease, went to my father's chambers. I had expected an argument before I could enter. But I found two new guards outside father's door, ones that I knew were loyal to my brother.

"Prince Cavan is expecting you, Mistress Kerrin," said one. They made no comment about the child I held in my arms. I set her down and placed her against the wall next to the guards. "Stay right here," I ordered. "And don't move. I'll be right back."

She grabbed my hand. "Promise?"

I couldn't help but smile. "Promise."

She stepped to the wall and put her back against it, seeming to settle in for a wait.

The inside of father's room smelled of sickness and I could see him lying in his bed. Even in the two weeks I'd been gone, he looked thinner and very pale. Cavan stood by the room's fireplace playing with his dagger. His special one. Swords had never really thrilled him. They were too big and bulky for his liking. But daggers....They were the weapon of royalty. He always carried three, one on each side of his belt and one in his boot. The one in the boot was coated with poison.

His eyes went up when he saw me.

I ignored him and went to my father's bedside. "What's wrong, Father? What happened?"

Father turned yellow eyes to me and tried to talk. But only garbled sounds came out. He raised his head weakly from his pillow and pointed a wavering arm at my brother. He held it only a moment or two before it fell to the bed. My father panted with the exertion.

I turned to Cavan. "What happened? He was well when I left."

Cavan stepped toward us, repeatedly flipping his dagger end over end and catching it. He ignored my question. He seemed angry. "Did you complete your mission? The servants say you have a child with you."

I turned to look at father. "The child *was* my mission. Apparently, there was another mistake and the anchor was wrong. There is no way she could have been the target." I looked back to him as he slowly approached, flipping the dagger end over end. His expression made me uneasy.

Cavan stopped his incessant motion and pointed the dagger toward the bed. "Father's dying. The physician thinks it's poison."

"Then why isn't the physician trying to make an antidote?"

My brother shrugged. "He tried, but it didn't work. I finally dismissed him."

"Then do you know who did this?"

He grinned. "Yes, I do."

Suddenly I knew without a shadow of doubt...my brother was behind it. And as much as I wanted to, I couldn't touch him. I began inching toward the door.

He gave the dagger a flip and pointed it in my direction. I knew what he was going to say. "*Huntress*, extend your arm."

The spell immediately seized me. I fought it, but it won as always. Slowly my right arm lifted.

He went to father's bed and pulled a ring from my father's hand. Then grinning, he slipped it on my finger.

"Don't...." I pleaded.

He looked up at me innocently. “Don’t what? Kill father? I’ve come too far to stop now.” He shook his head. “I think you’ve realized by now that I made up the rebel story and substituted Faydra’s scarf. I brought the girl’s hair too. Father was just taking too long to declare me his successor. I think he was afraid I would kill him. I can’t believe he distrusted me so.”

I felt my anger swell within me. “You made me kill Faydra when she was innocent. Our very own sister?”

He put his special dagger away and reached down to pull one from his boot. The poison one. “Oh yes. Father knew where Faydra was these past few years.” He stepped toward me. “He was even thinking of forgiving her for her past failures and inviting her back. He’s really gotten soft in his old age. But I couldn’t have her competing for the throne...nor her child.” He leaned in close so I could feel his hot breath. “And by the way, it was my suggestion to use the Huntress Collar on you. I had to take care of the bastard too.”

He then plunged the dagger into my right shoulder, leaving it embedded in my flesh. I groaned at the searing pain. And the poison...I could feel it burning as it spread through my blood. In minutes, I would be dead.

“You’ll be the perfect scapegoat.” He switched to a falsetto voice. “Oh it was terrible. She went berserk and killed father. I only saved myself by catching her with my dagger.” He leaned forward again and dropped back to his normal voice, deadly serious. “And don’t worry. I’ll entertain our little niece after you’re dead.” He smiled wickedly. “By my command, seek and kill. *Huntress.*”

The ring on my right hand slid up tight.

Despite the pain in my shoulder, the spell forced me to draw my blade and I turned toward the bed. I summoned all my resolve and willed myself to stop. Slowly, like some living statue, I ground to a halt.

“Kill him,” my brother shouted from behind me, concern creeping into his voice. My sword began to waiver and sweat beaded on my forehead as I struggled. But the poison was making me too weak. I wouldn’t be able to hold out.

I glanced at my sword and saw the remaining tear drop stain. "Faydra," I whispered aloud.

Immediately there was a brief flash of light and....

I was standing in a field dressed in my best shirt and vest. I could feel a gentle breeze, scented with spring flowers, tugging gently at my hair and rippling across the grass. Faydra stood before me wearing the same green dress she wore the day I killed her. She smiled at me and tears sprang to my eyes. It was so good to see her. And yet, I knew this was just a vision. This wasn't really her.

Faydra smiled at me. "My sister, I have just a moment with you. Know that I love you and will keep my promise. You are not responsible for my death, no more than a sword is guilty of how its owner chooses to use it. Feel no guilt over my death."

"But..." I started.

She held up a hand stopping me, her expression serious. "Time is too short. Cavan had used a spell of silence on the scarf, and as you approached, it would have prevented you hearing my counter command. It was a deadly trap. I had no way out, except to kill you. And I couldn't do that. The scoundrel was to be rid of at least one of us."

Faydra shook her head and moved closer. "But I am not innocent either. I will protect my child, and so I too must use you, just as Cavan did. I pray you forgive me. And with our father's death and my final command, I give you your freedom...And a choice." She reached forward and touched my cheek. "Please take care of my daughter. You're the only one strong enough to do it."

Suddenly, I was back in my body still straining against the spell. I heard the sound of water dancing on a hot iron and saw the tear drop stain melt away.

Immediately, my body burned white hot. Every fiber of my being burned in agony. Then just as suddenly, it was gone and I knew the poison had been magically removed. Then in a loud voice, I heard my dead sister's command: "*Huntress, stop. Instead, by my command, seek and kill Cavan.*"

The spell immediately reversed and the dagger in my shoulder drew in tight. Then for once in my life, I willingly worked with the collar as I focused on my new target. Cavan panicked and stepped back, but it was already too late. Before he could open his mouth, my sword found its new target and my brother died.

Panting, I dropped my sword and I fell to my knees; the dagger slipped from my shoulder of its own accord. I clamped my hand over the wound to slow the bleeding, but found it had already stopped. Another gift of Faydra's healing.

Hearing the noise within, the guards burst into the room with swords drawn. They saw my brother's body, my wounds and bloody sword. They were quick to figure out what had happened, and being my brother's men, I expected them to kill me on the spot.

Behind me came a soft whisper, but despite its weakness, it held the voice of command. "Do not...harm her...," said my father. "Cavan...poisoned me." He paused to swallow. "Get...captain...."

Seizing the opening my father had made, I reinforced the order. "You heard him! One of you fetch his captain, *now!*" They glanced at one another and realized where their best chances lay. One of them left out the door while the other covered my brother's body with a nearby cloak.

Father tried to raise his hand towards me. And I shuffled over on my knees to be closer to the bed. I took his damp hand in mine. "Rest, father, I'll get the physician."

He almost imperceptibly shook his head. "Too late..."

I heard little steps just before I felt a tiny body lean on me and wrap her arms around my neck. Veretie had disobeyed and came to find me.

I stood and despite my fatigue, I raised her in my arms. Father's tired eyes tracked me. He gazed at her seeming to drink in her likeness. "Faydra's...?"

I nodded. "She's your granddaughter. Her name is Veretie."

Father swallowed painfully. "Pretty...like her."

Just then the captain came running in, followed by several more guards. "Sire, what happened?"

Father weakly motioned him over. "Witness...." he

commanded in a whisper. He aimed a trembling finger in our direction. "Faydra's...daughter...my heir...." And then he turned his tired eyes on me. He took a labored breath. "Kerrin...." His eyes closed and the last word came out so soft, I was the only one to hear it.

"Regent."

And then father died.

I closed my eyes and couldn't help the sudden wetness filling them. This was the man I despised. I hated. And as I was discovering, somehow loved.

I blinked back tears and turned to the men in the room. "All of you witness King Liam's last order." I raised her as high as I could in my arms. "Veretie, daughter of Faydra, King Liam's oldest daughter, will be the new ruler of this land."

The captain nodded his understanding. "I so witness it." He and his guards all bowed formally to her. Veretie seemed to take the move in stride and bowed back to them from my arms.

Unable to hold her any longer, I placed her on the floor and sat down myself.

Veretie gave me a serious look, clearly concerned. "What will happen now?"

At first, I wasn't sure how to answer. Faydra had said I had a choice. And I had to admit I was a little angry with her. She had used me to spare the life of her child and place her on the throne. In that respect, she wasn't any different from Cavan. Now that the curse had run its course, I could walk away. For the first time in my life, I was truly free.

Then I remembered the laughter of my sister's voice and the friendship we had shared. No, it had been different. I found I didn't mind her last command, nor her last request.

I looked at Veretie's gentle face and realized that for me there was only one choice.

"I'm going to take care of you from now on," I said. "Or at least until you're old enough to rule. So don't worry, I'll protect you."

The child broke into a huge grin and threw her arms around my neck. "Mother said you would."

A VARIATION IN SILENCE

by Rebecca G. Eaker

My favorite place to vacation is a Benedictine convent, so I'm familiar with silence. I even prefer it when I write, unlike some authors who can actually make up playlists for what they listened to while writing their books. In this story Rebecca has come up with an interesting use of both silence and music.

When I asked for her biography, she sent me this.

"Growing up, I watched my father, Jessie Eaker, write several stories for SWORD AND SORCERESS. It seemed liked the coolest thing in the world to me and, to this day, I still treasure my signed copies of his work. It seems only fitting that now my first publication is in SWORD AND SORCERESS alongside my dad.

"I have always been a writer. At a young age, I started writing fantasy, recruiting friends and family to read my work and even making my little brother perform in a play I wrote. This love of writing carried into my high school years, when I would stay up long past my bedtime, just to pen a few pages. I later became a more serious writer, studying English and creative writing at Longwood University in Virginia, where I am now also working on my master's degree.

"I currently live in Richmond, Virginia, with my loving boyfriend, two cats, and one very noisy pug. I am now in my fifth year of teaching tenth- and twelfth-grade English, a career which certainly makes each day a unique sort of adventure."

For the girl who lived above the inn, all the world was dark and silent. She had never glimpsed the sunlight flickering among the trees in evening or heard the staccato song of crickets at nightfall. But she had been born this way—unable to see, unable to hear—and so darkness, silence meant nothing to her. For the girl, color was the golden smell of honeysuckle just outside the window and music was the wind that danced across her nose.

She spent many of her days one and the same, waking and sleeping when she pleased, later exploring her small corner of the world. With hands extended, she'd prance about the room, feeling rough cracks in the floorboards or soft folds in the bed's quilt. Sometimes her mother put lilies on the dresser and the girl held the flowers to her nose, tracing the papery leaves and silken petals with her fingers, tasting the fragrance in the air. Other times, she was content to wallow in the scents that drifted up from the inn below—meat and ale, grease and spice—and to feel the human rumblings that reached through walls and ceilings. But most of all things, she loved to stand by the window, feeling wind or rain or warm sunlight pass by, each like an old friend, each whispering of a world beyond the reach of her grasping fingers.

She lived her life, for the most part, alone. There was her mother, of course, who sometimes came, bringing turmoil into her peaceful world. Once the girl had wanted to understand her. But now, grown older, more independent, the girl considered her little more than a force like the wind, one that came and went but never stayed. Her visits, after all, were never very pleasant. Sometimes she brought something rough and wet to wipe the girl's face, and dumped water on her head until her hair ran down her back like streams of rain. And then she'd take her clothes and leave her with new ones that were still and chill and smelled of strong soap. Sometimes her mother brought food, but when the girl smeared crumbs and honey between her fingers, reveling in the sticky mess, her mother slapped her hands away and came at her with the rough, wet cloth again. The girl was just as happy to be left by herself.

But sometimes, as she stood at the window, breeze tickling her face, a strange feeling filled her, overpowering her so that she laid her head on the window sill. Water ran from her eyes. The wind, though gentle, understood her no more than her mother. And though she didn't have a word to name it, the girl understood what it was to be alone.

Far below the girl's window, on a narrow dirt street, a

Troubadour passed by. The Troubadour, whose name was Nolia, saw the girl in the window. But, presuming her to be any other wild-haired urchin, she took no notice. Nolia had dealt enough with children in her time.

So instead, she walked past the inn, humming an ancient tune. She hummed partly because music came more naturally than breath and partly because it filled the silence of her solitary travels. She liked the silence, of course—reveled in it, in fact—but after two dozen years of apprentices parading after her in a turmoil of noise and music, the silence was strange. And so she filled it with song.

As she came to the town square, she moved her hand to her pocket, tracing the smooth outline of her instrument, the olke. The olke lay, for the moment, in its resting form of a small flute. She was aware that most of the villagers had noticed her, recognizing her by the floppy, wide-brimmed hat that all Troubadours wore. And when a Troubadour made music, people always stopped to listen. She paused in the middle of the town square and casually cast her hat to the ground. In nearly the same motion, she drew out the olke and pressed it to her lips. At the chorus of the song—which was, in Nolia's opinion, the best part of any song—she began to play.

The villagers drew near, a few fishing coins from their pockets to throw into her hat. It was a tradition as old as song itself; to turn away from a Troubadour's song was bad luck and to listen without leaving a coin or two may as well be a curse. In return, Troubadours always stayed in the village for at least a week, playing simple spells. Spells of healing, spells of fortune.

Nolia was a veteran of this way of life. So she played a simple tune on the olke, one as old as human memory, as universal as laughter. She kept the olke in its simplest flute form, playing a sprightly rendition of the well-known song. The crowd muttered in anticipation, wondering what shape the olke would transform into, what surprises might be in store. Some were beginning to sing along when Nolia suddenly stopped playing and instead resumed humming.

She shoved the olke back into her pocket, laughing to herself as the crowd muttered in disappointment. They knew, however, that this was only a sampling of what Nolia could do. The real show, as always, would be in the evening when farmers had come in from their fields and shopkeepers could leave their stores.

As the audience turned away, Nolia swung her hat back atop her head and, in the relative quiet that surrounded her, she kept humming to herself.

The girl, deaf to the world and blind, somehow understood the music. It came upon her suddenly as she leaned upon the window sill, striking her so forcefully that she felt something in her head must have burst. She stumbled backward, hands pressed to her temples, the pressure of the music mounting inside her ears. The thrill of it coursed through her veins so that she trembled with each note, so that her heart beat in time with the music's pulse. When she breathed, the music seemed to breathe with her. It became part of her, and yet wasn't.

Frightened, curious, the girl groped about her. Her fingers reached toward the sound, trying to feel the warmth that raced through her head, trying to understand it through familiar senses. She wanted to grasp the music, let it pour through her fingers. She wanted to press it to her face and inhale its scent. But this thing, this mystery, could not be caught. It was everywhere and nowhere all at once.

She scarcely understood that this was a sense she'd never had before, a sense that brought her closer to the world, to people. She didn't know that outside a Troubadour played a song of journeys and kings and ancient magic. She knew only that it lit in her veins like fire and sunlight, that it warmed and caressed her and held her captive in its embrace.

The girl longed to know more, to chase after this phantom sensation, but she feared that if she chased it, it would flee. And so she sank down there in the middle of the floor, head cocked to one side. Of course, she didn't know it, but at that moment she was doing something she'd never done before.

She was listening.

With a song still on her lips and a spring in her step, Nolia entered the inn. At once, however, she noticed something peculiar: she stood now in a room crowded by a dozen tables and four times as many chairs but, surprisingly, not a single living soul. Nolia waited, watching dust drift across the room in the streaks of dusky sunlight. The place was, for an inn, eerily still.

"Hello?" Nolia called.

Upstairs, a door slammed. Feet pattered across the wooden floor.

"Coming! So sorry!" a voice called. A woman bounded down the stairs to Nolia's left. She was, perhaps, in her middle years and held herself with the air of one who is perpetually, and unsuccessfully, attempting five tasks at once. "I am *so* sorry. I didn't hear you enter."

"No trouble," Nolia said.

The woman came round from the stairs and gasped, quite dramatically, as she beheld Nolia's hat. "Oh, my! Madam Troubadour!" She curtseyed so deeply and so many times that, for a moment, Nolia feared surely she would fall to her knees and praise her as a god.

"I am indeed," Nolia said and tried to mask this awkward moment with a smile. "And if I may, I'd like to ask for permission to play in your inn this evening." In a wide, sweeping motion, she removed her hat. Now, it was her turn to curtsey.

"Why, I would be honored! Most honored! And I'll give you a room this evening free in return for so great a service!"

Nolia laughed and, with a hand, waved the notion away. "I'll take the room, but I'll be glad to pay for it. And for now, I'll take a table near the window and some tea, if you please."

"Certainly!" The innkeeper turned away and, in her haste, almost tripped on the tangle of her own feet.

Nolia watched her disappear into another room and wondered, though she knew it to be no business of her own, why the town's only inn was so utterly deserted.

With a shrug and a sigh, she chose a seat near the window so she could watch villagers pass by. All manner of people were out and about today: young wives and old men, merchants and craftsmen. She took particular interest in two children that darted by, smiles stretched across their ruddy faces. For a moment, but a moment only, she missed the sound of children's laughter.

The innkeeper returned shortly, precariously grasping a kettle in one hand and a cup and saucer in the other. "There you are," she said, setting them on the table. And, with a glimpse at Nolia's hat, added, "What brings you this way?"

Nolia poured herself some tea, leaning her face over the wafts of steam. "Oh, just traveling for traveling's sake. I just released my last apprentice. Would you believe I've trained eleven of those urchins? It seemed time to move, now, where I want, to find a bit of peace and solitude."

"Eleven apprentices!" the innkeeper said and her eyes lit with wonder. "You don't look nearly old enough."

"I thank you." Nolia laughed and ran a hand through her downy gray hair. "Do you have children?"

"One," the innkeeper said. She looked at the floor, eyes fixed on her feet. "A daughter."

"Imagine that times eleven. I'm surprised I don't look half in the grave."

The woman laughed, but all light and wonder had drained from her face. "Oh, one is plenty for me."

Nolia, habitually nosy, almost asked why. For her, of course, one could never have been enough. Her apprentices had driven her wild with questions, with mishap adventures, but in the end, for reasons beyond words, it had been worth it. Nolia wanted to tell the woman this, to tell her the wonders of a child's mind, but at that moment the door to the inn opened. The woman excused herself and darted away.

Instead Nolia sighed, staring down into her cup of tea, watching the vapors drift upward. She tried to enjoy the solitude, to revel in the silence. But when she sipped at her tea the taste on her tongue was somehow bitter.

The girl lay in the middle of the floor, stretched out into the shape of a crooked star, waiting for the music's return. It had disappeared as quickly as it had began, leaving her cold, her solitary heartbeat pounding relentlessly against her chest.

But after many empty minutes, nothing came. The girl pressed her hands to her ears, covering and uncovering them alternately, hoping to entice the music to return. She held her breath—lungs burning, chest aching with the strain—hoping the music would fill her stillness. And when that failed, she stood and stumbled to the window, reached far out into the open air. Only wind slipped past her fingers.

Try as she might, the girl could not summon the music.

An unbearable hum came now to her ears where the music had once been. It was as if the world had lost a dimension, as if it had gone flat. In those long, still moments, the girl learned yet another unfamiliar concept. Knowing now what music was, knowing how sound rushed through her veins and sent sparks through her blood, she understood the void that surrounded her. This terrible stillness, this emptiness had a name: it was silence.

And in those moments of quiet, the world lost its wonder. Nothing mattered, not the feel of the woodgrain on the floor nor the smell of pastries rising up from the kitchen. She didn't even care when the walls began to tremble as the lower level became full of people; she didn't care for the smell of the fields and shops the people brought with them. She leaned her head against the window sill and water came to her eyes as it had before, but now she knew why, now she knew that this was sadness that leaked from her eyes and dripped from her chin.

The world, for the girl, was broken.

Nolia sat on a stool in the dining hall of the inn, her hat on the floor before her. The room was crowded now with people—with farmers and merchants, shopkeepers and housewives—all come to hear her songs. They filled the chairs and sat on the tabletops and spilled out the front door, crowding around the open windows. All wanted to hear the Troubadour's magic, if only a few muffled, scattered notes. And so they crowded in, pressing closer to her as the frazzled innkeeper pushed her way about the room, taking orders.

Nolia took the olke from her pocket, smiling as a cheer rose up from the crowd. This was the first time in many years she would play without an apprentice accompanying her. She remembered, quite vividly, her last apprentice, and how for two years every time he played in public, he always forgot the notes. It was odd, for once, to have the show to herself. And yet, it was also a wonder. How long had it been since Nolia played alone?

She lifted the olke, in flute form, to her lips and began to play. The crowd fell still, holding their breaths to listen. Nolia chose first to play a song as old as dust or sky, a song that everyone knew and some sang along to. It was the song of a hero's journey. The olke began as a flute and as Nolia played, she worked and shaped it to fit the song. As the tempo picked up and livened, telling of the hero's triumph, she stretched and pulled the olke into a drum and she pounded out rhythm. When it told of his defeat, she pressed flat the drum and pulled it until it became a harp. Now the song became mournful and the olke became an ocarina, now a guitar, now a lute, now a small bell with a tinkling, silver sound. She worked and stretched and played and transformed the olke, telling this tale of wonder and music and finally, at the end, the olke again became a humble flute.

The crowd cheered, a few individuals pressing forward to throw coins into her hat. Their voices, their cries of joy, that was the real music to Nolia. She had lived selflessly for so many years, allowing her apprentices to bask in their young glory and take that praise for themselves. But now, she soaked up cheers and applause for the benefit of her own ego. It felt good to be selfish for once in her life. To live for herself.

Nolia nodded her thanks to the crowd and molded the olke into a harp again. This was her one Song, the one that she had written to gain the status of Master Troubadour. At first it had been the simple story of her own life, a rhythm of interwoven chords that represented her childhood, her training, her achievements as a Troubadour. But as she grew older, she added to this Song and it became a sort of theme and variation. There were eleven variations on the original theme, one for each of her apprentices. She had named each of the sections in her own mind, molding the song to the child's personality: Kye the Mischievous, Sarai with Eyes of Fire, Mindi the Ever-Pretending Innocent. One section was simple and mellow like her first apprentice, another flighty and energetic as her last. And as she played, wandering through eleven individual variations, she was filled with nostalgia. She remembered faces, habits, gestures. Her children.

And for a time, she forgot the crowd, absorbed in those memories, the variations of her lifetime. But, as she was nearing the end of the Song, she was pulled sharply back to reality. She heard a wild banging from upstairs and desperate, manic cries. But Troubadours, once they begin a Song, will not stop. And it was known well enough that to interrupt a Troubadour was one of the great taboos.

So Nolia played on, even though her notes echoed strangely in the hush that had fallen over the crowd.

The girl stumbled to her feet, hands flailing, searching in desperation for the untouchable. She moved twice about the room, feeling only familiar things—the bedsheets, the cold glass of the window, the smooth wood of the walls. And where was the music? Why could she feel it filling her head with warmth, but not touch it with her fingers? How could she move about the room and not come closer?

It was agonizing.

So she screamed, feeling the vibration in her throat, though she did not hear or know what she was doing. She knew only that, like the tears she cried, it was emotion pouring out of her.

Finally, she found the door, and here the music burned warmest. She banged and stomped and screamed until finally, something flew open and there was space where a wall had been—the door had opened. The girl stepped forward, the floor unfamiliar to her sensitive feet. The music was much closer here.

She ran, recklessly, and felt herself falling down ridges of wood—stairs—only just catching herself. And here the music was louder and her head burned with it and she was screaming, still now knowing it, her fingers groping at nothing.

And then hands grabbed her and pulled her away.

The girl howled louder but felt her cries fall flat as she was pressed against a body, someone who smelled faintly of flowers. It was her mother. And suddenly the girl was dragged away, though she writhed and struggled, and the burn of the music in her head began to fade.

Soon enough she was back in her room. Here, her mother patted her face and the girl recoiled when she tried to hold her. She retreated to a corner and began again to cry. But not just angry tears, great sobs that shook her small body. She had been so close to discovering the music, only to be ripped away. The unfairness of it made her insides ache, as if someone had ripped out some vital organ, leaving behind a gaping, throbbing wound.

She lay down on the floor, curling in on herself in a tight knot, head buried in the crook of her arm. She wished then that, somehow, she could simply disappear.

Nolia sat at the table in her room at the inn, counting the coins from her hat. They clinked and clattered as she poured them out, winking in the light of a nearby candle. She arranged them neatly into stacks, then arranged the stacks into neat rows, the rows into perfect squares. It was quite a pile, more than she'd made when she had apprentices—after all, many times those donations were in mere sympathy of a yet unlearned youth. Nolia felt a dull sense of pride in herself; it seemed she hadn't lost her touch after all, not even after all these years of allowing her apprentices their glory. She smiled, turning a coin over in her palm.

But not even the weight of the coin could keep her mind from wandering.

She thought of the girl who had stormed down the stairs, howling like something otherworldly, and it made sense now why the inn was so utterly deserted, what with a child that screamed like that. Nolia had spoken to the innkeeper—who bowed and sobbed and apologized profusely—and had learned that she, the innkeeper, was the mother. She had also learned that the girl was blind. And deaf.

Nolia should have been surprised. How could it be possible

that a deaf child could react to an olke's melody? For it was obvious to Nolia that this was exactly the case. The child was sound-touched: she could hear the whispering of the magic beyond the music. To some, perhaps, this would seem impossible. But to Nolia—who'd seen so much of the world that not much surprised her—it made an odd sort of sense. Though the music and magic of a Troubadour were connected, the magic was more like a sixth sense; it played off the sense of hearing but was more than just what ears could discern. Perhaps the girl had no sense of normal hearing, but she had this sixth sense, a kind of inner ear.

Nolia, wizened and practiced as she was, had never heard of a deaf Troubadour. An interesting contradiction indeed.

With a decided shake of her head, Nolia stopped that thought before it went further. "No, no, *no*," she said. She stood, scooping the coins into her hat and tossing it into a vacant chair. As fascinating as it was—a deaf girl who heard Troubadour's music—Nolia refused to let herself think of taking her as an apprentice. Nolia had just found freedom, was enjoying it, why should she be so eager to give it up? Besides, she was getting on in her years; her knees ached when it rained and her back pained her when she walked too much. Clearly, she had no energy to teach another child. She had earned a life of ease. And may the gods damn anyone who said otherwise.

She puffed out the candles and fell into bed, hoping to end the debate within herself. With the lights off, she lay in stillness, staring into the nighttime void. Sleep eluded her, calling forth musings and memories instead.

An image of her last apprentice came to mind, her white nightdress shining through the darkness as she sat in the corners of inns like these and practiced music late at night, rhythmic whispers issuing forth from her olke. The songs were never good of course, but Nolia never let her know she was listening and let the girl play on.

She'd had another apprentice, a boy, who had also played at night. But his goal had been to see how many people in an inn he could wake with a single bar of music. How angry he had made her with his joking! Even now Nolia remembered how she'd fuss and how he'd jut out his jaw, ignoring.

Nolia, with suddenly clarity, realized she was smiling.

"Stop it, Nolia. Just stop," the old Troubadour said to herself, rolling over onto her side. She yanked the covers up to her chin, burrowing beneath them. "*You* are an old fool."

Inevitably, that was when the banging began.

It came from a room nearby and mingled with it, Nolia heard the frazzled voice of the innkeeper mother. Nolia tried to pretend that if she lay there long enough the child would settle down, the cries would stop, and finally sleep would come.

The noise continued.

Nolia, with clenched teeth, warned herself to remain steadfast, concentrating on the pride she had felt earlier, thinking of the pile of coins that had glittered in the candlelight. She turned over again, covering her head with the pillow. But even that failed to drown out the screams and cries of the innkeeper's deaf-blind daughter.

As if she had no will of her own, Nolia felt herself roll out of bed. "I can't believe I'm doing this," she said, even then telling herself not to go. "I will help settle the child and nothing more."

In her night dress, hair rumpled, olke in hand, she trudged down the dark hall. She found the room with the screaming child easily enough and entered without knocking.

The innkeeper kneeled in the middle of the room, holding a girl of seven or eight by the shoulders. It was, of course, the same wild-haired urchin Nolia had seen in the window. The girl squirmed beneath her mother's grasp, mouth open wide, wailing as if wounded. Or as if her heart were broken.

The innkeeper didn't notice Nolia until she started to play the olke. Nolia played a sleepy tune, a lullaby, and, like the magic it was, the child was calm. Her screaming stopped at once and the child groped about her, fingers reaching toward the sound, searching for its comfort. When the mother tried to restrain her, Nolia nodded. The mother let her go.

The child wandered over to Nolia and turned her head upward. Nolia stared down into unseeing, watery eyes, dark and unblinking. The girl pulled at Nolia's skirts, the grasp of her fingers a plea for understanding. She knew from whence the music came and now she begged for help.

Nolia crouched, letting the girl touch her face and hands and the olke. Her touch expressed so many things: loneliness and desperation, curiosity and understanding. Nolia pitied her, this shell of a child who knew nothing of the world, pitied her because she was trapped, because it was the music that tormented her. Nolia stroked the child's head, knowing that after she left it was likely this child would never know music again; this girl would lose a precious part of herself. A Troubadour without music was like a flower without sunlight, it would surely wilt and wither away.

Unless Nolia helped, and she admitted, however reluctantly, that this girl *needed* her help, and so did this hopeless, struggling mother. The moment she admitted this she knew she had no choice in the matter. She had become a Troubadour to help people and to bring joy to their lives. She could not turn away.

And so she admitted defeat.

Nolia felt her freedom slipping away. But she knew that she would have to spend just a few more years as a teacher; this girl wouldn't need much more than six years of training to find her place in the world. And besides, this was uncharted territory, wasn't it? She might be the first Troubadour to have a deaf apprentice. Imagine what others might say. Nolia thought then of her Song and wondered, with interest, what a variation in silence would sound like.

Nolia smoothed the girl's rumpled hair and, with the corner of her sleeve, dried the girl's eyes. "I can't believe I'm going to do this," she muttered.

With the girl clinging to her skirts, Nolia turned and looked the innkeeper in the eye. "If I might," Nolia said, "I'd like to have this girl for my apprentice."

The girl didn't know what was happening, only that things were going to change. She knew, instinctively, that she was outside, somewhere open, from the wind that swirled around her.

It was the same wind as before, but this time it brought new things to her: the smell of pastures and crop fields and the fragrance of the distant woodland. The world lay stretched before her, wide and open and undiscovered.

But even without her old friend the wind, the girl knew she was not alone. A stranger held her hand, and it was the woman who carried the music with her. The girl went willingly, understanding somehow that soon there would be more sound, more music. The world would not be flat forever. There would no longer be silence, nor loneliness.

The stranger moved forward and, feeling the tug, the girl trailed after her. And so they walked on together—hand in hand—into the distance, a comfortable silence filling the narrow space between them.

THE TAVERN AT THE FORD

by Dave Smeds

Dave Smeds is the author of novels such as THE SORCERY WITHIN and THE SCHEMES OF DRAGONS, which will soon be followed by THE WIZARD'S NEMESIS. His short fiction has appeared in many anthologies, including over a dozen previous volumes of SWORD AND SORCERESS, and in such magazines as *Asimov's SF*, *Realms of Fantasy*, and *F&SF*. His most recent publication is the eBook short story collection *Raiding the Hoard of Enchantment*, a gathering of seven of his recent tales of high fantasy. "The Tavern at the Ford" is, chronologically speaking, the first tale of the characters Coil and Azure, but readers of SWORD AND SORCERESS 27 will already be familiar with them from their appearance in that volume.

Until that awful night, Azure had always assumed she would live out her entire life in the village. That's how it had been for generations.

Grandpa had shared the history one day while standing with her on the old stone bridge. "There used to be a ford there," he said, pointing to the willow flats where Coil and Azure liked to play. Grandpa's great-grandmother Cinnamon had drowned there while crossing the river. Her husband Fleet had built the bridge in her memory, working through his grief by making sure no one else would die that way.

Fleet and Cinnamon had been caravan folk. But the erection of the bridge caused more traders than ever before to cross the river at that spot. A village immediately sprang up. Fleet built an inn and bathhouse and grew wealthy. He passed down his holdings to his son, who passed them to his daughter. Grandpa was the next heir.

Azure missed her grandfather. He had taught her how to study the tavern customers while they chewed their food, quaffed their drinks, had their smokes. He made her see how even a small quirk revealed a person's nature. Eventually she had picked up the knack, but it was hard to be sure of it now that he was gone. Even at this moment she wanted to go down to the basement, put her hand on the engraving of his niche, and talk to his bones. But he would scold her for that, if he could. There were customers in the common room. Just old Chisel and Root, finishing their game of Pegs, but they were there, and therefore she was still on duty. She dipped her mop in the bucket and continued scrubbing beneath the corner bench.

The front door opened. A man stepped into the vestibule. He did not stop to hang his cloak. He advanced at once into the common room, his scabbarded sword waving behind him.

Chisel and Root straightened in their seats, their hands poised over the game board in that relaxed way that would let them seize the hilts of their own blades at the first sign of trouble. The stranger gave them a respectful nod. They returned it.

As the man caught sight of Azure, his expression wasn't like anything she had ever seen. Sad? Relieved? Proud? She wished Grandpa were here to explain.

"Eight years old now. Almost nine."

Azure nodded.

"Is your mother here?"

"I am."

The newcomer turned. Mama was standing in the archway that led to the kitchen. She, too, was wearing an expression that wasn't like anything Azure had ever seen.

The man gestured toward the kitchen. Mama nodded.

Azure started to follow, but her mother held up her hand. "Stay."

Azure lurched as if her sandals had been nailed to the floor.

She glanced at Chisel and Root. Brows high, they were regarding the archway. Always sober when they played Pegs, they both reached for their cups and seemed surprised to find they contained only tea.

Root raised an eyebrow at Azure and tilted his chin in the

direction of the kitchen.

"Are you the girl I know or not?"

She nodded. A moment later she was tiptoeing down the hallway.

Mama and the man were standing near the bread ovens. They were whispering. Azure only caught the man's final three words.

"He is dead."

Mama *slipped into his arms!* He held her. She trembled.

Azure was a tavern girl. She had seen Mama's lovers drape a fond arm around her waist at breakfast. This was something else. Suddenly Azure knew who this man was.

Mama noticed her hiding in the hallway shadow. To Azure's surprise, she wasn't angry. "Fetch Coil," she said. "It's time he met his father."

She had guessed wrong. But then—that talk of someone being dead?

"Azure. Hurry!"

Azure found her milk-brother in the scouring crib, rinsing out bowls. She was bursting to tell him everything, but if she uttered the words "your father" he would think she was playing a trick on him.

"You have to come *now.*"

He tossed the roughcloth in the bucket of washwater and followed at her heels.

The kids found the two adults up in the family quarters over the kitchen, hurriedly packing clothing, money, and other necessities of travel.

"This is Burnish," Mama said. "We have to go with him. Now. Tonight."

"Chisel and Root are still out there," Azure said.

"They can let themselves out. Go to the pantry and fill up a sack with food. Just a few quick things. Some bread. That round of cheese Vetch delivered today. A few apples. We'll meet you there."

"Come on," Azure said, tugging on Coil's damp shirt. He let himself be pulled along, like he hardly ever did. She knew why.

"Burnish," he murmured. "*The* Burnish?"

"Yes," she said.

Coil said nothing more until they were in the pantry. She had him hold the sack and began grabbing the items Mama had mentioned.

"Do I look like him?" Coil asked.

She tossed in a vial of salt as well.

"Yes," she decided.

He ran a forefinger down his nose as if measuring it. Azure would have said more, but a racket erupted in the common room. The children ran to see what was happening.

Azure was glad her bladder was empty. In the middle of the common room was a gigantic spider—a spider as tall as a man. Chisel and Root were hacking at its front legs with their swords.

The blades were bouncing off. Clanging. Leaving no mark on the creature.

The thing pointed a leg and thrust. The tip went right through Chisel and burst out his back.

"Run!" Coil yelled. He pulled Azure away.

They had barely made it back to the kitchen when they collided with her mother. "What—?" Mama blurted.

Coil tugged them both. "Don't stop here!"

The spider burst through the archway. Azure screamed.

Coil pulled Azure back toward the rear exit. Mama sprang forward!

—And was immediately stung in the chest by the spider. A flicker of fangs and it was done. Her knees started to buckle.

"Keep running!" yelled a man's voice. It was Burnish.

Coil pulled again and this time Azure fled just as fast. But both couldn't help looking back. They saw the spider rush at Burnish, who scampered up the stairs. The spider followed, squeezing its massive body into the passageway.

Mama was left there crumpled on the floor, braid knocked loose and lying like a dead snake beside her head.

Azure tugged free of Coil and rushed back to her mother's side. A moment later her milk-brother joined her.

"You have to escape," Mama whispered, barely able to talk.

"We can't leave you!" Azure protested. Coil nodded.

"There is more at stake here than you know. If you love me at all, *you will run*!" she hissed.

Azure blinked. "But—"

Noises of struggle reverberated down from above. Mama looked at Coil. As soon as their eyes met, he sobbed, grabbed the sack of food, and darted out the rear.

"Go."

Faint as it was, the word was clear. But Azure stayed where she was.

Suddenly Burnish tumbled out of the laundry chute. Without any hesitation, not even looking at Mama, he scooped up Azure, draped her over his shoulder, and propelled them both out the way Coil had gone.

"No, no, no, no!" Azure said, her voice wavering as she was jiggled up and down.

They made it to the lane between the tavern and the wheelwright shop. Coil was on his hands and knees in the middle of the lane. Apparently he had gone so fast he had stumbled. He stood up. The dust on the front of his shirt merged with the water from scrubbing the bowls, leaving mud.

Burnish tossed Azure to her feet, reaching to help Coil. As soon as she landed she grabbed the bag of food from the ground and hit him with it.

"We have to go back!"

"We can't," he said. He grabbed her and Coil and by the upper arms and yanked them onward like stubborn puppies on leashes. He was *strong*. She wanted to hit him again but it was all she could do to just hold on to the bag.

A waxing quarter moon hung over the wheelwright shop. Burnish tugged them to the ground in the deep shadows between the building and a parked vegetable cart. Their arrival made the small mule hitched to the cart flick up its ears. Azure knew that mule. It belonged to Root. It was the most placid animal she had ever met.

Through the wheels of the cart and the legs of the mule, Azure had a clear view of the back exit of the tavern. The spider burst into the open. It scurried into the lane. It turned this way and that.

The mule was no longer placid. It danced, struggling with its hobbles. The loaded cart, brakes locked, resisted the beast's attempt to surge forward. The dust it raised helped hide Azure, Coil, and Burnish even further.

The spider ignored the mule. It clambered onto the tavern roof and surveyed the area, but this did not give it a good vantage of their hiding place.

Azure made herself stay silent, even though she wanted very much to scream.

Finally the spider came down. It darted back into the tavern.

"Stay," Burnish whispered. "Don't move."

The spider reemerged, carrying a silk-wrapped bundle with its mandibles and forelegs. It raced off down the lane in the direction of the bridge.

The bundle was the size of a person.

"Isn't there any way to kill that thing?" Coil asked.

Burnish made a choked noise. "Yes," he said hoarsely. "If you can get around the armor."

Coil hesitated. Azure knew he was thinking about what they'd seen in the common room. Coil had always liked Chisel. The quarryman had lately spoken of making Coil his apprentice.

Chisel had been the toughest warrior in the village. Root had been almost as good.

Finally Coil found his voice again. "Are we going to follow it? What do we do about Mama?"

"We *have* to follow," Azure interjected. "We have to get her back!"

Burnish was wiping his eyes with his sleeve. "No. No, we can't follow."

"But she's still alive!" Azure said. She didn't actually know that, but her mother had been alive after getting stung. Maybe she still was.

"Maybe so. But I promise you, if we follow, we'll be caught, too. That won't help her much, will it?"

He really wasn't going to try to rescue her. And somehow Azure knew if she tried running after the spider, Burnish would tackle her and hold her back.

She stood up. She began crying so hard she almost made herself vomit. "This happened because of you! Why did you have to come here?"

Burnish put his hands firmly on her shoulders. He made her meet him eye to eye. She didn't want to look, but eventually she did. She couldn't entirely make out his expression in the dimness, but could hear him perfectly.

"The goddess's minion would have come whether I did or not," he said. "I thought we had a few hours. Probably a whole day. I was wrong. I am so terribly sorry for that."

Azure absorbed his words. She decided he was being truthful.

"What goddess?" Coil demanded.

"One that will not stay dead," Burnish answered.

Azure would always remember the next hour of her life, but even while it was passing it felt as though she were a sleepwalker having an unusually vivid dream. Nothing seemed real without her mother's presence.

Burnish said they had to get out of the village. The vegetable cart became the means. Just as Root would have done, they went to the riverside quay. Soon the night barge made its regular stop. The crew, a pair of brothers, happily accepted the fare from Burnish and helped tie down the cart in the center of the platform near the main stack of cargo. Minutes later they were floating away with the current. The barge was not due to stop again until dawn when it arrived at Bulltown. That was where Root would have disembarked and taken his load to the market plaza.

Coil finished giving the mule some carrots and came to sit with her and Burnish at the center of the barge. They were out of the hearing of the crew. The elder brother had retreated to the stern as rudder man and the younger to the prow to watch for submerged logs and other navigational obstacles.

"You're small for your age, but strong." Burnish ruffled Coil's hair. "That's how it was with me."

Coil never let Mama touch his head like that anymore. It really was odd how familiar Burnish seemed. The way he crinkled his eyes. The way he spread his fingers so widely when he reached for something.

"You keep looking at the banks," Coil said.

"Do I?"

"Yes."

"I'm looking for the spider," he confessed.

"Why?" Coil began studying the hollows where the moonlight didn't penetrate. "Does it know we're riding the barge?"

"If not, it soon will. Its mistress can sense what direction we're in. Once the spider consults with her, it will know where to hunt for us."

"Then why are we here?" Azure demanded.

"It's an excellent place to be for now. The goddess's sorcery made that spider big and strong and plated it with armor. Couldn't do that without making it heavy. It can't swim, and if it tried walking across the river bottom to reach the barge, it would get stuck in the mud. We're safe until we dock at Bulltown."

"What then?"

"Don't worry about that yet."

"Which goddess is it the spider serves?" Coil asked.

"Schrae."

"The one killed by her sister?"

"Yes. But somehow her consciousness was preserved in a vessel of wire and glass. Two centuries ago something or someone awakened her."

"Why did the goddess make the spider come *here*?" asked Azure.

"To free herself. She is still imprisoned in the vessel. To be fully free, and to be able to use all her powers, she has to create a real body for herself. The trick is, it has to be just like her old body, so she's been capturing and studying her descendants to see how they're made."

"Are *we* Schrae's descendants?" asked Coil.

"Yes." Burnish tapped himself on the chest. "I carry the blood. And because you are my son, you have it, too. And so do you, Azure. Your father was also a descendant. Sprawl was some sort of distant kinsman of mine."

"When she studies her descendants, does she kill them?"

"Yes. Apparently that's an unavoidable part of the process."

Azure began shaking. She had never liked the idea she might die someday, but to be tossed down on a slab and taken apart? By her own foremother?

"Why didn't Mama tell us?"

"It wasn't yet time. We hoped it might never be necessary."

"Why?" Azure choked. "Did you think Schrae would *give up*?!"

"No. We thought she'd succeed." Burnish's voice was gentle. "If in the past few years Schrae had found enough descendants for her needs, if she had restored herself, then she would have no more need to chase the descendants who were still at liberty."

"But then she'd be *back*," Coil pointed out. "That would be terrible."

"Yes. Her restoration would probably be the worst thing to happen to the world since the Long Snow. Now that the other gods have returned to the sky, who could stop her? But what would that be to us? Just a storm out at sea. The kings and masters of the great nations would be scrambling to assemble their armies to save their reigns, but you two would probably be sleeping in your beds right now, dreaming good dreams. Sprawl and I might be living in the village and learning to be proper fathers."

"But it didn't happen that way," Coil said.

"No. It did not. The goddess is still hunting. And we are her prey."

Azure found herself wishing she hadn't even been born. And that made her wonder. "Why did you sire us? Knowing what you knew?"

He sighed. "I had hoped your mother would explain, along with the rest of it. I don't really want to get into it right now."

"Why?"

"It's complicated."

"We have time," she said.

She was afraid the real answer was, *So Schrae could get you and not us.*

When he didn't respond, she gave up. She leaned back against a pickle barrel. Coil nestled in beside her. Burnish found a spare tarp and covered all three of them. When the younger brother wandered past to give the cargo a quick check, he ignored them as if they had gone to sleep.

An hour later, though, Azure and Coil were still wide awake when Burnish gestured at the left bank.

"Keep your heads down. Look carefully."

Along this portion of the river, the bluff on the left bank dropped sharply toward the water, almost as steep as a cliff. Azure spotted something scurrying along the heights, darting from a gully to a cluster of olive trees, and then to the shadow of a rock outcropping, avoiding the moonlit open stretches. It made no noise loud enough to be heard over the soughing of the nightwind, but the presence of something that huge and shambling could be *felt*.

Azure began shaking again. She slipped into the crook of Burnish's arm and torso. No matter that he didn't give good answers to questions, she needed an adult to hold her.

"Don't worry, child."

"How can you say that?"

"You know how to swim, don't you?"

"Of course." The question was stupid. She had, after all, grown up in a hot and dusty village next to a large river. She could hardly recall a summer day of her whole life when she had not taken a dip.

"Good. Keep watching the spider. I believe it will try to get ahead of us. We'll slip into the water. It will keep tracking the barge until it docks at Bulltown. It won't realize we're not aboard anymore."

The spider behaved as Burnish predicted. It scurried ahead of the barge until even Azure, who had the sharpest eyes, could not detect it.

The moon set. The river straightened until the elder brother was able to tie down the rudder and venture to the prow, where he and his brother began sharing a pipeful of ropebud. Burnish helped the children slip out from their places, leaving the tarp in place in such a way that it appeared to still be covering them. They slipped silently into the water and swam underwater until the brush on the right bank hung over their heads. Surfacing, they caught hold of branches and held themselves in place against the current until the barge drifted completely out of sight.

They waited a good long while in the shadow of the brush, but none of them saw any sign that the spider had backtracked. They swam across to the other side. The bluff was not as steep here. They clambered up the bank.

The wagon road paralleled the river here atop the bluff, but they did not use it. They proceeded into open country, Burnish obscuring the footprints they had made on the road while crossing it.

"Where will we go?" Azure asked.

"For now, back to your village. I left something there. It's not that far. The river wound us around. We'll take the straight way back."

"Is it safe to go there?"

"It should be. Schrae can't send the minion after us until it ambushes the barge at the dock, discovers we're not aboard, and comes back to get new instructions."

"What will happen to the bargemen?" Coil asked.

"They will take one look at that creature and jump off," Burnish said with conviction. "The minion will take no further interest in them."

They reached the village while it was still full dark. They moved along the outskirts, making no noises that might awaken dogs.

The light was still lit above the lintel of the tavern. Usually Mama extinguished it when the last patron left. The front door was slightly ajar, having mostly closed after the spider had gone through. Apparently no one had noticed these odd signs and checked inside. The spider's assault had happened just late enough in the evening that few would have ventured outdoors since. No one would be missing Chisel yet. His wife had died long ago and he had no offspring—one reason he was thinking of taking on Coil as his apprentice. Root lived up Ramble Creek near his vegetable fields. His family had no reason to expect him back from Bulltown until the end of the coming day.

The only sign of activity was the light from the windows and smoke from the chimneys of Vetch's bakery. Vetch himself would be inside kneading dough.

"We shouldn't let anyone know we're here," Burnish said, guessing Azure's thought.

"The whole village would fight for us if we asked."

"You saw what happened to the men in the tavern. Do you want any more people you know to die like that?"

She shuddered. "No."

Burnish led them around behind the inn to the base of the path that led up to the guest huts on the hill. The structures were all empty at the moment, though due to be filled in just one week when the leapfish began their seasonal run up the river.

"We'll wait indoors until dawn," Burnish said.

"The huts are locked. The keys are inside the inn," Azure said. "Should we get them?"

"No, let's not chance that. We may not need a key." He led them up to the very last pair of huts, the highest on the hill, tucked back away from the others, each with their own privies. Azure assumed he was going to break in, and braced for the noise that would make. But Burnish just went to the front door of the one on the left, cupped his fingers at its base, and lifted.

The door shifted upward. The lock released.

"Nine years and she never fixed that," he muttered. He opened the door and waved the children in.

The interior exuded a welcoming aroma of clean linens and sachets of herbs. Mama always kept the huts ready for the next guests. Azure had helped her freshen this one just five days back. Stepping inside was almost like coming home.

Coil wasn't so used to where things were. He bumped into the end of the bed and then Azure bumped into him.

"No lamps," Burnish warned.

"But I can't see anything," Coil complained.

"We don't need to see much. This is just a place to wait. Up on the bed with you. Keep your shoes on, though." The chair creaked as he settled into it.

Azure and Coil stretched out on top of the bedcovers. It was a far better bed than her pallet in the inn. Any other time lying there like that would lull her. Under the circumstances, the stillness only filled her with more questions.

Apparently it was the same for Coil, because all at once he asked, "Have you always had to run like this?"

"Not always like this," Burnish replied. "I had a happy childhood. I was seventeen before Schrae became aware I existed. And there have been other good times over these past thirteen years. I found Sprawl early in my roaming. We became like brothers. The road can be a fine place with the right comrade. Many men have spent their twenties roaming. Sometimes I think I might have chosen to live very much as I have in fact lived."

"But aren't you afraid all the time?" Coil asked.

"It's not a life for children. It's not what I wished for you."

"It's not what I wished for, either," Coil said. "Not even when I wished I could meet you."

Burnish was silent for so long Azure thought he was done, but then he added, "Sprawl and I both vowed never to sire offspring. We didn't want Schrae chasing them like she was chasing us."

"But we got born," Azure said.

"What happened?" Coil asked.

"I didn't want to speak of it, yet here we are in this hut. I suppose that's a sign that I should tell you."

"What about this hut?"

"This was where you were conceived, my boy. Azure was conceived on the same night in the hut next door."

"That can't be," Azure insisted. "Mama never uses these huts herself."

"I take it you know what these huts are used for."

"Everybody around here knows what these huts are used for." Mama made more money from the rental of these two huts than all the rest of the inn rooms combined.

"*I* don't," Coil blurted.

Azure wished it weren't dark, so she could tell if he was joking. Maybe he really didn't know. She talked about almost everything with Coil, but not about *that*. Not since she had figured out what *that* was.

"Shall I tell him?" Burnish asked.

"Yes," she murmured. *She* certainly didn't want to be the one to do it.

"You know how it is with livestock when the females come in season? How it is with cats and dogs? How at those times, they can't be kept apart?"

"Yes," Coil said. He sounded disgusted.

"It so happens that if a man and woman who already like one another have a cup of a certain tea, and if they then go to one of the bathhouses and breathe in the fumes after a certain elixir is added to the hot water, and if they then retire to one of these two huts, then the pair find themselves consumed by the same sort of craving for one another that lower mammals feel at breeding time."

"Mama wouldn't have done that," Azure said, louder than she meant to. "That's not how it happened!"

"I told you I didn't want to speak of it."

"What's going on?" Coil asked.

"You hog puddle, don't you see? He's saying Mama tricked them!"

"Don't call me a hog puddle." Coil poked her in the ribs. "And that wasn't what he said. Was it?"

Burnish was silent again.

"Oh, no," Coil mumbled.

"She had decided she wanted a child," Burnish said. "She didn't want a husband. Just a child. What better way, she thought, than wait until a particularly fine specimen of a man appeared in her tavern, and then see to it that he joined her for a night in one of these huts? He would be on his way in the morning and would never know all that went on. She would have a child and be able to carry on her life without some man ordering her around."

That was just the sort of thing Mama would do, Azure had to

admit. It even sounded like her saying it.

"If it had been as she imagined, we might have remembered that night as the best of our lives," Burnish continued. "We all liked Flora from the moment we met her. We being Sprawl, me, and my new sweetheart, Auburn. We had been in the village for a week, easing our road fatigue, certain we were far ahead of the goddess's hunters. Every evening the three of us would drink with Flora and talk. And laugh."

He reached over and clasped Azure's knee. "I have forgiven your mother long since. I hope you can manage to do the same. She should have told us, but she didn't see the harm. She knew Sprawl wanted to bed her. She only resorted to the tea and the elixir and the huts because she knew she was not quite in the fertile part of her cycle. The magic was the cure for that. She did not imagine Sprawl would care, given that he was never to know he had fathered a baby. She did not imagine Auburn and I would care, because she could see that Auburn and I were deeply in love, and we had even said we wanted children. Unfortunately we had not mentioned that we dared not fulfill that desire.

"You must not blame Sprawl for his part in making you, Azure. You, Coil, must not blame Auburn. Neither one realized they were under a spell, and both assumed it was safe to couple that night without those consequences. Let their ghosts rest in peace. Me, you can blame."

"Why you and not them?" Azure asked.

"Because I didn't drink the tea. I pretended to, out of politeness, but Flora had put honey in it to mask the unusual flavor. Honey makes my skin break out and sometimes even makes it hard for me to breathe. So I was not under a spell that night in the hut. I realized something was not normal. I had my wits. I just didn't use them.

"I wanted her, you see. Auburn was the woman I had never imagined I would be lucky enough to know. When she joined me in the bed in the state she was in, I chose not to worry. I took the gamble. We'd had to be so careful all those months. For one night, to just let go? It was irresistible."

"What happened then?" Coil asked.

"Sprawl and Auburn and I left the next day. A few fortnights later, Auburn began throwing up in the morning, and couldn't abide certain foods she had loved in the past. We realized what had happened. We knew that soon there would be two more descendants Schrae would want. From that point on, your safety was our foremost goal. Schrae can call upon certain magicks to track prey she has already identified. She can't use those methods if she doesn't know who to look for. We hoped to keep her from ever learning you existed.

"We did not want to appear to have any particular interest in this village. So we roamed far and wide until Auburn grew heavy with child. We came back here for the births. Flora had to be warned. You were born first, Azure. Three days later Auburn went into labor and..."

"And she died," Coil said. He had been told many times about his mother and why she could not raise him. Though in all the years Azure had overheard those same stories, she had always thought her mother and Auburn had known each other much longer. Her mother had let her think that, she supposed.

"Yes. She died." Azure wasn't sure she had ever heard a man sound so hollowed out. "And Sprawl and I left. Your mother raised you both while we stayed away to protect you. Flora did not expect to see either of us again. We all thought we would never stop running. Maybe we would be lucky and die naturally when we were old. Maybe Schrae would close in. We agreed to kill ourselves before letting her have us."

"But you came here after all."

"Yes. That minion—it is an ally more formidable than most Schrae has managed to create. It surprised us. Sprawl was captured. That's when I knew I had to come here. When the goddess...studies...her descendants, she does more than examine how they are made. She can harvest memories. Especially the strong memories. The ones her victims would most want to hide from her."

"The same minion that killed my father is the one after us?" Azure asked.

"Yes."

"I'm not going to be able to fall asleep," Coil declared.

The light of dawn began to glimmer beneath the ill-hung door. Burnish stood up.

"Time to go," he said.

They ate, used the privies, washed the crustiness from their faces.

"Follow me closely and quietly," Burnish told the children.

He led them over the hill behind the huts. This took them into the heathlands. Soon they could see no buildings or paddocks or tilled fields, because all of those were concentrated along the river or along the caravan route. Ahead, in the direction of the rising sun, the soil became sandy and the sources of water few and far between. No one had lived in that wilderness since the time of the barrowfolk. The people of the village used it only as a hunting ground for sage antelope or pheasant.

The three of them threaded through a tangle of knotlimb and came upon a small field of maregrass. A pair of handsome dun horses were grazing there.

The animals turned toward Burnish and nickered. He ambled to them and leaned his head and right hand against their necks in turn.

Azure and Coil approached.

"This is Bread," Burnish said of the slightly darker one. "And this is Butter."

"You had horses waiting?" Coil burst out. "Why didn't we use them last night?"

"Because they were spent," he answered, brushing his hand along Butter's dark mane. "I pushed them very hard to get here when I did. I would have pushed them even harder if I'd known how little time I had, but there's no fixing that now. They have carried Sprawl and me away from danger many times. I believe they are fresh enough now to do it for the three of us. Shall we see?"

He went to the edge of the clearing. Azure saw a pair of saddles half-hidden in the shade of a featherseed tree. Burnish whistled. Both horses came to him. He finished saddling both of them as fast as Azure had ever seen someone saddle just one horse. He checked their feet for burrs and waved the kids over to Butter.

"This was Sprawl's horse," he said. "He likes to let Bread take the lead, so just let him. Don't worry, he's gentle with children."

Azure hoped so. Neither she nor Coil had done much riding. Other people travelled the roads. Their kind were villagers. But Mama had insisted they learn how. Had she been worried they might someday urgently have to have those skills?

With Burnish's help, Coil vaulted up and took the reins. Azure was tossed up behind him. She didn't want to be in the back. It left her with nothing to hold on to except her milk-brother's waist. What if *he* lost his grip?

But off they went. She saw Burnish was right about Butter. The animal was easy to ride. Unfortunately that was not enough to let her relax.

What if the spider found them out here? Where could they hide?

Nowhere.

It did not go well.

Within a couple of hours at what Azure thought was too idle a pace, Burnish slowed the animals even further. He kept checking their gait. He called a stop. Dismounted. Massaged both horses' legs. Frowned.

"Get down," he told the kids.

They continued on foot, leading the horses.

"I'm scared." Azure had to say it. They were going too slow and the country was becoming more open, the thickets of scrub farther and farther apart. Every so often they had to cross high ground where they could be seen from miles away.

"The spider is tired, too," Burnish said.

"That makes me feel a lot better," Azure snapped. "It'll get us, but at least we made it *tired*!"

"Making that spider tired is important," Burnish said. "Now shut your mouth and keep walking."

It was the first time Burnish had raised his voice in anger at her. Azure found she was unable to say one word more.

They kept on, seldom riding, mostly walking, pausing only to water the horses. The sun sank toward the western horizon. That meant that when she looked back, as she constantly did, she easily spotted the giant eight-legged silhouette on top of the low ridge they had traversed just minutes earlier.

Burnish turned at the sound of her sharp inhalation.

"Well, that's it then," he said. "It comes down to a fight."

"I thought you didn't want to fight it," Azure said.

"I didn't want innocent villagers to die fighting it. I didn't want *you* to die—not if I could get you to safety first. But I knew someday I would have to try to kill that thing. I just wasn't sure until now that today was the day."

He pulled a little silver puzzle box from Bread's saddlebag and opened it, revealing what appeared to be a small, withered prune.

"What's that?" Coil asked.

"A sloe. The fruit of the blackthorn. I obtained it from an aged shaman of the north, who told me he picked it from a bush he had tended since he was a beardless apprentice. What sort of magic he worked over all those years is not something he would reveal, but he made certain promises about what I will be able to do if I eat it. It could be he was lying, but now I have no choice but to trust him."

"Will it help you kill the minion?" Azure asked.

"Yes."

"Then eat it!"

He put the sloe in his mouth. Chewed. Swallowed. Grimaced.

"Why the northlanders think sloes are edible I don't know."

"Did it work?" Coil asked.

Burnish convulsed. His knees buckled. He caught himself before collapsing, though.

"It's certainly doing *something.*" He straightened. Touched his belly. Grimaced again. "Let's assume it's going to do what the shaman promised. Here's what I want the two of you to do."

He had them mount up, Coil on Bread, and Azure on Butter.

"You angle off to the right," he told Coil. "You to the left," he told Azure. "Don't gallop or the horses won't last. I'll take the middle and run straight east. The spider will go for me. I look like the easiest victim, and it will assume it can deal with you at its leisure once it takes me down. It will find taking me down to be harder than it expects."

They all looked west. The spider was halfway down the slope, making for them at a ferocious speed.

Burnish removed a pair of coiled ropes from Bread's saddlebags and looped them around his shoulders.

"All right, then," he said.

He gave each horse a slap on the hindquarters. For the next minute, Azure had to concentrate on staying in the saddle and keeping the horse headed the right direction. It wanted to follow Bread. Finally she was able to look back.

Burnish was running away, but the spider was gaining so quickly it would soon catch up to him.

Azure slowed Butter to a walk. She was safe enough for the moment and watching was more important than adding distance. Off to the south she saw Coil doing the same thing.

Inevitably the spider closed to within a few of its body lengths away. Azure began holding her breath.

Burnish sped up.

Azure expelled the breath. Burnish should have been worn out by now, but he had doubled his pace.

The gap was still too close, and grew no wider as monster and man darted around scrub thickets and hurtled between clumps of bunch grass, kicking up sand.

Burnish stumbled and fell. The spider was nearly upon him by the time he regained his footing. He raced ahead just out of its reach. Azure put a hand over her mouth. That stumble couldn't have been part of the plan!

The pursuit went on like that. Azure tasted blood and realized she was gnawing the inside of her lower lip. The spider was *so close*—and yet it never quite managed to reach its target. Burnish somehow always managed to stay just out of reach.

Finally the spider's pace began to flag. After another half a league, it paused altogether. Burnish trudged a bit farther and stopped as well, panting. The spider burst forward. Burnish let it get near—too near as far as Azure was concerned—but his burst was superior, keeping him out of reach.

Azure began to see just how Burnish was manipulating the minion. Not toying with it, exactly. The thing was far too dangerous to toy with. But it was obvious by now that if all Burnish had wanted to do was run away, his enchanted speed would have had him out of sight by now.

Bit by bit, the spider's surges became short-lived. Finally it was crawling so sluggishly it was moving just one leg at a time.

Now, at last, Burnish showed just how fast he could be. He removed a coil of rope from his shoulder, made a lasso, and snared one of the spider's front legs, all so quickly Azure would have missed it if she hadn't just finished cleaning a speck of grit out of her left eye. Equally quickly, he anchored the rope around a stout tree.

The spider tried to shake its leg free, but it had barely started to do so before Burnish sped around behind it, snared one of its rear legs, and pulled the rope taut. He anchored that one to a boulder.

The spider thrashed. The movements were sluggish, but still very strong. Azure thought it might break free, but Burnish raced back and forth eliminating the slack from each line until the creature could hardly move. If anything, its struggles only made the ropes tighter around its legs.

Burnish beckoned Azure and Coil. The children rode toward him. At his warning signal, they left a margin of safety, but they came near enough that Burnish was able to run over to each horse and fetch additional ropes.

Soon he had every one of the spider's eight legs tightly secured.

Eight ropes, Azure noticed. Burnish had brought along precisely eight ropes. Before she had ever seen him stride through the vestibule of the tavern, the ropes had been there among the horses' gear.

The kids edged nearer. The spider was flailing, but between

the bindings and its own exhaustion, it couldn't get even a handspan off the ground.

Burnish laughed. "Just a spider after all. No stamina. Not like a mammal has stamina."

Coil spat in the monster's direction. "Kill it!"

Burnish drew his sword. He checked the blade's sharpness by dropping a strand of bunchgrass across the edge. The grass parted and fluttered in two pieces to the soil. He nodded.

But then he took a step back and turned to Coil and Azure. "Would you two like to do it?"

Hearing the question was like jumping from the hot pool in the inn's main bathhouse into the cold water one. Azure shivered. She met Burnish's gaze. He wasn't joking.

She shivered again.

"How?" she asked.

"There is no armor down in that gap between the abdomen and the thorax. See how thin the stalk is that connects the body parts? Thrust the sword into that gap. Saw through the stalk. The minion will die as any spider would die."

"We'd have to get on top of it," Azure said.

"Yes. So would I, to get the best angle. Shall I do it?"

"No!" Coil said. He backed up to get a running start and sprinted toward the spider. He had to clamber to make it, pulling himself up with hands and knees, but he made it.

Azure needed to take one deep breath before she could get her feet to move, but then she launched forward just as her milk-brother had done. In moments she was standing beside him atop the minion.

The creature writhed. As before it got no slack. It could pound its abdomen against the ground, and did, but could summon only a small portion of its strength. The shaking made the children dance up and down, but they were too nimble to be knocked off.

Burnish took off his sword belt, slid the blade back in the scabbard, and tossed the weapon to Coil. "Mind you don't cut yourself."

Coil drew the blade with care.

Azure knew he wouldn't make the first thrust without her, and she was right. He put his left hand around the grip and the right atop the pommel and waited for her to wrap her hands around his. Then they both pushed down at the same time. Hard.

The spider's chitin resisted for only a moment, its insides not at all. The children almost lost their balance as their hands plunged downward.

The spider hissed. She hadn't realized it could make sounds with its mouth.

It was in pain! Good!

Coil worked the blade back and forth, widening the cut. He stopped, wiped a bead of sweat off his forehead, and let Azure take over.

Back and forth, in and out. The creature hissed and flopped its abdomen up and down some more. The jiggling made Azure's teeth rattle.

Then the monster went still.

She stopped. Was that it?

Coil took over, sawing some more. Right. They had to make sure. She took another turn as well.

The stalk gave way. The abdomen settled into the hollow in the dirt created by the pounding. Azure tossed the sword into the clear. She and Coil jumped down.

Ichor oozed from the apertures of the severed parts. The substance reeked of vomit and dusty cobwebs. Coil covered his nose with his sleeve. Azure backed away. The horses snorted.

"Well done," Burnish murmured. "Well done."

Azure had trouble catching her breath. Her heart was pounding.

She expected that Burnish would pick up his sword and start cleaning off the mess before it did something awful to the steel. Instead, he stuck fingers as far down his throat as he could, and vomited.

Along with the remains of his most recent meal came what little was left of the sloe, along with several flecks of blood.

"Are you hurt?" she asked. "Is it bad?"

"I'll never live to be an old man. Not having eaten that fruit. But that's something to worry about if I get to be a middle-aged man. What's important is, I outlived *that* thing." He spat blood and bile at the eight-legged corpse.

"Is this it?" Coil asked, casting a nervous glance back the way from which the spider had come. "Does this mean we got away?"

"For now. The goddess has no servant left that could chase us down faster than we can vanish into those hills." He waved toward the east.

Azure shaded her eyes and looked to the west instead. Toward home.

"We can't go back," Burnish said.

"Not even now?"

"No. I want with all my heart to save your mother. But if we tried, we would fail. And we would die."

"She's *already* dead, isn't she?"

Burnish led Azure away from the cloud of stench and sat her down on one of the anchoring boulders. He took her hands in his and stared straight in her eyes. Coil hovered at his side.

"I don't believe Flora is dead. I believe Schrae will keep her alive in the hope of trapping us when we attempt to rescue her. Eventually the goddess will realize we're not coming. So she'll have a choice. Kill Flora, or let her go. I believe she'll let her go."

"Why would she do that?" Azure asked.

"Schrae is many things, but she is not stupid. She'll assign spies to follow Flora. But Flora doesn't know where we went. She'll go back to the inn. There's no reason why she wouldn't. Schrae will let her. The goddess knows you want to go back there. She will be watching. If you ever come within a few leagues of the village again, she'll know, just as she knew which direction to send the spider today. Our only hope is to keep moving beyond the places she expects us to be. As long as we have yet to be caught, Schrae will have no reason to kill your mother. By keeping ourselves safe, we keep her safe."

"You're just saying that," Azure protested.

"Let me put it to you this way—would you rather imagine your mother dead, or still alive and running the inn, holding out for a day when you can be reunited?"

"Alive," she admitted.

"There you go."

"But if I never see her again, it's *like* she's dead."

"Not at all. There is a very big difference." He stood. "But I understand how you feel. There is, in fact, one way you could see your mother again."

"How?"

"Schrae must be destroyed. Completely and permanently."

Grandpa would be proud of her, she thought. Because she was able to tell from the way Burnish said it he wasn't joking and wasn't playing a trick. He was saying it like he meant it.

"How?" Coil asked.

"I don't know," Burnish answered. "But at one time I wasn't sure how to destroy that minion. I learned how. I got it done. Did I not?"

"Yes. You did," Azure said.

"Killing the goddess will be much harder. But as long as we're alive, we may find the way."

Azure thought deeply about this as Burnish tended to his sword, retrieved his ropes, and checked the horses. She thought about it some more as Burnish set her and Coil back on Butter's saddle, mounted Bread, and led them onward.

Maybe her mother was alive. Maybe she wasn't. She would have to hope so.

She was certain of one thing. The goddess did need to die. And when it happened, she would be there to see it.

THE DAMSEL IN THE GARDEN

by Pauline J. Alama

Some sisters save their brothers by making shirts for them. Others take a more active approach. Pauline J. Alama is the author of the epic fantasy THE EYE OF NIGHT (Bantam Spectra 2002). Her work has appeared in volumes 18, 23, 25, and 26 of SWORD AND SORCERESS, as well as in *Realms of Fantasy*, *Abyss and Apex*, *Penumbra eZine*, and a number of anthologies. She studied medieval literature and has a particular fondness for the Old French Arthurian romances of Chrétien de Troyes, which influenced this story.

The dragon was bad enough, but when I'd cut off the last of its heads, I still had the bridge before me. And that was worse than a herd of dragons.

Over a burning river, the only footholds were hovering sword blades spaced so far apart, and so unevenly, that a mountain goat could have lost its footing. To make it a bit more interesting, the fire below the bridge had an annoying habit of spurting up at intervals perfectly timed to set one's nerves off-key. Crossing it would be like a caper with death. Luckily, I'd learned capering from the jongleurs who sometimes stopped at my father's hall along the way to more illustrious castles. I fancied I might have a better chance on the Bridge of Blades and Flame than a knight whose chivalric training had been more regular.

I considered leaving my armor and sword on the bank; they'd weigh me down as I leapt, and if I were really unlucky, they might get hot as branding irons. But I dared not trust that the Bridge of Blades and Flame was the last layer of deviltry wound around the Garden of Delights. Whatever bloodthirsty strategist had placed the dragon on the bank of the icy torrent, and the gulf of flame just beyond the dragon, might set a hungry lion or an assassin on the other side of the bridge. I kept my armor on. Muttering a quick prayer—God guard fools!—I leapt to the first blade-thin foothold, just missing the first jet of flame.

It was indeed a bit like dancing. Once I caught the rhythm of the fire's music, I could be almost safe on that ghastly bridge, leaping just in time to avoid each burst of flame. All the same, exhaustion was a formidable foe. By the time I reached the far side, I was in no state to fight off a lion or even a particularly determined lapdog. I collapsed on the bank, dazed. When I opened my eyes, I found an elegant lady offering me a hand up.

I accepted her help with thanks, too startled to be distrustful just yet. She looked as young as I was, and a good deal richer. She wore no silken headdress over her shining black hair, but that hair was a wealth in itself, the intricate braids cascading from her broad forehead to the silver belt at her hips. Her gown of crimson silk brocade must have cost a fortune, and the bodice that offset it was so thickly flowered with embroidery that I couldn't tell what color the cloth might be. And yet here she was, dressed fit to meet the king, lounging out in the garden where the dew might spoil her silk. How rich she must be to treat such finery so carelessly, I could scarcely imagine. This was my first journey far from Révie, and I had not yet seen much of the world.

She smiled at me, and her teeth, of course, were perfect. "Welcome, bold adventurer, to the Garden of Delights. You have passed the last test, the last peril, and arrived at the haven reserved for the bravest of the brave. You have swum the River of Pain, fought the many-headed dragon, and crossed the Bridge of Blades and Flame. All here is yours, O flower of knighthood, and all is for your delight, for this is the Garden of Delights."

"So I see," I said. "Someone told my brother Roland to come here seeking the Water of Life that heals all wounds."

"Yes, here flows the spring of the Water of Life," the lady said. "You can fill your vial before you return home, victorious hero. But meanwhile, rest and refresh yourself in this fair land." She laid a blossom-light hand on my shoulder. "All here is for your pleasure, good sir: the Water of Life, the shade of the bower, the fragrant apples, the sweet dark grapes—and me, the Damsel of the Garden of Delights. I also await your pleasure."

The damsel leaned against me. She was a head shorter than I, but something in her bearing convinced me she was nothing near as fragile a blossom as she appeared. Her deep blue eyes sought mine—foiled, of course, by the visor of my helm. I slid a hand around her waist, but kept myself masked. Playfully, she put a hand to my visor. "Let me look upon the face of my hero and plant a kiss of welcome on—oh!" the damsel cried as she unmasked me, "you're a girl!"

"That I am, Jezebel," I said, "so you can stop pressing your brocaded bosom against me." I clasped her to myself—an embrace she no longer desired—and glared into her too-perfect face. "Someone went to great expense to deck you out as bait. Virgin Mary's eyeteeth, an army of women must have labored over that embroidery!"

"I live a retired life here with little to occupy my time besides my embroidery," the Damsel said. "But you are not so constrained, good maid-at-arms. If the Garden of Delights does not please you, by all means, fill your flask and go your way."

"You're as anxious to be rid of me now as you were to detain me a moment ago," I said. "You wanted a man, and I doubt it was for the obvious reason. This garden is built on strong magic, and here you are in the center of it like a spider in her web. If you only wanted a lover, you needn't take nearly so much trouble: one glimpse of your pretty heart-shaped face in the church square would be enough. No. You—or more likely, whoever owns you—set out to lure men to this secluded place for a purpose."

"It's true that my Lady Ettarre of the Island commanded me to attract a knight into her service," the Damsel conceded, "and as I doubt a female would satisfy her—"

"*A* knight? Your lady wants *one* knight? *Why, then, have all my three brothers disappeared into this trap? WHERE ARE MY BROTHERS?*"

"Why, how should I know?"

"Because you lured those three fools here and you bound them to your service—with this!" I brandished the hazel wand I'd found in the back of her bodice when I pretended to embrace her.

"You—" For a moment I thought she would spit fire. Then, regaining her self-command, she laughed. "You've put too much faith in minstrels' tales if you think that twig can bind men-at-arms."

"Really? Then why did you keep it hidden in your bodice?"

"It must have gotten there by accident. Look, I'll show you how harmless it is." She reached for the wand, but not quickly enough.

"No you don't! I'm not fool enough to give a witch her wand back to use on me!"

"I'm *not* a witch. And *you're* a thief!" The Damsel of the Garden of Delights lunged toward the wand, but to no avail. It's nice to be tall: all I had to do was hold it above her head.

"A thief, am I? For taking an old twig that got into your clothes by mistake? Oh, that's droll, Jezebel. You're not only a witch, you're a wit."

"Stop calling me that!"

"A wit? Certainly. It wasn't so terribly witty."

"I'm *not* a Jezebel. I didn't want to kiss those sweaty, smelly, self-conceited knights. And I'm NOT A WITCH." The Damsel made such a lunge for the wand that she nearly tore one of her fashionably close-laced sleeves.

"Not a witch, eh? And this is not a wand, so you won't mind if I toss it into that bird's nest, high up in the tree?"

"Not a bit." The Damsel spoke with such sincere unconcern that I saw through her instantly.

"Ha. You could always climb up and get it afterward, couldn't you? Very well. You won't mind a bit if I mar it a little—chew on the end, perhaps?" I snapped at it teasingly, like a cat playing at fighting.

For answer, she kicked me in the shin. The armor I'd managed to scrounge from my brothers' leavings did not extend to my legs, and the damsel's shoes had nasty pointed toes. I didn't drop the wand, but I did let loose some of the choice language I'd learned in my travels. "That does it!" I said, when I was done cursing her and her shoemaker. "The wand pays for that kick!" And I brought my teeth down on it.

That was not the wisest thing I've ever done. It was like biting a bolt of lightning. Pain lanced through every fiber of my body. When I could see again, I realized I'd dropped the wand, and the witch was scrambling for it on the ground.

"Oh, no you don't!" I threw myself on her.

"Get off me, you great heavy brute!" she protested as we grappled. But at last she got the wand in her hand, its tip against my throat. "Be still, or I'll—I'll give you such pain you'll wish you'd been skewered and toasted on the bridge."

"What does it matter what I do now? You'll treat me as you did my brothers."

"I don't want to," the Damsel said. "But I will if you force me. Back away."

Wary of the wand, I disengaged myself from our tangle of arms and legs and gave her some room—but not so much that I couldn't close the distance quickly at need. "What good is it for me to back away? Surely you can bewitch me as well where I am."

"I won't, if you give me no reason," the damsel said. "My Lady Ettarre wants knights, not maidens. Leave now, and I'll let you go unharmed."

"Free my brothers and I'll leave gladly."

"I can't do that. My lady needs them."

"Whatever for?" I said. "Even my father scarcely knows what to do with them."

"She needs one-and-twenty knights of proven worth. Bound together by enchantments, they will become an unstoppable force to help her reclaim the inheritance that was denied to her. She has twenty now. I can't take three from their number when we're so close to completion."

"It's hard to imagine my brothers making such a difference in a battle," I said. "Between you and me, they're not very great swordsmen."

"I don't believe you," said the Damsel. "If they came here, as you say, then they fought the dragon and braved the Bridge of Blades and Flame. Only the flower of chivalry can attain the Garden of Delights."

"My brothers, the flower of chivalry?" I snorted. "I can outfence every one of them."

"Maybe they didn't come here after all," said the Damsel. "Maybe they only claimed to be searching for this garden, and went seeking their fortune instead. If they're not here, you can leave with a clear conscience."

Privately I had to consider the possibility. Given such a golden chance to get out from under Father's thumb, why shouldn't Roland, Raoul, and Berenger put as many miles between themselves and home as they could? But I had to brazen it out, or I'd never learn the truth. "Oh, you'd like me to believe that. You'd say anything to get rid of me."

The Damsel fumed for a few moments in silence. Then, "Come," she said, "see for yourself."

She led me down a pleasant stone-cobbled path from one glorious scene to another: a garden of roses that filled the September air with the heady scent of June; an arbor of grape vines, all bearing fruit; a bed of fragrant herbs; a grove of nut-trees; a broad orchard where every branch drooped with golden-skinned apples.

"Such a marvelous land!" I said. "It goes on and on, from beauty to beauty, from bounty to bounty. What inheritance could your Lady Ettarre wish to claim that could compare with what she already has?"

"Why should she be content with just this island, when by rights, all Loegris should bow to her?"

"All *Loegris*? What does she think she is?"

"She is the rightful sovereign—"

"Who told you *that?*"

The damsel's blush told me all I needed to know.

"She did herself, didn't she? Well, doesn't that just figure. All I can say is, I never heard of any Queen Ettarre."

"Who cares what *you've* heard of? Who are *you?*" the damsel shot back.

"Who are you?" I countered. "Tell me your name, and I'll tell you mine. Or don't you have a name, witch?"

"I'm *not* a witch."

"Then give me something else to call you. Witch."

"Isabeau." She scowled as if she had lost something, giving that away.

"Why the long face, Damsel Isabeau? *I* can't work spells on your name. But I'll even the score: my name's Ursula. My father's the lord of Révie, a rocky scrap of land at the back end of nowhere. When bards stay at our hall, he sometimes tells them he was cheated of a much wider inheritance. To his face, they all agree with him—but behind his back, they laugh."

"Well, no one laughs at my Lady Ettarre."

"Locked up in this inaccessible island, how would you know if they did?"

Isabeau stalked on in silence a while, but her pretty clear-skinned face changed from white to red, and her shapely hands clenched.

After a time, bored with the silence, I tried to strike up a conversation. "What's Lady Ettarre like? Is she a witch, too?"

"I am *not* a witch!"

"Right, *right*, and that twig's not a wand."

"I am a learned *enchantress*, educated according to the School of Salamanca. I know the spirit-lore of Solomon, the Enneads of Plotinus, the natural history of Pliny, the charm-lore of Africanus, the herb-lore of Hildegarde, the geometry of Euclid, and the algebra of the Arabs."

I was a bit impressed. Father didn't hold with book-learning. "You must have been at Salamanca all your life to have learned so much."

A look of discontent crossed the enchantress's features. "No, I was here all along. My grand— er, my lady taught me. She was at Salamanca in her youth."

"Ah. Well, this is a fair enough place to take root in."

"Take root!" Isabeau kicked a stone in the path. "As if I were one of these trees. I might as well be one. Did you travel from your homeland all alone?"

"Oh, yes."

"What was it like, traveling by yourself?"

"It seems almost heartless to say it, with my brothers missing, but this has been the best time I've ever had. Not that it hasn't been hard, too—sleeping outdoors, eating whatever I could find, fighting off the occasional brigand—but oh, the open road! The prospect of something new over every rise! And this armor—Roland's second-best—how handy it is to put my visor down and be mysterious: the knight without a face! People treat me like I'm someone important when they can't see it's just Maid Ursula, the squire's youngest brat."

Her blue eyes assessed me curiously. "You carry a sword. Why didn't you draw it on me when you had my wand?"

"Well, really, what do you take me for? I wouldn't kill you in cold blood, would I? You haven't done me any deadly harm—not that I know of," I added. "But rest assured, I know how to use that sword. My three brothers needed a fourth as sparring partner, so they taught me. Let me ask you a question in return, Isabeau. Why didn't you use that wand on me as soon as you got it back?"

"Because you never drew the sword on me," said the Damsel. "But trust me, Maid Ursula, I know how to use my weapon, too."

"I believe you," I said. "How did you come to be the Damsel of the Garden?"

"My mother was Lady Ettarre's daughter."

"She's your grandmother? Why do you call her Lady Ettarre, then?"

"When she chose me as her apprentice, my lady said it was better I should see her as mistress than as kin."

"She did, did she?"

"It was an honor to be so chosen."

"Huh."

"None of her children inherited her skill," Isabeau said a touch defensively. "None of her legitimate grandchildren, either. I outshone them *all*, legitimate and illegitimate. My lady said I was the *only* one worthy to inherit her knowledge."

"Then you must be the heir of all this beauteous land."

She looked sour. "And are you, then, heir of your own homeland, Ursula?"

"No, Damsel," I said. "No more than you are."

We came at last to a stand of willows near the brook. Isabeau's steps slowed. "We're almost there," she said. "The knights, they—they rest under the shadow of the willows. If you don't find your brothers there, will you promise me—promise to leave me in peace?"

My heart sank to my stomach. "There's something you don't want to show me. I promise nothing. Show me first."

Sighing, Isabeau led me across the brook at the ford.

Under the trailing branches of the willows stood an array of extraordinary statues: young men of marble, standing or sitting or reclining on the grass, leaning as if to embrace an unseen person. They were most marvelously lifelike. And as my eyes swept the crowd of marble forms, I knew one of them at a glance. "Berenger!" He stood, leaning slightly forward, looking downward fondly, as if into the face of a lover. I ran to him and cast my left arm about him. My right hand drew my sword, and the heat of fury rising through me could almost have melted it.

"Drawing steel?" said Isabeau, raising her wand. "You said you didn't want to kill me."

"That was when I believed you'd done no great evil."

"I didn't kill them! I mean, they're not dead."

"No," I choked out, "they're neither alive and free, nor dead and with God. They're in some godforsaken *nowhere*, like a little girl's dolls left carelessly under the bed. Like *things*."

"It's only until we get the twenty-first."

"And then what? Then they go *free*, I suppose, little witch?" I spat at her.

"Then they become Lady Ettarre's champions."

"Yes. Instead of standing spellbound, they'll march spell-kicked and spell-goaded, with no more choice where to go than a farmer gives his wheelbarrow."

"Only until my lady has her rightful inheritance."

"Which you claim is the whole realm. The realm and all its

people in the grip of a woman who thinks it fair to bind young men in living death. How can you lend yourself to this evil?"

"When did I have a choice?" Isabeau said.

"I don't know. But you've surely left Berenger no choice."

"So. Now we're foes, are we? Why don't you strike, then, swordswoman?" Isabeau taunted. "Afraid I'll strike back?"

I smacked her with the flat of the sword. She staggered and pointed the wand at me, chanting, and I braced myself for a bolt of lightning, a burst of flame, some huge, swift, and painful retaliation. That was stupid, a beginner's blunder. I ought to have gone on swinging. Never having faced magic before, I hadn't yet learned that it doesn't always come at once—especially when the magician is young and distracted by a muddle of emotions. When it looked to me as though all Isabeau's wand-waving was for naught, I recovered my wits enough to aim another blow at her. That was when the slow-building spell finally broke over me. It was like the rolling pains I had with the vomiting sickness one Shrovetide. It wrung every fiber of my body, from my heart outward. Before I quite knew how it happened, the ground came up and hit me in the back. When I could see anything but dancing sparks, I found Isabeau bending over me, her brow creased. "Ursula? Oh, God in heaven. I didn't mean to kill her."

"I'm not dead," I rasped out. I coughed, sat up, and nearly lost my breakfast on the grass.

She leveled her wand at me, but it wavered a trifle.

"Look, Isabeau," I said when I'd recovered, "you weren't trying to kill me. I don't want to kill you either. Must we be enemies?"

"What choice do we have?"

"Of course there's a choice," I said.

"I can't let them all go," she said. "Not till the twenty-first knight is bound will the perils of the crossing give way to let them pass. I could let *you* go, but the Bridge of Blades and Flame only holds one. By the time anyone else had a chance to cross, my lady would be aware of it. Her vengeance would be terrible."

"I don't understand you," I said. "You slave for her. You sin for her. She gives you nothing, and forgives you nothing. Why don't you defy her? Is your magic not strong enough?"

"For what?"

"To make this unstoppable force of proven knights your own, of course."

"Are you crazy?" Isabeau stared at me.

"Maybe," I said. "I fought the dragon. I crossed the cursed bridge. If my brothers are the flower of knighthood, so am I. So go ahead." I sheathed my sword. "I'm the twenty-first. Bind me."

It was almost worth the certainty that I was the world's biggest fool to see the look of astonishment on her face. For a moment she hovered, eyes wide as platters, mouth open. Then she smirked. "Kiss me."

"Pardon?"

"The spell's on my lips. If you trust me. If you dare."

I didn't trust her—not wholly. But what else could I do? Escape alone, leaving my brothers and all those other poor fools in bondage? I bent awkwardly toward her upturned face.

"At least you smell better than the others," said Isabeau, and kissed me.

I tried to open my mouth to return some jest—but my body no longer obeyed my commands. Isabeau chanted, tracing spirals and arabesques in the air with her wand, and I could look at nothing else. Then all the statues—all the knights—moved stiffly into ranks beside and behind me, and we marched.

The chasm of the Bridge of Blades and Flame was now nothing but an empty gulch. The Damsel in the Garden hitched up her skirts in one hand and made her way down one side of it with surprising ease, and we soldiers, bound by her will, lumbered afterward. The dragon I had beheaded raised a new head to glare at us, but Isabeau tossed a silvery scale into the River of Pain, and the beast stretched its neck over the river as a bridge for us. We all marched across and stood on the far shore, facing Isabeau, our captain.

"Well done, apprentice." The woman who spoke, straight-backed and regal, had not been there a moment before. Even smaller than Isabeau, her arms slender as a child's in her elegant tight-laced sleeves, she nonetheless gave an impression of compact power, like a cat poised to spring. Under her jeweled headdress and silk veil, her aged face was still beautiful; but her eyes were like sparks from flint, ready to set the world ablaze. "Now place them in my hands, child, so I may reclaim my rightful domain."

"One moment, Grandmother," said Isabeau placidly. "All is not yet ready." She spun widdershins, swept the wand with a great flourish, and shouted in some outlandish tongue. And suddenly twenty knights and I stretched our limbs and moved of our own accord. Most drew their swords—and then stopped, finding no one to attack but an old woman.

"What have you done?" Lady Ettarre cried.

"I've done all the evil I'm ever going to do at your bidding, Grandmother!" Isabeau broke the wand over her knee. I cringed, remembering how it had felt to bite the end. A singed smell confirmed my fears. Isabeau did not cry out, but wrung her scorched hands. Lady Ettarre surged toward her granddaughter, murder in her eyes, a wand in her hand—and there was Isabeau, all unarmed.

Without a better plan, I thrust myself between them.

"Ursula, you fool!" I heard, at the same moment that a world of pain descended on me. Every inch of my skin was on fire; my eyes ached; my ears ached; my stomach threatened to turn itself inside out. *This she meant for Isabeau, for her own grandchild*, I thought, and forced myself, through it all, to keep hurtling toward the old enchantress to disarm her or die trying. I landed squarely upon her and, through sheer weight, knocked her over like a ninepin. I heard shrieking, and was astonished to find it came from the enchantress, as if the moment I touched her, she shared all the agony her spell had inflicted on me. I hung on like death, scarcely knowing what went on around me, hoping I'd give Isabeau a chance to do something cleverer than I could manage.

"Ursula, get up," Isabeau said at last. "Please. Let her go."

"She aimed that spell at you, Isabeau."

"I know," Isabeau said, "but she's still my grandmother. Besides, I have her wand now."

Astonished, I lifted my anguished body off the old woman's, and found that once I let go of her, the pain ceased. Standing beside me, Isabeau pointed a wand of dark, knotted wood at Lady Ettarre. "Grandmother," she said.

"I told you to call me Lady," the old enchantress said.

"I'm not your apprentice anymore. I'm not the bait in your trap. I'm an enchantress in my own right."

"Will you bind me to your will, then, young adept?"

"Only if you make it necessary. Go back to your hall, to the grandchildren you care to acknowledge as kin. I'll never be your tool again." She stood over Lady Ettarre, wand in hand, until the old woman vanished as quietly as she had appeared. Then Isabeau turned to the knights. "Go now. Go free."

"Ursula! What are you doing here?" My oldest brother, Roland, had caught up with me.

"Rescuing you," I said.

"Who brought you here?" my second brother, Raoul, asked.

"Myself. You were all three imprisoned here. What did you expect me to do—wait for a miracle?"

"Well, at least you won't need to travel home unguarded," Roland said. And Berenger—even Berenger, my favorite—nodded agreement.

"Who said I need a guard? Who even said I'm going home?" I hadn't actually thought, till then, of not returning. But I could feel walls closing around me, and I knew I couldn't let myself be trapped again.

"Are you sure you wanted your brothers freed?" Isabeau spoke quietly at my elbow. "I could enchant them again."

"Only if they make it necessary," I said through clenched teeth. "Roland, Raoul, Berenger, I'm glad you're free. But I'm not going back with you."

I hadn't actually asked her—and she hadn't actually asked me—but somehow, we didn't need to speak of it. I found my steed where I'd left him, munching grass on the bank. I mounted, then pulled Isabeau up behind me—brocaded skirts and all—and we rode off to seek our fortunes.

GHOST SPIKE

by Jonathan Moeller

Jonathan Moeller is very glad to return to SWORD AND SORCERESS a seventh time with "Ghost Spike." When he wrote the first *Ghosts* story seven years ago, he did not suspect he would still be writing about Caina seven years later, but sometimes life has pleasant surprises.

Visit him on the web at http://www.jonathanmoeller.com, where you can find, among other things, six years of interviews with past SWORD AND SORCERESS contributors, and CHILD OF THE GHOSTS, a free full-length novel set in the world of "Ghost Spike."

"So my son has asked you to marry him," said Lord Corbould Maraeus, his voice thick with derision.

"He has," said Caina Amalas.

She sat in Corbould's solar. The old lord faced her, his face a mask of disapproval, his eyes like gray ice. Corbould Maraeus was the very image of the cold, stern Imperial lord, and one of the most powerful men in the Empire. If Emperor Alexius died tomorrow morning, Corbould might well become the new Emperor by afternoon.

And he did not like Caina. She was the Ghost circlemaster of the Imperial capital, the leader of the Emperor's spies and agents, and she had foiled Lord Corbould's plans more than once.

"You come to negotiate yourself?" said Corbould. "I am surprised your father did not come to speak for you."

"My father has been dead for eighteen years," said Caina. "I have no other living relatives. I am therefore head of my own noble House, and well within my rights to negotiate my own marriage."

"I am not surprised," said Corbould, "that Lucan wants to

marry you. He was always a wastrel and a fool. Little wonder he would become besotted with a murderous whore."

Caina felt her hand curl into a fist beneath the table, her fingers brushing against the skirt of her green gown. But not a hint of her anger touched her voice or face. She had faced things far more frightening than Corbould.

"You do your son a disservice," said Caina. "Lucan has spent the ten years since the murder of his wife hunting rogue magi and supernatural predators. Countless men, women, and children owe their lives to him."

"How terribly noble," said Corbould, "to run about playing the hero instead of doing the hard work of maintaining the Imperial peace. Countess, I shall be blunt. The Emperor finds you useful, so I tolerate your existence. And I concede that you are necessary to him. Politics is a dirty business. But I will not permit a creature like you to wed one of my blood."

"Why so squeamish?" Caina said. She had a vision of putting a throwing knife into Lord Corbould's throat, and shoved it aside. "You don't care about Lucan. I've heard it from your own lips."

"I don't," said Corbould. "But he will have children, as soon as I force the fool to take another wife. For the good of the Empire, House Maraeus must remain strong. And you will not give me grandchildren, Countess. I have my own sources of information. I know the magi murdered your father when you were eleven, and the attack left you unable to bear children. So if you wed Lucan, you would take away the one use he has to me. Let me be perfectly clear, Countess. The day you present me with a living grandchild, you can wed Lucan. Not before. Now get out of my sight."

And that was that.

Later that evening Caina stood before the door to Lucan's rooms at the Black Cuirass Inn.

She hesitated.

Perhaps Lord Corbould was right. Caina could not have children, and Lucan claimed that didn't bother him—but she did not entirely believe him. And what kind of life would he have, married to a woman like Caina, hunting outlaw sorcerers and slavers and assassins? He could have a different kind of life, one with children—and one with a wife who didn't have a score of vengeful enemies bent on her death.

Caina shook her head. She had tried to push Lucan away before, for his own good, but he had adamantly refused to be pushed.

She knocked at the door…and it swung open at her touch.

That alarmed her. Lucan was not quite as cautious as she was, but he was close, and he would never leave his door unlocked.

Caina stepped into his sitting room, and noticed things were amiss.

His weapons were gone, emptied from both the trunk by the balcony and the hidden compartments on the wall. His sword was gone from its stand. To judge from the disarray, he had left in haste.

A piece of paper lay on the center of the floor, alongside a length of white cord.

Caina picked up the paper and the white cord.

It was a note.

"My lord Lucan Maraeus," it read, "it has been ten years, and I have missed you sorely. But not as much, I think, as your wife. Livia used to scream for you to save her when I used the knives on her. Of course, it has been ten years—now she just screams. I wonder if she even remembers your name. Or her own.

"You slew my master Morneus, and it's time for you to pay that debt. Meet me at the Inn of the Golden Milestone by noon. Come alone. If you are late, or if you bring anyone with you, Livia will pay dearly for it.

"And if you tell anyone about this note—anyone—Livia will suffer for it. I know you've seduced the 'Ghost Countess' so famed among the rabble, and if you contact the Ghosts or the Imperial Guard…well. You failed Livia once. Don't fail her again."

The note was signed "Croanna."

Caina's hand clenched, the paper crumpling.

Lucan had told her the entire story. He had been married young, a political match arranged by Corbould to Livia of House Cycorus. Much to Lucan's surprise, they had come to love each other. And then Livia had seen the master magus Morneus practicing necromancy, torturing and murdering to fuel his spells. Morneus killed Livia to cover up his crimes. So Lucan struck down the necromancer and all his apprentices.

But one had gotten away.

A woman named Croanna.

A woman who had apparently taken Livia captive rather than murder her.

Caina examined the length of white cord. It was in fact a lock of hair. Platinum-blond hair, exactly as Lucan had described his dead wife's hair.

Caina closed her eyes for a moment, surprised at the intensity of the pain.

If Lucan's wife was still alive, then Caina had lost him.

The damned fool. He should have come to her. She had resources. She could have helped him...

Her eyes snapped open.

She was a Ghost, a spy and assassin of the Emperor. More, she was the Ghost circlemaster of the Imperial capital, with reliable agents at her call. And she had learned long ago that the surest way to combat grief was with action.

Lucan might be lost to her, but she would save his life.

She paused only long enough to help herself to some equipment from Lucan's stores, and hastened downstairs to the common room. The Black Cuirass Inn was not far from the Imperial Citadel, and catered to nobles visiting the capital on business. The innkeeper, a grim-faced Legion veteran named Appian, kept watch over a common room full of rich nobles eating their dinners. Caina caught his sleeve as he passed. Appian started to glare at her, but his expression quickly changed to respect.

Caina had a reputation.

Saving the Emperor from an assassin in front of a thousand witnesses had that effect.

"Countess Caina," said Appian, "a pleasure, but..."

"Lord Lucan received a message today," said Caina. "Who delivered it?"

Appian nodded. "A short fellow. Shabbily dressed. Looked sort of like a nobleman's seneschal fallen on rough times."

"Gnaeus?" said Caina. She knew the man. He was petty thief and a small-time spy, scratching out a living selling secrets to interested parties.

"Yes, him," said Appian. His mouth twisted with distaste. "In fact, he's right over there, by the door."

Caina headed for the door. Gnaeus himself lounged against the wall, looking over the crowds of nobles and their retainers. His eyes flicked to Caina, and all the blood drained out of his face.

He spun and raced out the door.

Caina cursed and sprinted after him.

Carriages rattled back and forth in the broad street, most making their way to the Imperial Citadel. Gnaeus twisted and ducked into an alley behind the Inn, and Caina followed. She was faster than Gnaeus, but her long skirt hindered her, and he would outrun her.

So she snatched a throwing knife from her sleeve and flung it. The handle smacked into Gnaeus's temple, and he stumbled, bouncing off the wall, and almost fell. That was all the opening Caina needed. She fell upon him, driving a palm into his face and a knee into his gut. Gnaeus crumpled, and she caught his arm, twisted it behind him, and drove him to his knees.

"Don't kill me!" wheezed Gnaeus, blood dripping from his nose. "I..."

"You shouldn't have run," said Caina, twisting his arm a bit more. "You delivered a message to Lord Lucan Maraeus today. Who gave it to you?"

Gnaeus hesitated. "I don't know what you're talking about."

Caina sighed. "Let me make this plain for you. Tell me, and I'll pay you." She dropped a gold coin in the dust at his knees, and then drew another knife. "Don't tell me, and I'll cut off pieces until you tell me. Decide. Now."

Gnaeus looked at the knife, and then at the coin. “I don’t know his name. But he paid me well to do it, said he’d kill me if I talked to anyone.”

“Describe him,” said Caina.

“Vicious sort,” said Gnaeus. “Wore red chain mail. Red tattoos around his eyes and mouth, too.”

Caina nodded, let Gnaeus fall to the ground, and hurried away without another word.

She recognized the description. Red Trajus, a mercenary not overly burdened with scruples, and a favorite hatchet man of the Magisterium, the brotherhood of the magi. The magi used Red Trajus and his company for their dirty work. And if Croanna had returned to the Empire, the magi could not be seen aiding an outlaw. So they would send Red Trajus to assist her.

That troubled Caina. Why would the Magisterium take the risk of aiding an outlaw magus? Perhaps they wanted Lucan dead even more badly than she had thought.

Her mouth thinned at that thought, and she hurried into the night.

She couldn’t take on Red Trajus herself.

But she knew where to find help.

But first, some preparations.

The Ghosts kept a safehouse near the Imperial Citadel, located in the cellar below the shop of a goldsmith who owed the Ghosts several favors, and Caina slipped inside unnoticed. She stripped out of the formal gown and into more suitable garb. Loose black clothing, fortified with hardened leather plates to ward off blades. A belt of throwing knives and other useful tools went around her waist, and daggers into her boots, and more throwing knives beneath her sleeves. A black mask hid her face.

Finally, her cloak. It had been created by the nightkeepers of the Ghosts, and it blended and merged with the shadows, rendering its wearer all but invisible. And as an added bonus, it shielded its wearer’s thoughts from mind-controlling sorcery.

Caina left the safehouse, stole a horse, and hastened through the capital’s dark alleys.

A short time later she arrived at the Street of Forges, where smiths labored endlessly to produce arms and armor for the Imperial Legions. Caina stopped before a large smithy, let the horse go, and climbed up the copper drainpipe. Within a window on the second floor she saw a man in his late forties and a woman in her early thirties eating dinner before a fireplace. The man had the look of a Legion veteran, with hard hands and hard gray eyes, and the thick arms and neck of a smith. His wife was pretty, despite the faint lines near her blue eyes.

Caina slipped open the window and dropped into the room.

The Legion veteran moved in an instant, a sword appearing in his hand, the tip resting at Caina's throat. The woman was on her feet as well, a crossbow ready in her grasp.

Caina reached up, drew back her hood, and removed her mask.

"Countess," said the Legion veteran, lowering his sword.

"Ark," said Caina, nodding at the woman. "Tanya."

"There's trouble," said Ark, "isn't there?"

Caina nodded. "I need your help. Both of you."

"You have it," said Ark.

"Whatever you ask of us," added Tanya, "it is yours."

Caina nodded. Ark and Tanya were both Ghosts, and would do whatever she asked. And Caina had rescued Tanya from slave traders years ago. Both would follow her into hell if she asked it of them.

She hoped it wouldn't come to that.

"An outlaw magus named Croanna returned to the capital," said Caina. "She's one of Morneus's apprentices."

Tanya's eyes widened. "The necromancer your Lucan slew."

Caina felt herself twitch, but nodded. "Lucan thought that Morneus killed his wife. Apparently, Croanna took her captive instead. She sent a note to Lucan, telling him to come or his wife would die. He went."

"Oh," said Tanya, "oh, Countess. I am sorry."

"Get our gear," said Ark, and Tanya nodded and went to a chest against the wall. "Do we have a plan?"

"Yes," said Caina. "Red Trajus delivered the note to Lucan."

Ark scowled. "The pet thug of the magi."

Caina nodded. "I know where he's staying. We'll find him and make him tell us where Croanna is hiding."

Ark grunted. "Red Trajus and his crew are nasty pieces of work. We may need help."

"No time," said Caina. "I don't know what Croanna has in mind for Lucan, and I don't want to find out." Croanna might have killed him already. Caina refused to think about that. "And once Red Trajus tells us where Croanna is, we'll kill her and rescue Lucan and Livia."

"Livia?" said Tanya, pulling weapons and armor from the chest.

"Lucan's wife," said Caina.

Tanya handed a chain mail hauberk to Ark, and began to pull on a leather jerkin studded with steel discs.

"Croanna might have lied," said Ark.

"Perhaps," said Caina. "But if Livia is alive, then Lucan will go back to her."

Ark tugged on the hauberk and strapped on a sword belt. "I'm surprised he hasn't asked you to marry him yet."

"He did," said Caina, voice quiet. "So I went to Lord Corbould, his father. He declined."

Ark nodded, lifting a massive Legion-issue shield, while Tanya tucked a pair of daggers and a quiver of crossbow bolts into her belt.

"Heartless old bastard," muttered Tanya. "You should marry Lucan anyway, just to spite him."

"No," said Caina. "I am a Ghost, and I do what I must for the good of the Empire. Corbould Maraeus is one of the Emperor's strongest allies. If I married Lucan without his permission, it would drive him away from the Emperor." She hesitated. "Even if...I wish it might be otherwise."

"I am sorry, Countess," said Tanya.

"But there's more going on here," said Caina, hoping to change the topic, "than just Croanna's vendetta against Lord Lucan."

"What do you mean?" said Tanya.

"Red Trajus works for the Magisterium," said Caina. "Not for outlaw magi. Which means that the high magi, maybe even the First Magus himself, ordered Red Trajus to help her."

"So the magi are up to something," said Tanya, shouldering her crossbow.

"And whatever it is," said Caina, "we're going to stop it. Let's go."

"Red Trajus owns an inn?" whispered Tanya.

They hid behind a stack of barrels in the mouth of an alley, the nearby docks reeking of salt and dead dish. A large inn of timber and stone stood across the street, and the sounds of carousing and off-key singing spilled into the street.

"He uses it as a base," said Caina. "Billets his men here when he's in the city. Stores captives in the cellar. And, of course, his men get free ale and whores when they're here."

Ark grunted. "There are at least sixty mercenaries in there."

"Most of them drunk," said Tanya.

"Aye," said Ark. "But those guards…there, and there. They're not drunk, and they look like they know their business."

"Of course they do," said Caina. "Trajus isn't a fool. The Ghosts have been watching him for years."

"Then how do we get him?" said Ark.

"Simple," said Caina. "We set in the inn on fire."

They stared at her.

"We…set the inn on fire?" said Tanya.

"Most of Trajus's men are drunk," said Caina. "We set the inn on fire, they'll panic and run into the street. We snatch Trajus, run for it, and question him."

"Why is it," said Ark, "that your plans always seem to involve setting buildings on fire?"

"I haven't burned down a building in years," said Caina.

"After I joined the Ghosts and started working with you," said Ark, "I set fire to more buildings than I did in twenty years with the Legion."

"It always worked, didn't it?" said Caina. "Wait here."

She slipped out from behind the barrels and crept across the street, gliding from shadow to shadow. The guards at the door kept close watch over their surroundings, but Caina had years of experience moving unseen, and the shadow-woven cloak. In a short time she circled around to the inn's back windows. It was child's play to slip the latch and climb into the inn's kitchen. Two stoves stood against the wall, pots of stew bubbling atop them.

Caina kicked both stoves over, found a jar of cooking oil, and flung it over the spilled coals.

The resultant flame was...rather more than she had hoped for.

"Fire!" she bellowed in the direction of the inn's common room. "Fire! Fire!"

Then she raced out the back door, circled the block, and rejoined Ark and Tanya. Flames already billowed out the inn's back door, and a stream of panicked, drunken mercenaries surged into the street.

"What did you do?" said Ark.

"Cooking oil," said Caina.

A thunderous bellow cut over the roar of the flames. "Buckets! Damn your hides, you dogs, get buckets! A brigade from the docks! Move, damn you!" A tall man wearing a red chain mail shirt paced back and forth, his pale face marked with crimson tattoos around the mouth and eyes.

Red Trajus.

"Ark," said Caina, scooping up some pebbles from the alley. "Tanya. Get ready."

Ark nodded and pressed himself against the wall, while Tanya crouched in the shadows.

Caina tossed one of the pebbles, and it bounced off the back of Trajus's head. He turned in irritation, scanning the alley, but saw nothing. Caina waited until he turned, then flicked another pebble. This one bounced off his earlobe. Again Trajus whirled in annoyance, and Caina's third pebble caught him right between the eyes.

He stormed forward in a rush, and Caina stepped out from behind the barrels, letting him see her.

He hesitated, his eyes narrowing as he took in the shadow-woven cloak, and then he grinned and lifted his blade.

"So," Trajus growled, "the Ghosts finally decided to burn down my inn?" Caina backed away, and Trajus followed, his sword point waving back and forth like an enraged serpent. "Well and good. The Magisterium offers a standing bounty of five hundred for the head of any Ghost..."

Ark surged out the darkness and seized Trajus's arms. The mercenary opened his mouth to shout, and Tanya leapt upon him, a dripping rag in her hand. She slapped it over his face, the fluid filling his nostrils and mouth.

Trajus went rigid, and then slumped unconscious in Ark's grip.

"Well done," said Caina. "Tie him up, and we'll take him someplace where we can have a private chat."

Caina knew of an abandoned warehouse in the docks, and they took Red Trajus there. Ark bound him to a chair, taking his weapons and armor.

"Wake him," said Caina.

Tanya pinched his nose closed and poured a vial of green fluid down his throat, and Red Trajus awoke, sputtering and cursing.

"Damn you all," he muttered, "'I'll have your hides, I'll..."

His bloodshot eyes darted back and forth, taking in Caina's cloak and the masks hiding Ark and Tanya's faces.

"Ah," he said, spitting. "So, the Ghosts have finally decided to assassinate me, eh? Well, the Magisterium will be displeased, and you do not want to face an angry magus..."

"Spare me," said Caina, speaking in the snarling rasp she used while disguised. "You're the Magisterium's rabid dog. Kill a dog, and a man simply finds another. But if we wanted to kill you, we'd have done so already."

Trajus smirked. "So you want information."

"Earlier today you delivered a note to a petty spy named Gnaeus," said Caina. "Who gave you the note and why?"

Trajus grinned.

"You're her, aren't you?" he said. "The one they call the Ghost Countess." He laughed. "She said you would get involved."

"She," said Caina. "You mean Croanna."

"Aye," said Trajus. "Tell me, is it true that every night you lure a different enemy of the Emperor to your bed, only to slit his throat while he lies exhausted in your embrace?"

Caina rolled her wrist, a throwing knife appearing in her hand. "We could skip to the end, if you like."

"No need," said Trajus, his eyes on the blade. "I'll tell you everything you want to know."

Caina frowned. He was far more cooperative than she had anticipated. She would have expected threats.

Not cooperation.

"Speak," she said.

"You know the Magisterium pays me to do their dirty work," said Trajus. "And one of the dirty jobs is killing outlaw magi...at least those that the high magi don't find useful. One day Croanna turned up in the capital with a captive."

Lucan's wife, no doubt. Croanna had been telling the truth. Caina was grateful the mask hid the pain on her face.

"I would have killed her," said Trajus, "but word came down from the First Magus himself. Said I was to assist her, quietly."

"Did he say why?" said Caina.

"No," said Trajus. "And I didn't ask. I'm paid to kill people, not to think."

"Then she's up to something," said Caina. "Something the First Magus thinks will be useful."

Trajus shrugged. "Like I said, I don't care. The crazy hag had only one job for me. Take a letter to a noble named Lucan Maraeus. The man plays the drunkard, but the high magi hate him, and he's dangerous. So I hired that rat Gnaeus to deliver the letter, and hung back to watch. Maraeus took off the minute he got the letter. Croanna was waiting for him in a carriage, and he climbed in, and that was that."

"Croanna," said Caina. "What is she like?"

"Dangerous," said Trajus. "All magi are, of course, but

she's...worse. Did you know she was old Morneus's student? He was a necromancer, and she was his favorite apprentice. And she spent her exile in Catekharon. The sorcerers of Catekharon are the finest artificers of enspelled devices in the world. Croanna learned from them, as well. She can make...things, enspelled things, from the blood and flesh of her victims."

And Lucan had been in this woman's clutches for hours.

"Where is she?" said Caina.

Trajus answered without hesitation. "She's hiding in the ruins of the Old Baths, where all those people died in the riots during the previous Emperor's reign. She said it's a place of power, that the energy of their deaths still lingers."

"Why are you telling me this?" said Caina.

Trajus smirked. "Because Croanna ordered me to do so."

"Did she," said Caina.

"She knew you would come for her one way or another," said Trajus.

"She should have hidden from me," said Caina.

Trajus laughed. "She's going to kill you. I've heard all about you, Countess. You've been giving the Magisterium fits for years. They've put a bounty of fifty thousand on your head, did you know that? No one's been able to collect, and I wasn't foolish enough to try." He smiled. "But Croanna is more dangerous than the other magi. She uses her head, not just her spells. And she's going to kill you, Countess."

"She is welcome to try," said Caina.

But the utter certainty in the mercenary's eyes chilled her.

"Cut him loose," said Caina. "Let him go."

Trajus blinked in surprise.

"We should kill him," said Ark.

"No point," said Caina. "Croanna already knows that we're coming." She nodded to Tanya, who cut the ropes binding Trajus. "But if you interfere, you will regret it. Though only briefly."

"Not to worry, Countess," said Trajus. "Croanna can handle you by herself, and if I interject myself, you'll probably kill me out of spite."

"Probably," said Caina. "You should stop working for the magi, while you still can."

Trajus snorted. "You should worry more about what Croanna is going to do to you."

He left without another word.

"I still think we should have killed him," said Ark.

"He isn't important," said Caina. "We need to deal with Croanna."

"How will we do that?" said Ark.

"We kill her, and quickly," said Caina. "And we do it ourselves. If Croanna's as powerful as Trajus claimed, and we bring a company of soldiers, we'll only get them killed. If she gets a chance to use her spells against us, we'll lose."

"But how will we defeat her?" said Tanya.

"Simple," said Caina. "We creep up and stab her in the back before she can cast any spells."

"Straightforward," said Ark.

"The best plans always are," said Caina. "Let's go."

The ruined Old Baths jutted in the night like skeletal fingers. Years ago, during the final turbulent years of the previous Emperor's reign, a riot had broken out. The Old Baths had caught fire, and hundreds of people had been killed when part of the structure collapsed. Ever since then, the site had been considered cursed, and no one had repaired the ruins for fear of drawing ill luck.

A perfect place, Caina supposed, for an outlaw magus to hide.

She sent Ark and Tanya to climb to the roof with their crossbows, and entered into the ruins herself, shadow-woven cloak flowing around her, boots making no sound against the tiled floor. Soot marred the elaborate reliefs upon the walls, and heaps of broken rubble covered the mosaics upon the floor. Statues of long-dead Emperors and lords stood at crooked, drunken angles.

A glimmer of light came from the center of the Baths.

The main chamber of the Baths had once boasted a great dome. Now the dome had half-collapsed into piles of rubble, and algae choked the stagnant pools, weeds rising between the cracked tiles. A dozen wooden tables stood in the center of the chamber, laden with jars, vials, books, scrolls. Caina scrambled up one of the rubble piles for a better look.

She saw Lucan at once.

He lay upon one of the tables, still alive, and Caina let out a long breath of relief. Yet he stared at the ceiling, blinking every so often, and his eyes were empty and glassy.

What had Croanna done to him?

A dark shape moved near one of the tables, and Caina laid eyes upon Croanna.

She was tall and gaunt, with glittering black eyes and ragged gray hair. Jewels gleamed upon her fingers and ears, and she wore rings in her ears, her eyebrows, her nose, her lips. No doubt every last one of them had been imbued with sorcerous power.

Caina slipped a throwing knife into her hand and crept to the bottom of the rubble heap, looking closer.

And Croanna looked up, her eyes narrowed.

"Ah," she said, her voice dusty. "That must be you, Countess. No need to hide further." She lifted her left hand, and Caina saw that she wore a strange glove made of steel rings and delicate chains. "Do you like it? One of the little toys I learned to make in Catekharon. It lets me sense the presence of any steel within a certain distance." She chuckled. "You are quite well armed, aren't you?"

Caina straightened up, the knife still in her hand.

Croanna's eyes fixed upon her. "You've come for Lucan, I suppose?"

"What have you done to him?" said Caina.

"Why, I've given him the chance to become famous," said Croanna. "Tomorrow morning he is going to kill the Emperor."

She smiled and gestured at Lucan, her sleeve falling away, and Caina saw a bronze spike driven through her left forearm, between the bones.

"You've mind-controlled him?" said Caina. "The Imperial Guard knows to look for the signs."

"Hardly," said Croanna. "Mind-controlling sorcery is

so...crude, so inelegant. What I've done is different. He is...sleepwalking, in fact. No one looking at him, or even speaking with him, will be any wiser. Tomorrow morning the Emperor will offer sacrifices to guarantee victory. Lord Corbould will be at his side, and Lucan will be there as well. And then he will strike the Emperor down. A son of Lord Corbould, murdering the Emperor before the assembled lords of the Empire...ah, that will mean civil war. Which will allow the Magisterium to retake its place as the rightful masters of the Empire."

Little wonder the First Magus had been willing to aid Croanna.

"Really," said Caina, taking a slow step forward. Another four or five paces, she judged, and she could put a throwing knife into Croanna's throat. "A bold plan."

"You, of course, will not be here to see it," said Croanna. "I will lay your head before the First Magus and take my place among the high magi." She cocked her head, her cold eyes glittering. "I had hoped to meet you. You would have made a tremendous magus. Regrettable that you are too clever for your own good."

"I would rather have been a swineherd," said Caina, taking another step. Another few paces...

"No doubt," said Croanna. "I know what you're doing, by the way. Trying to get close enough to pin me with a throwing knife?" She smiled. "I wouldn't recommend it."

"You're warded against steel, I suppose?" said Caina.

"Oh, no, no," said Croanna. "Most magi place too much reliance in their precious wards. Besides, I've no doubt that you have a silver-plated knife or two up your sleeve. In fact..." She took five quick steps forward, putting herself within reach of a throw. "Why don't you do it, Countess? A knife, right through my throat. Or the eye. Come, now. Surely you can do it."

Lucan groaned, and for a brief moment his placid expression dissolved into fear.

"Suppose I did put a knife through your throat?" said Caina. "What would happen?"

"Why don't I show you?" said Croanna. "Siona! To me!"

Something moved under one of the tables. A little girl, no more than nine or ten, crawled out, and got to her feet. She wore only a filthy gray shift, and her face and thin limbs showed obvious signs of abuse. The gray eyes she turned towards Caina were dark with hatred and rage.

A bronze spike had been driven through her left forearm.

But Caina hardly noticed that.

The girl's eyes, her gray eyes, were the exact color and shape of Lucan's eyes.

"Oh," said Caina. "That was clever."

"You understand?" said Croanna.

"It wasn't Lucan's wife you had," Caina said, her fingers tightening around the throwing knife. "It was his daughter."

"Indeed," said Croanna, stroking the girl's hair. "Livia Cycorus was pregnant when we killed her. Lucan never knew. My master cut the girl from the woman's body, believing a grandchild of Corbould Maraeus might one day be useful. And he was right...but not in quite the way he thought. Observe."

And before Caina could react, Croanna drew a dagger from her belt and drove it into her left hand. Blood welled over Croanna's palm, dripping upon the floor as she wrenched the blade free. She lifted her wounded hand, turning the palm towards Caina.

And then the wound vanished.

Siona shrieked, doubling over, left hand clutched to her chest. Blood welled out between her clenched fingers. She staggered back a step, and Caina saw the wound upon the girl's palm, a wound exactly the same shape as the one that had vanished from Croanna's hand.

"Go ahead, Countess," said Croanna. "Strike me down. And Lucan will watch his daughter die in front of him. Shortly before he watches you die in front of him, of course."

"You cruel coward," said Caina. "Hiding behind a child? That's why you lied to Lucan, isn't it? You knew that he would act rashly, if he thought that Livia was still alive. He never knew about the girl...because you took her from Livia." Her hand clenched around the throwing knife's hilt. "That is monstrous, even by the standards of the magi."

Croanna smiled and stroked Siona's hair again, the child huddling away from her touch. "It did work out rather well, didn't it? Lucan will murder the Emperor in front of a thousand witnesses. You dare not lift a weapon against me. A perfect trap...and all that is left for you to do, Countess, is to die."

She clapped her hands, and shadows began to move.

Men strode out of the darkness, armed and armored, Red Trajus at their head. For a moment Caina thought that Trajus had betrayed her. But then she saw the glassiness in their eyes, the placid calm of their expressions. Croanna had forced them into trances, as she had with Lucan.

Trajus should have listened to Caina when he had the chance.

"Of course, I had to test my sleepwalking spell before I employed it upon Lucan," said Croanna. "And dear Trajus and his men made excellent test subjects." She stepped behind the mercenaries, dragging Siona along. "Kill the Countess, quickly. No games."

Trajus and his men drew their swords, expressions still placid, and fanned out in a semicircle. Caina flung a throwing knife, her entire body snapping like a bowstring, and the blade buried itself in the throat of the nearest mercenary. The man went down with a scream, blood pouring from his throat, but the others continued without missing a beat. Caina yanked the daggers from her boots and backed towards the rubble heaps.

She glanced up at the broken dome, where Ark and Tanya crouched at the edge, and nodded.

Ark threw down one of the sealed flasks that Caina had taken from Lucan's rooms. Caina closed her eyes and looked away as it struck the ground at her feet, the liquid within spilling over the floor.

A liquid that burst into blinding white flame when exposed to air.

Croanna shrieked in pain, eyes screwed up against the light, and the mercenaries flinched, hands going to their faces. Caina sprang forward. She killed one mercenary with a quick thrust of her dagger, slashed the throat of another. Croanna stumbled back, hands raised in the beginnings of a spell, but Caina seized Siona and raced towards the table holding Lucan. If she could just wake him up, snap him out of the sleepwalking spell, they could escape together, they could find a way to break Croanna's spell over Siona...

"Stop her!" roared Croanna. Caina saw another troop of Trajus's mercenaries move to block the exit.

They had crossbows.

Caina cursed and ducked down behind a pile of rubble as the steel-headed bolts shot past her, sparking off the stone floor. She looked for a way out, cursing her folly. This hadn't just been a perfect trap for Lucan; it had been a perfect trap for her. She should not have come with just Ark and Tanya. She should have brought more men. She should have scouted ahead...

Siona stared up at her without blinking.

"Countess!" called Croanna. "This resistance is futile. Surrender now and I will kill you without undue pain."

Ark would go for help, Caina thought. But there was not enough time. Not nearly enough time.

Something tugged at her sleeve.

She looked down, saw Siona staring at her. The girl had the same hard gray eyes as Lucan, filled with grim determination. She lifted her arm and pointed at the bronze spike jutting from her flesh. Up close, Caina saw the sigils worked in the metal, symbols of sorcery and necromancy. Croanna had an identical spike in her left arm. Was that the means by which Croanna transferred her wounds to Siona?

Caina gripped the head of the spike.

"This is really going to hurt," whispered Caina.

Siona nodded, and Caina wrenched the spike free. The girl shrieked in pain, right hand flying to the gaping wound in her arm. The spike turned cold in Caina's hand, steam rising from the silver sigils.

And if Caina was right, Croanna was no longer protected. She peered around the edge of the rubble heap, hoping the magus stood within range of a knife throw. But Croanna stood well behind the ranks of the mercenaries.

"Last chance, Countess!" said Croanna. A note of amusement entered her voice. "Or I'll send Lucan to kill you himself." She laughed in delight. "Either you will kill him in front of his daughter...or he will cut down the woman he loves. A fitting end for an enemy of the Magisterium, no?"

Lucan rose from the table, drawing his sword, his eyes glassy and his expression serene.

Caina looked back and forth, her mind racing. She couldn't get past the mercenaries for the exit. She couldn't get past Lucan to strike down Croanna.

There was no way out of this trap but death.

She looked at the cold spike in her hand.

Caina gripped the spike in her right hand, braced her left arm against the rubble, and drove the spike into her forearm with all the strength she could muster. Pain exploded through her left arm, and she gasped, a wave of dizziness swimming through her.

The spike grew even colder, numbing her arm.

Siona's eyes went wide in alarm, and she shook her head, grabbing Caina's wrist. Caina shook her off and staggered to her feet, walking around the rubble pile, throwing back her cowl and mask. The mercenaries turned to look at her, Lucan raised her sword, and Croanna smiled.

"Ah," said Croanna. "You accept the inevitable, I see."

"In a way," said Caina, and raised the dagger in her right hand and cut her own throat.

She had cut so many throats in her time that she was almost curious to see what it felt like.

An explosion of fire in her throat.

Choking. Couldn't breathe. Drowning in her own blood. Darkness welled up to flood her version. Caina fell to one knee, heard Lucan screaming in rage and horror.

And then she fell backwards, the darkness swallowing everything.

So this was how it ended.

The spike in her arm burned.

Then light exploded in Caina's eyes, and breath burst through her lungs. Lucan knelt over her, eyes wide with shock, and helped her to sit up. Caina coughed up some blood, and found that she could breathe.

She grabbed at her throat, felt only smooth, unmarked skin.

"Gods," breathed Lucan. "You're alive. When I saw you cut your throat, I..."

"Help me up," said Caina.

She stood, saw the mercenaries staring at her in stunned horror.

"That's not possible," said Trajus. "You...you're a sorceress yourself, a..."

"Stop talking," said Caina, and walked past him.

Croanna lay twitching on the ground, blood pooling around her head, hands clutching at her torn throat. Her eyes rolled to meet Caina's, and the horrified realization filled them.

"You were wrong," said Caina, "I was too clever for your own good."

Croanna slumped against the floor and died.

"He was right, you know," said Lucan.

"Oh?" said Caina, adjusting the bandages on her left arm.

"Trajus," said Lucan. He held Siona, who leaned her head against her father's shoulder. "You are a sorceress. And you don't even need sorcery. I've seen you slay two master magi with my own eyes. With nothing more than tricks."

"And burning down the occasional inn," rumbled Ark.

"Also a trick," said Lucan.

Caina laughed. "It's called clear thinking, my dear. And if you like tricks, you should see what I will do to your father tomorrow."

"So," said Lord Corbould Maraeus. He looked every inch the Imperial lord, proud, imperious, and cold. "My wastrel son and his paramour the Ghost Countess. I see the two of you did not bother to attend the court. How nice it must be for the business of the Empire to be beneath your notice."

His icy eyes turned towards Siona, and puzzlement came over

his face.

"Lord Corbould of House Maraeus," said Caina, "I, Caina of House Amalas, present you with a living grandchild, Siona, daughter of Lucan and Livia Maraeus. Having presented you with a living grandchild, I accept your terms, and consent to wed your son."

She had the very great pleasure of seeing the astonishment on the old tyrant's face.

He stared at her for a long time, a hint of respect crossing his expression, and at last he nodded.

Caina smiled and held out her hand, and Lucan took it.

RU'S BAD DAY

by Lorie Calkins

Everyone has her own opinion of what constitutes a bad day, but some opinions are rather unconventional. Lorie lives in Kirkland, Washington, with her husband and two dogs. Despite her allergies, she keeps her Miniature Schnauzers, Magic and Chaos, who fill the void of the seemingly mandatory Writer's Cat. Her four kids are grown, and producing a fine crop of grandchildren. She likes to read, carve, crochet, spend time with the grandkids, and visit the ocean.

Ru stomped along the cliff edge, itching for a fight. It was a sunny spring day. Wildflowers tangled around her legs like a breeze-blown calico tablecloth, and delicate butterflies fluttered among the multicolored blossoms. The cheerful song of chickadees and finches filled the air, calling for mates. Fluffy white clouds skipped through the sky above with childish abandon. The entire day was disgustingly bright, sweet-smelling, and cheerful, and she had nothing to do but enjoy it. She wanted to growl and snarl and bite something. If she hadn't had a firm rule never to unsheathe her sword unless she meant to kill something, she would have slashed at everything along the path, cutting the heads off the flowers, blossoming bushes, and even the blasted chickadees, if they got too close! Grr. All this peaceful beauty was boring, boring, boring, and it was driving her crazy!

If it wasn't for the massive, churning waves hammering the boulders at the base of the cliff below her, she'd have lost her mind. She focused on the slam of each wave into the headland, and the slight shudder of the ground each pounding caused. If only something would happen, someone would attack, or maybe a volcano would bubble up from a crack in the earth! But no, there wasn't a soul in sight. It was as peaceful as a sheep pasture here. Oh, blast. It *was* a sheep pasture. She dropped her head into her hands, cringing as if from a stomach blow. The pleasantness of it all was unbearable!

With a roar louder than the crash of the waves, and a burst of sulfurous flame that charred the ground around her, something huge plummeted from the sky, straight at Ru. The heat of its flame pressed her backwards. The draft from its wings knocked her sideways. Glinting dagger-like talons flashed through the air, slitting the front of her tunic as she leaped back. Over the edge of the cliff.

Ru screamed cusswords in every language she could think of, grasping wildly at rocks, plants, roots. She fell. Dirt from her kicking feet clattered down the bare earth of the eroded cliff. Rocks dislodged and fell, bouncing with pops and crashes against the battered stones below. Ru clawed at the cliff edge with her hands, scrabbled at the crumbling dirt below it with her toes, and came to a halt. A slow slide, really. She glared at the sprays of colored flowers sticking through her fingers, as if they were the enemy, and not the only thing keeping her from certain death. A toe's niche in soft dirt, and the stubborn roots of two handfuls of wildflowers and sea grass were all that held her.

Above, on solid ground, the dragon peered down at her. She couldn't let go of the weeds to pull her sword, and she didn't have the leverage to fight from here anyway. The thing was going to toast her and eat her, if she didn't fall the rest of the way and drown or splatter. Well, things were looking up. This was not so boring.

"Mmmm-wwwmph," the dragon whimpered, blowing a puff of steam from its nose that gave a remarkable impression of consternation. "Ooo-oo," it warbled, stretching its neck out toward her, and laying its head on the ground. Was it disappointed it had spilled its dinner?

The giant head turned, and one enormous eye examined her. One very moist eye. If it hadn't been a dragon, she'd have thought it was about to cry. "Go away!" Ru hissed, wanting to shout it at the top of her lungs, but knowing her perch was too precarious. "Go eat those fat sheep behind you. Much easier picking than a stringy old swordswoman like me. Go fetch," she encouraged the dragon. *Hey,* she said to herself, *who are you calling old?! I'm in my twenties! I think. Probably. Not that old. No! Not old at all. Still in my prime.* Eh, this was no time to try to remember when the last birthday was.

Miraculously, the dragon pulled back from the cliff, and it sounded like he trotted away! Was it that easy? Had he lost interest?

A sheep thudded onto the dirt above her, baaing pitifully. The dragon's eye once again looked over the edge at her, happy and expectant. "Oh, blast," she sighed. "Can nothing go right today?" Several of the plants in her right hand pulled free of the dirt, and her toe slipped down a handspan in the rubble, cheering Ru somewhat. Not boring.

With another sigh, she shook her head at the dragon and said, "No sheep. Not for me. No," she said firmly.

The dragon seemed to deflate, laying its head sadly on the wriggling sheep. "Oww-oooo," it said.

Ru wanted to scream. Of all the stupid things to happen today. "Gaahhhh!" she vented. Flower stems broke in her left hand, and the toehold gave a bit more. *That's better,* she thought, adrenaline flooding her about-to-die-horribly system.

But the threat of dying was not the same as actually dying, which she did not want to experience today. Steeling herself for the humiliation, she looked up. "Hey, dragon," she said. "Want to play tug?" The huge beast eyed her questioningly. "Give me your, uh, paw…."

It tilted its head, then tilted it the other way. It blew out a puff of smoke with a stench like Hades. It wrinkled up its nose, as if trying to guess what she'd said. Then it pulled its slobbery, scaly lips back in a horrifying snarl, or, maybe, a smile. "Warrr-uuu," it said.

"Paw," Ru repeated firmly. "Hand, claw, talon, foot, paw!"

The dragon's smile disappeared, and it hunched its head back a bit.

"Good dragon," she said. "Good boy." Could this go any worse? The dragon did not, or would not, understand the command. She was going to have to put out her hand if she wanted it to reach for her. She gulped, feeling immensely better. She'd only have one try before she fell. This would be very dangerous. She could crash onto the rocks at any second. Even if the dragon pulled her up to safe ground, it might decide to eat her instead of playing. Pep talk over, she felt almost her old self. "Paw," she said again, letting go of the crushed wildflowers and reaching up toward the beast with her right hand. "Give me your paw."

The dragon sat up at attention, waving its tail in wide, joyous sweeps that nearly sent the sheep off the cliff onto her. "Paw!" she shrieked, as the last flowers in her left hand uprooted, her feet slipped away, and her life passed boringly before her eyes. A monstrous green-scaled thing like a massive tree root came down, and she grabbed onto a single gleaming claw of it as she fell. Her arm nearly pulled out of the socket, but she held on. "Pull!" Ru ordered, no longer willing to drag this out. "Get me up on land!"

The dragon lifted its foot, shaking the dangling swordswoman like a sticky bit of moss. She held on tightly until she was over solid ground, then dropped with a whoof of relief. She moved quickly away from the edge, and dusted herself off, glaring at the multicolored stains on her hands. "Blast. If anyone sees me, they'll think I've been picking flowers!" The dragon turned to her and bowed its front, waggling its haunches and flipping its tail back and forth. "Grr," it said.

"Are you kidding me?" Ru asked. "You want to play now?" She made as if to draw her sword.

"Arr—ooo!" it whooped, bouncing on its feet, and a sparkle of excitement in its eye.

"Blast. Don't you have anything dragonly to do, like steal a princess or obey an evil wizard?"

The dragon gave Ru a panicked look. "Urh-oh…." it said. Its eyes grew even bigger and rounder, if that was possible. Its jaw dropped open. "Roooo-ooo!" it moaned. Suddenly it grabbed Ru in its tree-root paw, and thrust itself violently into the sky. Ru was completely wrapped in scaly foot, except for the upper half of her head. Looking back, as she had no choice but to do, she saw the ill-used sheep trot back to its brethren, snatching a mouthful of flowers on the way. Stupid sheep. She sighed as deeply as she could, considering the constriction.

On the other hand, things were definitely looking up. She was away from the sheep and flowers, kidnapped by a dragon, and—flying over the open sea, where she'd quickly drown if she fell from the dragon's claws. Hey, this was almost getting good.

In nearly no time at all—a few hours at most—the dragon plumped Ru down on a rock island out in the ocean. From the look of the small square castle and one stubby tower, she guessed someone lived here—probably a wizard. Wizards were *so antisocial*. "All right, dragon, why did you bring me here? Your boss needs a slave? Someone to experiment on?" She fingered the hilt of her sword with anticipation. "I'll knock *that* notion out of his head."

The dragon galloped a short way up the hill toward the castle keep, then turned back to look at her. "No thanks," Ru said. "I don't feel like playing."

"Warrr-ooh," the dragon warbled, galloping back. "Oortle-oortle-oortle," it coaxed, turning to run off again, then coming back.

After several repeats of this, and one episode of the dragon trying to nip her clothes to pull her along with him, Ru sighed hugely and said, "Do you want me to follow you, boy?" There was something so eerily compelling about those words and the situation, that Ru felt as if she'd passed into an alternate reality for a moment. The feeling evaporated, and she trudged after the dragon.

The dragon coaxed, chivvied, and nudged her into the castle and up the stone stairs to the tower. There, she discovered the homeowner, stretched out on the floor in a room full of work tables and bad-smelling concoctions. "That's it?" she said, lifting her hands in exasperation. "You brought me here to bury some dead guy?" The body in question was fairly young, say, not-thirty-ish, in the way that she herself was…not-thirty-ish. Except for being dead, he was not repulsive. In fact, if his beard had been less tidy, and his clothes not so cringingly *scholarly*, and minus the deadness aspect, he looked like a guy she might deign to interact with at a tavern for an evening's amusement.

"Nuh-uh," said the dragon, whose head didn't fit through the doorway, and whose body pretty much occupied the entire stairwell of the tower—a tight fit. It blew a stiff puff of stench at the body, raising a twitch and a tiny snore from it. A weighted-open scroll rattled in the breeze, and Ru was able to glean enough from the weird mix of languages to have a sinking feeling of the situation. It was that kind of day.

As if to confirm her nasty inkling, the dragon made smoochy noises with its snout pressed against the doorway.

"Blast!" Ru said, along with a few more expressive terms. But she was a brave woman. She knew her duty when someone was in trouble. Might as well get it over with. She bent and kissed the wizard firmly on the mouth.

He opened his eyes and looked at her. "Uh, thanks," he said. "I guess that spell really backfired this time." He stood up, brushing himself off and avoiding Ru's gaze. "I take it Glassy brought you here to wake me. I, uh, hope it didn't put you out too much."

Ru glanced at the chortling, happy dragon. "Nah."

Crashing and yelling came from the castle proper, and Glassy backed out of the tower in a hurry. "You have guests?" Ru asked.

The wizard sighed. "No. Brigands. They attack every fortnight or so. They think I have the Philosopher's Stone."

Ru looked at him blankly.

"The secret of transmutation," he clarified.

Ru gestured for more.

"Turning lead into gold."

"Aha," she said. Then she brightened. "Brigands?" She grasped the hilt of her sword. "May I?"

"Be my guest."

There were a dozen of them, and Ru had a grand time. It almost made the rest of her day bearable. When they were dispatched, one way or another, she returned to the wizard. She found him asleep on the floor of his workroom again. Ru administered the required aid.

"Oops," said the wizard. "I can't figure out what's going wrong with this spell. I, uh, don't suppose you'd consider staying around a while, in case I—you know."

Ru screwed up her face into a thinking expression, ready to say no. "Oortle-oortle-oortle," said the dragon, spitting a sheep at her.

"Where did you get a sheep, Glassy? We don't have any sheep on this island."

"Huh," Ru said. "No sheep? How about wildflowers?"

"Nope, sorry. They refuse to grow on the rocks."

"And you say those brigands attack frequently?"

"Them or others. Always someone coming around looking for a fight. It's a nuisance."

"Not boring." She adjusted her sword belt. "So, you got any spare rooms?"

"It's a castle."

"Oh, yeah. What's for dinner?"

"Um,…sheep?"

"Good enough." Ru chased the sheep down the stairs. She said, "Want to play, dragon?"

THE VINE PRINCESS

by Steve Chapman

Shada always seems to find new and interesting ways to get into trouble, but this time she's reached a new personal best.

A lapsed musician and engineer, Steve Chapman lives with his wife and daughter at the New Jersey shore. Though he spends most days high above Times Square, in the evening he can hear the ocean. His fiction has appeared in the previous three volumes of SWORD AND SORCERESS, in the Harrow Press anthology MORTIS OPERANDI, and in *Penumbra eZine.*

Shada's heart hammered against her ribs, her hand dropping to her sword. She fought down the impulse to scream.

"The answer is *no*," Sienna repeated, as if Shada hadn't heard Gregory the first time. "Stay away from the envoy."

Shada was backed up against a priceless unicorn tapestry in Gregory's solarium, her fists and weapons useless against Sienna's mastery of rhetoric and protocol.

The sixteen-year old twins shared their mother's green eyes and olive skin but little else. Sienna's hair was dark where Shada's was gold, Sienna's violet dress the height of Court elegance where Shada was dressed, as usual, in combat leathers for the fight that usually found her.

The sisters stood glaring at each other like mismatched bookends.

"As Duchy Tremaine's new envoy to St. Navarre, Vander deGroat is protected by diplomatic protocol." Sir Gregory, gaunt and gray, tugged at his elaborate whiskers. "We cannot move on him without endangering our diplomats in Tremaine."

"Have you seen him fight on the proving grounds?" Shada

asked. DeGroat had demonstrated great skill with precisely the sort of exotic knives which had been removed from the corpses of the rulers of the two city-states to which he'd previously served as envoy. He was a covert assassin and his target was Shada's father. She was sure of it.

"I followed deGroat back to his chambers," Shada said. "He's there now with a Kasabian mercenary. We can catch them plotting."

Sienna sighed.

"The Solstice Blessing is tomorrow." Shada hated the quiver in her voice. "Father will be an easy target."

"Tremaine's army is powerful," Gregory said. "But because of St. Navarre's enchanted walls, it can't threaten us. Tremaine won't risk an assassination. So leave deGroat be."

So that she wouldn't slash the tapestry unicorn into priceless threads, Shada fled the solarium, out into the dark passages of the Citadel.

Halfway to her rooms she had an idea. A *terrible* idea. If she hadn't been so angry she would have rejected it in a too-loud heartbeat.

She headed for the Sanctum Stairs, the massive spiral staircase hewn into the white granite beneath the Citadel. As Shada descended the air grew humid, her breath visible. Halfway down she found the entrance to the Eldritch Passages.

The Passages had been created long before the Kings of St. Navarre adopted the Citadel as their seat of power, but each ruler had found uses for the magical corridors. Within them one could see and hear everything nearby while remaining invisible to those outside the passages. A spymaster's dream, they honeycombed the Citadel.

Time ran strangely within the Passages, and it was said some who entered never returned. Shada had never risked them without her sister, but now her father's life hung in the balance.

She placed her palm upon the topaz oval and spoke the words. A perfect circle of darkness beckoned.

She entered a tunnel barely five feet high. Though the walls and floor appeared black, she had the impression that she wasn't looking at rock or dirt, but rather a starless night sky. Veining this darkness were green vines dotted with small white flowers.

The rules of the Passages were simple, if cryptic. Follow only the known paths. Don't linger in any one spot. And if you see yourself, run.

Shada's path ascended through the lower corridors of the Citadel, and then into its living quarters. She passed through walls and floors, brushed unseen past courtiers, until she reached Vander deGroat's chambers.

She stood inside the envoy's room, yet was still within the transparent tunnel, its dimensions marked by flowering vines.

DeGroat arranged his cloaks before a full-length mirror. Beside him was a huge man with tattoos inked across his face. The Kasabian mercenary stared straight at Shada—her hand instinctively dropped to her sword—but there was no way he could see her. She wasn't actually in the room.

But she could see and hear everything.

The Kasabian chuckled, a sound like animals dying. "For a little Duchy, you don't lack ambition."

DeGroat glared as if he'd found the man on the bottom of his boot. "Can you do it?"

"It will be punishingly expensive."

"I'm punishingly wealthy." DeGroat gestured at his gold-trimmed clothing.

"I cannot guarantee the result."

"The result will be St. Navarre shattered, its people enslaved." DeGroat drew a scroll from his cloaks.

Shada's breath came fast and shallow. This was worse than she'd imagined. She leaned forward to glimpse the scroll, and then froze. Behind her, something moved.

The vines drew together, knotting into a doll-like shape. The figure gained nuance, blossoming into a life-size simulacrum, a girl of thorn and vine, white flowers for its eyes and mouth.

Shada recognized herself in its contours. She'd stayed too long.

She moved to draw her blade, but a creeper snagged her ankle. The floor of the passage, thick with vegetation, opened beneath her. She dropped three feet and jerked to a stop, her sword tumbling into darkness.

She hung by an ankle. The drop seemed to go on forever. Heart pounding, Shada looked up at the vine girl. "Please. I have to warn my father."

The vine released her. Shada fell into darkness.

She hit another tangle of vines. For an awful moment she feared they'd snap beneath her weight, but they gave and then pulled taut, holding her upside down like a fly in a spider's web. Vines curled around her, as if drawn to her warmth.

Faint light filtered down from above. The coils were strewn throughout the darkness, a shadowy lattice of green cords and white flowers. Below, Shada could see no bottom. She still hadn't heard the sword hit.

She fought down a wave of vertigo and tried to think. She'd have to climb out. She twisted about, managing a vertical sit up. Her legs were wrapped tight in vines and flowers. She dropped back down and reached for the dagger on her belt.

A vine snared her wrist.

She froze; her movement attracted the creepers. But panic bubbled in her muscles. She had to get her information back to Gregory.

Swords, shields, and armor hung in the vines around her. And strangely shaped objects of dirty white.

Human skeletons.

She stifled a cry. She had plenty of time before she starved to death.

A high-pitched whistle issued from the white flowers, as if they were singing. Petals slipped open, liquid dribbling from their centers. Drops fell on her boots and leathers, into her hair. Whatever they touched began to smolder.

A hard fist of fear formed in Shada's belly. She looked to the skeletons. These men hadn't starved to death. They'd been *dissolved.*

The flowers were drooling acid.

Shada thrashed in blind panic. Acid dribbled down, her leathers sizzling, her hair smoking. A single drop caught her bare hand. It felt like having a knife inserted between her knuckles.

More flowers bloomed. The acid would eat through her clothes in minutes.

She had to get to her dagger.

Shada twisted about, bringing her bound wrist beneath a dripping flower. She gritted her teeth. She waited an endless, agonizing moment for the acid to weaken the vine, and then yanked her arm free.

She grabbed the dagger from her belt and pulled herself upward, slashing flowers from the vines. Wrapping her left arm tight about a flowerless vine she cut away the creepers holding her legs.

For a breathless moment she dangled in the void.

Sliding the dagger into her belt, Shada got a solid grasp on the thicket of creepers and pulled herself up. She moved haltingly, unable to forget the empty space yawning below, but she was able to climb the vines as she would a tree.

It felt like hours before she hauled herself back up on to the floor of the Passage. DeGroat's room was empty. Her hands were abraded and bloody, her tunic in tatters. Clumps of her hair had burned away. She looked to the mirror and gasped.

It was empty.

For a moment she wondered if she was dead, or hallucinating, but then realized that because she was within the Passages she cast no reflection in deGroat's room.

She made two painful fists. She was alive. It was all that mattered.

There was no time to waste. DeGroat was up to something worse than assassination, and she had to stop him.

Shada traveled back hallways to Gregory's solarium, hoping to arrive unobserved. She'd tied her smoldering hair back, scrubbed the soot from her face with fingers and saliva, but she still looked like she'd been wrestling a dragon in a compost pile.

She rounded a corner and ran into Violette Aurola, her aunt and unofficial etiquette instructor.

Everything about Shada mortified her aunt. Their current,

uneasy peace was predicated on Shada maintaining minimum standards of decorum. Even at her worst, she'd never presented Aunt Vi with a look quite like this. She braced herself for a verbal smackdown and the withering report to her father that would follow.

But her aunt merely offered a tight smile. "You're on your way to bathe and change?"

Shada nodded.

"Hurry, then." Aunt Vi swept by.

Shada stared after her, astonished. Unwilling to take her good fortune for granted, she sprinted the rest of the way to the solarium.

"Shada." Gregory blanched at her appearance. "Whatever have you been up to?"

"DeGroat's plan's bigger than killing Father." Shada gulped air. "But it's probably still timed to the Solstice Blessing."

Gregory stared as if she had two heads.

"The hair's not as bad as it looks," she said. "I can have it cut and restyled before Father sees."

"Why are you back on deGroat?" Gregory stood up.

"He's with the Kasabian. The Solstice Blessing—"

"Was two weeks ago." Gregory said. "DeGroat was perfectly behaved, as were you. I thought we'd put all this behind us. I've been impressed with the change in your behavior."

"Two weeks?" Shada felt as if she stood on the lip of a precipice. It was impossible. "I spoke to you barely an hour ago."

Gregory moved toward the call bell.

She realized he was going to summon the Guard. Not to apprehend deGroat, but her.

"I heard them plotting." Shada moved to block him. "I'm not crazy."

It was said time ran differently in the Passages. Was it possible that an hour there had been weeks here? But even that wouldn't explain her presence at the Blessing.

Had deGroat cast a spell while she was in the Passages? Perhaps his plot was already in motion.

Shada turned and ran, as bells pealed across the Citadel.

Shada angled away from the royal chambers, cutting through the rooms behind King's Hall. She opened a door and stopped dead.

She was staring at herself.

This second Shada wore an emerald-studded dress the color of her eyes. Her hair, brushed out and radiantly blond, fell perfectly to her shoulders. A necklace of violet gemstones encircled her throat. She was beautiful.

Shada stood frozen, as if in a dream. She felt a punishing wistfulness, like she was looking at something wonderful that had been hers, but she'd long ago mislaid.

Five young soldiers, joking and laughing, vied for her double's attention. Shada knew all of them vaguely. They seemed to be having such a good time.

And if you see yourself, run.

This doppelganger had nothing to do with deGroat. Shada had created it herself, by staying too long in the Passages. It had tried to murder her and now it had taken her place.

A mixture of fear and anger rose like bile in her throat. She was going to make this creature terribly sorry it had chosen her for its game.

Bells chimed. Four soldiers headed through the opposite door, her double following. One boy remained. She tried to remember his name. Westin Charles.

She let the others depart then slipped inside. "Westin."

"Princess?" He blinked in the direction her double had left.

She drew him away from the door, feeling acutely aware of what a mess she looked. "How long have I been acting strangely?"

"Strangely?" His gaze took in her clothes, her hair. "What happened?"

"The girl you were flirting with tried to kill me," Shada said. "How long have I been dressing like my sister?"

Westin stared into her eyes. It was inappropriate and unnerving but she needed an answer.

"Since the Solstice Blessing."

The vine girl had taken over Shada's life for a fortnight and no one had noticed.

"It's a changeling from the Passages," she said. "Pretending to be me."

"Princess Shada." Westin looked at her too intently. "Forgive me, but how am I to know that she, rather than you, is the imposter?"

Shada registered this like a punch to the throat. "She's that convincing?"

"Utterly."

"Ask me about things we've done together."

"She knows all that. We were joking yesterday about last year's tournaments."

Shada felt a new sort of fear, a fist of ice at the base of her spine. The vine girl had her memories as well as her aspect?

But Westin believed her, Shada realized, and then she understood why. "You like her." Her laugh sounded like a sob. "You never liked me. That's the difference."

Westin reddened. "I'm yours to command, of course."

She didn't want someone to command. But she'd take what she could get. "Keep watch in case she circles back. I'm going to grab a sword from the storeroom. Then we'll tell Gregory what you've seen."

Shada found a sabre, tried to remove more soot from her face before a filthy mirror, and then raced back.

The room was empty.

"Westin?" she whispered.

A pile of material in the corner hadn't been there when she left. Shada poked at it, revealing the remains of a chainmail shirt doused in red goo. And beneath that bones. And a skull.

Westin's skull.

Shada couldn't breathe.

Behind her, a footfall. She turned to face her doppelganger.

"What I don't understand," the lovely Shada said, "is why *you* don't look like that. The flowers had you."

Shada stared into her own face. The dreamlike confusion felt like vertigo, like an earthquake affecting only her. "Who are you?"

"Shada. Daughter of Sisco." The imposter smiled. "Princess of St. Navarre."

"That may work on everyone else, but given that I'm—"

"You're no one." The vine girl carried no weapon but moved like a predator, light-footed and silent. "Perhaps you were Shada, once upon a time, but you've been careless."

Shada couldn't deny it. Now Westin was dead and a monster wearing her face was loose in the Citadel. She raised the saber. "Westin was my friend. I generally don't like killing unarmed—whatever you are. But in your case I'll make an exception."

"The boy was your subject. I made him your friend." The vine girl raised her hands. "And I'm not unarmed."

For a second split like a lightning stroke the girl vanished and the doll of vine and flower stood in her place. Then Shada's mirror image returned, vomiting vines from her mouth.

Shada slashed laterally, severing vines and flowers. But creepers darted past her guard, coiling about her forearms, circling her waist. She dropped the saber.

White flowers pressed tight against her. She gasped—this was how Westin had been dissolved so quickly. Her arms and legs trembled in panic.

The flowers opened.

Shada screamed. The doppelganger looked about. She must realize a scream yards away from King's Hall would bring the entire Guard.

The vines recoiled back into the mask-like face.

Heart pounding, Shada ran.

Shada didn't stop until she neared her own quarters. She couldn't fight the doppelganger alone. She hated to admit it, but there was only one person she could turn to.

She found her sister at her desk.

"Shada." Sienna barely looked up. "Nice hair."

Shada took a deep breath. "Before Solstice Blessing I entered the Passages to spy on deGroat but a doppelganger formed and tried to kill me with acid-spitting flowers but I escaped but now it's two weeks later and she's taken my place and you all think she's me."

Sienna turned back to her paperwork. "I figured as much."

"Excuse me?"

"Not the acid flowers." Sienna signed a document. "But you and I have gotten on famously for a fortnight. You're polite and thoughtful and do what you're told. My theory was demonic possession."

Some of the awful tension within Shada eased. Sienna knew her; everything else would fall into place. "Gregory doesn't know."

"I couldn't prove it so I haven't told anyone."

Shada swallowed her pride. "I need your help."

"The Mages should be able to figure out something." Sienna's brows knitted. "But Gregory's quite taken with the new you. You need to stay—"

The doors burst open. Red-cloaked guardsmen poured into the room.

"No!" Sienna leapt up. "Swords *down*."

"Swords will be lowered," Gregory marched through the doors, "When the imposter is dead."

Twelve blades ringed Shada. "Then bring her here. I'm Shada, as Sienna can attest."

"This is my sister." Sienna glared at Gregory.

"It's as you feared," Gregory said over his shoulder. "The vine toxin has clouded Sienna's mind."

The vine princess strode into the room, a picture of regal authority in her emerald gown and short sword. Her furious gaze fell on Shada. "This creature murdered Westin."

The long mirror stretching above the mantle captured them both. Princess Shada shook with righteous fury, her authority as effortless as her beauty, as deadly as the blade she held with an expert's grip. Who then was the soot-smeared ragamuffin at the mirror's other end?

Shada felt the vertigo return. She looked like nobody. She felt like nobody. Perhaps she had only dreamed of being Shada, and had awoken.

"Kill her," a Guardsman shouted.

"*This* is my sister." Sienna took Shada's hand. "If you don't believe me, have the mages sort them out. But if anyone harms my sister, I'll kill him myself."

Shada's eyes moistened. If Sienna insisted she was Shada, then she must be.

Gregory hesitated. The soldiers were distracted. One smart kick and Shada could grab a blade, slip between their legs and reach the door. Her muscles twitched. Her body wanted to do it.

But it would leave the vine girl triumphant in her place. There was no way to fight her way back to her life.

Gregory frowned. "It will be as you say, Sienna."

After hours of stoning against the cell wall, Shada's shale chip wasn't yet sharp enough.

She sat in the Citadel's deepest dungeon, at the very bottom of the Sanctum Stairs; the walls, floors, and ceiling carved from white cliff stone. Iron bars were all that separated her from the vine princess.

A conjurer was posted beyond the door. Shada assumed the mages couldn't distinguish between the two girls, so they were using her as bait. The imposter must eventually attempt to kill the true princess, and thus reveal herself.

The historically over-confident mages were no doubt sure they could stop the attack in time. Shada was dubious, but had come up with no better alternative than her chip.

"Shada." The doppelganger stood at the bars.

"You're willing to admit that I'm Shada?" Shada approached cautiously.

"I admit it. But so am I. That's our difficulty."

"I'm Shada. You're a homicidal weed. Not that difficult." Shada examined her duplicate. "You can kill me, but how would you explain my dissolved corpse? You wouldn't be princess for long."

"I'd think of a story. I'm quite persuasive. If I wanted you dead, you would be." The vine princess bowed her head. "I apologize for attacking you. And Westin. Most of me is Shada, but I still carry instincts from the dark place."

"You're *sorry*?" Shada wondered what new type of game they were playing.

The girl nodded. "No more violence. You're going to leave St. Navarre."

"That's never going to happen." Shada trembled with anger. "Why do you even want to be me?"

The vine princess' lacquered nails tapped iron bars. "What's your purpose, Shada?"

Shada held her stare. "I protect my people. That's why I'm going to drop you back down the hole you climbed out of. If you were really me, you'd know this."

"I know it well. You're going to cede me your place because I can do it better than you."

Shada laughed.

"Look at you," the vine princess said. "The King's daughter. You're smart and resourceful, brave and physically disciplined. And pretty, should you care to be. Yet you spend so much time complaining. Fighting with your allies. You have so much, so why are you so tiresome?"

Shada felt the peculiar urge to punch herself in the face. "You wouldn't understand."

"I want to be you because it's *wonderful*." The girl's smile turned radiant. "I have all your skills and memories. I care about everything you care about. I have everything but your terrible attitude."

"I don't make people happy. I keep them safe."

"Perhaps you'd do a better job if you didn't make so many people unhappy." The green eyes narrowed. "I'm your equal with a sword. But I can also use my vines. I can take down a cavalier bare-handed, but I can make him adore me, get information. I want to protect St. Navarre as much as you. But I can do it better."

The righteous anger churning Shada's stomach turned sour. Maybe the vine princess would be a better defender of St. Navarre. Shada didn't want to make people angry. It just happened, because everything seemed so hard. Because so many people wanted her to be different than she was.

For a moment Shada felt small and useless.

But then the image of Westin's skull filled her mind.

If the vine princess truly wanted to protect the city, she shouldn't have started out by murdering one of its soldiers.

"The way you protected Westin?" Shada spat.

The vine princess cast her gaze down. "The longer I'm here the more the Passage instincts fade." She looked up, eyes shining. "Soon I'll be nothing but you."

"You won't be," Shada realized as she said it. "I've had to claw for every inch of what I am. Everyone in the Citadel wants me to be the furthest thing from it." The taste of despair faded. She understood the difference between them. "You didn't have to fight for any of this."

"Maybe. But if you could have charmed Gregory as I have he would have stopped deGroat and I wouldn't be here."

Shada felt a stab of panic. She'd forgotten the envoy. "If you really love St. Navarre help me stop deGroat."

"What do you think I've been doing? I tailed the Kasabian into the deep caverns. He's placing fetishes."

Shada's mind raced. Fetishes meant sorcery, and the caverns housed the moon pool. A shiver passed through her. The moon pool was the source of the enchantment that made St. Navarre's walls impregnable.

"That scroll is an unbinding spell," the doppelganger said. "I was recruiting soldiers when you found me because deGroat's planning to use it tonight."

An unbinding spell in the caverns. Shada felt ill. DeGroat planned to destroy the moon pool. Without the walls' enchantment, St. Navarre would fall to Tremaine's army. This was how he intended to smash the city and enslave its people.

"You know what he's planning?" the vine princess asked.

"What happens if deGroat casts an unbinding in the caverns?"

The doppelganger gasped. "Father isn't the target. The entire city is."

Shada grabbed the bars. "I need to get out of here."

The doppelganger's face collapsed into a flat mask. Vines

pushed through the eyeholes.

Shada leapt backwards.

But the vines wrapped about the iron bars at the floor and ceiling, white flowers pulling tight against the brick that held them.

The vine princess was breaking them out.

Mortar began to smolder. Shada threw a sidekick. One bar snapped free of its anchor. Another kick and she was free.

The outer door opened; the conjurer's hands in motion to release a spell. Creepers tangled his ankles, toppled him to the floor. Vines coiled around him.

"No!" Shada whirled on the doppelganger.

The vines snaked back into her mask. "I wasn't going to kill him."

"Tell it to Westin."

"I apologized for that."

"And yet he's still dead." Shada stepped over the unconscious mage. "Where do you think you're going?"

The vine girl's face was dirty, her hair disheveled. She now looked too much like what Shada saw in the reflecting glass. "There's no time to get help or weapons. DeGroat and the Kasabian are professional killers. Go alone and you'll die."

At the bottom of the Sanctum Stairs, the deep caverns beckoned. They were spotted with patches of phosphorescent lichen that threw an eerie, emerald glow. Shada carefully picked her way over sand and moss-covered stone.

The tunnel opened into an enormous cavern, the ceiling high as a cathedral's. From its center silver moonlight poured through an opening, striking the body of water below.

The moon pool.

The thought of deGroat polluting it frightened Shada more than facing the envoy and the Kasabian without a weapon. She had to surprise them. With the doppelganger's help maybe she could beat them.

The question was whether in the next heartbeat she'd find herself bound in flowers.

Just ahead, deGroat stood on a ledge overlooking the shimmering pool, reading from the scroll. The silver moonlight filling the pool began to distort. Inky shadows moved in the water, agents of the unbinding.

"We have to stop him now," Shada whispered.

"I can't." The vine princess was shaking. "The moon pool's magic is too powerful. I can't change here. I can't call the vines. This close to the pool, I'm nothing but you."

"Stay here, then," Shada fumed. "Nothing but me is plenty."

She sprinted along the path and leapt down, landing on the ledge beside deGroat. The envoy looked up as Shada swept his legs out from under him. The scroll fell from his fingers.

Shada landed on top of him, chopping at his throat. He caught her wrist. She slammed her open palm into his face. DeGroat went limp beneath her.

She reached for the scroll.

A huge hand closed about her arm.

The Kasabian hauled Shada off deGroat, his blade angled to impale her. She kicked out, snapping his wrist. He dropped Shada and the sword.

As she struggled to her knees his arms wrapped about her waist. The mercenary crushed her against his chest. She couldn't breathe. Stars danced before her eyes.

He slammed her down into the wet sand.

The silver world spun. Shada desperately needed to breathe but couldn't seem to remember how.

She looked up and saw his spiked boot descending.

An emerald shadow plowed into the Kasabian, carrying him past Shada and down into the sand.

The mercenary sprang to his feet, absurdly graceful for his size. But the vine princess was just as quick, dancing around his jackhammer blows.

Shada raised her head. Her entire body ached, but nothing seemed to be broken.

The vine princess tripped on her dress. A blow caught her shoulder. The Kasabian leaned in, battering her with both fists.

Shada struggled to one knee. She had to get up.

The vine princess took punch after punch as she reached for the knife in the mercenary's boot. She grasped the hilt and sliced him across the thigh.

Scarlet splashed sand. The Kasbian howled and fell, bleeding out.

The vine princess eyed the dying man with satisfaction.

"Nice work." Shada crawled toward her.

"Wow, this *hurts*." The vine princess wiped blood from her face. Her left eye was purple and her dress splattered with blood.

"You could have let him kill me," Shada said. "Then gone at him."

The vine princess held her gaze. "I'm not your enemy, Shada."

"You saved St. Navarre." Shada could barely wrap her mind around it.

A crescent of silver emerged from below the doppelganger's ribs. She gasped and fell forwards.

DeGroat stood behind her, the curved knife in his hand. "I don't think there should be two of you."

Shada tried to stand. DeGroat drove his knife through her right thigh. She fell back on to the sand.

"Unlike the wound I gave your friend, this isn't fatal." DeGroat reached for the scroll. "I need one Shada alive for tomorrow's public executions."

Shada tried to get up, but DeGroat put a boot on her chest.

"Have you ever seen someone drawn and quartered?" The envoy grinned. "You're going to be quite the spectacle, Princess."

DeGroat began reading. Dark threads reappeared in the Moon Pool. Fractals of shadow flitted in and out of the moonlight, unbinding the pool's magic. St. Navarre's defenses were being destroyed and Shada could do nothing to stop it.

"Envoy." Behind deGroat, the vine princess rose like a revenant in the moonlight. "I'm not dead yet."

She could barely stand, but deGroat had to turn to face her, his foot slipping from Shada's chest.

Shada rolled on to one side, coiled up her remaining strength, and kicked out.

The crack of deGroat's kneecap breaking echoed across the cavern. His scream followed a heartbeat later. He tottered at the end of the ledge.

Shada's second kick sent him over. He fell into the shadow-streaked water, black threads coiling about him, unbinding the envoy and his scroll.

Now deGroat *really* screamed.

The unbinding collapsed, the shadow threads fading. The pool once again glittered with moonlight.

The doppelganger collapsed beside Shada.

Shada's leg ached, but the bleeding was light. She drew herself up one knee.

"I'm dying," the vine princess whispered.

"How can you die?" Dread uncoiled in Shada's belly. "You're made of vines."

"This close to the moon pool, I'm mortal."

The path back wound upward, studded with fissures and boulders. Shada felt as if her legs were made of rubber. She could barely stay conscious.

But her double had saved St. Navarre.

Every nerve in her leg screaming, Shada stood up. She wrapped an arm under the vine princess' shoulder and dragged her to her feet.

"Shada, I can't walk. *You* can't walk."

"Shut up." Shada's leg ached, but it worked.

Every step was agony, but slowly Shada dragged her double back to the base of the Stairs.

There she gasped. "You saved me?"

"How do you feel?" Shada sat beside her.

The doppelganger stared at her. "I feel like it's worth it. After so much time in the darkness I have people to care for. To protect. It's worth all the pain." She laughed. "You must think I'm ridiculous."

Shada knew exactly what she meant.

"Don't misunderstand me," the doppelganger said. "I'll go. I see that I can't take the place you've made."

Shada took her hand. "You have a place here. You won't be me, but we'll work something out."

The vine princess convulsed, spittle dribbling from her mouth.

Shada grabbed her shoulder. "What's wrong?"

"No." The doppelganger's entire body shook. "Please."

Shada heard a purposeful murmuring drifting down the Stairs. "Who's there?"

Gregory and robed mage appeared, the sorcerer making elaborate hand gestures.

"Help us!" Shada called.

The princess was suddenly light in her arms. Shada found that she held nothing but a bramble of dead vines and dried flowers.

The mage dropped his hands. "The exorcism has succeeded."

Shada looked into the mirror. She wore her dress uniform, a taut tunic of silver and scarlet, blue ribbons dangling from the shoulder. Her hair had been cut short, colored and styled to obscure the missing bits.

"Just got word." Sienna appeared in the glass. "DeGroat's army was a day's march away. Our cavalry took them by surprise."

Sienna kept talking, but Shada couldn't pay attention. The danger was past. That was all she needed to know.

She stared into her green eyes. If not for the vine princess deGroat would now rule St. Navarre. She'd had the skill to wrangle Gregory, the soldiers, and even Aunt Vi. How strange it must be to have the ability to do *that*.

"What was she?" Shada asked her sister. "Some kind of demon?"

Sienna drew closer. "It turns out there are no demons in the Passages."

"A ghost?" Did it matter? Shada didn't even know what she was asking.

"There's *nothing* in the Passages. Just some magical reflecting principle. Someone goes in; a doppelganger forms. It's born with the urge to supplant its originator, but once it does so it's pretty much just the person it replaced."

Shada shivered. That was ridiculous. The vine princess had appropriated her appearance and memories, but it had been nothing like her.

"The mages say there might be doppelgangers living among us, right now."

Shada thought of the skeletons, hanging in the vines.

"They might not even know," Sienna continued, fascinated, "that they're not the original person."

Shada thought of times before she'd dangled in the vines. Were those really *her* memories? It was hard to be sure. She felt a curious lightness at the thought.

She straightened her tunic and fixed her hair. The new cut was stylish, but would be easy to maintain. She tried on a dazzling smile and offered her sister her arm. "Shall we go see Gregory?"

TRADING GIFTS

by Rabia Gale

This story reminds me a bit of the folk tale "Stone Soup" where many individuals each contribute one small piece to the finished product. In this case, however, the product is something very different from soup.

Rabia Gale writes about flawed protagonists who never give up, magical gifts that lead to trouble, and things that fly. A native of Pakistan, she now lives in Northern Virginia where she reads, writes, eats chocolate, avoids housework, and homeschools her children. Visit her online home at www.rabiagale.com.

There was a checkpoint on the road to Serenai, on the narrow strip of land that tethered the almost-island to the continent. I looked down the road to the city, its tall white towers soaring skywards, red and gold banners flapping in the perpetual sea breeze. A green frill of flat land encircled the city, dropping to the sea in grey cliffs.

The scent of brine filled my nose, and salt stung my lips.

For the longest time, that had been the smell of homecoming.

I stroked Suki's nose. "What a great place for kite-flying."

The guards waved the farmer in front of me on. The wheels of his cart ground away, loose onions rolled around in the back.

Suki and I took his place. A guard prodded the packs on Suki's back.

"I make kites," I told him, as he rummaged through a stack of silk and paper shapes. "I'm here for the festival."

He grunted and pulled out a long bundle of bamboo strips.

"Those are for the frames."

The guard thrust them back onto Suki. The bundles tilted, and spools of string and ribbon spilled into the sandy road.

Silently I counted to five, then bent down to pick them up.

"Thank you." I flashed a smile at the guard who had done nothing to help.

He shrugged, already turning to the juggler who was next in line.

I urged Suki on, humming, trying to calm the fluttering of my heart.

I'd passed the first obstacle.

Most of the vendors and entertainers headed for the city gates and more checkpoints, but not me. I went down towards the sea, to where a tiny fishing village clung to grey rock and white sand. In a sheltered hollow, I relieved Suki of her burden, spreading out my materials in the short hardy grass.

I weighed down bird and butterfly shapes with rocks, set out ribbons in rainbow colors. Then I got to work making frames, bending the strong, flexible rods.

It wasn't long before the children found me.

They peeped out from behind rocks and scraggly bushes. I looked up and smiled, but my hands didn't stop their work. Emboldened, they drew closer, watching me with solemn eyes.

"Kites," breathed a wisp of a girl, in a voice of awe most people usually reserved for the sight of massive jewels.

"Indeed. Would you like one?"

"She ha'nt got any money," an older boy interjected, drawing the little girl back. Her face fell.

"Oh, I take all kinds of payment, not just money." I put out a wooden mug in front of me, as if I were a street performer. I looked at the little girl thoughtfully. "I bet you have a laugh like silver, a laugh like air. A laugh that makes other people happy to hear it. How about you pay me with a laugh?"

The girl let out a merry peal, her eyes sparkling. I grinned back. "Pick out a shape—any shape. And a ribbon."

A scramble and a skip, and she was back with a butterfly and purple ribbon.

"Now, who's next?" I asked, as I fit the butterfly to a frame.

"Me!" A boy pushed his way closer. He was a sturdy creature

with square hands and bare feet. His pockets bulged.

"You're good at finding things, aren't you? Small things, precious things, well-hidden things that most people overlook."

He grinned, showing a gap in his teeth. "Too good, says Ma!"

"Then give me something you found and we'll call it a deal."

A milky shell with an iridescent underside and soft curves went into the cup, and the boy picked out a beetle shape and green ribbon.

The children pressed around, clamoring for my attention. I beckoned them forward, one by one.

A girl with long brown hair lifting in the wind paid me in cartwheels and springs. A boy in much-mended clothes raced the others down to the beach and back, barely panting as he brought me an eagle for his kite. Two other girls gave me twirls and another boy gave me a spectacular leap.

I looked at the first girl's older brother. "I ha'nt good at nothing," he told me, low and sullen.

"Oh, yes, you are. You're good at looking after your sister, aren't you?"

He thought about it, then nodded. "Saved her once from the sea," he offered.

"More than once," interjected a curly-headed girl in a dress with shell buttons and embroidered fish at the hem.

"Tip a measure of courage and compassion into my cup," I said, "and pick a kite, boy."

"What about me?" asked the girl.

"Did you embroider those fish?"

She flushed with pleasure. "I did."

"Neat strong stitches. Lovely work. See that square of yellow fabric? And there's needles and thread in the small pack. Hem it for me, and embroider something nice in the corner."

She plopped down next to me, a frown of concentration between her brows as she sewed.

I asked a round-faced child to roar for me, and he filled the hollow with a din that would've put a lion to shame. Another boy boasted he was the best fire-maker in the village, and proceeded to demonstrate his skill.

The hollow emptied of children as I finished one kite after another. They left, running and whooping, and soon the sky was full of swooping rainbow shapes.

It made my heart glad to see it.

Soon there were only two children left. One was a tall boy in big, old boots and the other an entirely forgettable-looking girl of average face, average color, average height.

"You're good with animals," I told the tall boy, and produced a coin. "Could you take my mule and look after her for me? Will that be fine with your parents?"

His eyes widened at the money—he had probably never handled a silver coin in his life. "It's just me and my granddad, mem, but we'll put her in the byre with the cow. She'll be as snug as a rug!"

He stroked Suki, and she showed her approval by slobbering all over him. He had gentle hands. Suki would be safe with him.

Tears pricked my eyes, and I blinked them away furiously. "Be a good girl, Suki," I called as he led her away, his kite tucked under his arm.

That left just the girl.

She wouldn't meet my eyes, but neither did she leave. I knew the struggle going on inside of her; I'd seen it manifest in a hundred other children before her. The longing to share warring with the need to stay hidden, stay safe, stay *normal*.

"Look around," I invited. "Which kite would you like?"

Her gaze darted to a dragonfly, with a long iridescent body of green-blue silk and stiff translucent wings. "Will you take a pebble for it, mem?" She held out a dull grey stone, no different from the others that littered the clearing.

"I could," I told her, gravely. "But that's not something that's important to you, is it? It's not a testament to your skill, nor an indication of your passion. See those kites up there?" We both looked up at where the goldfish leapt and the butterflies danced. "They ride high and strong because the children thought the kites were worth paying for with the best they could give." She hung her head.

"You have a gift," I said gently. "A great, rare gift. If you choose to share it with me, I promise that it will remain between the two of us. Why do you think I sent all the rest away before talking to you?"

"I can't, mem," she muttered. "It's—unnatural."

"Unusual, I'll bet, but not unnatural. Show me."

She wavered, then dropped to her heels. Her face was resolute and a clear light burned in her eyes. She wasn't so forgettable now.

My heart leapt at the familiarity of that look. I'd seen the same expression on the face of a yellow-haired foreign-born boy, not much older than her.

She pulled a knife from her pocket, and a piece of wood. Her movements now were sure and confident, with none of her earlier hesitation. Her brown, work-roughened hands were covered in old cuts. "What shall I make for you, mem?"

My mind went blank. Then, recklessly, I said, "Make me a key. Make me a key so strong that it will open a prison without locks."

She gave me a crisp nod, and set to work. I worked, too, on the dragonfly kite, sneaking a glance at her every now and then. Her entire being was focused on the whittling, on the chips of bark and curls of wood, and the shape she gave to both the wood and her power.

Her power. It came to me with the scent of sap and green, oil and fresh-cut wood. I inhaled it, and thought, *Yes. This one.*

The sun touched the edge of the hollow, spilling light like golden yolk along the horizon. The girl was in shades of dim, turned wraithlike. Power wove itself into the thing in her hands.

I tied a last knot, and waited.

The girl rose, and came to me. I held out my cupped hands and she dropped the key into it.

It gleamed blackly. No longer wood, not quite metal, fluid and flickering with power. Tingles ran up my arms.

The girl was just a girl now, looking tired and drained. I'd forgotten how quickly the young and powerful ones get used up.

I almost regretted what I'd asked her to do. My fingers closed over the key, tucked it into my bodice, close to my heart.

"Will that do, mem?" she asked, shy and uncertain again. My heart almost broke at her innocence. She didn't know what a treasure she was, even living in Serenai's shadow.

"What's your name, child?"

"Pella."

"You must be very careful with your gift, Pella. Careful who you show it to, especially when you're young. Keep it hidden, until you're a grown woman and you've learned wisdom." She leaned forward, eager, like a sun-starved plant. How lonely her power had made her! "There will be those, even those who sit on the High Council, who will want to use you for their own ends. Don't give them the chance, Pella."

She nodded, eagerly. "I know who you mean." Her voice dropped to a whisper. "The Red Witch."

Oh, that hurt. I had only meant to help the children I'd sought out. But I'd failed them. Failed them all, not just Trell.

I smiled through it, a bittersweet twist of my mouth. "Yes, dear heart. And also the grey ladies of Serenai, with their soft voices and hard eyes. The mages of Pajorah who read your shadow, and the blind bell-ringers who catch your thoughts with their nets of music. Watch out for headmen and minor councilors and petty nobles. Beware of them all. Promise me that."

"I promise." Her eyes were wide.

"Good luck, child." I handed her the dragonfly kite. I'd wound silence and strength and patience into it. "Not even my kites last forever, but the ribbons will. Wear them in your hair. They will help protect you."

That night I sought my bed in a cave that I knew from long ago, its mouth facing the sea, hidden behind jagged rocks. I lay there, wide awake, listening to the rush and roar of water on the shore and the whistle of the wind above.

And in that noise I caught the thread of a golden song sung by a golden voice. A voice pure and powerful, even as its owner slowly died.

The next morning I spread out the red silk I'd used to bundle up all my other papers and cloth. I cut it into pieces with sharp silver scissors, then bent my last remaining bamboo strips into a frame. As I sewed and glued, I used the gifts the children had given me. Care and strength went into the kite's construction, along with the little girl's stitching. I gave it the leaping energy of the dancers, the endurance and swiftness of the runners. Even half-made, it writhed and skittered like a thing alive, impatient to be off.

"Soon, soon," I murmured to it as I sewed its yellow eyes and attached the milky-white shell above them to help it find its way. Its ribbons undulated, and its mouth opened in a soundless roar.

"Not yet, not yet." I gentled it, but I knew I could not contain it for long. The magic was strong but fleeting, like childhood itself.

Tonight was the night.

I stood on the cliff after sunset, in the star-dusted twilight, holding my kite. The wind whipped my hair across my face and the kite strained against my hold. I whispered the last words, the words of awakening.

The dragon came to life.

A fierce light leapt into its yellow eyes. Its hide rippled with silk and scales. It flexed its claws and opened its wings.

I flung myself onto its back. To my senses, its body flickered between warm solidity and a frightening, fragile lightness.

Then the dragon jumped into the air, and my stomach gave a lurch. I clung to its neck as it soared.

I reached out and touched the shell in its forehead, thinking about the boy I had found, the youth I had known. I thought of his golden voice. "Find him," I whispered.

The dragon, great-hearted construct that it was, flapped its mighty wings. Ribbons blew back from its body.

The walls of Serenai flashed below us. A sea of lights illuminated the city, its streets unrolling like dark ribbons. The dragon climbed higher, rising up the walls of the citadel at the heart of Serenai. I could've reached out to touch the grey wall if I wasn't holding on so tightly.

We exploded over the top, right above a sentinel's head. He staggered back, fell on his rump.

As the dragon soared ever higher, I heard the warning shouts.

I craned my neck up, looking at the tallest tower of the cluster. How long before the warning went to the grey ladies, how long before they figured out what was going on, how long before they sent someone to secure the tower?

How long before the dragon's speed and strength, heart and courage, given to it by children, gave out?

It had slowed, clawing its way up through air that had turned thick and murky as soup. I remembered the boy who'd saved his sister from the sea, and prayed that his courage and goodness would be enough.

We'd left all the other buildings far below us. The dragon hit the white walls of the tower and ran up it, its claws gouging stone. It found the sill and clung there, while I scrambled up and perched uncomfortably on the narrow ledge.

A small barred window stood in my way.

The last obstacle.

And behind it, a shadow.

"Kithri?" it whispered, in a voice so grey and tired I could've wept. I may have, but the wind lashed my tears away. "Is that you?"

"Yes. I'm here, Trell." *Finally.* "I'm sorry it took so long."

His slender hands clutched the bars, as if he needed their support to stay standing. His head was bowed. "The bars are made of oppression, Kithri. The whole chamber reeks of it."

I drew back, horrified. Oppression. No wonder Trell was so worn, no wonder they'd been able to control him. Denrys and the other grey ladies were slowly leaching the life from him.

The dragon! My heart beat madly as I saw its eyes dimming. Oppression was draining its power away, too.

"Give me your knife, Kithri. Slip it between the bars and let me end this."

"No." I plucked Pella's key from my bodice, gave it a desperate kiss, full of love and regret. "Stand back."

For a moment, he didn't move. Then his hands dropped, and

he staggered back.

Please work. I took the key that would open a prison with no locks and pressed it against the bars.

Lights pinpricked the key, ran in flickering strings all over the bars. I held my breath as the bars wavered, bent, melted and disappeared.

She'd done it. Pella had done it.

I reached in through the opening. The chamber inside was small, dark, foul-smelling. The lingering traces of oppression cast a shadow over my soul.

My poor Trell. Hatred rushed through my blood; my fingers crooked into claws, as I imagined gouging out Denrys' eyes. When had my former friend become so hard and cruel?

Instead I reached out to Trell and caught his hands in mine. His wrists were slender—like his voice, his body would forever be that of a boy's.

Together we got him through the window opening. We sat on the ledge, and the dragon, still clinging, looked at us with eyes once again aflame.

Oh, I loved those children.

I pushed Trell onto the dragon's back, then slid into place in front of him. He slumped against me, cheek on my shoulder.

"Now," I told the dragon. "Fly us to the sea."

The dragon let go of the sill. We plummeted.

The wind dragged away the shriek from my lips. Silk folded and bamboo bent alarmingly under us.

Behind me, Trell lifted his head and sang high and clear. The dragon solidified and flapped its wings, powerful muscles moving beneath us.

"Kithri...the birds..."

I looked, and there they were, a swarm of dark angry things, made of paper, fueled by the need to rip and rend.

Denrys' work.

I laughed, high, shaky, relieved. "Roar," I told the dragon. "Roar!"

The dragon's eyes rolled in fierce delight. Its mouth opened.

It roared.

The sound echoed off the tower walls. It boomed through the night. It blasted the paperlings away, sent them tumbling end over end, scattering them.

Dark shadows, large as eagles, swooped down on us. The dragon exhaled flame, and burning paper rained down on the citadel walls.

I thanked the fire-making boy. Up we spiraled, out of the reach of arrows, and headed out to sea.

"Where are we going, Kithri?"

"There's a ship waiting for us, with Nerrin and Dis and Mauris on it. It'll take you far away. You're free, Trell, you're *free*."

"You did it." He sounded stunned. "You got all of us out. What will you do now, Kithri?"

The wind whipped my face. The moon sailed above us, the sea heaved and murmured below. I thought of Pella and of others like her. "I'll do what I've always done, Trell.

"I'll find the children who have the gift. I'll find them, teach them, then set them free."

A DRINK OF DEADLY WINE

by Michael Spence & Elisabeth Waters

Marion always said that if you didn't send in your bio, she would make something up. You would think that I would be able to nag Michael into providing his, but so far no luck. So: Michael has spent the last year imprisoned in the body of a Terracotta Warrior as the exhibition traveled from Minneapolis (his home) to San Francisco. He communicated with me telepathically so we could collaborate on this story. So even though his online friends cannot fathom how he can have failed to see a single episode of *Game of Thrones*, there is a logical explanation.

This is another story in the "Treasures of Albion" series, although this time the treasure is Chinese. This happened before, with "Daughter of Heaven" in SWORD AND SORCERESS 23. That was the year both the Asian Art Museum in San Francisco and the Minneapolis Institute of Arts had the exhibit "Power and Glory: Court Arts of China's Ming Dynasty." Both Michael and I appear to be susceptible to Chinese art.

If you practice an unwanted task long enough, someone had once told Laurel, eventually a new perspective—perhaps even enlightenment—will click into place. That had never happened to her, and it certainly wasn't going to happen now.

Hush, she told herself as she prepared her calligraphy tools and sat down, cross-legged, before her writing table. It wouldn't do to be seen grumbling by one's teacher, even if technically one did outrank him.

This was as frustrating as it could be for an academic, she told herself. Appointed to the imperial court of China as the Guardian of the Scholar's Pin, she was expected to be a *Scholar*. Well, wasn't she? Back home in Albion, she was the youngest student ever to pass her Senior Ordeal and graduate as a full-fledged mage, a Senior Thaumaturge. She had even learned to speak fluent Mandarin there. That sounded like sufficient qualification for a scholar, no?

No. Not here in China. Here she was barely literate. The imperial civil service exam featured twenty thousand Chinese characters, and after three years she had yet to master even a fraction of them.

She pulled her hair back, twisted and pinned it with a decorative comb (the Scholar's Pin was safely in its box in the corner of her workroom). Weng-xiou, the Emperor's master calligrapher, smiled at her as she removed paper, ink stick, inkstone, and brushes from their case and set them beside the bowl of water on the table. After placing some water in the depression in the stone, she ground some ink from the stick and mixed it with the water.

A true scholar must master the Four Arts. Laurel would have to play something more complex than "Twinkle, twinkle, little star" on the *guqin*, a seven-stringed instrument that made her think of a dulcimer that had been put on the rack. She would have to be competent at the game of *weiqi*, which she had learned as "Go" and been slaughtered at the few times she'd played it back home. She would have to learn painting—*if only I had taken that as my required art course at the College of Wizardry! But no, I had to insist on needlework...*

And finally there was calligraphy. *Here we go, for the five hundredth try: "The Thousand-Character Essay."*

She took the brush delicately yet firmly under Weng-xiou's approving eye, dipped it in the ink, and touched it to the paper—

Click.

Under the brush, the line took form. It began as a tentative search for direction, then swelled to an enthusiastic boldness before swooping into a tight curve, ending up as a hair-thin swirl of the utmost gentility. *And thus it happened,* thought Laurel. *The divine breath touched the body of clay, "and man became a living soul—"*

"If I might interrupt such concentration," murmured Weng-xiou, his voice heavy with irony, "that does not resemble any of the Thousand Characters. What are you doing?"

Laurel lifted the brush from the paper and said, wonder in her voice, "I was thinking that when the ink from the brush meets the paper, it's like creating life. An observer sees only black marks. But they express energy, emotion...even character, really." She chuckled, imagining her brother, Stephen, saying, *They don't call them "characters" for nothing.* "I wonder if you could measure a person's virtue by the way he writes?"

The Emperor's master calligrapher paused. "Many pardons, O Daughter. I mistook your contemplation for frivolity with the brush. It seems you have grasped a core truth of what we are doing here: Expression is expression, in this medium no less than any other. And the expression of a mind represents and displays the life that exists in that mind."

The sound of a throat clearing drew their attention to the doorway, where a messenger stood. "Most respected Daughter of Heaven, you asked to be told when the Archer next appeared."

Laurel rinsed her brush and laid it carefully to dry. "Indeed I did. Master, if you would be so kind as to allow me to continue at another time?"

"But of course, O Daughter," Weng-xiou replied, rising and bowing briefly to her. This time, when he said, "I would be pleased," his tone suggested that perhaps he finally glimpsed a reward for his patience. He smiled and took his leave.

Laurel arose and went to a map on the wall of what she had declared to be her workroom. Two identical maps depicted the capital city and its environs, but one had a rather random assortment of different colored pins, while the second bore a pattern of yellow pins. Each pin identified a site where a statue wearing ancient military armor had been spotted; from each pin a string led to the margin of the map and an image drawn by a witness at that location. Each image showed a soldier wearing what appeared to be garb typical of the army of Qin Shi-huang, the First Emperor. Several military personnel she had consulted in the Emperor's court had identified the figure as an archer, although it bore no weapons.

The pins traced a path from the outskirts, where the statue was first seen, in toward the Forbidden City, the home of the Emperor and his court.

Her home.

"Please come in," she said to the messenger. "Who has seen the Archer this time? And where?"

A different voice sounded, with echoes that could not be entirely accounted for by the room's acoustics. "A great many people, I fear," it said. "The court is by no means deserted this day." The messenger, who had not spoken, took a few timid steps into the workroom. Laurel's eyes widened as, behind him, another figure entered. He bore himself as a soldier would, at once suggesting both complete competence and unmixed humility. Indeed, he was the very model of an former era's fighting man...if the model were made of clay.

For clay he undeniably was. The material was the same that Laurel had seen used for roof tiles and water pipes, called "baked earth" by many. Normally such material was a reddish-brown color, but the figure who stood at the doorway also held a tinge of green, reminding Laurel of the stains that marred her clothing after unruly childhood evenings spent outdoors.

She imagined her brother Stephen's voice chuckling: *They say soldiers aren't born, they're made. Now I believe it*. If there was a possible pun in any situation, Stephen would find it. She had to remind herself not to throw things at him when they chatted through the scrying mirror. While she didn't believe in the automatic "seven years' bad luck"—that depended on the composition and provenance of the mirror—she was no gambler.

The other voice, with the strange echoes, spoke again. "The worthy emissary says you are the Daughter of Heaven, and a wizard. If this humble servant may be bold enough to request a few moments of the Daughter's time, it would be most appreciated."

Laurel motioned to the messenger, who was inching his way out the door, and indicated that he should stay. Nervously he obeyed, taking up station just inside the door, ready to bolt. To the clay soldier she motioned toward two chairs by a small round table and said, “Can you sit down?” Inwardly she cringed. *Who do I think this is, Jacob Marley? No, wait, it’s a legitimate question.*

At the other’s nod she said, “Please do, then. And let us not stand on ceremony. I grant that you are a humble servant and I honor you for it. But you are yourself, and it will save us time if you speak directly. Is that understood?” Again the soldier nodded. “Very well. I realize that formal court etiquette has its routines, but I gather you have urgent business that has brought you here. Let us get to it. Would you like tea?”

“No, thank you, my lady. This humb—*I* am proof against liquids, but have no taste for them.”

Nor would court dignity be served by the sloshing noises that would result, she realized. Ah, well. At least some etiquette had been upheld. “How may you and I serve the Son of Heaven?”

“You see,” the archer began, “that this armor does not match the garb of the warriors standing outside your residence. That is because...I...represent a different era in your history. Nor am I the only one of my kind. There are—”

Laurel held up a hand. “There are thousands of your fellows buried with the First Emperor, near the city of Xi’an, which was Chang’an.” She had thought the sculpted warrior’s face incapable of displaying emotion, but the look of surprise showed otherwise.

Deciding not to attempt to explain an archeological dig to someone for whom her ancient history was his very recent past, she said simply, “These soldiers, which those in the court refer to as the ‘terracotta army,’ were discovered years ago, and some of them have been recently brought here so that the Son of Heaven might have them in the Imperial Palace.”

The Archer looked alarmed. “They are actually *here*, in the home of the Son of Heaven?”

“They are in a workshop between the west gate and the watchtower south of it. Why?”

“Someone is tampering with them,” the Archer said gravely. “I am a shaman; I was appointed to guard over the rest of the warriors, and thus I know when several of them have been cut off from the rest. There are three that I cannot contact: a light infantryman; a charioteer, and—"

"—a cavalryman," Laurel sighed. "They're on the other map." Rising, she led him to the wall where the maps were fastened side by side. "You're the map with the yellow pins."

"I see," he said. "You were tracing my journey here. But they," he frowned at the other map, "appear to be wandering aimlessly."

"While it's true that they do not appear to have a destination," Laurel agreed, "they have been sighted at various points in the city outside the gates. The cavalryman keeps taking horses, and I assure you their owners are *not* happy. The Fist of Heaven has been dealing with them."

"*Trying* to deal with them." A new voice came from the doorway. "So far I'm a step behind the warriors—especially the one who takes horses—and for some odd reason I can't seem to persuade the subjects of the Son of Heaven that having their horses appropriated by clay soldiers of the First Emperor is an honor."

"Have some tea," Laurel said.

"That would be most welcome," the Fist of Heaven said, crossing to the chairs. Over his shoulder he said to the messenger still standing next to the door, "You may go." The man left the room perhaps a bit more quickly than etiquette required. Laurel poured tea for both herself and her fellow Guardian and sat next to him. Both of them watched the Archer studying the map that showed the wanderings of the other warriors.

"And yesterday," the Fist sighed, "some idiot shipped up a chariot they found. The unloaded it from the train, turned their back for what they all swear was just a few minutes—"

"—which they would swear had it been a few hours, but may still be true," Laurel said. "I take it the charioteer now has something to drive?"

"He seems to be out of practice. It's thoroughly tangled in some bushes in the east park, and he's nowhere to be found." He took another sip of tea and looked at the figure still studying the map. "Archer, can you find the missing warriors?"

The Archer turned and looked at him steadily. "By what right do you command me?"

"First, it was a request, not a command. Second, I Serve." He drew a short silver knife from his belt and held it in front of his heart, balanced on his open palms.

At the sight of the knife the Archer's eyes opened wide, and he hurried across the room to bow deeply. "Your pardon, O Fist of Heaven! I beg you to forgive my ignorance."

"Granted. Now, what can you tell us?"

"Very little, I fear." The Archer dropped to one knee and sat on his heel with the air of one who had spent much of his life in that position. "I catch the image of a woman performing some rite, and after that I cannot reach them."

"A woman?" asked the Fist, narrowing his eyes.

"Oh, no!" Laurel exclaimed. She and the Fist exchanged glances. "She wasn't in Albion—"

"For the Power and Glory Exhibit? So someone told her—inaccurately—what you did there."

"What?" The Archer was obviously confused. "And who?"

"Lady anything-that-stupid-round-eyes-can-do-I-can-do-better is a member of the Emperor's court, and the Power and Glory Exhibit was a collection of lesser treasures sent to Albion, where I grew up. One of the terracotta warriors was in it, and I *pretended* to bring him to life. It was an *illusion*. The real warrior was in his place the entire time."

"Unfortunately, there is a sorceress here at court who..."

"She's jealous," Laurel said. "If they had offered *her* the Scholar's Pin she'd have accepted it on the spot."

"Which is why it would never have been offered to her." The Fist frowned. "If she animated the warriors, can she control them?"

"That would be the purpose of such dark magic," the Archer said, "but if she can control them, why is she not doing so?"

"She probably botched whatever spell she used," Laurel said in disgust. "This won't be the first time we've had to deal with her mistakes."

"If we can prove she did this," the Fist of Heaven said grimly, "it will be the last time. The Son of Heaven will have her executed for *this*. We'll have to find a way to prove what she did, though."

"Will the Son of Heaven not execute her on your word?" the Archer asked in astonishment.

I guess the stories of how ruthless the First Emperor was are true. "It's not that simple these days," Laurel explained. "The Son of Heaven dispenses justice, and justice must not only be done, it must be *seen* to be done." She turned to the Fist and added, "You're being pessimistic. We don't have to prove she did it; all we have to do is give her an opportunity to brag about having done it."

"Very well," said the Archer. "But we must still find them. That is why I have come to you. I do not know this city, and it is larger than any I have seen."

Laurel went over to a cabinet standing along one wall, and opened a door to reveal a mirror. "What can you tell us about these soldiers, Arch— do you have a name?"

"Indeed, O Daughter. I am Zhan."

"Thank you, Zhan. If these were men, we might have some clearer ideas about—"

"But they *are* men, my lady!" said Zhan. "*I* am a man. We are baked-earth for my Emperor's purpose, but I assure you, we are true men. Yun-peng is the cavalryman, Li-qing is the charioteer, and Song is the infantryman."

The Fist chuckled. "Knowing that makes it somewhat easier. What do soldiers most want to do when they're not in battle?"

He and Laurel looked at each other. "We check the taverns."

Zhan nodded. "That makes sense. Song always said that if we wanted to find him, we should look anywhere there are wine and women to be found."

"Really?" said Laurel. *I am* not *telling Stephen about this.*

When the Daughter of Heaven and the Fist of Heaven walked into the Hall of Supreme Harmony for Court that night, the archer Zhan walked silently behind them.

"I see you've *finally* managed to raise *one* of them," a

scornful female voice said into the silence. "I raised three of them. Weeks ago."

"Really?" Laurel forced herself to sound skeptical. "Why should we believe you? I don't see them with you."

"How did you encompass such a feat," the Fist of Heaven asked, "if indeed you did?" He didn't sound as though he believed it either.

"I admit it took some research," Lady Mei-ying said as she strode forward into the circle of lamplight, her tone of voice clearly adding, *since that's what* true *scholars do*. "And I found it: the Vintage of Life!" From the sleeve of her robe she took a small bottle filled with a purple fluid. "With this we can bring all the statues to life to serve you, my Emperor!"

Zhan stepped forward. When he spoke, everyone but Laurel and the Fist gasped. This was clearly not something the other figures had done. "If I may beg the Son of Heaven's indulgence, may I examine this Wine of Life?"

From his throne the Emperor nodded, and extended his hand, palm upward, to Lady Mei-ying. Powerless to refuse, she placed the bottle in his hand, and he held it out to Zhan. The archer took the bottle, held it up to the nearest lamp to judge its translucency, and then unstoppered the bottle and held it under his nose—which surprised Laurel, who would have sworn he did not breathe, nor need to. Then he replaced the stopper, and made as if to dash the bottle to the floor, holding himself back barely in time. Clutching the bottle, he did something that made the courtiers fall to the ground in horror.

He howled. It was the howl of a savage battle's last survivor; of a man who has discovered the burning ruin of his village. It froze the blood in Laurel's veins—or at least she would have sworn it had.

"*O Blessed Son of Heaven!*" the clay warrior shouted, in the voice of one who spoke to an emperor but not to *his* Emperor—the resonance within him turning his voice into thunder. "Believe not her who speaks! I know this liquid. Whatever she may call it, *it is the wine of death!*"

"Lady Mei-ying," said Laurel, who with the Fist had

remained standing, "how is this used to animate a...statue?"

Hesitantly the other rose to her feet. "It is a ritual that climaxes in touching the liquid to the lips of the warrior," she said, trying to recapture the proud voice she had used earlier. "It drinks the liquid, and then it can move."

Again Zhan howled. "Son of Heaven! Let me tell you what your most worthy predecessor—my Emperor—has done! These warriors you have pulled from their station are *not* lifeless statues, as this woman supposes. They are an army—an army of thousands, preserved against the day of the Crisis that is coming! They are not dead, no—*they never died.* Their breath has been *almost* completely taken away and stored elsewhere by his wizards—but *not* fully away. It remains connected to them by the thinnest of threads, to be called back when the Crisis comes. Until then, the body without the breath is but clay—such clay, treated with the arts of my Emperor's wizards, that it is preserved until that time. When the time comes, then at my Emperor's command their breath shall return to them, and they shall be fully restored, in the fullness of their youth, at the peak of their training, ready to do battle in his service!

"And *this woman...*" —he swept his arm aside, finger pointing toward Mei-ying— "this woman *has cut the thread!* She has not brought my fellow warriors back to life, no! She has *murdered* them!"

While he spoke, servants quietly brought the clay warriors into the hall on litters. Seeing them, Zhan fell to his knees. "All you here, bear witness! This was Song, the infantryman, who cheered his fellows in their dark times. This was Yun-peng, the best horseman in his unit. And this was Li-qing, from whose chariot attacks were mounted. I had the pleasure of riding with him myself, and let me tell you, his technique was the smoothest and yet fastest I have ever known. And now..." he gazed sadly at them, "now they are gone. These bodies bear the imprint of their spirits, but those spirits are no longer here.

"Goodbye, my companions. I shall miss you." He rose to his feet, looked the Emperor wordlessly in the eye, and then for the first time turned to face Lady Mei-ying directly.

"*MURDERER!*"

Silence, like that following a thunderstorm, lasted several minutes. "Supreme harmony," always a wishful goal, was for the moment banished.

"'Thou hast showed thy people heavy things: thou hast given us a drink of deadly wine,'" Laurel murmured. At the Fist's inquisitive glance she said, "It's a sacred text in Albion. I'll explain later."

The Emperor did not clear his throat. He did not need to. At his slight movement the court sprang to attention. "Injustice has been done. Is that your conclusion as well?" he said, looking at Laurel and the Fist.

"It is, O Son of Heaven," said Laurel. The Emperor seemed satisfied with the Fist's nod. Laurel put her hand on Zhan's arm. The terracotta felt cool to the touch, but she could feel the energy and turmoil within. Zhan turned to her and smiled weakly.

The stunned Mei-ying, who had not attempted to escape, appeared not even to notice as guardsmen restrained her. "It now remains," said the Emperor, "for justice to be administered. In this case, which I trust will remain unique in this lifetime, I invite suggestions."

The Fist stepped forward. "Although it is an inadequate restitution," he said, "it may be possible for Lady Mei-ying to take the place of one of these warriors and serve in his stead." The Emperor glanced at several of the court's wizards, one of whom said, "Theoretically it is possible, O Son of Heaven. Indeed, we have proof standing before us." He bowed to Zhan, who returned the bow.

The Emperor turned to Zhan. "Would that be agreeable?"

Zhan bowed slightly to him, and to the Fist said, "I see what you are offering, and I appreciate it. But if you are the soldier I believe you are, you know the answer." The Fist nodded. Of course.

"I do have a suggestion," said Laurel. "May I have two cups, please?" A servant brought them, and she took the bottle from Zhan and divided its contents between the two containers. She set one aside and held the other one up before the Emperor. "Even though they no longer suit the First Emperor's plan, I believe we can reactivate these figures for service to the present Empire, as Lady Mei-ying proposed. We must have your decision, however. One procedure would make them servants of the truth, whatever it might be. The other procedure would make them your personal servants, to do your will and your will alone, whatever *it* might be. Which do you select?"

The hubbub that followed this question was considerable. *Where is the choice? The truth is what the Son of Heaven says it is! Who would dare to say him nay?* The Emperor himself was about to speak, no doubt along similar lines, when his eyes met Laurel's. An eyebrow lifted, as if to say, *Are you challenging me? That would be most unwise.*

Laurel attempted to appear as innocent and affirming as possible. *No challenge whatever, my lord! I am on your side. But I need to hear your answer.*

If the courtiers were surprised to see the Emperor pause before answering, they were stunned when he stood before replying. In a clear but gentle voice he announced, "The Daughter of Heaven is most wise. In all the land there is no power above mine...and yet power for its own sake is a trap, one into which I have watched too many fall. My divinely-bestowed power is worthless unless it is directed toward noble ends. I choose to accept the phrasing presented by the Daughter: 'servant of the truth.' As much as I have ability to do, I cannot turn black into white, day into night, or winter snow into spring rain. The world is what it is, and I must rule within that reality. I serve the truth, and were it otherwise I should not be worthy of this throne. In accord with this fact," he said to Laurel, "I choose your first procedure. They are to serve the truth."

As the hubbub momentarily returned, the Fist whispered to Laurel, "I strongly suspect that very few will venture to argue with him as to whose vision of the truth is the correct one."

She hoped that was true. At the same time, as the Emperor reseated himself and glanced at her, she gave him an encouraging nod. *I would very much like to introduce you to*

Lord Logas sometime.

To Zhan she whispered, "Are you comfortable with this?"

He replied, "They are now simply clay statues, as the Lady has believed all along. There is nothing for me to say about them. Do as you wish."

To Weng-xiou, standing at the far end of the hall, she called, "Master Calligrapher! I have some language that must be inscribed on the foreheads of these warriors. Please assist us."

The master made his way forward. When he reached Laurel, however, he said softly, "I would be most willing to help—but if it is magic you have in mind, I should remind you that yours is the mind, the vision to be expressed here. My work would be of little effect, no?"

She bowed to him. "Forgive me, master. You are wise."

"I believe that word has already been claimed for today." Smiling, he offered her his kit and stepped back into the throng.

Laurel selected a brush and, using the purple liquid as ink, drew three symbols on the forehead of each of the three clay figures. Then she beckoned to the Fist of Heaven, who used his silver knife to extract something from behind the lips of each figure. His incisions resealed themselves, as they had done previously. "Command them," Laurel told him. "They are yours."

They did indeed respond to his command. The courtiers fell back as he led the warriors away to stand well behind the throne.

Taking the second cup, Laurel presented it to the Emperor. "As for Mei-ying, I can only propose that the punishment fit the crime."

The Emperor shot an enquiring glance at Zhan, who with some surprise nodded. He then commanded the chief of his guardsmen, who took the cup over to where they held the sorceress. As the chief held out the cup to her, the Emperor said, "You will drink every drop."

Mei-ying's eyes remained wide open, as they had been for the last few minutes, but she could not disobey the Son of Heaven. She drained the cup.

For a moment nothing happened. Mei-ying, relieved, began to

breathe in a deep sigh of relief, when suddenly her body convulsed in huge spasms. The guards held her arms tightly; she did not even have time to look over at Laurel before the last convulsion hit her, she shrieked in terror, and fell lifeless in their grip.

Nothing else would be accomplished that evening. The Emperor left the throne room for his residence, and everyone else followed in order of rank. The only exception was Laurel, who did not move throughout all the proceedings. When everyone else was gone she stood in the center of the Hall of Supreme Harmony, staring toward the corner where the Fist of Heaven had stationed the three terracotta soldiers before he and Zhan took them to their new resting place.

Mei-ying's shriek continued to resound through her thoughts. It troubled her, as doubtless it would trouble everyone who had watched the sorceress die. But it bothered Laurel especially, because she was certain she had heard the shriek come from more than one direction—accompanied by familiar echoes.

Clay sculptures couldn't shriek. Of course they couldn't.

"It's eating at me now," she told Stephen's image in the mirror back in her rooms. "Could she somehow be trapped inside them? Unable to move, unable to talk, unable to do anything about what she sees?"

Stephen, in his workroom at the College, considered. "As one of your wizards said, theoretically I suppose it's possible. If so, it's her own doing; she shouldn't have gotten so attached to her work." When Laura glared at him, he put up his hands and said, "I'm serious! The way you describe her, Mei-ying was obsessed with one-upping you—okay, *three*-upping you in this case. She invested not only her time, but her will and her passion and her mind in this project. She truly put herself into the magic she worked on those figures. I wouldn't be surprised if she were still there."

"So what can I do?"

"What need you do? Nothing. As Lord Logas would say, that's a crisis for another era."

That reminded her. "The suspended soldiers are going back to Xi'an, all of them—except the three, of course. I don't know what this Crisis is that they're to be ready for, and neither does Zhan. But he's told us he will respond to visits from time to time—as long as we allow him to wake up properly."

Stephen chuckled. "Bring coffee. So tell me: how did you know the golem rituals would work in this situation?"

Laurel laughed weakly. "I didn't, at first. When we went to try to capture the three, I thought, clay men, why not? Maybe they were enough like the medieval golems that would it work…. We saw that when the Fist broke or cut the soldiers with the Knife they healed themselves automatically, so I had him poke a hole in each one's cheek and I shot this inside." She held up a crumpled piece of paper, torn from her calligraphy practice.

"A spitball?" he said incredulously.

"Close. Anyway, it worked. Weng-xiou asked if he could see one after he saw us remove them. He was impressed. 'Congratulations, Daughter,' he said. 'You have mastered the command for STOP. I commend you.'" She chuckled. "As if everything else hadn't already made my day, that topped it.

"So after that, yes, I was sure the rest of the lore would apply. I wrote *aleph-mem-taw* on their foreheads, *emet*, 'truth'—see, I remembered, which is much easier with a language that has only twenty-two characters, and when I commanded them to rise and obey Li—uh, the Fist of Heaven, they did."

Stephen nodded. "And if the Emperor had made the other choice..."

"I would have done the very same thing, but within a few days that aleph would've been erased, and *emet* would become *met*—'dead.' Oh, the magic didn't last? What a pity. And I would still have learned something I needed to know about the Emperor."

"Logas will be proud. And just think, I can now tell everyone here at the University that you're making head-lines!"

Her hand was halfway to a jade paperweight before she remembered there was a mirror between them.

PROMISES AND PASTRY

by Melissa Mead

This story illustrates the main editorial difference between me and Marion. She didn't like "recycled fairy tales"—in fact, that was one of the paragraphs on her rejection list. I, on the other hand, like to see new twists given to old tales, as long as they are well done. This story certainly qualifies.

Melissa Mead lives in Upstate New York, and she loves messing with fairy tales. You can see more of what she's up to at her website, http://carpelibris.wordpress.com.

I'd just taken a loaf of rosemary bread out of the oven when the old woman appeared in the kitchen.

She looked like an old woman, like the kindest pink-cheeked, white-haired granny possible, but her eyes gave her away. They always do. All the Good Folk of our land have silver eyes, like mirrors with a fathomless hole in the middle, taking everything in and giving nothing back. All their magic can't change that.

Besides, benevolent grannies don't just appear from empty air.

"I'm your fairy godmother, Ella dear," she said.

I stood there with the bread peel in my hands and a smile pasted onto my face, wondering what I'd done to attract her attention.

"I know how you've yearned to go to the prince's ball tomorrow night, and I'm here to help you do just that." Her smile shone brighter than the copper I'd spent hours polishing.

My heart sank. Yes, my plans had involved going to that ball. Through the servant's entrance, the way I'd been sneaking out to do for months. Cook was expecting me. I'd slowly earned her respect through hard work and more skill with spices than she'd expected from "gentry." For weeks, my yearnings had involved getting away from my stepmother and stepsisters and doing what I loved best in the gloriously-equipped royal kitchens. Had I really been foolish enough to speak them aloud? I was sure that my ostensible benefactor's plans didn't involve kitchens.

"I don't want to be disrespectful, but I thought that the Good Folk didn't like the word 'fairy,'" I said, playing for time.

She didn't. I saw her wince when I spoke the word, but her smile replaced it almost instantly.

"Merely a word, my dear. What do names matter? And I am your godmother. Your dear mother swore this when you were born."

Worse and worse. What had Mother done? And names didn't matter? To a fairy? Something strange was going on.

"Mother never told me about you, Godmother," I said, careful to keep any hint of skepticism or reproach out of my voice. Saying "Where were you when she died? Or when Father did? Or when Stepmother decided to use me to replace the entire household staff?" could end not only my plans, but my life. If the rumors were true, it might even do worse than that.

I hadn't been careful enough. Those mirror eyes glittered.

"You're refusing my gifts?"

I didn't know what happened to people who refused a fairy's gifts, but I'd seen what happened to people who accepted them. Ida, the Squire's milkmaid, had worn a real silk dress to marry her sweetheart, just like she'd wished. Then her husband was hanged for stealing the dress. The next day, they found Ida's body five miles downriver. She'd barely begun showing.

"I'm overwhelmed," I said, which was true. "I mean—to have someone as powerful as you just show up—I really don't deserve this."

"It's your destiny," the fairy godmother assured me. "You were born to marry the prince.

"Born to?" I had a horrible feeling that now I knew what Mother had done. And why she had died so young.

"Enough talk. This wish has been a long time waiting. Put

down that bread, child! Your hands—what have you been doing with them? Such dark circles under your eyes—haven't you been sleeping? And young ladies shouldn't have muscular limbs, like some common laborer."

I was proud of my strong arms and legs. Of my ability to heft full cast-iron kettles and churn cream until the butter came, and make the old iron stove heat evenly. My stepmother and stepsisters, who'd never cleaned a stove in their lives, turned up their noses at the sight of my sooty clothing. I didn't care. I wasn't the sheltered, ornamental thing I'd been before Father's ruin. I had a real skill, one that stopped the neighbors from pitying my scorched and flour-spotted dresses and had them swooning over my baking instead. It didn't excuse Stepmother's cruelty or her daughters' scorn, but it was a consolation I didn't want to give up.

"Perhaps some other young lady would be more worthy of your gifts," I suggested.

This time I had gone too far. The air of the kitchen crackled. I felt a pressure on my mouth, like a shushing finger held to my lips. "What happened?" I exclaimed. My voice sounded oddly muted and flat.

"Take your hands away from your mouth, girl. I can't see your lips. That's better. Don't worry; the spell will wear off in time for you to say "I do." And I haven't done anything to you directly, my darling saucy godchild. I've just stopped your voice from traveling further than an inch from your lips. Now; be a good girl and let me make you happy. You'll want a pretty dress, of course. Something pale pink. No, you've let your complexion go too much for such a dainty color. Blue, then. Trimmed with blush roses. And more for your hair. Look into my eyes!"

Startled, I did. Those otherworldly mirrors reflected back my astonished face, crowned with a pink wreath that prickled my forehead. A sudden weight of satin dragged against my body.

"Beautiful!" A full-length mirror appeared next to the icebox, displaying the whole frothy, lace-trimmed creation, complete with slippers the color of my godmother's eyes gleaming beneath the hem.

"The slippers are my own creation." She beamed. "Windows, as it were. No, not for peeking up your dress. Don't look like that. They simply show me the area around you. The palace is such a big, imposing place, I can't have you wandering off. And if you do, the thorns in your headdress will give you a little reminder to get back on track."

I shuddered.

"Now, I have to go arrange suitable transport for tomorrow night. I suggest you get to work on your hair. It's a disaster. You'll have to arrange it more becomingly. I've laid a little extra enchantment on your washtub to keep the water hot, and left you some much better soap than that harsh yellow lump you were using. Until tomorrow, my little flower!"

And she was gone, leaving me in that absurd froth of a dress. My carefully-baked loaf lay cold on the counter, and Stepmother's summoning bell was jangling at a furious volume. I stripped off the ball dress, wreath, and slippers, hurried into my other work dress, and ran to answer it.

Not being able to talk had one benefit. Once I convinced Stepmother and her daughters that I was ill with a sore throat, they left me alone for the night rather than risk getting sick. I scrubbed with my fairy godmother's rose-scented soap (no sense wasting it), slipped out the back way, and ran the mile to the palace. The sun hadn't quite set, and I hoped that Cook would be far too busy to notice my tardiness.

I was right. The other kitchenmaids teased me for smelling like a fine lady's rose garden, but Cook waved me in without my having to say a word. The ovens roared at full blast, pouring forth roasted beef and fowl, and loaves of bread enough to build a wall. Two girls were pushing thick soup through a stretched tammy. Others stirred pots, chopped vegetables, and minced forcemeat.

I went to work on a batch of salmon pastries, without joining in the usual chatter. The others commented on my silence, but I just grinned and turned my attention back to the intricacies of working with puff pastry. My stepsisters would have berated me for ignoring them, but these girls, my friends, just shrugged and let me work.

I worked all night, and stumbled home to collapse on my cot and sleep like a stone. Fortunately, when Stepmother stormed downstairs to harangue me for ignoring her summons, she took my heat-flushed cheeks as a sign of fever and declared that no one was to enter the kitchen.

My fairy godmother entered anyway, of course. As soon as Stepmother's carriage had rattled off to the ball, she appeared.

"Up, lazy child!" she exclaimed with false gaiety. "Get dressed! You only have until midnight!"

To do what? I managed to convey the question with a look of silent bewilderment.

"To win over the prince, of course! Your destiny demands that you both fall in love before midnight, or all my hard work will be for nothing. Your dear mother would be appalled."

While she bustled me into that bouquet of a ballgown, I pondered. She wasn't granting my wish; she was granting my mother's. Her dearest wish had been for her daughter to marry a prince.

I wish she'd told me. Mine had been, for the longest time, to have my mother back. Now it was to get away. Away from this house, from Stepmother and her endless demands, from her whining, mocking daughters. And from the fairy godmother I'd never wished for.

I have to admit, her magic was impressive—and reminded me that despite her taste in dresses, my godmother was one of the Fae, older than mankind and more powerful than the prince, king and queen combined. She led me outside (and when I quietly tried balking, a thorn jabbed me in the forehead, hard enough to draw a bead of blood.)

At her command, a pumpkin growing near the house tore itself from its vine and rolled to her feet like a dog coming to heel. There it swelled and grew, becoming as large as a coach. While it was growing, my godmother called fieldmice from their burrows and began an odious transformation. The poor things squealed and shrieked as their bodies re-formed, their tiny substance stretching to fill an illusion of horse-ness. I turned away, nauseated, to see that the coach-sized pumpkin had become a coach in truth. My godmother, smiling beatifically the whole time, manhandled me into it. I felt as manipulated as the poor mice.

But as the coach rolled away, guided by unseen hands, I had time to think. The fairy hadn't come with me. Something was restraining her. And what happened at midnight? If I could keep away from the prince until after twelve o' clock, I hoped I might just get free of whatever curse my mother had unwittingly set in motion.

The bewitched coach stopped in front of the palace. I tried to steal around to the servant's entrance. My crown of roses drew more blood. And this time, the crown wouldn't come off. Nor would the gloves, or those treacherous, spying shoes. Or that overblown dress. Before anyone could catch me trying to strip off my clothing on the palace lawn, I steeled myself and entered by the front way.

A trumpet blast startled me. (Not, alas, right out of my shoes.) The major domo looked expectantly at me. His silence attracted more attention than a shout would have.

Of course. He was waiting to announce my name. But the fairy's prohibition was still in effect, and I wasn't about to press my mouth to his ear in order to be heard. I smiled and inclined my head, and tried not to blush as I descended the staircase into the gaslit ballroom.

After an entrance like that, I had no hope of retreating to a quiet corner, much less the kitchen. Young gallants swarmed from all sides, begging the honor of signing my dance card.

"Gentlemen."

That one quiet word, delivered in a matter-of-fact voice, parted the whole crowd. The speaker strode past the men surrounding me, and studied me with frank curiosity. I studied him back. Yes, I stared at the prince. In this ballroom, in this dress, washed ghostly by the gaslight, deprived of my voice and name, I felt unreal. This other girl, this Not-Ella, didn't quite exist, and could stare at royalty with impunity.

The prince's mouth quirked up at my scrutiny. He had a nice face. Brown eyes—warm brown, like cinnamon. A quick smile. He wore the formal crimson and gold uniform of the royal family easily, as easily as I wore my baking apron. A silvery coronet circled his wavy hair. I thought it would have looked better in gold, to match the uniform, but overall he made a fine picture.

"May I have the honor of this dance, Miss?" He extended his hand.

I hesitated. Dancing with the prince only put me one step closer to completing whatever my godless godmother had planned. But my crown of roses dug its thorny claws into my forehead, and the prince looked hurt and baffled by my silence. I had no real excuse to refuse him, and no way to leave. I relented and allowed myself to be swept onto the dance floor.

"I'm Prince Theodore," he said, unnecessarily. Everyone knew about the prince, and story of Their Majesties' long, barren years of praying for an heir. Of their rumored meetings of sorcerers and astrologers.

And their longed-for heir was now wearing a coronet that shone like my enchanted shoes.

I stumbled. Officially, the Royal Family had nothing to do with the Fae. Fairy bargains were the stuff of peasants' tales and nursery warnings. Officially, making deals with the Fae was a crime. A sin. The Church claimed that it involved selling one's soul. Officially, no respectable person would do such a thing.

But my mother, a respectable merchant's wife, had made one. I suspected I knew how Their Majesties had gotten their heir.

"Are you all right?" said Prince Theodore.

I nodded, hoping that no trace of my treacherous thoughts showed on my face.

The prince's silver coronet winked in the light of the chandeliers. No, not silver. Glass. Mirrored. Like the shoes I wore.

The prince noticed my gaze. "Darn thing pinches horribly," he said, guiding me through a turn. "But it's expected." He looked at me sidelong, as though about to divulge a great secret. "Sometimes, when I'm in a temper, I could swear it burns.

Ridiculous, no? If I'm stubborn enough, it leaves blisters. Father says I'm just not used to wearing it."

I shook my head, laid a hand on his arm to guide him away from the worst of the crowd, and signaled for him to watch. Then I turned my back on him and walked away.

The thorns dug in at once. I kept walking. They clawed harder. One more step. Two. Three. A drop of blood trickled down my forehead. Hiding it with my hand, I walked back to the puzzled prince.

"What was that all about?"

I moved my hand. He gasped. I motioned for him to be quiet.

He produced a spotless white handkerchief from his pocket. Gently, apologetically, he wiped away the blood. "Fae curse?"

I nodded.

"And your voice, too?"

I motioned him closer. I could feel myself blushing, but after all, he'd touched my face. I was only whispering in his ear. "Until I obey."

"What do they want you to do?"

I blushed even harder.

He looked grim, and waltzed me back to my seat as the song ended. "Mother and Father won't admit it, but the Fae really rule this kingdom. Even people who won't bargain with them are afraid of them. They're everywhere."

I started to nod. Then I grabbed my dance card, with its stub of pencil, and wrote "None here."

"You're right. They can't set foot in the castle. Miss...?" He bent his head again for my name.

"Miss Ella, will you violate every rule of courtesy and dance with me some more? We seem to have much in common."

I pointed to his coronet and gave him a cheerful "You're the prince!" grin. And though plenty of young gentlemen looked disgruntled when we danced off again, none objected.

"Tell me truthfully, Miss Ella," he said, the music of a rousing quadrille drowning out his voice. "Did you bargain with the Fae to wed me?"

Of course he would assume that. He was the prince, after all.

And not bad-looking, either. Most girls would jump at the chance just to dance with him. I responded with a firm headshake. He chuckled.

"You don't have to be so adamant about not wanting me. Was the wish your own?"

If he thought my other reply was decisive, this one nearly snapped my neck.

"Neither was mine. So; someone else made bargains with your life. Can they be summoned to court?"

I was surprised to find tears stinging my eyes. Mother had cared for me, sang silly songs with me, told me she loved me with nearly her last breath. Despite her foolish bargain, I still missed her.

"Someone you cared for. And they're gone?" he asked, more gently than I ever would have expected from a prince.

I nodded.

"Yet the bargain stands. And you're tied to me." He looked grim. "I think the Fae may have found their way into the palace. Through you. You may not be looking to marry me, but someone expects you to, right? And those thorns will hurt you badly if you don't. Possibly even kill you."

Nod.

"I suppose marrying wouldn't be too terrible. We seem to be getting along well enough."

I remembered poor Ida's waterlogged body, the catcalls and jeers from the streets on the day of her husband's hanging. What fate would they inflict upon the prince? And his family. Whatever the Fae had planned, it would leave the kingdom without an heir, leaving an opening for whatever the Fae convinced the desperate townspeople to accept. This kind, gentle young man didn't deserve to be their pawn.

I laughed a silent, bitter laugh, tears of anger and frustration pouring down my face.

"It would kill you, your Highness," I whispered in his ear.

Prince Theodore glared at the roses in my hair. "And it wouldn't be pleasant for you either, I suspect. But how do they know? This castle is warded against all supernatural beings.

We'd know if one got in here. How do they know when you walk away from me?"

I held out a mirror-shod foot.

"Ah. I've heard that the Fae use mirrors and crystals to spy on people. They...Wait, the set's ending. May I escort you for refreshments? It will be easier for us to talk sitting than dancing."

The salmon puffs I'd helped make had come out perfectly. The prince had three.

"You're examining those pastries as though you'd made them yourself and were waiting for someone to judge them," he said.

I blushed, and at his encouragement, whispered my secret aspirations.

"Now I'll have to try all your creations," he said. "These are wonderful—and I don't even like salmon! Here; have some."

It felt strange to be eating the ball supper instead of preparing it, and even stranger to have the prince approving of both my cooking and my secret wish. Even with thoughts of fairy plots filling my mind, I savored each taste, making notes to myself of tricks I wanted to learn after I got out of this bargain.

If I could. This was about more than one mother's romantic wish for her daughter. Official declarations or no, people believed in fairy godmothers. A thousand seemingly innocent wishes granted, with consequences coming years or months later, so no one connected the wish to the tragedy…

"Can you take the shoes off?" Princc Theodore asked.

I shook my head. Thorns prickled my forehead, as though they'd been listening.

"May I try?"

The shoe felt glued on. But glued, not nailed. I gestured for him to pull harder.

"I don't want to hurt you."

If I'd spoken to the prince in the commanding tone my gesture implied, I'd have been jailed for treason. He pulled. The shoe moved ever so slightly. He pulled harder. I thanked the fates that my forced muteness kept me from screaming aloud.

Silk stockings tore, and took a layer of my sole with them. One shoe slid free. Theodore looked up at me and grinned.

"One more, and then you can help me with this cursed coronet." He tugged at it. "It looks made of the same stuff as your shoes, and it won't come off either. I may have to shave myself bald. Your other foot, please."

Just as he took hold of the second shoe, the palace clock began to chime midnight.

What had my fairy godmother said about midnight? I was hardly falling upon Theodore and declaring him my one true love. Surely thwarting the Fae's plan couldn't be as simple as not getting betrothed tonight?

Then the pain started. Not one thorn. Dozens, digging deeper by the second. Blood trickled down my forehead. The prince dropped my foot.

"Good God! Ella!"

I clawed at the wreath. Petals flew, but the thorns clamped down. They were going to kill me unless I begged Theodore to marry me right that instant. I'd be able to speak those words, I knew.

I ran. If the thorns were going to impale me, better somewhere far from here, where I couldn't succumb to the curse. And where Theodore wouldn't have to watch my punishment.

I've scalded myself with boiling fat and burnt myself on red-hot iron, but nothing hurt as badly as those thorns, unless it was my flayed foot. Half blinded from blood and the sudden change from bright ballroom to night, I stumbled from the castle's paved paths onto cooler grass. My head and foot were both on fire. Surely thorns couldn't pierce my skull?

The last chime faded away. I'd done it. I might bleed to death now, but I was free of my fairy godmother.

"Look at you, you naughty girl. You've gotten blood all over your pretty dress."

My godmother's voice dripped poisoned honey. Her hands gripped my arm, pulled me forward.

"Most girls dream of marrying a prince. Of course, you're not most girls. You're the seventh generation of a hopelessly romantic family. Wishes right down the family tree, in every generation. Everything was going so well, until your mother died before her wish came true. Do you know what happens when you leave a wish unfulfilled?"

I didn't know, and I didn't care. My head spun. My body felt too heavy to carry, and wintery cold. And it had all been for nothing.

I expected my fairy godmother to strike me dead, or at least turn me into something slimy and easily squashed. Instead, she led me to a cottage and pushed an overstuffed chair under me before I collapsed.

"This will never do," she said. I felt both revulsion and dizzying relief as the thorns slipped from my skin and the crown of roses crumbled to dust. The remaining shoe dropped from my stinging foot.

"Playing hard to get? That really isn't necessary. Oh, don't expect me to believe that you were really running away! You two were getting along so well, dancing so close, whispering sweet nothings to each other. You're really quite fond of the boy, I can tell. You'll have just enough time to get yourself prettied up before he arrives. The washroom's in there. I'll take care of the dress. Go on now."

I didn't move. Some part of me took satisfaction from the small defiance. Most of me was just plain exhausted.

My fairy godmother's lips thinned. Her mirrored eyes tried to lock onto me. I closed mine.

"Very well."

She didn't touch me, but the air around me might as well have grown hands. Something swept through my hair, combing out the tangles and sticky blood, and leaving it smooth. I felt bathed in air, cleansed and once again rose-scented. I sighed and opened my eyes.

That fluffy cloud of a dress was back, and infuriatingly spotless. The shoes were gone, thank goodness. So was the flowery crown, but I had a horrible suspicion that the invisible hands would find some other way of making me obey. Something that wouldn't leave bloodstains on the dress.

Despite my godmother's glare, I actually started drifting off. I woke at the pounding on the door.

My godmother didn't move to open it. She just stood there smiling while a royal guardsman kicked it open and Prince Theodore rushed in, my discarded slipper in his hand.

"How nice of you to return my property, your Highness," she said.

"Ella! You're as pale as paper. And there's blood in this shoe. Are you all right?"

I smiled, tried to stand to greet him, and fell back into the chair.

"Poor thing." My fairy godmother sighed. "It's every girl's dream to dance with a prince. She must be overwhelmed from awe."

"From blood loss, more likely." Theodore caught my hands in his. His were so warm. "Let her go."

My fairy godmother laughed. "I'm not keeping her!" The door slammed shut. The bolt slid home. Outside, I could hear frantic guardsmen pounding on oak. "I'm keeping both of you. Just until you agree to marry each other."

Now I sprang up. Rage can work wonders for blood loss. Theodore's hand went to his hip—he'd clearly rushed out without a sword, and was regretting it.

"Two families making wishes for generation after generation...Your Highness, haven't you wished for a girl unlike the court beauties? And what girl wouldn't wish to have you for a husband? Would it would be so dreadful to grant my goddaughter's wish? If you offer, I'll grant her leave to say I Do."

"What would be dreadful, Madam, would be to grant your wish. Dreadful for the entire kingdom."

The coronet flared. Theodore gasped. His hands flew instinctively to pull off the burning circlet and jerked away, blistered. The smell of burnt hair overpowered the scent of roses. I stamped my foot.

"What is it, my dear? You want this charming young man to marry you? To grant your wish?"

I didn't look at her. I looked at Theodore, willing him to understand what I was trying to tell him. At the word "wish," I nodded vigorously.

You don't grow up to be a successful prince without being able to pick up on nuances. Prince Theodore went down on one knee before me.

"Miss Ella," he said, as charmingly as he could manage despite the pain, "would you give me the honor of granting your greatest wish?"

My fairy godmother looked ready to burst with triumph. The band on my throat loosened.

"I do!" I shouted.

Prince Theodore ripped off the coronet—now dull—and flung it away. The frilly gown became my old brown dress and apron. The cottage door crashed open, and the guardsmen grabbed hold of my fairy godmother. She twisted in their grip, looking incredulous.

"So that's what happens when a wish goes unfulfilled," I said. It felt so good to speak aloud again! "It limits your power. That's why you wanted me back before midnight. And when your victims actually say no to you...well, I doubt you have the power to turn a pumpkin into pie right now."

"But...you said 'I Do!' I granted your wish!"

"My late mother's wish, not mine. My wish is to become the prince's chef, not his wife. No offense meant, your Highness."

"None taken. I do hope that you are capable of turning pumpkins into pies?"

"Absolutely."

"Then I'll officially welcome you to my staff tomorrow." He gestured to the guardsmen to take the fuming fairy godmother away.

"You look better in the apron," said the Prince. "More like yourself. I don't mean that disrespectfully..."

"I understand, Your Highness. And you're right. I feel more like myself."

We looked anywhere but at each other.

"It might not have been so bad, granting your mother's wish," he said.

"Maybe not. But I suppose there are alliances and things to be considered."

"There always are. Miss Ella?"

"Yes, Your Highness?"

"Please, call me Theodore. I give you official permission."

"Thank you...Theodore."

No, it wouldn't have been so bad, if it hadn't been for the fairy's machinations. Perhaps in a few years...

I bowed, and Theodore and I headed back to the castle. Home. I smiled.

One wish at a time.

WHERE THERE'S SMOKE

by Michael H. Payne

As I promised in the Introduction, here is another story in the continuing adventures of Cluny and her familiars. Michael is still a library clerk, college radio host, church cantor/guitarist, and webcartoonist, but he is now also a recipient of the *Kevin O'Donnell, Jr. Service to SFWA Award*, for 20 years of "keeping a desultory eye on SFWA's Circulating Book Plan." That's not as easy as he makes it sound, so congratulations are well deserved. This year's Cluny story harkens back to her first two adventures: "Familiars," originally published in SWORD AND SORCERESS 19 and reprinted in THE URSA MAJOR AWARDS ANTHOLOGY, and "Immolation," originally published in the Ursa Major follow-up anthology WHAT HAPPENS NEXT. Both these collections are available from Furplanet Books.

Sudden crackling twitched Cluny's ears, memories sparking through her of harvesting termites from the fallen trees back home on her parents' nut farm.

The sound kept growing louder, though, its vibrations taking on a supernatural edge that prickled her fur and pulled her out of her notes. Looking up from the floor in front of the bookcase where she lay sprawled across Magistrix Gosstelain's treatise on the numenistic forces inherent within the mind/brain interface, she said, "Uhh, guys? I think we might have a—"

A cabbage-sized mass of flame burst into the air above Crocker's desk, made him cry out and nearly tip over in his chair. "The fools!" came a shout, and Shtasith whooshed from the fireplace, his black and gold wings flaring. "They shall rue this attempted invasion of our inmost sanctum!"

But the fireball vanished with a camphor-scented pop, an envelope drifting down to settle on top of the evocation problem

Cluny had given Crocker to solve. "Huh," he said, picking the envelope up. "Anybody expecting any mail?"

Cluny scurried over the carpet, grabbed Crocker's robe, and swung herself onto the desk's blotter pad, her whiskers still ringing from the sheer—and unnecessary—amount of power she'd just felt flexing, piercing, and resealing the very structure of time and space, all apparently to drop off a letter. "Careful, Crocker," she said, flicking her claws to summon the basic defensive spells the last few months had taught her to always have standing by.

He was squinting close at the envelope. "It's addressed to you, Cluny. And it's from—" His eyes moved to where the return address should be and went wide, his scent souring with fear. "OK, that's it. We're doomed."

Shtasith swooped over to land on Crocker's shoulder. "Silence, simian! Your histrionics do nothing but bring shame upon—" His neck snaked down to the envelope, and his eyes went wide as well. "This cannot be!" he hissed.

Unable to keep from scowling, Cluny cleared her throat. Crocker's panicked gaze jumped to her, then he slapped the envelope onto the blotter pad, his hands springing away like it had suddenly become burning hot. The wavering letters in the center did indeed spell out *Novice Cluny, Huahuo House, Huxley College*. But the three words written in the upper left-hand corner made Cluny's every hair stand on end.

"The Ifriti Ranee, is it?" Master Gollantz nodded at the envelope still lying where Crocker had slid it across his desk. "You haven't opened it, I see."

"No, sir." Cluny fiddled with the edge of the pocket she'd sewn for herself along the front of Crocker's robes, her human familiar shivering where he sat, Shtasith draped over Crocker's shoulders like he was trying to hide his serpentine body behind Crocker's head. "I mean, considering what happened the *last* time we were in the Realms of Fire, I...well, we may have panicked a little."

The Magister Magistrorum's brambly eyebrows rose, and

Cluny felt her ears blush as she recalled their frenzied rush to the administration building: her clinging to Crocker's robes, the letter wrapped in the strongest ward bubble she could muster; Crocker sprinting with the bubble tucked under one arm like someone much more athletically inclined; Shtasith darting ahead of them bugling, "Make way, imbeciles! Make way!"

Fortunately, at 3:30 on the afternoon of the autumnal equinox, the campus was far from crowded—orientation week didn't even start for another ten days, and classes wouldn't kick in till the week after *that*. Besides, Cluny figured that everyone expected odd behavior from Terrence Crocker, by all accounts both the most powerful and the most disturbed wizardry student Huxley had seen in centuries. And yes, those accounts were wrong in almost every respect, but one thing she'd learned from Shtasith over the past six months was how useful other people's misapprehensions could sometimes be....

"As I recall," Master Gollantz said, tapping one long finger on the desk beside the envelope and snapping Cluny's attention back to the here and now, "the Ifriti Ranee declared you blameless for what happened while you were disposing of the magical water you'd left all over her magma fields." A tight smile twitched his beard. "I've even heard it said that the ifrit who was killed in the flood that day was not exactly her Majesty's favorite person. Perhaps you knew Lord Hypabyssal while you were a denizen of the Fire Realms, Shtasith?"

"No!" The firedrake exploded from the back of Crocker's neck, his wings beating faster than a hummingbird's, Cluny's link to him suddenly a tiny, itchy sandstorm in the back of her brain. The feeling was gone immediately, though, Shtasith's snout curling as he settled unruffled onto Crocker's shoulder again. "Do not sully the air of your lungs with that creature's name, Master Gollantz! His final annihilation can only have brought good to the Elemental Planes, and I am proud to be associated with those who take the credit for that deed!"

Cluny blinked up at him, and Crocker gave him a sideways glance, too. "So, what?" he asked, waving a hand at the envelope. "You think they're inviting us to a party?"

Shtasith's snout curled even more, but Master Gollantz clearing his throat stopped any further comments. "Tell me, Novice Cluny." The magister pressed his fingertips together. "What do you suppose would be the easiest and most effective way to discover what her Majesty has sent to you here?"

With a swallow, Cluny nodded and scampered down Crocker's robes to Master Gollantz's desk. So much had happened in the eight months since they'd accidentally summoned the Ifriti Ranee, but Cluny would never forget the gaseous stink of the Fire Realms and the panic it inspired in her: slinging spells she scarcely knew that first time to save herself and Crocker from getting sucked into the lava; her Majesty finally grabbing them, dumping them at Master Gollantz's feet, then demanding they return to fix the damage they'd caused; their efforts during that second visit going awry somehow and causing the flood that had killed her Majesty's cousin....

The envelope almost seemed to glow in the afternoon light drifting from the windows lining the walls above Master Gollantz's bookcases; a flex of her claws lifted the thick paper into the air, and a slash split open its top edge. Nothing burst from it—no death magic or fire imps or poison gas or anything—and narrowing her levitation spell, Cluny pulled out a folded piece of parchment.

Not a whisper from her two familiars behind her, but she could feel their magic wrapped around hers, the wonderful warm blanket sensation that came from Crocker and the much spikier power that Shtasith had brought to their partnership. "It's—" She opened the page, turned it so the writing would be right-side up. "—an invitation?"

Master Gollantz sat forward, and Cluny read aloud: "To the Esteemed Novice Cluny, her Two Familiars, and Guest. Your Presence is Requested at a Show Trial to be held in your Honor the Evening of the Autumnal Equinox at Her Majesty's Hall of Justice, downtown Darbijwe, the Fire Realms. Verdict of Not Guilty to be followed by Light Repast and Dancing. Dress: Optional."

A moment of silence, then: "Huh," from Crocker. "I guess it

is a party."

"It's not a party," Cluny said for what had to have been the fourteenth time.

Crocker frowned from under the floppy green hat he'd conjured atop his head and tapped the invitation resting on the desk's blotter pad. "It says 'light repast and dancing,' Cluny." He jerked his chin at the fireplace. "Besides, the Teakettle says they do show trials all the *time* in the Realms of Fire! And it's not like we hafta worry about them finding us guilty when her Majesty already said we aren't!"

Glancing at the fireplace, Cluny squirmed, feeling itchy again. Master Gollantz had volunteered to come along as their guest, an offer Cluny had immediately and gratefully accepted, and Shtasith had made several vaguely reassuring comments on the walk home about how her Majesty's will was law in the Fire Realms and how she never reneged on a promise. But Master Gollantz had looked especially grim as he'd told them he'd be by their dorm room promptly at 6:30, and Shtasith had zoomed straight into the chimney when they'd gotten back, his fiery power all banked and broody in the back of Cluny's head.

She blew out a breath. Too many times recently, Cluny had seen how the idea of an animal wizard with a human familiar drove seemingly rational beings to odd and sometimes dangerous behavior, and with someone as powerful and capricious as the Ifriti Ranee knowing her secret, she would need the support of her two closest friends now more than ever. "Shtasith?" she called. "Master Gollantz will be here soon if...if there's anything you need to say that you don't want him to hear."

"What?" Crocker looked from Cluny to the fireplace. "You think he's not telling us ev'rything?"

"I don't know," Cluny had to admit. She waved a paw, tried to straighten the weirdly fluttering strands of power connecting her to the firedrake, and raised her voice again. "Please, Shtasith. Is there any reason we *shouldn't* accept her Majesty's invitation?"

"We have no choice," that sibilant voice echoed from the

smoke-darkened bricks. “One of the four elemental rulers of all creation has summoned us. We can no more resist her than we can stop the sun from rising.”

Cluny blinked, but Crocker gave another of his little snorts. “OK, first? That whole ‘four elemental rulers of creation’ thing is pretty much bogus. I mean, just because she’s in charge of the Fire Realms doesn’t make the Ifriti Ranee any closer to the divine wellspring of the universe or whatever. And second, Shtasith, you don’t keep secrets from us! You *can’t*! We’re all three in this thing together, and, well—” He stopped, looked over at Cluny. “It might be you don’t know about the standfast spell.” He cocked his head and shrugged.

A chill rustled Cluny’s fur as she realized what Crocker must be planning. She wasn’t sure she liked it, but after half a heartbeat, she nodded. Crocker nodded back, strode across the room, and squatted in front of the hearthstone. “You listening, Teakettle?” Leaning forward, he reached up the chimney, and Cluny couldn’t keep from wincing at the squawk that followed, Crocker wrenching Shtasith out with a scattering of soot.

“Unhand me, simian!” But Crocker had apparently learned a few things, too, in the time Shtasith had been with them: a glowing net sprang from his hands to wrap around the firedrake, Shtasith squirming unsuccessfully against it. “This indignity will not go unanswered! I shall fall upon you when you sleep, and I promise you I shall then—!”

“You’ll listen!” Crocker’s voice, cold and sharp, bit at Cluny’s ears. But she kept them upright and tried her best to look as serious as Crocker sounded. “The standfast spell’s so basic, they teach it here first semester, back before me and Cluny had even figured out she was the wizard and I was the familiar.” He jabbed a finger into Shtasith’s snout, the firedrake’s eyes red and spinning. “It’s simple, but it lets wizards crack open the heads of their familiars and rummage around inside. It feels like white-hot knives slicing into you and your wizard both, but it shows her everything you ever thought and everything you ever did. *Everything*.”

Shtasith’s eyes got even wider. “You...you cannot be

serious!" He craned his neck, peered through the glowing mesh of the net at Cluny. "Mistress! Chastise the simian for his untruthfulness!"

This time, she didn't have to fake her scowl. "What did you call me?"

"Not mistress! Cluny, I mean!" His magic fizzed and sparked. "But this is madness! How can such a spell exist?? And how—??" His sudden fear burst like chalk dust against her whiskers. "How could you ever...ever—?"

"She had to." Crocker shivered, and Cluny almost told him to drop the whole ploy. Except, well, the panic radiating from Shtasith convinced her that he really *was* hiding something they needed to know.... "The second time we went to the Fire Realms," Crocker was going on. "We had to undo this spell I'd cast, but since I had no idea what I'd done, Cluny and Master Gollantz couldn't unravel it. The Ifriti Ranee was gonna kill us if we didn't, though, so Cluny had to...had to claw through my brain to get at the info." His voice broke. "Trust me, Teakettle, you do *not* wanna make her do that to you."

None of which was a lie exactly, but the growing terror on Shtasith's face made Cluny take a breath. "That's not quite what happened that day."

"True," Shtasith said, his voice trembling. "In fact, my Cluny, even *you* do not truly know what happened that day. For while I have meant these past months to relate the tale, no opportunity ever presented itself, and I reassured myself that, since we would never likely encounter the Ifriti Ranee, I had no urgent necessity to drag you into—"

A loud knock stopped him, the door rattling and swinging open to reveal Master Gollantz in the hallway, his black and purple formal robes more severe-looking than Cluny remembered. "Novices? It's time."

The transport spell Master Gollantz constructed in their room was the same one he'd built in his office when he'd taken them to the Fire Realms on their second trip. But even though Cluny could see and understand more of its intricate structure this time, she still felt very much the novice watching a master at work.

She found it so fascinating, it almost distracted her from Shtasith, physically coiled along Crocker's shoulders above her and aetherically pressing into her brain as jagged as a pawful of shattered glass. Her tail twitching, her claws digging into the cloth of Crocker's breast pocket, she wanted to stop Master Gollantz, ask him to step outside for a moment till Shtasith could tell them whatever had happened between him and the Ifriti Ranee, but, well, they were on a schedule, and—

"Novices?" Master Gollantz stood among the invisibly glowing balusters of the transport spell, his hand raised to grasp the section of empty air where the trigger rested. "Might I suggest you bring the invitation? One ought not to take chances when the rulers of realms are involved."

Cluny braced herself, Crocker turning, reaching for the parchment, tucking it into one of his side pockets. Master Gollantz nodded, took the trigger, and pulled it downward, the very fabric of reality unzipping as it moved, the wooden paneled walls and off-white curtains of their still sparsely-decorated dorm room peeling away to reveal—

A cacophony of color, searing reds, yellows, and oranges swirling to fill the space around her, the hot, dry, brimstone-laced air digging into Cluny's lungs like it wanted to suck every bit of moisture out of her. Shouting, chanting, screaming hit her next, her ears pulling flat against her head, her whiskers sweeping every protection spell she'd ever even considered learning out to surround herself and her familiars to stop whatever was going on here from overwhelming them and—

"Welcome!" a blast-furnace of a voice roared.

Forcing herself to settle down, Cluny managed to focus on what was actually happening instead of what her jittering nerves were telling her: banners, she could see now, in every fiery shade billowing from the marble walls of the room where they'd appeared, the black and white stone floor strewn with some sort of flower petals, shimmering like the first golden touch of dawn on a summer morning. Nothing that was going to kill them, in other words, and dialing her panic back one more step allowed her to make out the rows of ifriti, phoenixes, imps and other more globular elemental types standing below the banners and cheering, smiles on the faces of those who had faces.

And at the far end of the room, rising from her throne like a volcanic eruption given humanoid shape, the Ifriti Ranee spread the magma flow of her arms, the hooting and applause cutting off almost immediately. "Exactly on time, too, Cluny, Crocker, and Shtasith! And how lovely! I see you've brought Hieronymus Gollantz as your guest!"

"Your Majesty." Master Gollantz bowed, and when Cluny's still-shaky sense of balance started skewing, she realized with a quick stab of relief that it was just Crocker bowing, too. "It is truly an honor to be in your presence once again."

"Of course it is!" Her Majesty glided forward, the lava from her chest down suddenly seizing up to form a pumice-gray gown over her hourglass figure; a snap of her blazing fingers, though, and the gown burst into a vibrant, flamingo pink. "And on this celebratory occasion, all such positive emotions shall be doubled and then trebled!" She planted her big fists on her hips and let out a laugh as robust as a fusillade of cannons. "Perhaps even quadrupled for you, Novice Crocker, considering the absolutely and entirely appropriate headgear with which you have adorned yourself!"

Swallowing, Cluny stared up at her Majesty—taller than most of the trees back home, she was fairly sure—and wanted with every shiver of her heart to believe all this good humor. But Shtasith's touch in her head, normally a leaping flame of energy, guttered like a nearly-quenched wick, and Cluny found she could barely summon a smile.

Fortunately, Crocker didn't seem to be feeling quite so oppressed. "You're too kind, your Majesty," he said, and Cluny almost found herself grinning when he pushed his ridiculous hat a little farther forward over his dark, curly hair. "*Some* of my colleagues were a little worried that maybe a hat of this caliber wouldn't sit well in a 'court of law' situation. But I'm glad to know that my inherent sense of fashion was once again right on the money."

The withering look Master Gollantz gave Crocker forced a chuckle from Cluny's throat, and her Majesty clapped her hands. "*That's* the spirit! Come, and we shall begin this evening's festivities!" A flick of her wrist blasted magma into the wall behind the throne, that whole side of the room shattering like fire-ravaged wood to reveal a courtyard outside. Open glass carriages hitched to gigantic bombardier beetles stood in serried ranks under a sky about as dark, Cluny figured, as it ever got in the Realms of Fire. "Let us away to the Hall of Justice!" her Majesty continued, striding for the hole she'd just made. "Our three guests of honor shall ride with me, and the rest of you will follow!"

Moving in her Majesty's wake, Cluny felt very glad she wasn't walking. At least Crocker had worn his good boots, she noted, and bracing herself in his breast pocket, she cast an extra layer of protection magic over his hands as he scrambled down the tumbled chunks of marble to the courtyard below. The heat rising from the stones due to her Majesty's passage made Cluny's whiskers sweat, so she quickly summoned up several cooling spells as well: living with Shtasith had made learning them *very* necessary.

Speaking of whom—Turning, she dug her claws into the front of Crocker's robes and stretched herself up to his left shoulder, the firedrake's wedge of a head tucked there against Crocker's neck, his normally solid black eyes flecked with red and darting around like he was tracking multiple targets. "Shtasith," she whispered, "all that stuff Crocker was saying about the standfast spell! You've got to know I would never do anything to hurt—!"

"Foolishness!" His sharp but quiet hiss struck her almost as hard as a slap. "We must discard such pointless thoughts, my Cluny, and be vigilant instead! All here is not as it seems!"

She blinked at him, but before she could ask any of the questions that started popping into her head, the jerky ride leveled out, and she craned her neck around to see that Crocker had arrived at the base of the Ifriti Ranee's landslide, a blue flame of an imp pulling open the door of the nearest glass carriage for her Majesty. Except it wasn't *glass*, Cluny realized from the way the light of her Majesty's lava refracted through the thing: each and every one of the several dozen carriages lined up here had to be carved from solid diamond.

"Come!" her Majesty said again, settling onto the carriage's single bench and giving the space to her right a surprisingly delicate pat. "I will tell you the order of this evening's events."

Crocker clambered up and sat beside her, the tension Cluny could feel from him so well masked, she doubted anyone not aetherically connected to him would have any idea how phony his grin was. "It's the 'light repast' part *I'm* looking forward to," he said, rubbing his hands together.

The imp closed the door, whooshed to hover over the bombardier beetle, and extruded a whip-like filament of fire. Stroking this against the beetle's flank got the creature scuttling forward, and the carriage rolled smoothly from the courtyard, past a line of diamond-coated fire elementals, and out an arched gateway onto a street, more guards holding back a cheering crowd of wyverns, firebirds and other such folk.

"To begin," her Majesty said, waving a flickering hand, "we shall process in this fashion to the Hall of Justice. There, we will be met by a group of Lord Hypabyssal's former partisans. For the sake of, oh, shall we say domestic tranquility, I have agreed to their demands that I formally exonerate you of any blame in my unfortunate cousin's death only after they've presented their evidence to the contrary."

Cluny's ears folded. "Evidence?"

Her Majesty looked down and smiled in a way that made all of Cluny's nerves scream *predator!* "Fear not. They have not one iota of solid proof." Her smile got wider and even scarier. "Is that not the case, Shtasith?"

The split-second of silence that followed wasn't silent at all, not with the crowd cheering and the carriages rumbling and the bombardier beetles snorting. But it was still as soundless a moment as Cluny had ever known. "As your Majesty says," Shtasith muttered so softly, Cluny didn't think the ranee could've heard it.

Her Majesty nodded, though, her smile now more triumphant than anything else, turned to wave to the crowd again, and—

The explosion hit so suddenly and so powerfully, the only warning Cluny got was the word *Shield!* bursting through her brain in Master Gollantz's voice. Her claws flicked half a spell, then a massive weight of water engulfed her, surging over and around and swallowing the entire world.

Stomping down her chittering panic, she completed the motions, felt the shield bubble form above her breastbone, grabbed it with her magic, and pumped. Ozone-sharp air struck her whiskers, and she gasped it in, her panic sinking a bit further when two more gasps from above and behind told her that Crocker and Shtasith were both inside the shield and alive. "What's happening??" Crocker shouted.

But Shtasith shouted louder. "Unensorcelled water! It will absorb and dissipate every ounce of her Majesty's—!"

A muffled clap of thunder, and the water vanished, shouts and screams tangling in her ears along with Master Gollantz's voice suddenly right there beside her: "Cluny! Crocker! Shtasith! Are you unharmed??"

His voice gave her something to grab onto, something to use as an anchor to keep her mind from spinning completely out of control. Because filling the carriage seat next to Crocker, the spot where the Ifriti Ranee had been sitting a moment before, was nothing but a cold and inert lump of basalt.

"Impossible!" Master Gollantz shouted over the uproar. He leaped to his feet at the stone slab that served as the defendant's table, and Cluny, huddled inside Crocker's breast pocket, found she couldn't stop shivering. Not that her fur or his robes were still wet after two hours in a courtroom packed with sapient chunks of lava and other fiery folk. But being charged with regicide, she'd discovered pretty quickly, wasn't doing her already jangled nerves any good at all.

From the carved obsidian throne looming ahead of Cluny and to her right, the new Ifriti Ranee banged her stone gavel, her lava a pale and gangly spurt when compared to the former Ifriti

Ranee—Lady Felsic had been the previous ranee's second cousin twice removed or something, but Cluny didn't really remember much of the quick coronation ceremony earlier. She was only now starting to think again, she realized, after the shock of the attack and the announcement by the city coroner that the several tons of water had so quickly and completely denuded her Majesty of magic that she was now irretrievably dead.

Those watching in the gallery quieted slowly, and the prosecutor, an ifrit with a diamond pince-nez, raised one molten eyebrow. "I hope you'll forgive me, Magister Gollantz," he drawled, "but I fail to see the distinction you seem to be—"

"Novice Cluny," Master Gollantz interrupted with a wave of his hand, "is indeed one of the most powerful students of wizardry I've ever had the pleasure to mentor, but she and her familiars are just that: students! Not only hadn't they a *reason* to attack the former ranee, they hadn't the *ability*! The spell I felt forming out there—!"

"These so-called students." Her Majesty didn't have her predecessor's sheer volume, but her voice still carried easily though the overheated air. "Were they not the ones who summoned the flood of water that killed my cousin, Lord Hypabyssal?"

Master Gollantz turned to her, and Cluny could almost smell the effort it took him not to yell. "Yes, your Majesty, they are. But—"

"Then how," she cut in, "can you maintain that they could not have summoned the flood of water that has just killed my cousin, our former ranee?"

Master Gollantz began speaking then about spell levels, about the magnitude of the magic used in this attack, about how Cluny currently lacked the control to deliberately overcome the natural defenses of *any* fully-grown ifrit, let alone an ifrit who had ruled the entirety of the Fire Realms for close to six hundred years, but Cluny found she couldn't concentrate, overwhelmingly glad that the magister had come along with them: she never would have guessed that he was fully accredited as an attorney in all the Elemental Planes.

But then *everything* had gotten so difficult to believe all of a sudden! How could the Ifriti Ranee have been so utterly destroyed? And who could've done it? And what did it mean that they'd chosen the same method that Cluny and Crocker had accidentally used on Lord Hypabyssal eight months ago?

The more she thought about these questions, the itchier she got. Clearly, she was being set up, but she just didn't have enough information to draw any further conclusions. Of course, she did have a source of information huddled along the back of Crocker's neck, but in order to talk with him openly, she would need to—

Not giving herself time to reconsider, she straightened in Crocker's pocket, reached her paws up as if she were stretching, touched claws to both Crocker and Shtasith's chins, and cast the standfast spell.

When she'd done this before, the sensory illusion that had resulted had been one of being swept away in a raging river, but this time, she felt herself blasted sideways by a massive gust of wind, a cyclone suddenly whirling her away, trying to spin her ears over tail through a gray and cloud-choked sky.

None of it was real, she knew, so she centered herself, drew the buffeting air into her lungs, pirouetted in place, and blew the power of it out between her teeth, used it to propel her imaginary body backwards in an arc till the swirl of her inner ear told her she was rushing downward, something dark and seemingly solid forming beneath her. A flick of her whiskers made the wind spin her again, and she landed on all fours, the bare stone floor cracking under the impact of her claws.

Looking up, she saw the same small unfurnished room that she'd fetched up in the *last* time she'd cast this spell, the sky outside the arched glass doorway to her right a sheer, afternoon blue. She puffed a breath, heard two more gasps, and glancing to her left, she saw Crocker and Shtasith each sitting up in a corner of the room, her familiars now both exactly as tall as the other, either Crocker shrunk to firedrake size or Shtasith grown to just shy of six feet long.

Of course, the spell had again made her a little larger than them, and pushing herself onto her hind legs, Cluny couldn't help grinning at their wide-eyed stares. "Ummm," Crocker said after a few heartbeats. "You're not gonna kiss me again, are you?"

Cluny folded her arms. "Am I going to have to?"

That got a little grin from *him*, and he cocked his head. "It's just I was thinking how it might be even more awkward this time, what with three of us being here and all."

"Where—?" Shtasith's neck ridges were fully extended, his wings quivering behind him. "What is this place? I...we're within a magical construct of some sort, aren't we?"

She stepped toward him, motioned with one paw for Crocker to join them, then rested the other paw on Shtasith's forearm. "We're inside the standfast spell," she told him. "While we're here, time hardly passes outside, but someone in that courtroom will notice pretty quickly that I'm working magic. So we need to know *now*, Shtasith." She reached for Crocker's shoulder when he came up beside them, and without her even prompting him, he set a hand on the firedrake's other arm. "What were you saying back in the room before Master Gollantz interrupted you?"

Shtasith swung his head back and forth between them, then lowered it with a sigh. "I spent my first twenty years as her Majesty's private immolator, and on her orders...it was *I* who sabotaged your spell eight months ago, my Cluny, and killed Lord Hypabyssal." His head snapped back up, his fear so thick and sour, Cluny couldn't keep her whiskers from folding. "It was before I'd ever met you, and her Majesty—" His voice broke. "She banished me from the Fire Realms to save herself and me from the wrath of Lord Hypabyssal's partisans." His neck ridges began to flex like spiny little wings. "They've obviously discerned my involvement in his death and are striking at all around me in their attempt to garner vengeance."

"Huh." Crocker looked at her, his mouth sideways. "So whadda we do? Throw the Teakettle at 'em and run?"

"Actually?" Cluny tapped her claws against Shtasith's scales, the firedrake's words connecting in her mind with what Master Gollantz had been saying earlier about the raw power this attack would have required. "We might need to make it look like we're doing that. I'll just—" Swallowing, she looked down at her two familiars, both dearer to her than anyone else she'd ever known. "I'll need you guys to trust me."

They both answered at the same time: "Well, yeah!" from Crocker, and "Of course!" from Shtasith.

She squeezed their shoulders. "'Cause I'm pretty sure—"

Magical discharge spiked her fur, and the air itself cracked, shattering around her, Cluny slapped backwards by Master Gollantz's voice shouting, "Novice Cluny!"

Back inside Crocker's breast pocket, she blinked at the magister's angry face, the ifrit prosecutor glaring behind him. "Might I recommend, novice," he continued, even drier than the dehumidified heat of the courtroom, "that when your life is at stake, you endeavor to remain focused on the here and now?"

Nodding, Cluny forced away all her doubts—if she was right, she had to act quickly while the remnants of the standfast spell still connected her so intimately to her familiars—and said, "Yes, sir. It's just...I have new information I must present!"

A quiet sigh from the new ranee. "If this is some ploy to display your clients' childishness, Magister Gollantz, I—"

"If it please the court!" Leaping from Crocker's pocket to the stone slab of the table, Cluny flared her power and, popping off a prayer to the gods of evocation that she'd understood the basics of Magistrix Gosstelain's theory about the magical properties of the mind/brain interface, she dug deep into Crocker, deep into Shtasith, deep into herself, threw out a massive matrix of energy pulled from their unique three-way connection, and coupled it to the fireball spell she'd developed for Crocker during their first semester, the spell that had accidentally summoned the Ifriti Ranee to their dorm room. "I bid your Majesty appear!" Cluny shouted.

Every square inch of the courtroom burst into flame for an instant, but, well, since nearly everyone there was *already* on fire in some way or another, the only cries Cluny heard were from herself and her two familiars as invisible knives slashed through her and sprayed their power out like blood from a ripped-open artery. Collapsing, Cluny fought to stay conscious, heard a rumble from her left, snapped her head over, and saw the air crack the way it had when Master Gollantz had nullified her standfast spell. The cracks widened, a layer of empty space crumbling away, and there in the front corner of the courtroom stood the former Ifriti Ranee, rage contorting her glowering face, her fists bunching and her muscles bulging.

"Court's adjourned!" her Majesty shouted, and she swooped forward, those fists wrapping around Cluny, crushing her with a pain like none she'd ever known.

"You little vermin." The voice was gentle, nearly a caress amidst the waves of agony wracking Cluny. "That a thing such as you would dare set itself against me—"

"No!" The pain was real, Cluny knew, but not somatic; she was lying unbroken on a stone floor, her physical senses told her, the Ifriti Ranee towering above her while Shtasith and Crocker sprawled to her left. But the fiery tendrils of her Majesty's wrath biting and clawing along her every nerve paralyzed her: just moving her jaw to get that one word out made her want to start screaming again.

"No?" Her Majesty crouched, a smile parting the magma of her face. "You contradict me now?"

A fresh inferno roared through Cluny, and this time she let herself scream: "Please! You can have him! Just let us go and you can have him!"

The whole world seemed to freeze, then the tides of torment pulled back the barest inch. "I beg your pardon?" those gentle tones asked.

Offering a prayer to the Squirrel Mother that this would work—"Shtasith," Cluny panted. "This has all been about him, hasn't it? About you getting him back?" She struggled to push herself onto her hind legs so she could turn and bow raggedly to the Ifriti Ranee. "Let Crocker and me go, and I'll sever our connection, renounce my claim, and disavow him as my familiar."

Another frozen moment, and every last wisp of pain whisked

away, let Cluny gasp in her first full breath in she didn't know how long. Their gasps once again let Cluny know that Crocker and Shtasith were largely unhurt, but she didn't look over, didn't move her attention from the black and white of the granite floor.

"You can truly release him?" the ranee asked. "And let me assure you, mortal, that any attempted tricks on your part will almost definitely cause me to become upset."

The clench in Cluny's stomach relaxed a hair's breadth, but things could still go disastrously wrong...."Master Gollantz will be able to confirm what I'm saying, your Majesty."

"Which makes me even *more* suspicious." From the corner of her eye, Cluny saw the black claws of her Majesty's feet dig into the stone. "Still..."

A rustle like a breeze through an autumn tree, and the wonderful scent of old books washed over her. "Cluny!" Master Gollantz cried out. "Your Majesty! I must protest this treatment of my student! She's done nothing—!"

"Oh, now, *really*, Gollantz." Something that might have been respect crept into her Majesty's voice. "You and I have known each other far too long for such bluster. So just answer me: can this student of yours in fact disavow Shtasith as her familiar and set him free?"

Still not daring to look up, Cluny felt her various internal clenches tighten. Master Gollantz wouldn't lie. He *couldn't*. Everything depended on him telling the truth.

So when he sighed with what could only be resignation, Cluny nearly cheered. "Yes," he said. "The bonds between novices are always loose. I've known students to dismiss five or six familiars before finding a compatible pairing."

"Very well." Smoke wafted down around Cluny. "Release to me my Immolator."

The command pressed against her with a physical weight; dipping her bow a bit deeper, Cluny straightened and turned to Crocker and Shtasith, Crocker flat on his stomach and staring open-mouthed from under that stupid green hat, Shtasith nothing but a ball of scaly legs and tail.

And for all that this was about as right as her haphazard plan could possibly go, she hadn't had a chance to tell either of them what she was doing. Still, with the Ifriti Ranee's gaze focused on her hot enough to make her whiskers start sweating again, all Cluny could do was trust them. "I'm so, so sorry, Shtasith," she whispered, and with a flick of her claws, she cut the threads of power between them, staggered sideways when the sweet, strong force of him wrenched away from her.

"Oh!" The shadows in the room stretched as the ranee moved to Cluny's side, Cluny swaying, looking up at the lava of her Majesty's eyes swirling more brightly. "I definitely felt *that*." She sniffed the air and nodded. "Honestly done, Novice Cluny. And now that my Immolator is back in my service, all will be well again. You may go."

"No."

At first, Cluny thought the word had escaped her own throat, her body rebelling at the horrible, lopsided feel of the magic sloshing through her. But with only the warm, steady grip of Crocker's power keeping her upright, she knew she couldn't've spoken, and the way Crocker and Master Gollantz were staring at Shtasith, the firedrake unrolling to glare at the Ifriti Ranee—

"I beg your pardon?" her Majesty asked.

Shtasith leaped from the floor, his wings a blur, and swooped to hover in the sulfurous air between Cluny and the Ifriti Ranee. "I will not serve you, your Majesty," he said. "Not should you fall to your knees and *beg*."

Shock seeped across the ranee's face like water freezing a magma flow, and Shtasith crooked a needle-sized claw at her. "I loved you once and called you my Queen. But you merely used that love, absorbed it, and weakened me to such an extent that when you at last betrayed and abandoned me, I was unable to do anything but betray and abandon you in return."

He dropped to the floor beside Cluny, and she found her heart was fluttering even faster than his wings had been. "In loving my Cluny, however, I have found a friend and a partner—" Whirling, he wrapped his coils around her, Cluny gasping as he hoisted her aloft and settled with her on Crocker's back. "*Two* friends and partners! And the strength they have allowed me to cultivate within myself, it will brook neither betrayal nor abandonment!" His snaky neck snapped his head around, his solid black gaze hitting Cluny's as welcome as a summer breeze, and his power sprang back into place, plugging the holes within her. "So you will *not* disavow me, my Cluny! Neither now nor in the future!"

"Yes!" Crocker shouted. Stretched out on the stone floor beneath them, he slapped a palm, vanished in a shower of sparks, and reappeared sitting cross-legged in nearly the same place, his arms flailing out to scoop Cluny and Shtasith against his chest. "You *tell* 'em, Teakettle!"

Complete once more, Cluny let herself bask in the feeling for two seconds, then she wriggled free from most of Crocker's grasp and shoved herself around to look up, up, up at the Ifriti Ranee, her molten complexion darkening, the temperature and air pressure in the room suddenly spiking upward.

Unable to keep her ears from folding, all Cluny could do was hope. After all, trusting Crocker and Shtasith was one thing. But having to trust the ranee after everything she'd already tried to do to them today?

Several more seconds drifted by, Cluny not looking away from her Majesty's eyes, glowering like the last coals of an abandoned bonfire. Then—"Take them away, Gollantz," the Ifriti Ranee said, her voice also ashes. "See to it that they do not return."

The room went fuzzy around her, then became the first room they'd appeared in all those hours ago, the banners limp against the walls, a team of salamanders busily rebuilding the wall behind her Majesty's throne.

Crocker clambered to his feet, and Cluny let herself slide down the front of his robe into her waiting pocket with a sigh. "Stay awake, Novice Cluny," Master Gollantz muttered, stooping to grasp the trigger of his transport spell. "I find I have a few questions concerning this affair."

That got a groan from Crocker and a hiss from Shtasith, but Cluny couldn't keep from laughing. "Tomorrow morning, maybe, sir? So I don't find myself facing a mutiny?"

Barely able to keep her eyes open, Cluny watched Master Gollantz zip the Material Realm's reality back into place before he dismantled the spell. Scowling, he stepped to the door and said, "Nine o'clock in my office, novices. Here's hoping I don't need to call on certain friends of mine in the diplomatic corps to smooth this thing over..."

As soon as the door clicked shut behind the magister, Crocker folded backwards onto the bed, Cluny too exhausted to move from his breast pocket while Shtasith fluttered up just long enough to miss the impact, then dropped to drape himself across Crocker's chest. "OK," Crocker said. "Now that we've seen where me and the Teakettle grew up, I'm gonna propose we spend our vacations at Cluny's folks' nut farm from now on." He raised a hand. "All in favor?"

"Aye," Shtasith breathed, the steam of it rolling gently over Cluny. "But...how did you know, my Cluny?"

"I didn't." She coughed a laugh. "I just couldn't figure out why anyone strong enough to kill her Majesty would want to frame *us*, especially when killing an Elemental Ruler pretty much qualifies you to become an Elemental Ruler yourself."

"Whoa." Crocker's voice: Cluny lolled her head up, saw Shtasith looking back at Crocker, his head propped on his pillow. "We woulda been in charge of the Fire Realms?"

Shtasith snorted. "Once Lady Felsic had taken the throne, she would never have allowed our Cluny to live."

"Exactly." Another little clench twinged Cluny's stomach, but she breathed it away. "As soon as you told us you used to work for the ranee, Shtasith, I realized she staged her own death in order to get you back. Just outright killing me would've caused an interplanar incident, but this way, her successor would *have* to find me guilty and kill me or risk me becoming a symbolic rival for the crown. After I was dead, the ranee could reappear with some story about finally fighting off my spell, retake her title, and get you as well." She smiled at the firedrake. "'Cause everybody wants you on their team."

"Got that right," Crocker said with a yawn.

Shtasith's eyes slitted shut, and Cluny almost thought she could hear him purr. "Thank you," he whispered.

Snuggling deeper into her pocket, Cluny flicked a claw to douse the overhead light and closed her eyes, too.

JUSTICE

by Suzan Harden

Pontius Pilate asked "What is truth?" and finally sent Jesus to die. In this story the question is "What is justice?" along with what role mercy and understanding should play in a "just" decision.

Suzan Harden is the author of the urban fantasy series *Bloodlines*, and she is working hard on the sixth book, ZOMBIE GODDESS. She currently lives in southeastern Texas with a husband who supports her ice cream and book addictions, a kid who thinks she's too enamored with the undead, and a beagle who just wants his belly scratched. That's the nice thing about dogs. Their wants are simple and easy to understand.

The tinkling bells that lined her cloak announced the girl's presence as I ate my breakfast. "Justice Anthea, may I speak with you privately?"

Most Orrin inns were incredibly noisy, but the crowd here grew even more boisterous. It wasn't often a priestess of Love addressed a priestess of Balance in a public business. Not that I could tell if her cloak was the appropriate red silk. At least, not the way most people saw the color. But the clientele went out of their way to speak loudly and ignore us.

The dry musk of pigs underlaid her expensive perfume. I spooned the last bit of eggs into my mouth. Even if her odor hadn't given her away, she didn't bother to sit or give her name as an equal should.

Maybe she was too cocky about her deception. Or she was too frightened.

After dabbing the corners of my mouth, I smiled. I couldn't see her face with the heavy veil she wore, but I delayed long enough to detect her bare hands shift from dark gold to bright orange as they heated with her nervousness.

I should have waited for Luc to return from the bathhouse, but curiosity got the better of me. "Of course, sister." I held out my own hand, which she took and assisted me in rising from the bench. Just as anyone with decency, or the appearance of such, would help a blind woman to her lodging.

We carefully climbed the steps to the room Luc and I rented for the week, her to demonstrate her solicitude to the crowd in the common area, me to maintain the illusion of my sightlessness. Once we gained the second floor and I released my hold on the banister, my free hand slipped into the folds of my robes and grasped the handle of my dagger.

I led the way into the sleeping chamber.

"Justice, I have—"

To anyone else, my actions flowed so fast they would have seemed magic. With a swift kick, I shut the door. Before it slammed, I shoved the girl against the cheap plaster that covered the walls, my left forearm pressed against her throat. The tip of my dagger flipped up her veil before the point settled at the fragile join of her ear and jaw.

I didn't need her sharp gasp to know my hood had fallen back with the speed of my movements.

"Goddess, what are you?" The tremor in her voice matched the rapid throb of her artery under my blade. Everyone expected the milky white orbs of the sightless, like the rest of my order. Only Luc ever had the courage to tell me that no human's eyes were the color of blood.

"A better question is why a pig herder thought she could pass for a priestess of Love."

"Please forgive me, Justice. I didn't know how else to seek your help without the entire town—" Her sob could have been faked.

"You know the penalty for impersonating a priest or priestess of the Twelve," I ground out. "Who did you steal the robes from?"

"I didn't take them! They were my mother's."

I jerked away from the girl. I knew better than to release a potential threat. Thirty years of blasted training.

But her mother hadn't sold her. The way my mother had sold me at the tender age of three winters.

The hiss of steel on leather whispered on the other side of the door. No doubt the inn's patrons had enjoyed telling the story to Luc when he returned from his errand. I touched his mind and warned him of our guest. He sheathed his sword and slipped inside our room.

"Maybe you'd better start at the beginning, child." The rumble of his voice at my back reassured me.

The girl edged around me. "M'lord. I—I need your help. My betrothed has been kidnapped."

Wonderful. A cock-and-bull story. "Why haven't you gone to the magistrate's office?"

Her hair rustled as she looked at me, then back at Luc. "His own parents did the deed, Lord, Lady. He is Marco DiMara."

A bitter laugh erupted from my throat. A pig herder promised to the scion of one of the richest families in all of the land of Issura? "You really expect us to believe that load of—"

Luc cut me off. "You understand I will truth-bind you?"

"Yes, m'Lord." It was the first time I heard confidence in the girl's voice.

In less than three heartbeats, Luc had muttered the words of his spell. Brilliant oranges, reds and yellows of active magic surrounded the girl. She sat on the edge of our bed. The slide of skin over skin as she rubbed her hands set my nerves on edge.

"I am Katarina DiLove. My mother kept me after my birth eighteen winters ago, and I served as her handmaid until her death from the wasting sickness last summer. I have no great magics, nor did I wish to stay at the temple.

"My small talent is in the care of animals. I am—" Her voice faltered as the spell prodded her. "Was apprenticed with Jovis, the city's veterinarian. I met Marco last fall. His horse had broken a leg in a hunting accident, and I healed the poor creature."

Luc whistled, a high, surprised sound. My estimation of the

girl tilted. A true healer had more than a *little* talent.

Katarina didn't seem to notice our reactions. "He courted me. I told him I had no dowry other than the death gift from my mother, but he said it didn't matter. That he loved me no matter the difference between our stations.

"I was to meet him at the Wilding God's clearing two nights ago. He wasn't there, but Mistress DiMara was. She said that I would pay for seducing her son. That she and her husband would ensure I never saw him again. That if by happenstance we did meet, he would not know me.

"Yesterday morning, Master Jovis released me from my contract. He said I could sleep in the pig barn last night, but it would be best for both of us if I left the city."

Katarina's voice turned hard. "The DiMaras own the magistrate. He would not help if I had gone to him. Brother Kam sent me to you."

"Disguised as a priestess?"

"No. That was my idea."

Once her story finished spilling. Katarina sucked in a wretched breath and began sobbing in earnest. I questioned her for nearly half of a candle mark, but her story did not alter one whit, nor could she give us more details.

I sat down next to the girl, her sobs now reduced to hiccups. She not so subtly scooted away. I couldn't fault her. The reaction to me, to my eyes, was due to my own foolishness.

"There may not be anything we can do," I said. "It may be as simple as Marco's parents threatening to disown him if he continues with his plans to marry you, and he buckled to their wishes."

"But Marco isn't like that!"

"We'll look into it. That is all I can promise." I reached into a pocket of my robes and produced two gold pieces. "Go to Nastine. That's the next stop on my circuit. Tell the adherents at the temple of Balance I sent you, and wait for me. Nothing more. I'll be there next week with my findings."

She bobbed her head. "It is more than I expected." After a moment's hesitation, she whispered, "About my own transgression, Justice—"

"I discover you've impersonated a priestess again, and I'll behead you myself."

"Yes, Justice." The acknowledgement was my only thanks. Luc received a hug from her before she fled through the sleeping room's door.

He sealed the door behind the girl and cast a privacy spell. Warmth filled me. I knew where his actions led.

"Well?" He unlaced the ties of my formal cloak.

I sighed as he eased the material from my shoulders. "The girl's only telling the truth as she knows it. She's low on facts and high on conjecture."

"A veterinarian is not going to release a true healer from her contract without cause. Or some damn good incentive." He pressed a tiny kiss along my neckline with each word, stroked the scars along my back.

"So you believe it bears investigation?"

He chuckled against my skin. "I know you. You would have her stripped and flogged for the impersonation if you suspected her story false. And since you've already pardoned one transgression this morning…"

I sighed as he unwound my breast band. "Whatever happened to the days when our vocations fought demons and otherworldly menaces instead of dealing with jilted lovers?"

"Maybe the Goddess is trying to teach you patience with boring cases."

I slapped at his hands. "Luc, we have to be at court by third morning." My protest was token, and we both knew it.

"It's only second hour. We have plenty of time." As if he cued them, the city bells rang.

I sighed and let him press me to the bedcovers.

The port city of Orrin was far too big not to have its own temple adjudicator. After the elderly resident justice had passed in the spring, the Reverend Mother assigned Orrin to my circuit. I couldn't say she ignored my entreaties or those of Kam, the old priest at the Temple of Light across the city's main thoroughfare.

She always sent us both polite replies that she searched for the right candidate for the position.

Even though I spent a week out of every month in Orrin, I wasn't insane enough to take up residence in the temple facilities. The minute I did, the old hen would permanently assign me the position, and Luc and I would be parted forever. Besides, this city held too many bitter memories.

As usual, I heard the capital cases first that morning. I only had to execute one man. When I returned from the back courtyard after his beheading, I slipped my sword through the clasped hands of the Goddess's statue behind my chair. Odd how a bloody blade in the grip of a basalt figure subdued the crowd and kept order.

By the end of the afternoon, my grim humor had evaporated, and I wondered if I could die of boredom. The accused turned into a giant parade of disorderly conduct charges. At first evening, I called a halt to the proceedings.

The resident clerk approached me as the main hall cleared. "There's only a day and a half of civil cases left, m'lady." From her high voice and jovial attitude, she was still quite young.

I snorted. "And by morning, there will be another pile of criminal cases because some fleet arrived today, and all the crews decided to drink their pay."

She shrugged. "Sailors, m'lady."

Luc approached and handed me my cleaned sword. "Ready for evening meal?"

Bless him. The blade slid into my back scabbard with a satisfying *snick*. I had changed my clothes at the mid-day break, not that bloodstains were obvious in my traditional robes. Or so everyone said.

Even cold and dried, the spots left a slight temperature variation from the cloth. To me, they stood as mute badges to my position.

"Good eventide." I nodded to the clerk before Luc wrapped my arm around his.

As we stepped outside, I welcomed the cool air after the stuffiness of court. The business district's administrative offices and most of the temples were quiet for the night. Only the Temple of Love, three cross streets down, was brightly lit. The raucous laughter of men and the lighter giggling of the priestesses spilled from its front courtyard.

I paused, taking in the glow of oil lamps and torches. Then there were the sounds. Noises all too similar to the ones I made when Luc lay with me.

"Sentimental, Justice?" he whispered in my ear.

"No. I'm thankful my mother sold me every time I pass one of those places." She really had done me a favor though it felt like a wretched abandonment to the child I had been. But considering I couldn't keep my own vow of chastity to Balance—

I tugged on his arm, and we started across the street. "Come. I'm hungry." I left the rest of my feelings unsaid. It was too dangerous to speak the words aloud on an open street.

Dinner with Brother Kam was always a pleasant affair, but tonight, his jocularity seemed forced. After telling a particularly obscene story concerning a former mayor, two milkmaids, and a cow, he exhaled and sipped his wine.

He toyed with the stem for a long moment before he said, "I wish you would reconsider accepting the temple seat here in Orrin, Anthea."

I felt Luc's attention on me and I nodded my agreement. He rose and circled the room.

Brother Kam said nothing as Luc warded the room against anyone overhearing this conversation.

"Does this have anything to do with the DiMara family?" I asked.

Brother Kam's face blazed red. He reached for the wine pitcher and refilled his goblet. "According to the city's gossipmongers, Lord and Lady DiMara have been petitioning a match with one of the Queen's granddaughters for their son Marco. Needless to say, their attempts have been politely, but firmly, rebuffed."

He took a deep swallow of wine before continuing. "Three

days ago, Marco came to me for advice on a young apprentice he was enamored with. Even though I told him to forget about her, he was quite insistent he loved her." A self-deprecating chuckle echoed from Kam's chest. "I asked him why he didn't seek the guidance of the priestesses down the street. He told me he needed straight answers, not flowery speech."

"And?" I prompted.

Brother Kam looked at me squarely, one of the few who knew the truth about me and was unafraid to gaze upon my failed attempt at sight. "I told him if he was serious, he would collect any money he could lay his hands on and flee with his paramour to Cant. Lady DiMara would never countenance a match between any of her children and a mere animal healer, much less a bastard child of the Spring Rituals."

He took another swallow of wine. "Yesterday, the veterinarian Jovis came to me. It was before noon, and the man was more intoxicated than adherents of the Mother at a harvest. The man *never* drinks because he never knows when he might be summoned." He slammed his hand against the surface of the table.

"What did he tell you?" Luc said.

"Nothing." Kam waved his hand in the air. "He couldn't tell me a blessed thing. He was under some kind of compulsion I could not break." He stared at the tapestry of Light decorating the far wall. "He tried. God help him, he tried to tell me, but I found a secondary spell designed to kill him if he managed to defeat the primary compulsion.

"This morning, Marco's paramour showed up on my doorstep."

Luc relayed our own encounter with Katarina. Kam grunted and poured another goblet of wine.

My palms formed a blade, and I rested my chin against my fingertips. "This doesn't make sense. Why go to such lengths to stop Marco?"

"Oh, the story gets better." Anger coated Kam's words. "Shortly after I sent Katarina to speak to you, Lord DiMara arrived, claiming Marco wishes to take temple vows."

"He's of age, is he not?" Luc said.

"Yes." Kam shook his head. "I cannot refuse an honest supplicant. But…"

Luc's own rage flicked at the back of my mind. Katarina's story fell into place. The DiMaras had set a very neat trap for their son.

None of the temples would condone a memory block of this type, not even those of the God of Thieves. Only a second-rate sorcerer would agree to such a perversity, therefore the spell would eventually fail. By the time poor Marco realized what had happened to him, he would be sworn to the God.

And only the Temples of Light and Balance required their priests and priestesses to remain chaste.

Coldness swept through me, though I wasn't sure if it was concern for the young lovers or my and Luc's own violation of our vows. "Do you have the list of non-temple affiliated talents for Orrin?"

Kam pulled a scroll from his robes and handed it to Luc, who read off the names. Part of me was pleased Katarina had done the smart thing and registered. The rest of the practitioners listed bore some thought. They ranged from a minor prince with limited talent and no hope for the throne to several bastards from the other temples.

I stood. "Thank you for your hospitality, Brother Kam, but it is getting late."

"Thank you for listening to my nonsense." Relief danced along the old man's words. "If I can be of assistance…"

I squeezed his hand. "You've been more than enough help."

"Brother Luc?"

We paused at Kam's querulous tone. "Yes?"

"I'm grateful for your assistance, but my old bones cannot perform this office much longer. If Justice Anthea decides to settle in Orrin, may I present your name to the Reverend Father as my replacement?"

Luc tilted his head. "I would be honored, Brother."

Luc paced our room at the inn. Every curse word in the

records poured from his mouth.

I sat cross-legged on the bed and rubbed my temples at the growing headache. His tirade was difficult to shut out, made meditation impossible. "Any hope that your tantrum will end soon?"

He paused in mid-step. "It's one thing when your parents sell you to the temples, but this—"

"Is illegal. I'm not disagreeing with you, but we need to find Marco before the memory block is performed. The DiMaras have had to rush, haven't thought out their plan thoroughly. And why punish Marco, instead of quietly killing Katarina? This type of revenge is too personal."

"A way to keep the other DiMara children in line? Make them work harder at seducing a member of the royal family?"

"Maybe. Read the names to me again."

The parchment rustled, a counterpoint to Luc's bass as he repeated each name on the list. He tossed the scroll on the bed. "It's too many. We don't have time to check out each one. We can try a tracking spell on Marco."

I pressed my hands together and rested my elbows on my crossed knees. "If this unknown sorcerer has a lick of common sense and any real power, he is shielding both his presence and Marco's. If we try to track either of them, it will alert our unknown idiot that we're looking. And if he can't perform the memory block in time, he may decide slitting Marco's throat and fleeing is his best option for survival."

"The Wilding God's clearing? Lady DiMara?"

I smiled. "That was my thought."

The bells rang third night while we crossed the city. Black trousers and long-sleeved tunics allowed us to blend with the shadows. As for evading the night watch and accessing one of the city gates, three generations of peacetime in Issura made the men and women a little too complacent. Besides, they never expect anyone to *leave* the city this late.

Luc and I jogged to the clearing. While the Lord of Wild Things had an altar within every city, a copse outside of the walls was always set aside for him.

Luc stumbled twice on roots. For me, the blue trees and their yellow canopies were as bright as daytime. Sometimes I suspected he teased me when he claimed the trunks were brown and the leaves green to him. However, I had no doubts that nighttime for him was like the dark to which I was born.

"Here?" he asked when we reached the clearing.

I looked up at the bright red owl perched on the branch above us. "Only if you want droppings down your collar."

Luc grunted and followed while I found an appropriate spot. I sat cross-legged, my hands on my knees and concentrated.

The matrons of my order say that in the beginning, the universe was perfectly balanced, and that in the end, perfect balance will be achieved again. Translated, their teachings meant we could see the past, and sometimes, even the future.

What we needed was two nights ago. Katarina's meeting with Lady DiMara.

Cold filled the glade as I plucked the strings of time. Luminous eyes and hot bodies surrounded us. This was not my Goddess's place, and the wild creatures watched.

Luc circled the glade, asking for the Wilding God's indulgence, while I rewound the last two sunsets. Ghostly figures, both human and animal, entered and left the holy circle. All of them walking, hopping, crawling backwards. I would have laughed if a young man's life and soul weren't at stake.

"There," Luc said. "Hold there."

I saw nothing but shadows. However, he moved quickly, marking the spot with his own magic.

"I have her trail."

At his affirmation, I let the threads of the past slip, and the world snapped back to the correct moment. We thanked Lord Wilding for his indulgence, and his children skittered and leapt back through the yellow foliage from whence they came.

The soft orange glow of Luc's spell disappeared down a different path than the one directly from the city. We followed it a short distance before it hit the National Road, the main route through the land. The same road we had arrived on only yesterday.

The tracking spell threaded north towards the capital and south toward the rest of the port cities along the coast. Luc cursed and kicked a cobblestone. I knew his words before he said them. "We shouldn't split up."

I set my fists on my hips. "Do you seriously believe each of us alone cannot handle our culprit, much less a petty, pampered aristocrat?"

He made a low sound of displeasure deep in his chest. "A candle mark. No more. We meet back here in two."

"Fine," I agreed before I pivoted and ran south.

Near the end of the agreed candle mark, I despaired of finding the point of Lady DiMara's journey. Marco had to be relatively close in order to present him to Kam on the morrow.

I jogged around a bend in the road when the orange trail made a sharp right turn. The driveway would be nearly hidden by the foliage from most humans' sight as well as my own if not for Luc's spell.

I picked my way through the brush to side of the drive but kept an eye on the trail. Through a break in the trees, a dark purple monolith rose from the bluffs. A manor house from its outline, yet I encountered no guards.

The gardens and yard were unkempt and overgrown. Since the DiMaras prided themselves on appearances, this could not possibly one of their holdings. Or had I totally misread the situation?

Above me, leaves rustled. I glanced up, half-expecting a night predator. Instead of the warm glow of a living creature, something cold black perched on the limb.

Something I'd never seen before.

I stepped away from the tree. More of these creatures gathered in the surrounding branches. Automatically, my hand reached for my sword hilt. The rasp of pulling the reinforced steel normally reassured me, but there was something *wrong* with these things.

Crickets stopped chirping. The rustling mice paused as they scavenged for seeds. The night itself seemed to hold its breath.

I swung as the first creature leapt. My sword connected, but the blow felt like nothing I experienced before. As if I'd struck stone, only to have the creature melt after jarring my arm.

Its fellows followed, and I found myself buried under a multitude of frigid bodies. When a fist struck my temple, it remained stone. I couldn't stop my fall into a different kind of blackness.

Strange muttering infiltrated my aching head. I tried to raise my hand, only to find it fettered by cuffs linked to heavy chains.

"Oh, good. You're awake." The clap of pleasure sounded as loud as a crack of thunder directly overhead.

Very carefully, I pushed myself upright. Nausea threatened, but I couldn't afford to give in to my head injury. Taking stock, I found I had been left only with my trousers, tunic and undergarments. Matching shackles encircled my bare ankles.

Soft lavender light emanated from the walls, the same kind I'd seen on damp stones in caves. A man crouched before me, but my attention was drawn by one of the cold shadow creatures perched on a bookcase. Suspicion of what it may be gnawed on my gut.

The man unshielded a candle. The flare of white-hot light drove a spike of agony through my head, and I ducked my eyes against my shoulder.

"You react to light the same as a normal person. What are you, my dear?"

The tug to answer his question frightened me more than his shadow pets. He was definitely not as much as a fool as I'd thought if he'd laid a truth spell on me while I was unconscious.

"A human." To my relief, my answer did not result in a cascade of pain. He had the talent and knowledge to cast such a spell, but he hadn't been trained in logic or questioning.

His chuckle sounded like one of an elderly uncle indulging his favorite niece. "I mean, how did you get your unusual red eyes?"

"I gave them to myself."

"Why?"

I couldn't wiggle out of this answer. A bitter laugh poured

from my lips. "It was my poor attempt nearly twenty winters ago to restore my sight so I would be released from the Temple of Balance. I received ten lashes for the temerity to circumvent the Goddess's will."

His face turned from pale orange to crimson. All joviality fled him. "Who are you? What is your name? Your rank?"

Again, the pull on my soul to spill my secrets. If I resisted, he'd know I was hiding something, assuming the spell didn't kill me. Maybe he'd think twice about his actions with the truth.

My chin lifted. "Justice Anthea, the circuit judge assigned to Orrin until the Reverend Mother of Balance names a permanent justice."

The man jumped to his feet. He must be younger than my original estimation.

From the bookcase, an odd, guttural noise came from the creature.

"No, you can't eat her," the man snapped. "Be silent. I need to think."

"Is that a demon?" I wanted my captor to say it wasn't. *Goddess, I take back this morning's jest with all my heart and soul.*

He ignored both of us, set the candleholder on a table, and started to pace the workroom.

Or dungeon, I decided. It was a good six strides long and an equal number in width. Deep blue chains hung at regular intervals along the wall to which I was shackled.

I tried to call for Luc, but my mental shout bounced off the shielding spell. It only added to the ache in my head. The demon, for surely that is what it was, growled. Since he'd already decided he wanted to eat me, I took his warning under due consideration.

Interesting that I didn't recognize it, but the descriptions of demons were based on normal human sight. I needed to add my observations about complete lack of body heat to the temple's chronicles. If I survived the night, that was.

From the occasional word I picked out from my captor's muttering, he had schemed as far ahead as Lord and Lady

DiMara. Which is to say, barely at all.

"Might I make a suggestion?"

He halted and from the odd feeling on the back of my neck, he glared at me. "What?"

"You were planning to block Marco DiMara's memory. If you haven't yet, you should cast the spell on us both."

"Why would I do that?"

I was correct in my original assessment that he was an idiot. However, it didn't make him any less dangerous, and I needed to buy time for Luc to find us.

I sighed. "If neither Marco or I remember you, you cannot be charged with kidnapping or holding us prisoner. We both live, and you'll still get your payment from Lady DiMara."

"I already received my payment in advance. I am not stupid."

I sent a silent prayer of thanks to the Goddess that he didn't phrase his words in the form of a question. "And you won't be hunted like a dog for murdering a priestess," I pointed out.

He turned to the demon. "Bring the youth in here, and do *not* eat him."

The demon jumped down from the bookcase. Instead of exiting the room properly, it seemed to dissolve before it slid through the crack between the door and the frame. Interesting. Hopefully, the creature would take the time to open the door when it returned with Marco, or my efforts to keep the boy alive would be for nothing.

"What is your name, sir?"

"Uhn-uh." My mysterious sorcerer waggled his index finger. "I'm not falling for that."

I gave him a smile, as polite of one as I could muster. "I would need your true name to cause any mischief." I shrugged. And became painfully aware of a huge bruise on my shoulder. However, I didn't let the smile waver. "Besides, I won't remember the name you give me anyway."

"Who knows you are here?"

My smile fell. "Only you and your demons," I said. Thank the Goddess, he couldn't properly ask a question. "All you have to do is leave me on the National Road with the gear I came with, and you'll be perfectly safe."

He made a derisive sound. "If you are a circuit justice, where is your partner priest of Light?"

I clenched my jaw. The pain started in my belly, similar to eating the obscenely hot peppers of the arid regions of Cant. It quickly escalated to what I suspected a glowing poker shoved through my gut would feel like. I fell to my side. My body curled into a ball. "Heading north on the road, tracking Lady DiMara," I gasped.

"Stupid, stupid bitch."

It took a moment for his meaning to penetrate the dissipating haze of pain while he shouted for his demons. He referred to the noblewoman, not me.

I pushed myself back to a sitting position. If only he'd leave the dungeon, I could pull out one of my remaining hairpins and pick the Goddess forsaken locks.

Instead, the door swung open with such force, it crashed into the stone wall. Two of the demons dragged in a struggling man. I was sure the third demon behind them was the one who desired to pick his teeth with my bones.

From the hot bruises on the man's face and hands, he'd fought his captors. He shouted imprecations at the demons with every step they took until he was chained next to me.

"Marco, it will be all right."

He grew silent at my attempted reassurance and addressed our captor. "Are you insane, Samael? Did my mother pay you to kidnap her as well?"

Now, I had a name. One Luc had read from the list.

"Shut your mouth," Samael shrieked. "Or I'll have the demons eat your tongue."

I stared at him. "Samael DiRoy. Youngest son of the Crown Prince. Scholar and herbalist. Magical talent limited to languages." *Goddess help us, he had the demons place the spells on the veterinarian Jovis.* "How in the names of the Twelve did you manage to summon demons?"

"Jealous because I can, Priestess?" he hissed.

"Not particularly." I winced as I replied. *Bloody Sword, this truth spell will be the death of me.* "Actually, I'm impressed. All such texts were supposedly destroyed by the Temples a century ago."

My fawning tone hit his ego just right. "I found a tome tucked away in the rare books section of the capital library. I translated a few phrases, realized it was a grimoire on the forbidden magics, and I smuggled it out."

"But, Prince Samael, why bother with this child—" I gestured at Marco "—when you can *command demons*?"

"I need the money." His boasting shifted into whining. "Do you have any idea of how expensive summoning and feeding these things are?"

An awful suspicion grew in me. "Do Marco's parents know about the demons?"

"Of course." Samael's confidence chilled me more thoroughly than the demons' touch.

"Holy Mother," Marco swore. "They want you to raise a demon army for them once I'm out of the way."

I wanted to kick the youth for giving voice to my fears. We were both dead now.

Samael slowly shook his head. "I'm so sorry. For both of you. I'll make this as easy as possible." He pulled a knife from the worktable.

My dagger.

I curled and pretended to cower against the wall. I prayed there was enough slack in my chains, prayed that the stories I heard as a child of the demons' weaknesses were true. I had to be faster than the three demons in the room.

He approached me and reached for my hair. I slammed my heels into his knees. With a sickening crunch, tendons tore and bones shattered. He screamed. My dagger slipped from his hand as he collapsed and clattered against the stone floor.

I swept one of the arm chains around his throat and yanked him against my chest. The first demon, the one who wanted to taste my flesh, crouched inches from our faces.

"Back away, or I snap his neck," I growled.

It huffed before it said something to the others in their

guttural language. All three edged away from us. Their actions confirmed one of the old tales. They needed the sorcerer who summoned them alive in order to remain in this plane.

And if I killed a member of the royal family without benefit of a trial, I'd find my neck on the business end of another justice's sword.

The problem of getting Marco and myself out of this dungeon persisted. I rolled the possibilities through my mind, a process that became more difficult by the moment for reasons that had nothing to do with Samael's hoarse cries. With a sickening realization, I understood my situation. My head injury was worse than I originally suspected. Blood pooled inside my skull, and the growing pressure would kill me if we didn't escape soon.

"Where's the key?" I tightened and released the chain to gain his attention.

"If I tell you, you'll kill me," he whimpered.

Telling the idiot he was dead already wouldn't improve the situation. "I can grant you clemency if you cooperate," I said through clenched teeth.

"Don't bargain with him, Justice."

From the corner of my eye, I found Marco had already picked the locks to his wrist cuffs. Goddess bless the boy. He'd had the presence of mind to snatch my dagger when it fell.

The steel would be ruined once he was finished, but I didn't care. It was by far the least of our worries.

Marco quickly released the locks on my shackles while I kept a tight hold of the chain around Samael's neck. He stayed close to me when the demons started muttering under their breath.

"I need your help to lift him," I whispered.

Marco was no dandy. He hauled the sorcerer upright, and Samael screamed at the pressure on his ruined knees.

I gained my feet, only a rush of vertigo threatened to knock me down again. Clutching the wall, I made my way to the worktable. Relief swept through me when my fingers wrapped around the pommel of my sword. Feeling around the wooden surface produced a great many objects, none of which were my boots or the sword's sheath. We couldn't waste any more time.

"Stick to the wall," I muttered.

"Yes, m'lady." Marco replaced the chain with his arm and dragged the sorcerer, keeping him between us and the demons.

"Over there." I pointed at the opposing corner with my sword. The stones were only cold under my right foot. My left was numb.

The first demon spat an obvious insult, but he and his fellows edged around the dungeon while we made our way to the door. The instant we were through, I slammed the door shut and slid the iron bolt into place. The heavy wood shivered as the demons threw themselves against it. The barrier wouldn't last long.

Somehow, we climbed the stairs and exited the front door of the manor house. We backed slowly down the drive, the young nobleman literally dragging the screaming sorcerer. My own footing became more unsure.

"They're coming," Marco murmured.

Black shadows climbed the surrounding trees and swung through branches toward us.

I'd never killed someone without an appropriate trial. A growing disquiet said Samael's death would be the only way for Marco to survive. Deep down, I acknowledged I would never be greeted by the goddess at my passing, much less make it back to Orrin

"Luc, I'm so sorry," I whispered.

Anthea!

Luc. I nearly collapsed when the pounding of hoofs raced toward us from the main road.

"Marco!"

I recognized the feminine voice that shouted. The name was out of my reach. I'd sent her away, hadn't I?

"Here!" For all our shouting, the cold shadows would reach us before Luc. I couldn't fight them off before. I couldn't let an innocent die.

"Drop him, Marco."

The boy complied, and the sorcerer shrieked.

"Samael DiRoy, you have been charged with using forbidden magic by your own admission." My hands shook. I wished it was rage and fear instead of my injury.

"I, Marco DiMara, hereby affirm the justice's account, having heard the confession myself." The ritual response of a priest of Light.

I wanted to weep with relief. Marco was a good boy. A smart boy. I hoped he'd find his happiness.

Luc. So many things I wanted to say to him. So many things he needed to know.

A wave of frigid air hit me. "Samael DiRoy, you are found guilty of using forbidden magic. The sentence is death."

Wordless cries were his only answer. Marco held him down by the shoulders.

I prayed the old stories were true. That demons hadn't tricked me in the dungeon.

I slammed the sword point into the base of Samael's skull. Shrieks of demon outrage echoed through the woods. With muffled pops, the black shadows disappeared from this plane of existence.

Hands caught me as I pitched forward over the corpse of my deadly idiot. My last thought was that I was finally *free*.

The scent of vanilla and cinnamon twined around me. My eyes fluttered open. The dark blues and greens of a marble ceiling met my gaze.

"Where am I?" My voice was a hoarse croak.

"You're in the bedroom of the Justice of Orrin. Here, drink this." Familiar hands held up my head.

I gratefully sipped the water.

"Do you have a headache?"

I had to think about it since my entire head seemed to be wrapped in cotton. "No." Recognition slipped into place.

Luc.

"Good. Katarina needed to eat and sleep. The girl hasn't left your side. She's beside herself with guilt for putting you at the mercy of demons."

"She—" It took me a moment to pull the threads of memory from the tangled skein my mind had become. "I sent her to

Nastine."

"She disobeyed you and went to Kam again."

Luc filled in the events after I'd executed Samael and passed out. He returned to the city after he searched for me and spotted a demon watching the road. He gathered as many wardens from the temples as he could. Katarina insisted on accompanying the rescue party.

Which turned out to be fortunate, or unfortunate from my point of view, since she kept me alive long enough for them to return me to Orrin and find a trained healer.

The senior physician of Orrin insisted she become his apprentice since Master Jovis had released her. Samael's death dissolved the demons' compulsion on Jovis, who denied he'd terminated her contract willingly. Just another civil matter on the docket.

Luc's companions hadn't found the grimoire Samael used at the abandoned manor house. The Temples of Thief and Wilding worked together and tracked the blasted thing to Lord and Lady DiMara's estate. They had been captured after a brief fight between their household retainers and the temple wardens.

"And me?" I whispered.

"Technically, you're under house arrest for the murder of a member of the royal family. The Reverend Mother of Balance arrives later tonight. The trials will be tomorrow."

The noise from the crowds that thronged outside of the Temple of Balance echoed in the cavernous interior until the Reverend Mother ordered the main doors closed. A trial for treason outside of the capital was unusual. Two on the same day was unprecedented. In such severe matters, the highest-ranking priest or priestess of each of the Twelve temples of Orrin sat as one.

Like the DiMaras, I stood in the accused box, stripped of all accoutrements of my rank. Instead, I wore a plain gray shift. No hood covered my face this time. The whispers were equally divided by the DiMaras' attempt to seize the throne through dark magic and my appearance. Even the wardens guarding us looked uneasy.

I could feel Luc sitting with the rest of the spectators, but I didn't dare look in his direction. The milky white eyes of the Reverend Mother bore into me for a moment before she banged the hilt of her sword on the altar to begin the proceedings.

The first trial took less than a candlemark.

Brother Kam stood and read the verdicts. The only thing that saved Lord DiMara from a death sentence was he didn't know about the demons, and he certainly didn't know his wife had stolen the grimoire from Samael. They had convinced her she was a much better overlord than the sorcerer.

Lord DiMara hung his head and wept quietly as the wardens escorted him from the court. Lady DiMara screamed obscenities until the Reverend Mother ordered her taken to the back of the temple.

"As the persons immediately wronged by the actions of the guilty, I hereby order that all titles, possessions and estates of the guilty, minus the tithe to the crown, pass to Marco and Katarina DiMara." She leaned back in her chair. "I suppose congratulations are in order."

I closed my eyes and sent a prayer of thanks to the Twelve for watching over the two lovers.

"Anthea DiLove, you have been charged with treason by way of murder, specifically Lord Samael DiRoy, third cousin to our beloved liege."

I opened my eyes and raised my chin. I'd done what I had to save Marco from being forced into temple life as Luc and I had been. Or worse, eaten by the demons. I wouldn't—I couldn't—change a thing.

"Lady Justice, may I speak on behalf of the accused?" There was a twinge of nervousness in Marco's voice.

"Both Brother Luc and Anthea DiLove have given their statements in this matter, Lord DiMara." Unlike the boy's, the Reverend Mother's tone was ice cold and steady.

"As have I, m'lady." He crossed from the witness area to stand in front of the judges. "If it weren't for Justice Anthea's quick thinking, we'd be neck deep in another demon war. Surely this court can take the good of her actions into account. Justice should be tempered by mercy."

"Do you presume to lecture me in my own hall?"

Everyone, including the rest of the judge's panel cringed at the echoes against the marble.

"No, m'lady. I ask for clemency. Orrin has been without a permanent justice for a quarter of a year. I swear responsibility if you would appoint Justice Anthea."

"No!" Nausea threatened. Surely the demons had hit Marco on the head as well.

The gallery of spectators erupted at my outburst. The Reverend Mother pounded her sword pommel repeatedly for order before the crowd settled.

"Do you understand what you are offering, child?"

"Should she commit any further offenses, I will share in her punishment." This time, his voice rang out like a confident nobleman's.

The Reverend Mother turned to me. "Anthea DiLove, you have tried to escape service to our goddess from the time you could use a privy by yourself. You should know by now it is not that easy." Gleeful satisfaction danced in her words. "Unless any of my colleagues have objections?"

A collective murmur of agreement issued from her fellow judges.

"Anthea DiLove, you are hereby sentenced to serve as the justice of the Temple of Balance for the city of Orrin for the remainder of your natural life."

Four days later, Luc and I were riding to Nastine. The Reverend Mother gave me a week to catch up on the town's caseload before I was required to return to Orrin. He and I took a little used track instead of the National Road. We had too much to discuss.

"What if we took all the money we can lay our hands on and head south to Cant?" I tilted my head upward, enjoying the caress of the summer sun.

Luc laughed, a hearty sound that flushed birds from the

surrounding foliage. "You can't do that anymore than I could."

"Someone will find out about us eventually," I pointed out. "If you take the permanent position in Orrin, discovery is even more likely."

"What makes you think someone doesn't already know?" His words were so soft I barely heard them over the clomping of the horses' hooves.

"I don't understand."

"Why didn't you have Katarina flogged for impersonating a priestess?"

His change of subject threw me off. "That had nothing to do—"

"Maybe it does. So why didn't you?"

It wasn't a truth spell that tugged at my heart. "Maybe because I hoped someone would show us compassion someday." Then I understood.

Neither of us said anything more the rest of the ride to Nastine.

PEARL OF TEARS

by Deborah J. Ross

In this story we see again the Pearl of Fire, from the story by that name in SWORD AND SORCERESS 22.

Deborah J. Ross writes and edits fantasy and science fiction. She's a former SFWA Secretary and current member of Book View Café. Her short fiction has appeared in *F&SF*, *Asimov's*, STAR WARS: TALES FROM JABBA'S PALACE, *Realms of Fantasy*, SWORD AND SORCERESS, and various other anthologies and magazines. Her most recent books include the Darkover novel THE CHILDREN OF KINGS (with Marion Zimmer Bradley); COLLABORATORS, an occupation-and-resistance story with a gender-fluid alien race (as Deborah Wheeler); and THE SEVEN-PETALED SHIELD, an epic fantasy trilogy. She's on Twitter and Facebook as herself, and you can follow her blog at http://www.deborahjross.blogspot.com.

My brother was slain by a woman without a soul.

I had loved him above my other kin, for our mother died at my birthing and Father—the Lord of Eaglehurst—had no use for a mewling, sickly daughter. When I was older, my nurse told me that my brother had looked down at me in my cradle—even now, I can picture those gray eyes so like my own, that hint of a smile at one corner of his mouth—and I had ceased my fitful wailing. "She's beautiful," he had whispered. And so I was, in those rainwater eyes, if in no others.

When our soldiers returned from that bleak winter battle, I went running down the steps from the great manor house, half-tripping on my skirts. What was left of our defense force filled the stone-paved courtyard. Father had already gone down to them, his azure cloak bright against the mud of their forest gear. Half our horses were gone and those remaining bore oozing gashes. The men were worse off, exhausted, slashed and battered, their eyes hollow.

"Where is Joram? Where is my brother?" I ran from one to the other. The first soldier I asked gave no sign he'd heard me, nor did the next. Father ignored me, bent deep in discussion with the captains. I caught a phrase, *the Dragon of Sharaya*, and the very sound turned my bones to jelly.

The sky opened and the clouds bore down upon us, shrouding the house and all the fields around. I went among the wounded, washing and bandaging, spooning cups of broth, and holding hands as they grew cold and still. I tried not to think about Joram, wounded or dead, with no one to comfort him. I felt nothing but emptiness, and so I filled it with work. Father shut himself up in his war room, which had once been Mother's solarium, and plotted retaliation. I sensed his anger like a rumbling through the stones beneath my feet, growing and gnawing.

The next morning, when the rain had lifted, a Sharayan rider approached under a banner of truce. Unbidden, I slipped into the room where Father received him, praying for news of Joram. Perhaps if I knew with certainty that he was dead, I might be able to grieve. I might be able to hate. The message startled all of us, Father and captains and me, for it was an offer to return the bodies of our fallen.

For a long moment, no one spoke. Such a thing had never been done, or if it had, it was long ago and not by our old enemy. Sharaya was ruthless and without mercy, everyone knew that. It must be a ruse, a trap. My father did not believe the Duke would keep a truce, and so would not agree to let any enemy force approach us unhindered. After what I had seen, I did not think we could stand against the Dragon, not even if every last one of us were to band together.

In the end, however, the messenger convinced Father to set his own conditions as to time and place and who might be present. Father accepted, although the entire offer now appeared to be the prelude to a demand for total surrender. The only choice was to refuse, and not even Father at his most furious would throw away the chance to give proper rites to our own dead. So that very day, he rode out with a company of picked men to bring my brother home. I was left yet once again, not knowing what to feel or how to hope. I filled my hours with nursing and thoughts that *they could not return, not so soon, surely now, what could have befallen them, what must I do if-if-if,* until finally, finally, came the signal from the lookouts and the sound of hooves clattering on the courtyard stones. I rushed to the window of the infirmary chamber and threw it open.

Below, I spied two men easing a body down from where it had been slung facedown over the saddle of Joram's horse. I could not make out the face, only the soaked clothing and the water-stained leather. The russet hair, drenched and tangled like riverweed, dripped onto the courtyard stones. In life, it had been the color of mine, or perhaps brighter.

I clenched my fingers around the window sash until my joints creaked and breath came like fire in my throat. It would have been better if I had fainted or shrieked or raged.

She'd done this, the Dragon of Sharaya. And now I had nothing to live for except to see her suffer.

The words were said, the rites performed, and the bodies were covered with new-dug soil. The priest recited words of peace, that Joram and the others were now beyond all pain, all sorrow. I thought, *Funerals are not for the dead but the living,* and did not know which I was.

Sharaya kept their word to leave us unmolested, but the armistice did not last. We'd been sore hurt in the last year, and those who came to take the place of the trained warriors were unseasoned or unsound in body. A few women, accustomed to defending their flocks and strong from hard labor, volunteered. They were not swordswomen but archers and pike-wielders, sling-throwers and sentries. I pleaded with Father to let me join them, so that I might learn to defend our home. And, although I did not say so to him, that I might have a chance, no matter how remote, to put an end to the Dragon.

He said no. Of course, he said no. He had never counted me

of any worth, the daughter who had cost the life of his lady and any future sons she might bear, and he did not do so now. *Stay out of the way,* he meant. *Keep to women's work. Maybe the Dragon will spare you if she sees you are of no account.*

I cut my hair, bound my breasts, and combed through the attic until I found a chest with Joram's outgrown, discarded clothing. The shirt was too broad across the shoulders and the pants too long, but I had some skill with a needle and managed to alter them so that they would not attract undue attention. The fabric still bore the faint smell of wild herbs, and a few dried flower petals clung to the threads. I wondered when he'd last worn it, where he'd gone on those days when he'd come home smiling, if he'd lain on his back in a meadow dotted with blossoms, if some country girl or smallholder's daughter had made him smile.

When I presented myself at the first training session, no one challenged me. I roughened my voice and affected an accent similar to that of the forest folk. The only one who looked at me with any suspicion, and even that was but a moment's, was one of our few remaining officers. Herel he was named, for the small swift falcons of the highlands, and his family had served mine for generations. In peaceful times, he would already have retired to enjoy his grandchildren. He watched as each of us displayed our skill—or lack of it—with sword, bow, spear, hammer, and staff. I was too small to handle a weapon that required strength, but he could not afford to discard any resource.

There wasn't much time for training, only for fighting one delaying action after another as best we could. Very soon, I discovered that although I had little skill, I had no fear. I didn't care what happened to me as long as I had an enemy in front of me. It wasn't fury that drove me on, or desperation, but something far colder. That very fearlessness kept me alive until I attained a measure of competence at arms. I still couldn't hold my own against a trained swordsman, but I was quick and light, more an assassin or a cutthroat thief than an honest duelist. To everyone's surprise, I developed a talent for tracking, for moving so quietly that my presence often went unknown until I was almost upon my quarry. Such a gift served us poorly, however, for there was no need to stalk the Sharaya Dragon.

She led her forces against us again and again, bold and relentless, and each time there were fewer of us left to stand against her. She always rode in front, mounted on a horse that looked as if it had been ridden through hell. We lost more territory, and more, until we battled before the smoking ruin that had been the great house.

Herel still led us, although he had not recovered from a festering leg wound some weeks back. He sat astride one of the few good horses left to us, shouting out encouragement. In the past, I had been assigned to a party of lightly-armed fighters who fought together, harrying and skirmishing rather than engaging head-on, but as my comrades fell, I snatched up a spear from its fallen bearer and joined the others defending our captain. All the while, I searched for the figure that haunted my nightmares.

Come to me, come to me...

It seemed to me then that the tumult of fighting quieted and a path opened in the enemy forces.

I could not mistake the Dragon. Who else disdained helmet and shield? Who else raised her sword in salute even as the blood of the slain—*our* slain—dripped from it?

Come to me... I tightened my grasp on my spear. Likely I would have only a single chance.

Just then, just at the moment when surely she must have seen the hatred on my face and known that she was mine and I was hers, she paused. Did she sense a threat from the side? One of our best remaining fighters hurled himself forward and thrust the point of his sword under the edge of her breastplate. The stroke would have felled a raging bear, but the blade slid away, as if her very flesh were adamantine. She twisted in the saddle and beheaded him with a single stroke. His body remained upright for a terrible moment and then toppled like an uprooted tree.

I felt the life go out of his body as if from my own. Was this how Joram had died, with so little effort, such casual slaughter?

Then, as if shaken from a stupor or suddenly disenchanted, the Sharayans took up the fight again. The heart had gone out of our own forces. I knew what they were thinking, because the same despair howled through my own mind: The great house was lost. Even without the Dragon, we faced overwhelming opposition. Our deaths would serve nothing.

"Retreat!" Herel shouted, gesturing with his sword. *Retreat while we still can.*

As for myself, I was glad enough to leave that place. I would have the revenge I craved, I swore to my brother's memory, but not now. Not here.

We ran like rabbits with the hounds of Sharaya on our tails. I heard a scream behind us but did not risk a glance to see who it was. Sooner than I hoped, the pursuit fell away. They could have had us all if they had been determined, but the habit of following the Dragon was too strong. I imagined their exultation, their certainty that in time, they would trap us all.

Some hours later, Herel brought us to a stumbling, panting halt. Men and horses trembled on the brink of exhaustion. He'd taken us north, toward the mountains, but we had not yet traveled beyond familiar lands. Some of us knew these woods and the paths through them, the meadows and ravines, the caves. We sheltered in one of the caves, not deep but well-hidden.

I set to work ordering the camp, checking who was wounded and how badly, making an inventory of what little we had managed to carry away. Nobody questioned my orders; they were all too numb to think clearly, and I needed to be doing something.

Dusk fell quickly in the forest and a chill arose from the surrounding rock. A couple of the men who'd somehow escaped injury found enough fallen wood for a fire. I decided to risk it. The wounded would benefit from the warmth and the light would comfort the dying.

Gradually the others drifted off to sleep. I shifted closer to the fire, now an occasional flicker of light against the embers. I folded my arms around my knees and tried to make sense of what I had witnessed on this day. Everything I had been told about the Dragon of Sharaya—and disbelieved as superstition or battlefield exaggeration—was true. She could not be slain by ordinary means. The sword had struck true and yet had not touched her. Was she then a demon, a thing of supernatural power? A dragon in the shape of a woman?

What hope had I of avenging my brother's death, I who was not even a mediocre sword fighter?

Clothing rustled, drawing my attention. Herel, who lay nearby and close to the fire, propped himself on one elbow. "It is not defeat, my lady, for we will fight another day."

With what weapons—against a dragon? I thought bitterly. And then, *"my lady"?*

He must have seen the surprise on my face, for he continued, still keeping his voice low, "Your brother did not have a twin, and you are as like to him. Yet in this you are unalike. Hatred, not love of home and lord, drives you."

I did not waste my breath with false denials. "You think I should have stayed at home, embroidering holiday shirts? Should I throw down my knife and crawl to whatever lord will give me sanctuary?"

"I think you will not rest until you stand before the Dragon of Sharaya, no matter what I say."

I sat up straighter. Here was a man who would tell me the truth. "What is she, this Dragon? Is she even human?"

Herel studied me for a long moment, perhaps weighing the guilt of sending me to certain death. "Her name is Rayzel, daughter of the Duke of Sharaya. It is said she bears a magical talisman, a proof against all bodily harm. If that is true, it is a miracle we resisted her this long. My own father told stories of the old Duke, her grandfather. Or maybe her great-grandfather, who can tell? No foe could stand against him, but he sought only to protect his own lands. Lady Rayzel..."

I had seen her face, so lacking in human emotion. Perhaps the talisman granted her invulnerability of the heart as well as the flesh. "She would see the entire world in flames."

He nodded, as if I had spoken his thought. I tried to remember when the war had changed from traditional raiding to this campaign of annihilation. Before Joram was killed, it had seemed far away and happening to someone else. Certainly, he had been able to spare an afternoon now and again for his secret courtship.

My only chance would be to take the talisman from her, most likely by trickery or stealth. My size, which had served me poorly in combat, might yet be my greatest asset. Few swordsmen took me seriously, but I could move quickly and silently. I'd make an excellent thief.

"Tell me about this talisman," I said to Herel. "What does it look like? Where does she carry it?"

"It is said to be a Pearl of surpassing beauty, in appearance like none other. When roused by blood, it glows like fire-licked bronze. Or so it is said," he added, his voice made hoarse by weariness.

"*So it is said*," I repeated. "Have you yourself seen it?"

He looked away, into the shadows. I regretted stirring sorrowful memories, but I needed to know. "I have seen...something. I am not sure what. But Rayzel of Sharaya does wear a silver chain about her neck. That much I have seen with my own eyes."

Hope flared, the first I'd known since the day Joram died. This Pearl might render its wearer invulnerable to sword and spear, but it was a physical item, a bauble. And once it hung around my own neck, Sharaya would pay.

Those few of us who survived the fall of Eaglehurst lived as outlaws in the remote areas of brush and forest, never staying long in any campsite, always looking over our shoulders for fear we would see the Dragon, her sword gleaming like red-gold, coming after us. Herel died the first winter of a lung fever, and some looked to me as the next leader. I wanted no obligation, no loyalty to anything but my own vengeance. By this time, even the few veterans acknowledged my skill. I had earned a place with them not by bloodline—for none of them knew who I truly was—but by blood.

I still wore Joram's clothing, although with each passing season, it became more worn and less like the garb of a nobly-born youth. I suppose I became tattered and weathered as well. Certainly, it seemed that the men treated me as one of them, as my brother would have been. Sometimes I felt as if I were carrying on with his life and not my own, fighting and fleeing, speaking the names of the dead around the evening fires. I would remember why I was here instead of him, and what quarry I hunted, and why I must never rest.

After a time, we gained a measure of respite from Sharayan patrols. I took this as a sign that I might now resume my own hunt. We dared to emerge from the broken lands and scrub forests where we had hidden ourselves. The others were weary of constant vigilance and poverty, of cold and poor food and rarely a song. So we made our way back towards Eaglehurst, to the lands we once had known. We went warily, not only out of fear of discovery but because we did not want to bring retribution on any village that aided us.

At one of these places, the largest and most prosperous we'd visited, we ventured into the single inn and traded our few coins for ale and new-baked bread. The villagers and a few travelers regarded us with mild interest and, when they were satisfied we offered neither threat nor the promise of exciting tales, went back to their own business. I settled on a table next to the least taciturn of the travelers. He was of Herel's age, grizzled but not mean-eyed, a trader in small metal items like pans and sewing needles.

"What news from the road?" I asked. "We've been a-forest so long, there's much we've not heard."

His gaze swept over me, but lightly. He took me for an unbearded youth, and I did not disabuse him of that notion. "Like there'll be peace for a time."

"Why is that? Has Sharaya run out of enemies to pick a quarrel with?"

The traveler shook his head. "It's called Greater Sharaya now, and any man fool enough to go up against her is long since food for worms. Seems the new Duke's got no stomach for campaigns and prefers to sit home, toasting his toes."

One of my company, overhearing our talk, moved closer. "Might as well, with the Dragon on guard." He looked as if he'd like to spit the bitterness out of his mouth from speaking the name.

"Word is," and here the trader lowered his voice and leaned close, "the Dragon's gone as well."

"Gone?" I echoed.

"Gone?" the Eaglehurst man said. "What happened to her? How can she just disappear?"

She wasn't dead, that much I was certain, because *I* was destined to kill her. For the first time in my exile, I felt afraid that she might have gone beyond my reach.

Where? Where? The thought rampaged through my skull. The trader drew back, and I realized I'd been glaring at him, as if I could wrest the answer by the force of my will.

"If Sharaya is appeased and the Dragon is gone," my comrade said, clearly turning over the notion in his mind, "then we can go home again."

Home, someone else repeated, or perhaps I heard it only in my heart. "Go home," I told my company. "Be at rest."

Where would she have gone and why? The reason did not interest me, only the direction, and I sat long in the inn's room, gazing into my half-drunk tankard, wondering where to begin.

I ventured into Sharaya itself, working when I could and picking pockets when I must. I used the money to buy ale for anyone who would gossip, and after a time, I put together bits of stories. A woman fitting Rayzel's description had been seen bargaining for fare on one of the boats that followed the river down out of the mountains. As I followed her path, I puzzled over what could have brought her to leave behind family, home, safety, the privilege of a noble birth. These things had been taken from me, but she had *chosen* to walk away. There was no current threat to Sharaya, nor was there likely to be. Was this a sort of expiation, a penance? The very idea was so beyond reason as to be laughable. And yet, I saw a bizarre justice in her wanderings. Everything I had wished for her, a redoubling of my own exile and suffering, she now took upon herself.

But it was not enough. It would never be enough.

The mountains fell away into sloping pastures and then fields of millet and barley. At every town, every crossroads, I asked after her, always dreading the discovery that I had either lost the trail or my quarry would turn out to be someone besides Rayzel, some poor woman driven from her home, perhaps a mercenary looking for employment. So far, my luck held.

The way led south, across the withered, rock-strewn badlands. I stood on the outskirts of the last trading town, little more than a collection of tents clustered around an ancient well, and looked out over the caravan route. This far, I had trusted to my own sturdy feet, with an occasional ride on a farmer's cart. Hot wind stirred the sand that had blown up from the desert. My lips were already parched. I had a little money, but not enough to buy a camel, and no horse could cross such an arid, desolate place. This same wind would scour my corpse. For a moment, the image of dry bones half-buried in sand rose up in my mind, only they were not mine. They were *hers*, and yet I felt no exultation, no relief that the desert had been my executioner.

As I turned back toward the town, I reminded myself that such thoughts were fruitless, not to mention self-indulgent. I would have to find a means of earning money or a caravan willing to hire me. Tracking and petty theft would undoubtedly not be in high demand, but I wasn't afraid of hard work.

Now and again I'd seen women on the road, tall and strong, swords slung over their backs, but I'd been traveling as a youth for so long now, no one questioned my disguise, and I felt it safer to continue. As I looked for employment, I gave my name as Joram, in part to keep my own purpose alive. Because I had experience with horses, I found a position at one of the stable yards, with room and one meal a day in addition to my trivial pay. Best of all, I had a good reason to strike up conversations with the caravaneers, if not the masters then their assistants. We talked about the roads, the weather, the state of their beasts, where they were going, and all the best gossip from afar. Sooner or later, I would casually ask whether a swordswoman had taken passage with them across the sands.

No, no, and *no* were the responses as the moon changed in her phases and one day became much like the others. One day, when the question had become wearisome in its repetition, *yes.*

A camel-boy and I were sitting on the worn step behind the kitchen of the adjacent inn, sipping warm ale as the sun dipped toward the west. *Yes,* they'd sold a camel to a woman of such a description. I must have just missed her departure, so the time was right.

"Where did she go?" I asked.

"Only one place to go, 'cross the sands—Ixtalpi, it's called, the city where madmen and demons mingle on the streets. And gamblers. It sits at the foot of the Viridon Mountains, that spew forth fire and ash, or so it is said." The boy spat into the dust.

It sounded like the perfect place for the Dragon of Sharaya.

"*It is said?*" I repeated, an idea nudging my mind. "You have not seen these marvels for yourself?"

The boy shook his head, and I saw that he was even younger than I'd first thought. Young and far from his own home.

Carefully, least I disturb the luck that at last seemed to be coming my way, I gave him to understand that I very much wished to see such sights, if only there might be some other to take my place here, with its warm bed and daily meal. Before we'd finished our ale, we'd struck a bargain to swap places. The caravan-master was only too happy to exchange a frightened, homesick boy for the strapping youth I appeared to be.

The mountains were everything the boy had intimated, dark and jagged. Black mists curled about their peaks, but whether they were natural fog or some demonic vapors, I could not tell. Ixtalpi itself was a warren, its buildings huddled at the base of the slopes. The afternoon was wearing into dusk when we arrived, and a lurid red light tinged the western horizon.

I collected my wages and ventured into the town. Not wanting to squander my meager purse, I selected an inn that was neither ostentatiously luxurious nor overly dilapidated. The price of a single room was more than I expected, but I dared not share one with half a dozen men, all of us jammed into one bed and the floor, and likely a few of them interested in a closer intimacy with a beardless youth. The inn keeper might have thought my modesty laughable, but he accepted my coin. I had come too far to risk failure from something as simple as being exposed as a woman, and yet I could not bring myself to discard my disguise. In some way I barely understood, I had become Joram, and to set that aside now felt like a betrayal.

The overpriced room came with a meal, so I settled in the common room, pretending to focus on the trencher of surprisingly spicy shredded meat, pickled vegetables, and a grain I did not recognize. All the while, I listened to the conversations around me, trying to sense the temper of the town and the best way to inquire after another traveler. That first night, I heard nothing of any value, except that my quarry was evidently not the only woman with a sword in this part of the world. What she might do if she suspected someone was on her track, I could not imagine. All the way, I'd been far enough behind her and so well-disguised, it was hard to imagine she'd detected me. And why should she? Eaglehurst was destroyed, any man capable of standing up to Sharaya long dead.

By day, I strolled through the markets and stockyards. I didn't expect to hear anything of value, and therefore was not disappointed. My real work took place at night, when I drifted from one tavern to another. As often as not, a round of cheap ale would yield an hour's gossip, tales from the road and far-off places, and also not a few stories of doings within Ixtalpi itself. I dispensed my coin slowly, for I had no idea how long I must make it last. I heard stories of horse races, knife fights, snake-wrestling contests, and the birth of a two-headed camel calf. Most of the reports of gambling were either so exaggerated or so dull I paid them little attention. Then, on the third night, I heard something that piqued my interest.

A game of castles and dice...a young couple from Raë on the Western Sea, mercenaries by the sound of them...a woman with a sword, "a hard one, that"...

Bets rose as one by one the other players dropped out, and the couple won and won. The woman with the sword played as if she cared nothing for winning, as if she had nothing worth losing.

Then, when it seemed the game was over, one final bet: a gem bound in silver wire, hanging on a chain around the swordswoman's neck.

"Glowed like a bed of coals, it did," my storyteller said.

"Aye," said his companion. "I'd not touch the thing, for all I've seen it with my own eyes." As he said this, he made a sign to ward off evil.

"What happened?" I asked in the silence that followed. "Who won?"

"Why them young couple, of course. Took off the next day to who knows where, proud as peacocks. Up to no good, but so long as they keep their trouble to themselves, what do I care?"

"Just as well," his friend agreed.

I stared into my half-empty tankard, unable to believe what I'd just heard. She'd *lost* the Pearl? In a *game?* What kind of madwoman was she? Or maybe she wasn't mad at all, but so sickened by what she'd done, she no longer cared for living? Had she, after all these years and so much bloodshed, developed a conscience?

Or was I the fool to think that was possible?

"Where..." I began, my throat suddenly dry, "where did she go?"

My two informants exchanged shrugs and glances, as if to say that anyone mad enough to follow that woman deserved whatever ill fortune they brought upon themselves. The friendlier of the two unbent enough to suggest that if it had been him who lost such a pretty bauble, he'd be on his way to get it back, one way or another. This made as much sense to me as any other aspect of the whole fantastical story. I paid for another round for the two of them and returned to my own inn, where I settled my account and told the owner I would be departing before dawn. I might have a long way to go, but instinct told me that at last I was nearing my quarry.

The trail led me downslope, out of the Viridon Mountains and through a crossroads. I'd heard it said that the doors to the lands of the dead swing open at such places during certain times of the year, and as I searched the dry ground for a sign of her passage, I felt a breath, a whisper on my face. It felt as if Joram urged me toward the less-traveled road. His guidance proved good, for before long, I spotted the print of a boot I now knew to be hers. She'd stepped out of the center of the trail, and so the track had not been overlain by others.

There had been little enough traffic on this road as it narrowed, soon only wide enough for a single line of mules or a small cart. I followed slowly, attending to the story left in scuffed dust, bent leaves, the moisture remaining in the animal dung, the occasional depression left by a boot when the wearer had strayed into the looser soil to either side. I knew this game well, and I was very good at it. I read what had gone before, not only the beasts and men but the order in which they had passed. First had come the narrow-wheeled cart and three ponies, one of them unshod, and as many men. They traveled at a pace so as not to overtax the animals: a trading party about their ordinary business. Two sets of footprints overlay those of the cart and ponies, one smaller and lighter than the other. They paused behind brush at turns where they might be seen by the traders. As they went on, their pace hastened, as shown by the depth of the heel strikes in the dirt. They became bolder, less wary.

At first, I wondered if one of them were Rayzel of Sharaya, until I saw a third set of prints. They were clearly made by a tall, strong woman...and she was following the couple, who in their turn were on the trail of the trading party. Their lead was two days but no more.

I straightened up from examining the overlapping prints. In a fair game or a crooked one, she'd lost the Pearl. Now she wanted it back. She was stalking the young couple even as they hurried after the traders. To the west, the sun was rapidly slipping behind the forested hills. Dusk would come early in this place. Although it galled me to think that Rayzel might even now be lengthening the distance between us, I found a place to rest for the night. I had waited this long. I could wait a time longer.

Anticipation woke me well before dawn. I broke my fast, drank from my small supply of water, scrubbed my teeth with a frayed stick, and returned to the chase. The morning air was clear, still cool from the night. Once, a long time ago, I would have said this was a wonderful day to be alive, with the sun bright on the leaves and the scent of wild herbs on the breeze. I wished Joram might have lived to enjoy it with me, and I supposed he was, in the sense I carried him with me.

Once my muscles were warm, I picked up my pace, running when the trail permitted it. It wound along the contours of the hillside, so that often what lay ahead was hidden until the last moment. Around one such twist in the trail, I came upon the remains of a campsite. Here the cart had been placed between two arms of rock. Here, the campfire. Here, the picketed ponies. From one end of the site to the other, I marked the traces of a struggle. I touched my fingertips to the darkened splotches in the earth, knowing before I smelled the reside that it was blood, and not old blood, either. Four men had died here, the three traders and one more. They'd been laid out on the dirt and then dragged to a grassy slope, where a shallow pit marked their common grave. The earth was still moist under a thin crust.

How could Rayzel have done this? I demanded of the empty sky. Then I remembered, *Of course. She is not a mortal woman, with a heart to care for travelers. She is a dragon, the Dragon of Sharaya.*

The cart was missing, as were the ponies, and I assumed she had taken them as booty, along with the trade goods. Why not? Ever since I'd known of her, she'd taken whatever she wanted: lands, flocks, men's lives. To my surprise, she was not alone. The woman from the couple traveled with her, and clearly this woman did not stumble or lag as a captive would. That she went freely startled me. Even more surprising was the evidence that these two had sat together, as close as comrades, as trail-sisters. This was not the behavior of a victor and her spoils.

For the first time in my long quest, I felt a tremor of doubt. I had thought the powers of this Pearl were of the body only. I had not dreamt that it might also enslave the mind. How could I fight such evil? I could not slit its throat in the night. Not only might I fail, I might become subject to what I most hated.

On the other hand, what was there for me, besides this chase?

Who would I be if I turned back now? The last, defeated heir to once-great Eaglehurst? A traitor to my brother's memory, and now to my very self?

Slowly I wrestled my way back to an approximation of courage. I hadn't imagined the end of my long search would be easy. I admitted to myself that I'd had no thought of what would become of me once I confronted the Dragon of Sharaya. Perhaps that meant I would not survive, that I intended to finish her at the cost of my own paltry life. That must be why I had carried Joram's ghost, his very appearance, all these years—because I myself had no separate existence.

The trail crested the hills and then dipped into the valley beyond. I had no knowledge of these lands, but I could feel the vitality rising from the meadows. Birds nested in the surrounding groves, and rabbits darted away at my approach. Two heavily-pregnant does looked up from their browsing before bounding into the shadowed forest. Occasionally I glimpsed rolling pastures below and once, distantly, a herd of red-brown cattle.

Because I kept to a more rapid pace than my quarry and because the two women had lingered at the first campsite for the better part of a day, I gained on them rapidly. Now a new worry came to me, that they might reach a town or other settlement before I caught up with them, a place where they might gain allies. The last thing I wanted when I stood before Rayzel and demanded her life in payment for her crimes was an audience. So I hurried throughout that afternoon, sometimes scrambling down slopes and over rocks, risking injury and pushing myself for more speed.

My efforts paid off, for as twilight drew close, I saw that they had set up camp in a little grove that bordered the pastureland. I didn't know the type of tree, short and spreading, leaves massing dark in the gathering night, but suspected there was a water source there as well. I made out the cart, the women tending to the ponies, and then the flare and warm orange light of a fire.

In the forests of Eaglehurst, I had learned to move like a whisper through the underbrush, so softly that not even a hunting owl marked my passage. Now I drew my stealth around me like a cloak. I became a shadow against shadow, a flicker in the gloaming. I had no reason to think the two suspected my presence, but with a little care and skill, I would make sure that did not happen.

I breathed so softly and stepped so silently that I heard their voices long before I got an unobstructed view of their camp. Two women, of course. Of that I had already been certain. But as I paused to listen, I heard something that I did not expect.

One of them was weeping, long shuddering sobs that surely arose from the very pit of despair, that place bereft of hope, of thought, of words. That in itself was not surprising, for who would not weep in the company of the Dragon of Sharaya?

No, what brought me up short were the soft murmurs of the other woman, the gentle phrases, the tone of voice that rose and fell as a mother might sing to a fretful child.

Rayzel, the Dragon of Sharaya, was *comforting* the other woman.

How could this be? Had the world so disarranged itself, that the sky and earth had lost all reason?

Heart yammering in my ears, I stumbled forward. Only by long habit and fortune did I keep hold of my dagger. A moment later, I was glad I hadn't dropped it. The Dragon lived by her own law, but she was not beyond mine.

Only a thin screen of lacy branches stood between me and the campsite, a veil scarcely worth the effort of brushing it aside. In the light of the fire and what remained in the western sky, I could see the women clearly. I had not erred, for there was Rayzel, wearing the trail-worn garb of a sword-soldier. There was no mistaking that strong build, that hair, that line of brow and cheek. The other woman, the one curled into a ball, half on Rayzel's lap, wrapped in Rayzel's arms, she must be the one from Raë. Her body shuddered with the force of her sobs, and Rayzel rocked her, held her tight.

"Hush now," Rayzel said softly. "You did not kill those men of your own choice, but that is over now..."

"...never be free of it..."

"You must go on. That's what your lover would have wanted for you, is it not? Would he not forgive you for what was not your fault?"

The light shifted on Rayzel's body and I saw it then, hanging from a chain around her neck.

The Pearl.

The thing that had made her invincible, that had brought about the destruction of everything I loved—my home, my own hopes, my brother's life.

Before I had made a conscious choice, I darted into the camp. Rayzel was vulnerable at this moment, her arms encumbered by the other woman. Even with magically-enhanced reflexes, it would take her a moment to get to her feet and draw her sword.

She noticed me, her head coming up. Her gaze met mine. I moved to close the distance, but she didn't shove the other woman aside. It was as if she had no care to defend herself. Something in her posture, a stillness that bordered on surrender, made me pause when nothing else would have. I stood for an instant, dagger clenched low beside my knee where it could not be easily spotted, muscles primed for a lunge and a quick upward strike.

Now the other woman reacted, pulling away from Rayzel with a whimper. She scuttled away from the fire to hide herself in the shadows. It was just the two of us, the Dragon of Sharaya and me. I tightened my grip on the dagger, drew a breath like fire into my lungs, and—

—and before I could take that next step, the step that would commit me to the attack, her expression changed. The hardness fell away, and I looked into the face of a young girl, the girl she had once been, not beautiful, but radiant and open of heart. Even as my brother had been. Even as I had been.

"Joram?"

The astonishment in her voice held me fast, and I realized then that my brother and I had so resembled one another, and I had so assiduously taken on his manner and appearance, that she saw him instead of me. Yet I heard not a trace of fear in her cry, as would arise from confronting the ghost of a man she had slain.

No, what I heard so clearly was wonder, wonder and joy. I might have brought her death—that was yet to be decided—but I had also brought her the thing her heart desired more than any other—to see her beloved one last time.

For there was not the slightest doubt in my mind that she had known Joram and had loved him with the fervent innocence of first love. No matter what came afterwards, he had left an indelible imprint on her heart.

Rayzel blinked, and the young girl she had been faded into the battle-hardened woman. She made no effort to rise, as if granting me leave to do what I would. Try as I might, however, I could find no trace of the implacable Dragon, the one who had brought about the destruction of Eaglehurst. I discerned endurance and sorrows as deep as my own, and I also saw compassion.

"You are not Joram," she said, and it seemed to me that she would a thousand times have preferred to meet his ghost, vengeful or not, than any living person.

I straightened slightly. "His sister."

"Sister? I did not know he had a sister. Might I know your name?"

I told her, although I had not spoken it for so long, my tongue did not recognize it.

She hesitated, which surprised me even more deeply. "I suppose you have come to avenge him. And that you will not believe me if I say that I would give anything to exchange places with him."

"Fine words."

She smiled a little, but sadly, and shifted so that she knelt before me. Her hands were empty. If she had a weapon about her, she made no attempt to draw it. Moving slowly, she slipped the chain over her head and let the Pearl fall to the earth. It glowed as if it bore a living ember at its heart, but the light was uneasy, as if a subtle intelligence, a *hunger,* burned there also.

What had she said to the other woman? *Not your choice, not your fault...*

"Now I am as mortal as you," she said. "My life is yours to take, as recompense for what you have lost. I ask only one thing—that you bury the Pearl with me. That you make no claim on it for yourself. I have done enough harm to your family. I would not have you carry the curse as well."

What kind of trick is this? I wondered, and realized there was no deception in her voice, no falsehood. What would it cost me to grant her this one thing? I wanted justice for my brother, for Eaglehurst and its people. For all my life as a bandit and thief, I had no interest in turning into the one who had brought so much harm to so many.

When I agreed, she smiled again, like the sun emerging from behind a cloud. "You are indeed Joram's sister, to have such kindness in you."

If I had had any doubt that she had known him, known the heart and core of who he'd been, it vanished. "How could you do it—how could you," the words stumbled over one another, "knowing him?"

In answer, she looked down at the smoldering red light of the Pearl. If everything I had learned was true, the gem had made her invincible, immortal. I had not imagined what else it might have brought—or driven—her to become. I could almost hear her wish that Sharaya and not Eaglehurst had burned, that she had led an ordinary woman's life, that her own death at my hands might in the smallest way compensate for all the grief she'd caused.

My legs threatened to give way beneath me. I understood then that she had not killed Joram and all the others. This *thing* had. Now it was about to take her life as well, using me as its instrument.

I let my dagger fall. The blade landed on the links of the chain with a hollow, clashing sound. The camp was empty except for the two of us. The Raë woman had fled.

I lowered myself beside Rayzel. I had thought that getting close enough to slip my blade between her ribs would be the hardest part. I'd had no idea, no idea at all, what she'd endured all these years.

"If I bury that," I said, pointing, "it might not stay buried." Someone might dig it up. I'd heard enough tales about cursed objects to know they had ways of becoming found. I didn't think it was possible to destroy this one, or Rayzel would long since have done it.

She nodded in a friendly way, as if in that moment we had shifted from being bitter enemies to allies. "I thought to carry it, in time to...to tame it."

"How can you tame something like that?"

"Not with sword or whip," she replied, and again I heard such sadness in her voice, my own throat threatened to close up. She looked at me again, and her eyes were bright. "With memories. With tears."

Tears for Joram? Tears for the loss of her home, her own kin? Tears for the sweet young girl she had once been?

Tears for me?

I had seen that she'd loved him. What I had not realized until that moment was that *he* had loved *her*. But he hadn't been able to save her.

I could...if I would.

And if I chose not to, if I turned my back on the girl my brother had loved, who then would be the victor?

Not Eaglehurst, in ashes.

Not Joram.

Not me.

The *Pearl* would win, and its hunger would claim even more lives.

Together, Rayzel and Joram had found a moment of joy. I could either snuff out its very memory or I could set it free.

I picked up the Pearl, handling it by the chain only, and let the gem come to rest on her opened hand. There it pulsed once, twice, as if it had a heart of its own. A hungering heart. A dragon heart.

With both hands, I closed Rayzel's fingers around the Pearl. "Then I will help you tame the Pearl."

She drew back in surprise. Clearly, she'd expected death, a slow one of revenge or a quick one of mercy. "Why would you offer such a thing?"

"Because," I said, leaning forward to kiss her as a sister,

"surely we have enough tears between us."

"Enough tears, yes," she repeated, and kissed me in turn. "Enough tears to quench even a Pearl of Fire."

WHAT'S IN A NAME?

by Katharina Schuschke

Katharina has a knack for short and funny stories. Her story "Summer Flu" was the ending story in SWORD AND SORCERESS 26, and I'm delighted to have this one to end SWORD AND SORCERESS 28. It still makes me laugh despite the number of times I've read it.

Katharina is 47 years old and still enjoys working as a computer consultant—thanks to the fascinating people she meets that way. She has yet not succumbed to the "obligatory cat" and has no pets apart from the spiders in the garden. Those who are interested can find more about her at marzipanmuffin.livejournal.com.

She would like to dedicate this story to Cyrano, "who's got a strange sense of humor (and who told me he liked my story)."

"What's in a name? that which we call a rose
By any other name would smell as sweet."
(Shakespeare, Romeo and Juliet)

Sure, but would a "bouquet of borckls" be quite as romantic?

I'm an editor—I know about the power of names. Name the heroine or hero wrong and the best plot just falls flat on its face—tragedy turning into farce.

Yes, I'm the infamous editor responsible for the last-minute corrections to the urban fantasy *Blood Rose*. When Henrietta wrote that book, a dastardly godling had sunk its hooks quite deeply into her. The creature wanted its name spread and known. For to be believed in would give it its first foothold for gaining a power base.

Henrietta, being her inimitable self, wrote some kick-ass dialogue even when in the grip of despair. So, *Blood Rose* is a dark and stark fantasy—but even so, her odd sense of humor lurks through. I didn't notice anything amiss, and the godling might have gotten away with its plot.

But the thing was too greedy and wanted to feed off Henrietta. It forced her to attempt suicide and was ready to feed on her life energy and last-minute remorse. Henrietta fought it—in the end successfully—and managed to call me. I got an ambulance to her in time and, when I went through her desk for info on her insurance, I found some pretty disquieting personal notes about what had been happening.

My first thought was to stop publication of *Blood Rose*. But then I had my moment of mad inspiration, which is why *Blood Rose* was published—with one minor last-second editorial change: the name of the godling.

I wiped all copies of the original manuscript. I've got friends in low places (aka tech support), so even backups got cleaned up.

The book went into print. Critics laughed their heads off, having a field day making fun of the book—and incidentally making enough people curious that the book became a quite satisfying success—isn't it fun when even literary critics turn out to be useful?

Thousands of readers laughed—and one obnoxious godling of despair disappeared. There's still despair in the world. But it's our own, it can be fought. No godling gets fat on it.

And the moral of the story is… name the evil godling in an urban fantasy wrong in just the right way and you'll not only have surprising success, you'll also get rid of the damned thing through ridicule.

So, if you feel a bout of despair coming on—think of "Mupfi, God of Despair." Have a good laugh!

CPSIA information can be obtained at www.ICGtesting.com
Printed in the USA
LVOW07s2004270514

387448LV00052B/1702/P

9 781938 185311